Morris Automated Information Network

0 1029 0434483 9

W9-DFR-795

Fic
Pol   Pollen, Bella
       Hunting unicorns

PARSIPPANY - TROY HILLS

PUBLIC LIBRARY SYSTEM

OCT 2 2 2004

Main Library
292 Parsippany Road
Parsippany, NJ 07054
973-887-5150

www.parsippanylibrary.org

Hunting Unicorns

BY THE SAME AUTHOR

All About Men

B Movies, Blue Love

bella pollen

Hunting Unicorns

THOMAS DUNNE BOOKS
ST. MARTIN'S PRESS ✠ NEW YORK

THOMAS DUNNE BOOKS.
An imprint of St. Martin's Press.

HUNTING UNICORNS. Copyright © 2003 by Bella Pollen. All rights reserved. Printed in the United States of America. No part of this book may be used or reproduced in any manner whatsoever without written permission except in the case of brief quotations embodied in critical articles or reviews. For information, address St. Martin's Press, 175 Fifth Avenue, New York, N.Y. 10010.

The publishers gratefully acknowledge permission to reproduce copyright material from:

The Decline and Fall of the British Aristocracy, David Cannadine, Picador (1990)

"The Stately Homes of England," Noël Coward—refrain, *Operette* (musical, 1938). *The Columbia World of Quotations.* Copyright © 1996 Columbia University Press

Christiane Amanpour: "News is part of our communal experience . . . " Part of a speech made at the Edward R. Murrow awards ceremony of the Radio Television News Directors Association held September 13, 2000, in Minneapolis. Grateful permission received from Christiane Amanpour, CNN's Chief Foreign Correspondent.

Every effort has been made to trace all copyright holders but if any has been inadvertently overlooked the author and publishers will be pleased to make the necessary arrangements at the first opportunity.

www.stmartins.com

Library of Congress Cataloging-in-Publication Data

Pollen, Bella
    Hunting unicorns / Bella Pollen.—1st U.S. ed.
       p. cm.
    ISBN 0-312-32764-1
    EAN 978-0312-32764-4
    1. Aristocracy (Social class)—Fiction. 2. Americans—England—Fiction.
3. Women journalists—Fiction. 4. London (England)—Fiction. 5. Nobility—
Fiction. 6. Brothers—Fiction. I. Title.

PR6116.O55H86 2004
823'.92—dc22   2004041341

First published in Great Britain by Macmillan, an imprint of Pan Macmillan Ltd.

First U.S. Edition: July 2004

10 9 8 7 6 5 4 3 2 1

To Andy

who had faith I could do it

To Carole and Susie

who saw me through it

The families who in their heyday were the lords of the earth are now often strangers in their own land. The lions of yesteryear have become the unicorns of today.

— David Cannadine,
The Decline and Fall of the British Aristocracy

We live in strange times. The millennium is upon us. I belong to two worlds, the past and the future. I am what is more or less defunct yet I have not understood what I am to become.

— Daniel Lytton-Jones

daniel

My mother and father drank. Water, whisky, wine. It was all the same to them. Any time, anyplace, anywhere. Curiously they never appeared drunk. Instead they existed in a semi-inebriated world, never allowing themselves to fall below a certain level of intoxication as though to do so would be bad manners — like appearing at breakfast not quite fully clothed. They had two children. Two small boys who watched their parents drink. Both grew up to be deeply affected by this habit. That is to say Rory became a teetotaller, and I, an alcoholic.

The first time I took myself off to a meeting I wrote this down — just in case it was the sort of place where you were pressured into a confession, but it's not like that here. Your peers don't pressure you so much as bore you into submission. The first meeting was so inexcusably dull I swore it would be the last and it would have been had it not been for the eleventh-hour appearance of the fantastically pretty girl. Some gorgeous accident left the chair next to me vacant and one whiff of her scent; earthy, flowery, sold me on the merits of AA and had there been a year's contract

I would have signed on the dotted line there and then. But she didn't turn up to the following meeting nor the one after that. In ten minutes we're supposed to be starting this week's session and there's still no sign of her. I've now made a major management decision. If she doesn't come through the door within, say, five minutes . . . I'm off to the pub. I don't have the energy for this bollocks. There are more pressing matters to be dealt with – the nuts and bolts that actually underpin people's lives. Right now, there's all this stuff waiting on my desk – articles to be written, mail to be opened, bills to be paid . . .

This afternoon, for instance, I was supposed to turn in my piece for the *Spectator*. The editor called, screaming obscenities a couple of hours ago. It's not that it's a difficult piece to write. The subject matter is interesting enough but I seem to have no words to put to it.

For some time now I've been juggling the various incompatible factions in my life but lately it seems I'm in danger of dropping a ball or two. The fact is, I'm having trouble writing under the influence of sobriety. Usually I'm unable to contemplate any kind of work until I've downed a half bottle of red wine. Alcohol gets the blood to the head, unblocks the channels. As words flow, I write them down and print them out. Then I send them off and get paid for my trouble. This is a system and it works, but now that I'm semi-programme, quasi-AA or, more specifically, no alcohol before the six o'clock watershed, the system seems to have crashed.

*

They say that the moment you realize you're an alcoholic is the moment you're scared of living without alcohol. Perhaps this is true for some people but not for me. I have known since childhood I was an alcoholic, since long before I ever tasted the stuff. I am what's known as a genetic junkie. Much of what I have in life is inherited, unfortunately not all of it good. Whatever the distinguishing feature that ties other families together, ours is a gene, a wayward one that has ripped through our family tree like a tornado, dropping the fruit of our ancestors to the ground, leaving generations of us destined to become rotten, pickled and canned.

Rory expends much energy fighting this gene, I on the other hand have embraced it. I don't see the point in not. To spend your life struggling against your own DNA seems pretty damn futile. It's who I am. It's on the swab from the inside of my cheek, it's in my blood, in every bead of sweat and no doubt in every puff of carbon dioxide I exhaled into that police breathalyser last night.

'But we're the generation that can kick it,' Rory says.

But you can't kick it, as you can be sure I'll be telling the group one day, because it ain't no football. Besides, I'm not convinced it should be kicked. Instability is the root of creativity and I like to believe there is a chink in the circle of life – an uneven join on the curve where the top of the genetic pool meets the bottom. This is the place from which flawed geniuses come, where my family, with its mix of the charmed and the damned, belong. Somewhere on this isolated ledge lies the answers to all the contradictions on earth.

*

A dozen people fill the room now, swapping goodwill and drinking coffee out of plastic cups. Attending AA is not unlike going to the theatre. You do it because it's supposed to be good for you – or more accurately, somebody else thinks it's good for you. Your parents, friends, people you don't want to hurt, have almost certainly bought tickets and you go to keep them happy. The theatre analogy doesn't end there. Once in a meeting, there are uncomfortable displays of emotions, an interval between speakers. There are the stars, producers, an audience and prima donnas to entertain them and, oh Good Lord, there's the fantastically pretty girl walking through the door . . .

Her name is Kate. She touches the arm of someone she knows and nods. They give her a brochure, which she doesn't read. Today she's wearing a blue cotton shirt and pencil skirt. I like the way she moves in this skirt. Demure, yet . . . not.

I watch Kate out of the corner of my eye, mentally staking my claim on the chair nearest her. Suddenly, without warning, it's time and the talking stops. I look for Kate but she's disappeared. Everyone sits. I cast around panicked, the mulish child who can't get the hang of musical chairs. There are two seats left, but not together. I'm on the verge of bolting when Kate pushes in through the swinging door from the loo. Her eyes are red from crying. Somewhere along the line, some bastard has been mean to her. I want to be that bastard so that I can make it up to her. She sits down and crosses her legs. There is a ladder in her tights. It starts 5 inches above her knee and disappears up her skirt – God only knows where it might end. Dear Lord she's sexy, I am intoxicated by her beauty, I am overwhelmed by her suffering. If I don't sleep with her soon I will go mad.

The meeting gets underway. Kate was on holiday last week. This I learn from her share: 'Lisbon. Good tapas. A chance to escape.' So far she's given no reason as to why she's slipped on the banana skin of rack and ruin. She flicks her black hair over one shoulder, her eyes are the colour of mulberries.

Who's next? I look around. Whose boil-in-the-bag emotions need reheating this week? Whose family must now carry the burden of their child's dysfunction on top of their own. It's tempting to leap to my feet. *We've had them all*, I could say, *great granny kept a lion, Howard held poker parties dressed as a rat. Uncle Conrad drank himself to death, as did Uncle William. Robert took drugs. Dinah lay on her bed and swallowed pill after pill. Peter walked up to the top of the valley and put a gun to his head. John died of a brain tumour the size of a cantaloupe . . . We're a careless family. We lose a lot of people.* But I keep quiet, holding back for the real loonies and eventually Mad Millicent takes the chair. She has hair like a Brillo pad and believes herself to be Peter Mandelson's bodyguard. We're all a bit bored of her and she soon senses it. Eventually she falls silent then hauls a bottle of Evian water from her knapsack and stares at it incredulously.

Next we get Stan. 'It has come to my attention,' he begins, 'that certain people in this fellowship have been b'littlin' me,' he fixes his eye on Kate who hugs her knees to her chest. She has a fading bruise on her left calf, and intensely white skin through which her veins shine and flow like rivers on a map. 'Well,' Stan continues, 'I should like it known that I am carrying a long sharp knife and should anyone b'little me again, I'll stick 'em like a pig.' He wipes the spittle from his mouth. 'Fanks for listening.'

I have a brainwave. In the break I will ask Kate to be my sponsor. This means I can legitimately ring her up day or night to discuss my disintegration.

'I can't be your sponsor,' she says, eyes narrowing with suspicion.

'Why not?'

'It's crossing the boundaries. You don't even know me.'

'Ah but I don't know anybody here.' I turn my palms up to the ceiling, charming yet helpless.

'This isn't about sobriety,' she says quietly and furiously.

I'm floored that she's on to me so quickly. 'What is it about then?'

'It's about you wanting to sleep with me.'

I've completely gone off Kate now that she's got no sense of humour. If you can't even connect with people on a basic level, what hope is there for any of us here?

'I'll be your sponsor, mate.'

I turn to find a man the size of a small country accosting me.

'I've been sober for a year now,' he says, 'I'm ready to take you on.'

Raymond is black, schizophrenic and has spent most of his adult life in prison. It's going to be hard to say no.

I spend the second half of the meeting contemplating Raymond's neck. The thing must measure minimum a foot and a half circumference. In fact there's no way of deciphering where his neck ends and his head begins.

After the meeting he says, 'Call me anytime you need help,' and crushes me to his chest.

'You can't be on the bloody programme if you're drinking,' Benj says in the pub.

'I'm half on the programme. Half AA. I'm *A*.'

'That's like announcing you're half pregnant. There are certain things you just can't do in halves.' Benj, unshaved and apparently unwashed since the last time I saw him, is doing the crossword puzzle in the *Telegraph*, his third pint of bitter in front of him. When he takes a swig, his Adam's apple rises up and down in his throat like a miniature elevator. Rake thin, Benj looks like someone standing in front of a circus mirror, all extruded. I tear open a bag of crisps.

'The world is full of legitimate halves. Half dead, half decent, half-cooked. Half-witted . . .' I'm having my first drink of the day. A glass of red wine. It tastes pure and delicious and, God knows, I feel like I've earned the thing.

'I don't know why you're bothering frankly.' Benj turns his attention to the obituaries.

I glance fondly at the miffed expression on his face. Benj and I are first cousins, and we've been muckers, drinking and otherwise, since we were at prep school together. He is not taking kindly to my partial desertion.

'Half-baked, halfway, half-cocked.' I scribble with alacrity. The piece for the *Spectator* is flowing.

'They say the moment you realize you're scared of living without alcohol means you are an alcoholic.' Benj says.

'Demi-tasse, demi-cappucine, demi-monde.' I throw down

my pen. The piece is finished. I down the glass of wine to celebrate and order two more.

'Does Rory know you're *demi*-AA?' Benj enquires.

'Why? Am I not functioning magnificently on my new ration of alcohol? Am I not coping beautifully under such trying circumstances?'

'Uhuh,' he doesn't look up from the paper.

'Am I not achieving work deadlines, keeping appointments?'

'Speaking of which,' Benj says, 'weren't you meant to be having supper at home tonight?'

Bollocks. I scuttle off. Home, temporarily is chez Rory – not the most ideal of situations for either of us, but a couple of months ago I received one of those estate agent letters. Did I want to rent out my property to some wanker banker and his wife for an extortionate sum of money? If I remember correctly, the original thinking behind agreeing to this (apart from it paying off some frankly pressing, not to mention depressing debts) was that having calculated assignments abroad, weekends at home, and the rest of the time over at my rather obliging girlfriend's flat, I could probably wing it financially for a further six months. When my girlfriend threw both me and my clothes out, Rory seized his chance. I won't bore you with the details of our row but we ended up with a neat exchange of consonants for vowels. B&B from him in return for a commitment to AA from me. Rory, sobriety's bodyguard, has officially assigned himself to my case.

Metaphorically speaking, my little brother and I are

twins. We might be separated by thirteen months but we're the head and tail of the same coin. What I lack, he boasts and vice versa, our weakness and strengths balancing each other out. More importantly I have always lived in his head and he in mine, and thus united we have managed to make sense of the world. But as I drift further over a river he will not cross, things have changed.

Rory doesn't dare be too stony-faced when I finally buzz the door because his fiancée's just arrived from Italy. The purpose of dinner is for us to bond. I suspect neither of them fall for the story I make up about Kate having a breakdown in the meeting but they're gracious enough to pretend, in fact they positively radiate welcome and for a moment I have to muster every ounce of loyalty not to turn tail and flee.

'Would you like to drink something?' Leona says, then blushing adds, 'a Coca Cola?' I grin and kiss her on the cheek.

Leona whips dishes in and out of the oven with strong honey-coloured arms. She's a beauty all right. Cool skin, pale hair, hot Italian blood. Too healthy looking for my taste, I prefer Kate's bruised vulnerability, but at one point I catch the look Rory sends her across the kitchen. I realize the bastard's actually in love and I feel enormously proud of him.

'Are you taking Leona to Hell Hall this weekend?' I ask.

'Over my dead body.' Rory pretends not to see my frown and I do not push it but here we come to the point of separation. Our paths have diverged and discussions about

Hell Hall, about inheritance, matters of tax, our parents, their drinking, their hopelessness, my perceived hopelessness, are all places we no longer go together, emotionally, conversationally, and certainly not physically.

Rory believes he has escaped. Imagines it is possible. He has sworn not to be tied down, and of course, that's his prerogative – but it's also, I believe, his loss. It's different for me. Hell Hall, as our family home has come to be known, is one of the most beautiful places on earth, a place about which I'm passionate – which is just as well really as I cannot escape. I am the eldest son.

The rest of dinner passes pleasantly enough, I badly want a drink but there's just enough Coke to fill my glass, just enough perfunctory gossip to fill the gaps left by other forbidden subjects and by the time we finish it's mercifully late. When Rory takes Leona to bed, he steers her from the room with his thumb and forefinger round the back of her neck.

After an hour or two of television I doze. When I wake, edgy and twitching, it's somewhere between night and day. This has long been a moment of desperation for me. A bad sleeper as a child, irrationally scared of the dark, and now scared of the demons the dark allows me to conjure, I know from the moment my brain registers wakefulness that I will do almost anything for a drink . . .

It takes me a while to find where Rory's stashed it but eventually I triumph with two bottles of wine from the depths of the cleaning cupboard, hidden on a shelf behind the Ajax and Domestos.

*

Later, opening the kitchen bin to throw out the empty bottles, I knock against the drainer. A pile of saucepans clatter to the floor. I stack them back on the sink.

'What's up?' Rory is standing in the doorway looking sleepy and crumpled.

I try to keep the alcohol from my voice when I answer, then I think damn him – why should I? We talk, but as so often these past few months it soon turns to argument and God knows I am weary of it. He tells me I am following tracks in the snow and I tell him I'm no fan of these father/son style 'chats' because we've been so close all our lives and none of this ever mattered. As he lectures I close my eyes, strip back the years until I see two small boys, arms linked, dressed in woolly jumpers with embroidered initials. R and D. Now I look at him shaking his head angrily and I wonder what the hell happened to us. Two things occur to me. The first is that somewhere along the line, wires have been crossed. Rory seems to have responsibility whilst I have the responsibilities and the second is my fear that Rory is growing up whereas I am clearly regressing and I know then and there that I have to get out of the house before I either cry or end up clocking the little bastard.

As I'm unchaining the bike from the railings I remember that I meant to tell Rory he will not escape his roots, no matter how hard he tries. There is something of the father in every son. The gene might be dormant, but it's lying in wait. Then I recognize the fear and indecision in his eyes as he hesitates in the doorway and I see that he knows this already.

I head for Highgate, for the cemetery. The street lights are fading, the sky lightening. I pass an old man sweeping dust from one side of the road to the other and a dumpy matron jogging, her grey tracksuit stained greyer with sweat. Past Primrose Hill, the streets are empty and the city belongs to me. The exertion of pedalling sends all remaining alcohol straight to my head. Despite the freezing temperature I feel gloriously warm. Tabasco is running through my veins. My brain spins with all the things to do in life and in this one perfect moment all of them seem possible.

Then the moment passes. Crosswinds blow against my face. I put my head down, grip the handlebars – peddle for all life's worth up the hill. It's late autumn and the leaves are whirling. They fall against my face, slight, light, like oiled pieces of skin. Dawn breaks quickly as if the tip of a paintbrush had touched a dab of orange to wet blotting paper. I look into the sun's weak rays to suck some warmth onto my face.

Wait a second, where did that bastard come from? A white van has shot over the crossing and through the give-way sign. I squeeze the brake lever, nearly projecting myself over the handlebars. The bicycle stops, leaving just enough space for the van to swing through its turn. I give the driver a nod, but he doesn't nod back. In fact he doesn't wave, smile, salute or show appreciation of any kind – he just revs off down the street belching fumes from his exhaust. I stay still, breathing heavily, balancing the heel of my boot against the tarmac. As a spectator at this scene I might have an impending sense of doom. I might watch my face, catch the flicker of irritation that becomes a slow burn of anger at one human being's total lack of consideration towards

another. I might warn myself that to seek revenge, given
the disparity in our chosen mode of transport, is to dice
with death but from where I'm standing it doesn't seem
that way at all. Fuelled by the mix of self righteousness and
idiocy that only the truly pissed can muster, it just seems
like the right thing to do.

It takes only a minute to catch the van. A taxi stops to
eject its passenger, the van slows behind. I pedal out into
the middle of the road, fly past his open window, shout,
'Manners, you wanker.'

The driver's head turns but I am sailing on through the
dawn chill, laughing, untouchable.

Or at least so I think.

By the time I see it, the bus is virtually on top of me.
Christ, CHRIST, what happened? It swerves, I swerve and
for a split second I think I'm home free but I haven't
accounted for its tail end, haven't accounted for the fact
that the thing moves together, has no mind of its own. It
is, of course, just a bus, a thirty ton piece of metal, and I
realize absolutely that it's going to hit me and I know too
that whatever happens I don't want to go down. Up is an
option, down under this monstrosity is not. If I'm going to
go, let it be through the air, like an eagle, not squashed
underfoot like some irrelevant bug.

The bus hits. There's no pain, it's all too big for pain.
There's just a tremendous force, like being fired from a
cannon, and really not so unpleasant as you might imagine.
There's an explosion of red, a deep, deep red, and a colour
too vivid to be borne. I close my eyes but I can still see
through the skin. I can see through the windscreen of the
bus, into the driver's black eyes, through his body into his

beating heart. For a second, suspended in time I can see everything, all that defines my life, everything I love.

Overhead the air darkens, the weather changes fast and furious. Clouds hurtle through the sky. I feel a great burst of passion towards life, and its momentum carries me home. I am standing in the lake-field. The soil is damp between my toes. I can smell the earth, smell the honeysuckle lifting off the river breeze. I see the woods, the park, the great oak tree bowed in the fox cover. I see my father, stripped to the waist, axe in hand. I see the elms falling. There's a rushing in my ears, the sound the wind might make as it blows through the flowers of a horse chestnut – then there is nothing.

maggie

I have to confess that my basic knowledge of London's geography comes from playing Monopoly. My father, never the most switched on of shoppers, mistakenly bought the English version for Christmas one year. My mother disapproved of the game – vaguely distrusting it as a training in capitalism – but I loved that the makers identified places by colours. It reminded me of a car game I used to play with my dad. He would describe in detail a city he had worked in, then make me blur my eyes and tell him what colour it represented – Madrid, for instance, was brown, Bangkok was orange, Washington white and New York was . . . well one of the reasons I love living in New York so much is that we could never pinpoint its colour. It's a kaleidoscopic mix of shades, smells, sounds and race. Millions of multicoloured stitches that make up one small but fantastic pocket of humanity.

Maybe it wasn't the ideal present for an only child but I loved Monopoly. I saw it less as a training in capitalism than a crash course in survival. It's surprising what tips you can pick up from a game. How to land on Chance and grab Opportunity. How to get out of jail free. I can still feel the adrenaline buzz of being down to your last buck and making a run for it through those lethal trouble hotspots — the triple-hotelled properties.

I remember the colours of every card. Fleet Street was red, Piccadilly was yellow. Now, peering through my cab window at the damp streets of London, I assumed due to the grand nature of the offices to which I was heading they'd be situated in the royal blue hues of Park Lane and Mayfair. Turned out they were somewhere called Edgware Road, a street not actually featured in the game at all, which, as I wound down the window to take a better look, was unsurprising. With its shops selling carpets and lanterns, its profusion of hookah smokers sitting around outside juice bars playing backgammon, it felt more like some souk in Beirut than a mere traffic jam from Oxford Circus.

'It is very . . . ah . . . *Arab*,' Alexander Massey confirmed looking furtively behind me to the dark hallway as he opened the door.

Overweight, old school and upper class, Massey was the author of five anthologies of obituaries and a leading expert on Burke's Peerage (a publication listing everything you always wanted to know about the titles of England's aristocracy but were too afraid to ask) and I was praying he was going to be able to help me.

It was January, the first month of the Millennium and the world was recovering from its conflicting feelings of relief that earth hadn't exploded and its disappointment that nothing had fundamentally changed. I'd been in London for less than a week and already run into trouble. My crew was arriving in a couple of days but I had nothing to film.

I work for *Newsline*. You probably know it, most people do. *Newsline* is a current affairs, news and issues program that leans towards story journalism rather than information journalism – sort of a younger and smaller cousin of *60 Minutes*. We specialize in exposing scandal and exploding myths. We target corrupt government bodies, insensitive public companies, institutions and monopolies. I love working there, as a show, it just isn't afraid to kick ass.

This all started last November when I was running to a meeting in the *Newsline* offices. It was the Thursday before Thanksgiving weekend and New York was in its usual bi-thematic state of shivering outside and sweltering inside. Thanksgiving always feels like the practice run for Christmas and true to form the Santas were out in force, hitching wide leather belts over even wider beer bellies. It seemed that the whole of Manhattan was making the rush to Grand Central, off to family weekends and stuffed turkey dinners, but my parents had never been big on family occasions, and public holidays tended to prompt special derision for the over-commercial, greeting-card sentimentality of the American People. Besides, Alan Soloman, *Newsline*'s senior producer, had called me in for a meeting and when Alan scheduled meetings no one went home early.

A week before Thanksgiving, I'd made Alan a presentation; a story I really wanted to pursue in the Middle East. Alan had been ambivalent about letting me go, but now I was hoping to get it green-lighted.

A big man, weathered and broad, Alan pulled down the shutters in his office then perched on the side of his desk, tapping dried cranberries from the packet – a token nod to his high cholesterol. A CBS executive was sitting in on the meeting. I couldn't remember his name but since the sale of *Newsline* to CBS a year ago, network grands fromages were becoming a familiar sight around the place. The television fizzed then cleared. On screen were scenes of mayhem. I recognized them straight away. This was footage taken when England's Labour Government had finally succeeded in pushing through the abolition of the hereditary peers in the House of Lords. My grandfather had been Irish and ever since the British Parliamentary channel had been made available on cable I'd been alternately horrified and amused by the antics of the Houses of Parliament. I assumed Alan was inviting criticism of somebody else's rough-cut, a trick he pulled from time to time to keep correspondents on their toes. This segment looked like Ed's work. With his hand-tooled leather shoes, fussy little dogs and penchant for antiques, a piece in England would be right up Ed's alley.

The action cut to the chambers where tempers seemed more frayed than usual, in fact it looked as if a fist fight was on the verge of breaking out between members. The shot changed again to a line of aging peers handing in their security passes. One had tears in his eyes. Alan freeze-framed the image with the push of a button.

'Up until now the House of Lords has had the power to pass and initiate laws purely through their hereditary right. So it got us thinking . . . with the loss of this last vestige of political power, what influence do the aristocracy of England have left?'

Only then it dawned on me this wasn't a rough at all, Alan was pitching me a story.

'Wait a minute,' I glanced at him suspiciously, 'what about the piece I proposed?'

He didn't meet my eye. 'We have enough people out there right now, Maggie. Instead, we thought it might be revealing if you went over and interviewed some of the heads of England's more influential upper-class families . . .'

I couldn't believe I'd heard him right. The story I'd pitched was on honour killings in the Yemen.

'But England is cold, wet, formal.' I pleaded. 'Couldn't I please have desert, heat, scorpions? Couldn't I at least have something a teeny bit more relevant?'

'One thousand years of aristocratic rule. This is the end of an era, Maggie, this is *historically* relevant.'

'Added bonus we get a nice tour round England's country houses,' the executive threw in, 'keep the female viewers on the hook.'

Alan must have caught the look on my face. 'I know, Maggie, I know,' there was regret in his voice and it stopped me short of total rebellion, 'but the hard reality is, we have to chase the ratings like everybody else. Look, deliver me this piece and next time round you'll get the assignment you want but for now, go revisit Brideshead in the twenty-first century.'

Revisit Brideshead in the twenty-first century. That was my brief – whatever it meant. I guess it could have been worse. In television it seemed to be happening more and more – hard news stories were being ignored in favour of mushy high-rating segments. At least I wasn't being sent to see how some mother in Baltimore was coping with quintuplets or how Buttons, the heroic dog, had pulled a kid out of a hole. I'd never been to England and besides, when I'd calmed down enough to think straight, I realized I had a heady ulterior motive for spending a little time in Europe. I figured I'd just go and make the best of it.

Course, it hadn't turned out that simple. I'd done meticulous research in New York, but as soon as I arrived in London, permissions I'd spent weeks negotiating had been cancelled. The British, it seemed, were notoriously camera shy.

Access, to a journalist, is like blood to a vampire. If you cannot get to the people you're interested in, you try to get to their friends. If you can't find a whistleblower you're dead in the water.

At that point I could have called in to *Newsline* with a blank. It sometimes happens, you chase a story as far as you can then it dies on you. 'The dog won't hunt' as Clinton would say. You might have thought I'd be happy to find a legitimate reason for backing out of an assignment I'd felt railroaded into in the first place, but I couldn't do it. I hated giving up on a story.

Despite the market feel of the Edgware Road below us, Massey's offices offices were dry, stuffy and very small. Books and paperwork were strewn on every surface, and a stressed-looking assistant was struggling with a copying machine in the reception area. Through an open window came the resonant wailing of middle eastern pop music. 'The . . . er . . . *ethnicity* makes it very tricky at lunchtime you know,' Massey said leading the way down the narrow corridor to his office – a box-sized room smelling of pipe tobacco and decorated cheek to jowl with framed cartoons from *Punch* magazine. 'I've tried some of these places, but I never know what to *order*. I can't tell you how intimidating it is *not to know*.'

I took one of the leather-bound volumes of Burke's Peerage from his shelf and opened it curiously. Alexander Massey was reputed to know the names and genealogy of every great family in England – if he couldn't help me, then nobody could.

'Do you mind me asking, is anyone actually interested in this stuff anymore?'

'Oh you'd be surprised,' Massey said affably. 'Hotels, shop owners, that kind of thing. The sort of people listed here,' he tapped the front cover, 'can get very shirty about being wrongly addressed, you know.'

'You publish this annually?' The book weighed a ton.

'The great problem with the war,' Massey regarded the ringing phone with something approaching dismay, 'apart from bombs coming down of course, was a shortage of paper, that's when we decided to bring it out every five years instead of three. Now it's growing in popularity all the time.' He plucked the receiver gingerly from its cradle.

There was something a little Graham Greene about Alexander Massey – Our Man In The Edgware Road, keeping watch on his tiny piece of the empire, wearing his white linen suit in the perishing cold of a London winter. Actually, Massey was punctiliously dressed in neat fawn-coloured pants and corduroy jacket. In a way he was disappointing. I'd been hoping he was going to be a fantastic snob, instead he was gentle and self-effacing.

'Quite so, quite so,' he was saying into the receiver, 'to read of one's own death, whether over breakfast or not is, naturally, terribly distressing, but a genuine editorial mistake I can assure you,' he threw me a pained expression. 'No, no I'm quite sure that's not the case. I feel confident that your son must have been as distraught as everybody else . . . ah . . . sent a removal van for the furniture did he? Yes, I do see. That does present things in a slightly different light . . . yes, yes of course I'll send a written apology.'

'Well, rings the changes I suppose,' he positioned the phone back on his desk. 'Usually get it in the neck for leaving out births.'

'Don't people mind their addresses being printed?' I scanned through the tiny print of the book. 'Aren't they worried about getting robbed or stalked?'

'Dear me,' Massey said vaguely, 'well yes, I suppose there is a danger, but in my experience the criminal fraternity prefer browsing *Hello!* magazine for that sort of thing.' He took the list from my hand. 'Now these are the people you're interested in, are they? Let's see,' he switched on the brass light by his elbow and studied the names. 'Fermoy . . . yes, made their fortune selling black crêpe for Queen Victoria's funeral. He thumbed through the wafer-thin pages, 'Hartfield, oddly enough I was at prep school with. Just been voted out of the Lords. Makes cider now I believe . . . Bevan, as I'm sure you're aware, is cousin to the queen.'

'Really? A close one?'

'Oh yes.' He smoothed his finger gently along the book's binding. 'Eighth Earl of Bevan, family name Lytton-Jones, Danby also of Clandoyle. Issue two sons, eldest recently deceased—'

'Look, I know it sounds really pushy,' I rummaged in

my tote bag for a pen, 'but is there any way you could help get me in with these people?' The idea was to visit some of these fallen lords in their homes. See how they lived, find out what they stood for, what they believed in.

'Well now,' Massey cleared his throat, 'I'm only interested in genealogy, I'm a bit of a dry stick when it comes to the people themselves. Besides I think you'll find that the real top dogs, the sort you're after, would never allow themselves to be filmed.'

I pondered on this. I live in an age and a country consumed with celebrity. It's simply a national obsession. People will bare all and usually for nothing. The very idea of discretion seems archaic. When you ring up sources in America and say you work for a television show, you can barely shut them up.

'Do you have *any* influence? Could you get me any kind of access?'

'You'll have to find someone who's familiar to that world,' Massey said, 'someone they trust. It would of course entirely depend on the thrust of your piece but I'm afraid the answer is you probably won't get access. Why would they agree? What could you possibly offer them?' He closed the book. 'I'm sorry.'

As I headed out through the corridor I remembered something and doubled back.

'Moutabal,' I said.

Massey turned from the shelf.

'It's like an eggplant dip, and hummus is really nice too. Also check out the lamb kebab in pitta but make sure you order it with the chilli and sesame sauce, and don't touch the mayonnaise.'

Massey's brow cleared. 'Right,' he said beaming, 'splendid, thank you.'

'You're welcome.'

'Hang on.' He patted through the debris on the desk for a pen and scribbled a name on a piece of paper. 'Look, take this . . . an acquaintance of mine. I can't guarantee it, but it's just possible he may be able to help you.'

I want to see them starving,
The so called working class
Their wages weekly halving
Their women stewing grass
When I ride out each morning
In one of my new suits
I want to find them fawning
To clean my car and boots.

— Philip Larkin

daniel

It's wrong to say that time is a great healer. It isn't. What happens is that you get used to things. It's a question of survival and to survive you adapt. Rory is only beginning to understand that now. 18 October 1999. The price of petrol rose, a BSE outbreak was confirmed in France, twins were born to a sexagenarian, and a lesser-known journalist went down under a bus.

For over a year now, Rory's been living in a state of arrested insanity and how much longer it might continue he has no clue. All points of reference are gone. How many ounces to the pound? How many weeks in the year? How many inches to the foot? Oh God, let someone push back the clock for him because nothing makes sense any more.

Death results in isolation for the living and there are days when he must resolve to hang on until he returns to the safety of his own home, when it's all he can do to keep his temper at bay, when he considers himself a danger to society at large and if the authorities only knew what kind of lunatic was roaming the street they'd have him whisked straight off to a secure unit before any damage was done. These are the days that induce much self-pity, but Rory can be excused from wallowing because ask anybody who knows about these things – grief can bend your knees. Grief can bring you down.

As he sets off to the bakery where he buys his breakfast every morning he wonders whether people can actually see the fuse protruding from the cannonball that doubles up as his head – and if so, whether some mischievous child might do him a favour, take it upon themselves to light it then, cheers, it would all be over. On bad days he wonders why, on looking at his reflection in a mirror, he doesn't see the actual iron ball or the hand grenade with its accompanying pin, but the face that stares back at him is always the same bland mask and he considers himself a tribute to that great English skill of hiding emotion. Having said that, it's a bloody unreasonable way to live. If you're blind, you get a white stick. If you've got a gammy leg you get a disabled sticker for parking on double yellow lines. A hand grenade for a head is a genuine disability and it would be easier if the general public were made aware of it. Perhaps he could start a trend – the lovesick could stitch a heart on their sleeve, the bitter, tape a soggy chip to their shoulder. If there were more obvious clues to why people behaved the way they did, the world would surely be a nicer place.

Tomorrow it's Rory's thirty-eighth birthday but he feels ten thousand years old. His life has split in two and the chasm he's slipped into has fundamentally changed him. Leaving aside the loss of his sense of humour, which both he and I are praying will return shortly, Rory, in his best moments, used to be someone who believed in love at first sight, who thought that the hole in the ozone layer might self-heal. Now fate has flipped him up and landed him wrong side down on the face of pessimism. It's not that he doesn't get angry, just that he feels he must restrain it; or that he doesn't have passion, only that he feels he should conceal it. His irritability is taken out on things and events he can't control, pigeons that shit on him or stupid phone operators. Only last week, infuriated by drunk party-goers repeatedly ordering a taxi from the phone box outside his window, he took an unloaded shotgun and told them if they didn't bugger off, he'd blow their heads off. This was no solitary incident. Over the last year the list of people he'd like to kill has been endless and varied, and though gradually diminishing, still includes, for the record, most of his clients, all members of his immediate family, Alison his secretary and, very particularly, the lady in the bakery, who has persisted in asking him every day since the accident whether he's feeling better.

They find him surly, of course. A year ago he would have flirted with the baker lady good-naturedly, a year ago he would have flirted with the sticky bun had it been the good lady's day off — Rory's charm is natural and used to be applied indiscriminately. Now it is held strictly in reserve.

He shovels a sausage roll into his mouth reflecting that today looks set to be one of those days. He's just spent the night on the sofa, and on waking this morning found the channel changer wedged between his knees and the screen a buzzing pop art of black and white. He hates these endless nights. In his dreams I am laughing, full of life, always dancing away from him, out of reach while he can neither move nor speak. In these dreams it is Rory, not I, who is dead.

maggie

'*The middle classes view us as profligate and idle, nothing short of money-grabbing buffoons hiding behind our family's coat of arms . . .*'

'Wow.' I pushed my glasses further up my nose and took a closer look. I was in the bowels of the BBC watching footage of an old aristocrat, and whoever had executed the camerawork for this piece of film had done a stunning job. You could almost see the spider veins on the man's cheek pulsing with indignation.

Massey's acquaintance had put me in touch with a producer called Simon Brannigan who'd made a documentary about politicians' wives. 'Slaves to their Class'. Simon was a defensive left-winger with a media crew cut and a muscular intensity that hinted at daily gym workouts. He reminded me of an activist my mother hung out with for a while when I was a kid, who spent a disproportionate part of his day standing on his head against the wall.

My mother was one of the original pioneer feminist film-makers — and when I say pioneer, I'm not joking. Her devastating documentary about female circumcision in Somalia had strong men fainting at its Academy screening.

Needless to say, it didn't win, too controversial or maybe, as Mom always maintained, the board were guilty of anti-female bias.

Simon Brannigan's documentary was not exactly partisan itself, guilty of just about every kind of bias — class, wealth and gender — but it was also compulsive viewing. 'I can't get anyone to talk to me.' I told him. 'Where's aristo.com when you need it. How did you get this kind of access?'

'With great difficulty. Your problem is that you're trying to set up a lot of people fast.' He grimaced. 'Don't forget my film took two years to make. You've got to keep chiselling away . . . by the way, what is the thrust of your piece? What's your hook?'

The thrust of my piece. Massey had asked the same question.

The thing was I wasn't really sure.

Were the English aristocracy a dying breed who after centuries of appalling behaviour were finally getting their comeuppance?

I didn't know, but probably.

Was I sympathetic to the loss of their immense houses from death duties?

Not particularly.

Was I worried that they might forfeit the right to wear sharply tailored red jackets and tear foxes limb from limb?

It wasn't keeping me awake at night.

Would this attitude endear me to the landed gentry?

Well obviously not.

'Though, funnily enough, what you just said . . .' Brannigan was frowning.

'What did I just say?'

'Your quip about aristo.com.' He tapped his pencil against his forehead as though trying to dislodge some snippet of information. 'I did hear, well apparently there *is* now some agency.'

'There is?' I said hopefully, feeling around in my pocket for a Kleenex. I'd managed to contract a really first-class cold since I'd arrived and had been begging Tylenol stand-ins and hot drinks off the long-suffering hotel staff for the last couple of days.

'What you have to understand,' Simon said, 'is that these old farts are increasingly having to face the commercializing of their estates.'

'Yeah right,' I grinned. 'Poor destitute things,' The vast residence of Brannigan's indignant peer had now filled the screen. 'So what does this agency do?'

'Takes advantage of just that. The guy who runs this business is supposedly brilliant at getting a foot through the door in return for cash or, in your case, a few million viewers who might—'

'One day be paying tourists?'

'Exactly, that's about the gist of it.'

'Great. So do you know how I get hold of this guy? What kind of set-up is he running?'

'As I said, the agency wasn't around when I made *Slaves* but I imagine he's some new dot-com e-commerce wide boy who's bought himself a well-cut suit, learnt his dukes from his earls and is now busy exploiting them both. And frankly,' Simon looked at me and smiled broadly, 'the very best of luck to him.'

daniel

Outside number eight Connelly Mews, a small street tucked discreetly into a corner of south west London, Rory trips over a bunch of cable lying on the cobbled ground. 'Mind out,' shouts the builder switching off his drill. He repositions a sign *'Incorporating Stately Locations'* under the existing sign 'R. L. Jones' and moves aside to allow Rory to enter.

'Oh dear, you look terrible,' Alison says.

Rory grunts.

'Nice cup of coffee?'

'No thanks,' Rory throws his jacket on the table.

'How about tea? I've just heated the pot.'

Rory shakes his head.

'Breakfast? I could pop out.'

Rory doesn't bother to answer.

Alison looks crestfallen. Twenty-six going on forty, Alison could almost be pretty if it wasn't for the slight squint that made her appear as though she was permanently in bright sunlight. Alison is Rory's 'assistant' for want of a better word and every morning she arrives early to open up the studio and tidy the place. Every morning she snaps the blinds, makes fresh coffee, sometimes she even puts flowers, bought out of her own pay cheque, into a vase on Rory's desk but my little brother, in his current mode of self-pity has yet to notice these minor acts of worship. He has yet to really notice Alison at all, though with her placid brown eyes she reminds him vaguely of an orphaned heifer we once rescued as boys. We named her Ginger Rogers and bottle fed her for nearly two months. Every day we led her round the lake-field on a rope and scratched the velvety space between her ears. One Sunday about seven months later, Rory asked what we were having for lunch. 'Ginger,' my mother replied, her upbringing on the West Coast of Ireland having given her an entirely unsentimental outlook on life.

'You've had four more calls,' Alison says. 'Lord Carnegie, the Marquess of Nanthaven, uh, your mother twice about her dry cleaning and . . .' but as Rory takes the messages from her hand she feels the brush of his skin and it starts. Deep inside her the heat wells up, registering first as a tingling in her stomach then around her breasts. Gathering speed, it creeps up her neck before finally hitting her face full on. The colour that suffuses her cheeks can only be imagined because by the time she normally escapes to the loo to check in the mirror it has generally subsided.

'And,' she says shakily, 'your ten o'clock appointment is a little bit . . .'

'Cancelled?' Rory says hopefully.

Alison glances warningly towards the office door behind which the sound of muffled crying can be heard.

'Upset,' she says faintly and, as Rory turns, it takes all

her strength of character not to remove the tiny piece of shaving tissue glued by blood to his neck. Instead she takes herself off to the bathroom and weeps three or four mascaraed tears before wiping them away in a practised manner with the palm of her hand.

In Rory's office a couple in their late fifties perch upright on the tightly upholstered sofa. They look apprehensively to the door as it opens. The Penningtons both wear an identical expression, that of people who don't deal with disappointments, but instead simply absorb them. They are reasonably new clients for the reasonably new business of Stately Locations. Rory took them on two months ago but since then, they've been to see him a staggering nine times. There's not much to set them apart from Rory's other clients – many of whom once represented the great names of England, but who are now lost individuals, virtual foreigners in their own country, and the journey that has brought them to Rory's door is littered with death duties, bitter sacrifices, noblesse oblige and Lloyds. All Rory's clients have different stories to tell, but their endings are identical and are faced with the same look of bewilderment, the same gentle sense of defeat. They're all Penningtons, Rory's clients, and in every Pennington, Rory sees our parents.

'My boy, good to see you.' Lord Pennington pushes himself to his feet and rings Rory's hand. 'You're looking well.'

'Thank you.' Rory says, but he has decided the problem of these people must be faced head on.

'Look, Lord Pennington, as I mentioned before, you really mustn't trouble yourself coming in so often, I'd be more than happy to discuss potential bookings on the telephone.'

'No trouble at all, dear boy,' Lord Pennington says blithely, 'I'm sure you're far too busy to waste time telephoning clients all day long.'

Rory grinds his teeth and stretches for a file on his desk which is, I note, strewn with sob story letters from 'Venice in Peril' and 'Friends of Highgate Cemetery' etc. It's hard to believe Rory has become a soft touch for this sort of thing – but then let's be honest, Rory views his life differently now – and this is just as well. These days he has inherited the role of eldest son and all the fun and games that go with it.

'Right well. ITV are looking for a location for *Middlemarch*,' Rory reads from his file. 'A couple from New Jersey will die happy if only they can sleep in a king's bed. Apparently any old king will do . . . the splendidly loaded Mr and Mrs Lieberman from Palm Springs are interested in buying a title and are willing to pay really exciting amounts of money for it . . . and an American TV team are researching some icky Anglophilic piece.'

The Penningtons bow their heads, predictably uncheered by Rory's unique brand of sarcasm. 'Dell computers are looking for somewhere to host a retreat.' There's no attempt to keep the boredom from Rory's voice, 'and finally some gossip magazine needs a ballroom in which to photograph a "quality" soap person.'

He glances up. Until now he's managed to avoid the

ludicrous expression of misery on Lady Pennington's face, which is taut with the effort of not crumpling.

'Look,' Rory relents, 'I know it's a nightmare having strangers in your home but . . .' Rory tries in vain to dredge up the mitigating circumstances that have forced him to commit to this hellish job but finds himself at a loss.

The truth is the business of Stately Locations has not panned out exactly as Rory foresaw. When conceived eight months ago in a reckless bid to help the parents, it made sense. People like the Penningtons desperately needed money if they were to keep their homes. In return interested parties with cash would be able to appreciate the history and beauty of some of England's great houses, not normally open to the public. This notion proved depressingly naïve. The reality is that Stately Locations appeals to rich Americans prepared to pay for their slice of culture, or worse, scabby journalists intent on a scoop. Oh the business is lucrative all right, but it's repellent.

'It's not that,' Lord Pennington interrupts, 'it's . . . well . . . you see . . .' He falls into an uncomfortable silence.

'The thing is . . .' Lady Pennington attempts to clear her personal puissance for the second time.

I hope and pray with every fibre of my body she will not burst into tears. Last time the Penningtons came they brought with them an envelope of receipts. 'Life is so costly,' they said, 'bills so high, capital almost gone.' Tears had flowed, handkerchiefs had been wrung out. When Rory suggested they write down their major expenses it transpired they still had a cook, a chauffeur, a housekeeper and a butler.

When he instructed them to fire three out of four, I thought the paramedics might have to be called.

'We've tried to economize as you suggested. We got rid of the car,' Lord Pennington finally gets it out, 'oh . . . this is all so embarrassing,' he hangs his head.

'The thing is,' Lady Pennington looks beseechingly at Rory, 'taxis home have proved *surprisingly* expensive.'

'But Lady Pennington,' Rory is aghast, 'home is over two hundred miles away.'

'Yes, of course it is,' she says, wide eyed, blinking rapidly, 'but you said—'

'When I suggested public transport, I had in mind uh,' he looks at their uncomprehending faces, 'well . . . uh . . . a coach.'

Lord and Lady Pennington could not look more shocked had they just been informed of the second coming of the Lord.

'A coach?' they repeat blankly. It really is a revelation to them that this degree of cost cutting might exist.

'Well, well.' Lord Pennington gets to his feet. 'What a weight off the old shoulders.'

He grips Rory's hand, 'Always feel so much better after these little sessions, don't we, my dear?' He pats his wife clumsily on the shoulder. She, in turn, beams mistily at Rory.

'Lord Pennington, Lady Pennington . . . with great respect,' Rory breaks off, 'look you really must try to understand,' he says wildly, 'this is a locations finding agency, not a bloody counselling service.'

'Absolutely.' Lord Pennington says, 'Quite right, quite

right. Point entirely taken, totally understood.' He steers his wife towards the door. 'Same time next week then?'

Believe me, if I had the power, I'd go down there, take hold of Rory's head and bang it against the wall for him.

maggie

When I got back to my room in the Cadogan Hotel, Jay was lying on the bed. 'Jesus,' he said. 'Do these trolls in congress actually believe the bumper sticker drivel they spout?' He was stretched out on top of the chintzy counter-pane, reading the *Wall Street Journal*, glasses on his nose. His hair was flat where he'd been sleeping on it, and he'd been using his old leather briefcase as an extra pillow. His beat-up Nikes had been tossed onto the floor by the armchair. I sat on the bed and grinned at him. There was no point in asking him how he'd broken into my room. Hotels were, after all, his speciality.

Jay was my lover. We'd met at a human rights convention at the Kennedy Centre in Washington. Before I worked at *Newsline*, I spent five years at WKM TV, a small but respected local station up in Maine, where I did time writing, producing then field producing before I finally made correspondent. Anyway, a local counsellor with whom I'd become friendly while researching a story was speaking and had invited me to come along. It was going to be one of those off the chart scary evenings so I don't know how I talked myself into saying yes, let alone turning up. Some people have an irrational fear of spiders and mice, but my own room 101 is filled with people in tuxedos drinking champagne and engaging in small talk.

Even the time I picked up an award for a story I'd worked on I was at the ceremony, crouching in the loo with a cigarette for most of the evening, so when my name was announced I didn't hear it. Coming back into the room I couldn't think why everyone was looking around expectantly and clapping. I was so discombobulated that when I eventually staggered up to the mike I could only admit that I had to pee rather than say I had to smoke. For obvious reasons that night still ranks as both the best and worst of my life.

So when I walked into the Kennedy Centre that evening a couple of years ago, I wished for a moment that I'd come with a guide, someone who would hold my arm and steer me through. But a career in television, its accompanying obsession with stories and weeks spent holed up in editing rooms, not to mention the sheer amount of travel – well being single just seems to go with the territory. It was OK. Manhattan is one of the few places you can live alone and not feel lonely. People are all around you, life is happening everywhere. If you're on a Kansas farm, hours from the nearest town, you might be excused for microwaving puppies or pickling the heads of wayward hitchhikers. Real loneliness mitigates all sorts of crimes. In fact, if you think about it, a crime of passion must be a luxury for a lonely person.

Anyway the point was that I had this *moment* standing alone in that big room. What if I was one of those women who never had long relationships, who never got married or had kids? I'd always loved being attached to nothing and no one — considering it an incredible freedom — but for ever?

The talk began. Courtesy of my friend I'd been placed in the front row so there was to be no escape. After nearly two hours of speeches, I became aware of the man next to me shifting uncomfortably in his seat. The speaker had just shown slides of mass graves in Rwanda and there was a prolonged and uneasy silence in the room during which my fidgety neighbour leaned towards me and produced a partially inflated whoopee cushion. 'Would it be inappropriate do you think,' he whispered, 'if I were to let this off now?' This was so out of left field that by the time I recovered he was up on stage. He introduced himself as Jay Alder. He was valedictorian of the event and admitted, almost sheepishly, that he had worked for Doctors without Borders for twenty years. He then proceeded to speak for forty minutes without notes and I was totally mesmerized.

By the time I'd come out of my trance the evening had descended into the kind of social maelstrom that leaves me stranded. I stood in its hub, conversation and laughter washing over me, and clutched the program of speakers I'd found on my seat. Jay's picture was on the back. He had thick grey hair and looks that were strong, rather than handsome. He'd drawn himself a Biro goatee and scribbled the caption 'In need of major refurbishment'. I felt my face heating up. It was as though he was already asking me to move in.

He appeared at my elbow. 'Do you know what you look like standing there?'

'What?' I accepted the glass of red wine he was holding out.

'Like an alien who's landed on earth and only just discovered they don't know how to breathe oxygen.'

He was staying at the Elliot Hotel. It was late by the time we got there. The restaurant was virtually empty. My shoes were pinching. My shift kept shifting.

He said, 'You don't look all that comfortable.'

I told him I thought I might be a freak of nature.

'How so?'

'Because when I'm dressed up as a butterfly, all I want to do is turn back into a caterpillar.'

He laughed.

'Besides . . . I borrowed this dress and I hate it.'

'There's a simple solution to every problem,' he said and nodded to the waiter for the check.

Later Jay said, 'Of course this would be an entirely inappropriate relationship.'

I was already having inappropriate thoughts about the word relationship so I didn't answer.

'Although I realize a man of my age must be almost irresistible for you.'

Lying in the darkness I couldn't see his face but I heard the irony in his voice.

'OK, so just how old are you?'

'Old enough to know better,' he said.

'What do you suggest then?'

He lit a cigarette. 'Maybe I can adopt you.'

The next morning, packing to leave, he said he would try to call, but it might be difficult.

'Sure,' I said lightly.

'It won't be for the usual reasons.'

Round up the usual suspects, I nearly said.

I assumed he couldn't call me because he was married. When I discovered he wasn't, I didn't feel relieved. Instead I was shocked to discover I hadn't felt guilty in the first place. I soon understood why a relationship would be impossible. His life was crazy, genuinely crazy, his world unrecognizable. Half his time was spent bearing witness to some of the world's most atrocious crimes, the other half, to keep a semblance of normality, he had to force himself to pretend those crimes weren't happening. Whenever I saw him, I wondered at the huge effort required to move seamlessly from one reality to the other.

Soon after I got back from Washington, I found an aeroplane sick bag amongst my post. On the back was a stamp from Nicaragua and on the front he'd scribbled, 'Can I get you out of my mind? The hell I can, but I'm working on it.'

Please don't work too hard, I thought.

daniel

Look I don't want you thinking that Rory is just some pastiche of a Hooray with a loser's job, because he's not. Stately Locations is not his first choice of career, truth be told it's not his choice of career at all. What he was by trade, and continues to be whenever he gets the chance, is an archaeologist, and a pretty good one at that. An obsession with age, which began in childhood with counting rings in trees, teeth in horses, layers in sedimentary rock and even the dry wrinkles on our mother's elbow, grew into a passion for dead things, restoration and travel, but despite being consultant to the V&A, it's a job that has never paid much, and certainly not enough for his current needs. So when the first telephone call Alison puts through to his office this morning is from the museum who want to know whether he'd be prepared to go to Turkey on a three month dig, his inability to accept leaves him even more frustrated than when he arrived.

Frustrated he should not be. Last night, I can report, he spent a night of unadulterated passion with Stella – at least let's qualify this phrase by describing it as a night of reasonable although uninspired sex. Still, this is not to be sniffed at – representing as it does a grand breakthrough for Rory. It would not be an understatement to say that Rory, since the sudden departure of Leona from his life, has been no Tom Jones. There have been precious few pants slung onto the sweaty stage of his libido. Stella is a beautiful, sharp girl who paints and works the London scene with equal ardour though somewhat less equal skill. Unfortunately Stella is also a girl who must take before she can give and I can tell you from personal experience that a sexual encounter with her might be fulfilling for the body but tends to leave the mind emptier than ever. When she asks him, whilst applying toner to her neck, whether he thinks she looks older in the harsh light of day, you can almost see him mentally scarpering off in the opposite direction.

By the time Rory has extricated himself from Stella's morning neurotics and made his way through the rain to Connelly Mews it's ten o'clock and a parking ticket is waiting on the windscreen of his Rover. As he peels it off, a garbage truck rolling through a puddle sprays him with the dregs of London's sewage. Now, hanging up the phone on the V&A, he sits at his desk and in general thinks evil things of the world.

On the other side of the glass partition Alison looks at him longingly. The more broken he seems, the more she yearns to fix him. Her dreams are feverish, peppered with images of stroking away his pain. She imagines clasping him to her bosom as he cries himself dry, at which point she will lead him to bed, remove his clothing and perform a little gentle oral sex in a further effort to exorcise his demons. In her fantasy he is the innocent who's languished twenty years in jail, the castaway marooned on an inhospitable island, or even the shell-shocked soldier returning from war. Whoever he is, she is there for him because he is, apart from his rotten temper, nearly perfect and she sometimes wonders whether her heart might burst with love.

In the meantime she pours a mug of coffee, spoons in four sugars then securing the morning's post under her arm, scuttles timidly to his office. She speculates whether a knock is appropriate, decides it is, but is not rewarded with an answer. Plucking up courage she turns the handle.

Rory barely looks up. Alison places the coffee on his desk and finding no further excuse to stay, has little choice but to go. Then luck smiles on her. Her gaze falls on the small pools of water gathering upon the floor.

'Oh,' she says happily, 'you're soaked.' She advances on him fussily.

'No, no,' Rory pushes his chair back and holds up his hands, 'I'm fine.'

'You should take those off you know, you'll catch a cold.'

'Back off, Alison,' Rory gives her a look.

'Or even flu,' Alison quavers.

The look turns to a glare. Rory points at his chin, 'See this?'

Alison creeps a bit closer.

'What is this?'

'A chin?'

'And on the chinny chin chin?'

How she hates him at moments like this. Her verbal artillery is not armed with the necessary warheads to combat such nuclear sarcasm.

'A spot . . . uh no . . . a hair?' She takes a deep breath. 'OK I understand what you're saying. You have stubble, you're not a baby.' She attempts a dignified exit.

'Thank you,' Rory calls after her. 'Thank you for being so, so understanding.' He is in fact behaving exactly like a baby but doesn't care. Alison is maddening. He lobs the mail into the in tray and is in the process of ripping into a brown paper package when the door opens for the second time. Alison is again bearing down on him.

'Give me the trousers,' she says.

He looks at the towel in her hand. The pile has been rubbed bare but he can just make out a pattern of frolicking highland terriers.

'I'm not putting that on.'

'You've only got that girl for the accounting job.'

'I don't care.'

'Your trousers will be dry by then, I'll put them on the radiator.'

'Absolutely not.'

'Someone has to look after you, Rory.' Bravely, Alison stands her ground.

'Oh for Christ's sake,' he explodes.

Alison waits patiently while Rory yanks down his trousers. He snatches the towel from her and wraps it round his waist.

Alison plucks the wet trousers from the floor and turns away triumphantly.

'I have a mother,' Rory shouts after her. 'God knows I don't need another one.'

He reaches for a pair of scissors and stabs at the brown package. Inside are two silver foil containers, one marked 'bread and butter pudding' the other 'cheese and onion pie'. Rory's face lights up. He reads the accompanying note, 'To keep the wolf from the door! Happy Birthday, Love Nanny'.

maggie

Jay was gone by the time I surfaced. I pulled the pillow towards me and groaned. Almost always he had to leave before I did. Almost always I wished he could stay. These trysts left me with nothing more tangible than the imprint of his hands on my skin, his smell on the sheets.

I had never once asked how he managed to track me down so successfully. With anybody else, the assumption that I would always be pleased to see him might have seemed like gross arrogance, but not with Jay.

Before Christmas, Jay had left for East Timor where the previous summer Doctors without Borders had been evicted along with all other humanitarian organizations. He re-established health care facilities for the displaced population before travelling on to Bosnia, where he was now based. London was a lot closer to Sarajevo than New York. Jay was a pretty good ulterior motive for staying in England.

All I wanted to do was drift back to sleep but I'd been in negotiations with Simon Brannigan's aristo 'wide boy' and was supposed to be meeting him at his agency to pick up an itinerary covering the next few weeks. I crawled out of bed and padded into the bathroom, standing under a cold shower to force myself awake. There'd been a time at *Newsline* when we would not have been put up in hotels with marble bathrooms and gold shower fixtures. Those were the days when *Newsline* was struggling and when some of the stories it ran caused advertisers to yank their budgets. A segment Alan once put out about abortion lost him three hundred thousand dollars and it took a long time to prove to advertisers that contentious subject matter delivered viewers. Contentious subject matter was the reason I went to work for *Newsline* in the first place. Jay was right. To hell with the puff piece.

'So how's it going?' he'd asked. We'd been lying on the bed, the television tuned into CNN. The crew had finally showed up that morning and I'd whisked them straight from the airport to the Houses of Parliament where we had an appointment to film Lord Canaver. He was a stately old peer and supposedly an expert on Northern Ireland. He'd agreed to be interviewed when I'd done the original research but the minute we started filming he pulled out just like all the others. I was beginning to panic. I almost didn't care what we got on film as long it was something. We ended up trailing him halfway across London before eventually being turned away at his club.

'Is it because I'm not wearing a jacket?' I asked the porter. OK so I was being facetious. I knew full well White's was a gentleman's club.

The porter gave me a supercilious once-over.

'Madam,' he said, 'Jackets are for potatoes, gentlemen wear coats and ladies are simply not welcome.'

'You got to hand it to these people,' I reached for the water by the bed, 'for dinosaurs, they've lasted pretty well.'

Jay was channel-hopping looking for the same report from a different source. Jay's daily media diet consisted of snacks of NBC, ABC, CNN before embarking on a main course of newspapers, the *New York Times*, *Wall Street Journal* and the *Washington Post*. 'If there's more than one version of the truth, that means there is no truth,' he was fond of saying.

'I'm surprised Alan sent you. *Newsline* is built on reliable typecasting. He must know he's better off keeping you on the front line with an Uzi.'

'Well, I guess I got the sticky end of the lollipop this time.'

'I tell you why you didn't get your Middle East piece.' Jay switched off the television. 'Some advertising focus group had told CBS to tell their executives to tell your boss that a puff piece shot in grand old houses is exactly what's needed to recapture the twenty to thirty demographic.'

Jay's current *bête noire* was America's obsession with demographics – and to be fair he had a point. I recently heard even Barbara Walters say on *20/20* that once you've reached the age of forty-nine it is statistically proven that you use the same toothpaste for the rest of your life.

'I like your White's club story. There's opportunity there.'

'Like what?

'Like, let's see,' he rubbed his fingers around his temples, a habit he had when he was tired, 'there's snobbery, debauchery, Christ, there's even lunacy if you want it. Come on, you said it yourself, this is the English aristocracy we're talking about, a group of people living in ivory towers whose time has come and gone. Just what is their point any more – if any?'

'They're hardly falling over each other to tell me. I'm having problems enough with access as it is.'

'So do a little sleuthing. Ask the right questions, do what you're good at and blow a little smoke up their butts. Give these people enough rope, Maggie, and sooner or later, I guarantee you, they'll hang themselves.'

daniel

'What do you mean you didn't allow them in to any of the main rooms?' Rory asks. 'Surely that's what they were paying to see?' He presses his Biro into the notepad. 'Yes, but you must understand, you *are* doing this for the money, Lady Harcourt . . . no, it's because you *are* broke . . . quite penniless in fact.' From the other end of the line come the unmistakable sounds of his client's impending breakdown. Lady Harcourt is victim of the usual: heavy taxes, bad investments and an astonishing ability to bury her head in the sand. She has inherited a large but severely encumbered estate to which Rory recently organized a visit by a busload of wealthy Japanese widows prone to extravagant tipping. From the sound of it this outing has not been a resounding success.

'No, no, please, Lady Harcourt, I beg you, don't start crying again. Let me have a word with Benj, I'm sure we can sort something out.' He endures a few more tearful burblings before he lucks out with the dialling tone.

'Where the fuck is Benj?' He slams out of the office. 'I *told* him to go with them. Lady Harcourt is *not* used to dealing with, and I quote, *"The Great Unwashed"*. She's a die-hard Grade One for crying out loud.'

Grade One and Grade Two in Stately Locations does not imply, as you might be forgiven for thinking, the architectural integrity of clients' houses, but rather, their owners' level of skill in dealing with the General Public — Grade One being the most inept. Rory looks with exasperation at Benj's empty desk, overflowing with coffee-ringed paperwork. 'Why am I insane enough to employ him?'

'Because certain of our clients find me rather reassuring,' Benj says. He has been unwilling, during Rory's tantrum, to move from his position on the floor, primarily because it affords him a great view up Alison's skirt. This has to be one of the better early morning views Benj has enjoyed for quite some time.

He's not in a good way my cousin, Benj. He's been a fuck-up all his life, who wouldn't be with his background. An only child, the product of generations of stifled upbringing, it's not surprising he's lost and feckless; what *is* surprising is that he's lost and feckless with quite so much charm. He's always had a drinking habit, but recently this habit has sloshed over into the more hazardous category of dipsomania. Most evenings he quaffs himself into a stupor then wakes the next morning in a strange place, no memory whatsoever of how he got there. When this happens people tend to rescue him. Like a puppy, they feed him, check the name on his leash and someone, usually Rory, is called to fetch him home.

A few months ago, having driven all the way to Wimbledon Greyhound Track, only to find half a dozen canteen ladies ironing Benj's rumpled jacket and frying him a second egg, Rory decided enough was enough. He bought him a desk, gave him a chair and forced him into some compulsory hard labour.

'Well most of our clients can't find you *at all*,' Rory says, grabbing him under the arms, 'you're about as bloody competent as a bag of snot.'

'Yes, you're quite right, Rory,' Benj allows himself to be heaved into a sitting position. He rummages in his coat, whose pocket bag has finally given way and deposited its contents; a corkscrew, one honeyed date and a paperback edition of *Lord of the Flies* into the lining where they now sit, evenly distributed along the hem like old-fashioned tailors' weights.

'Did he sleep on the floor?' Alison whispers. Not privy to the full depravity of Benj's lifestyle she is aghast at such a notion, 'Has he been *drinking*?'

And for a moment Rory looks helpless.

Had he been drinking? They'd asked him the same question at the morgue. The problem is you can't breathalyse the dead. A post-mortem reveals me to be only twice over the limit but over whose limit pray? Was it not Winston Churchill who said, 'I have always taken more out of alcohol than it has taken out of me.' Considering all the lethal things you get up to when really plastered, to be exiled from life when you're only partially tipsy surely qualifies for the cliché of being hanged for the crimes you don't commit.

Benj has now found the remains of a kebab he'd stowed in his coat last night. He fails to notice the disgusted expression on Rory's face until he's mid-chew.

'Sorry, Rory,' he says meekly, offering it up as though it

were a quarter pound of fine Iranian sevruga. 'Have you had breakfast?'

Rory grabs the kebab from Benj and hurls it to the other side of the studio – at which precise point the outside door to the office opens and a girl walks in. Benj and Alison stand open-mouthed, like a couple of wax dummies. The kebab looks set to hit her but she dodges athletically and it smacks against the wall leaving a grease mark on the paint. Rory recovers first. He looks at the girl by the door, then double takes and stares at her. Despite the messy ponytail, the face scraped clean of make-up, she is unusually pretty for an accountant. 'Yes?' he says, sickeningly pleasant all of a sudden. 'Can I help you?'

He sits her down at the chair in front of his desk. 'So . . .' he begins then stops almost at once, at a loss apparently for an intelligible follow-on. Mechanically his finger goes into the bread and butter pudding. 'You're an American!'

'Uh. Yeah,' she says, eyes busy taking in the damp shirt, the bare legs sprawling loosely under the desk.

'Been in London long?'

'Uh, no. Not that long.'

'Like it so far?'

'Oh sure . . . it's great.'

'It's a good city to live in and . . .' he trails off, seemingly mesmerized by a tiny piece of skin on the left-hand side of her neck, 'But ah . . . you're all legit and everything I assume.'

'I beg your pardon?'

'I mean you've got your papers and everything?'

'Well I've got everything I need right here,' she pulls her knapsack onto her lap, 'if that's what you mean.'

'Good, perfect,' Rory says, 'because we don't want customs and immigration dragging you off your first day do we?'

'Uh . . .' she narrows her eyes questioningly, 'no . . . not really.' There's a long pause. Her ponytail has worked its way loose. She sweeps her hair into a knot and secures it with the elastic. 'The thing is,' she says carefully, as though weighing up the possibility that she's dealing with the village idiot, 'I'll be pretty much ready to get going in the next few days. So I was wondering, really, well . . . is everything under control, I mean . . . are you organized?'

'Organized?' Rory queries. 'Well, no, not really. In fact I would have to say, truthfully . . . not at all.' He leans over the desk, 'You see if we were organized chances are we wouldn't really need you now would we?'

She's openly staring at him now, clearly thinking that her original assessment was correct – he *is* a little simple . . . then suddenly she twigs.

'You have absolutely no idea why I'm here do you?'

'I . . .' Rory is completely thrown. 'Of course I do.' but he's looking at the wide forehead, at those strange eyes, brown, even hazel in the light and almost slanted really and he's thinking, *Forget no work papers, forget customs, it would be plain distracting to have her around the office.*

The telephone starts ringing. 'They'll get that next door.' Rory shifts uneasily in his chair

They don't.

The ringing continues.

Rory straightens a single piece of paper on his desk in

an effort to regain control of the meeting – and still the ringing continues. The girl's eyes slide towards the telephone.

Rory snatches it up. 'Yes.'

'Benj here,' comes the stage whisper. Benj is sitting on the floor in the reception area, his body hunched around the receiver. 'I'm actually still on the premises . . . and I realize of course that you're busy.'

'Yes.' Rory swivels his chair towards the wall.

'I was just wondering whether now would be a good time to tell you that—'

'Yes.' From the corner of his eye Rory watches the girl as she wanders over to the bookshelf and begins inspecting the spines of his archaeological books.

'Those uh . . . Americans are coming for their itinerary today as opposed to uh . . . tomorrow.' Benj clears his throat. 'As I might have perhaps originally led you to believe.'

'I see, how very helpful of you, thank you so very much.' Fuming, Rory places the receiver down. He tips his chair back and gropes for a package in the in tray on the ledge behind him. 'Maggie Munroe.' He reads off the label. The girl turns from the bookcase. She's wearing khaki combat trousers and a standard white T-shirt. Up until this point Rory has been oblivious to his own rather more eccentric form of dress. Grimly he tightens the towel around his waist. 'Robert Jones,' he says, putting out a hand, 'well, Rory most people call me. Maybe we'd better start again.'

'Fine by me,' she shakes it. Then things get a little awkward. He has of course meant to let go of her hand in the traditional manner but as she sits down he finds he's still holding on to it — moreover for a short moment it looks like it's all he can do not to clamber over the desk and sink his teeth into her neck. In the nick of time he pulls himself together.

'Right then,' he gives his head a little shake, 'you're with *Newsline*, and you're here to do a piece about the aristocracy for which you have given us . . . ah yes,' his eyes scan the paperwork, 'the usual brief — pomp, circumstance, some grand interiors and a duke or two.'

'You seem a little surprised.'

'Let's just say you weren't exactly who, or rather what, I was expecting.'

'Really,' she smiles, 'what were you expecting?'

Well for this not to be batted back at him for a start. He is now confused. Is she being direct, or is she flirting? He's played this game before of course, it's just that he's forgotten the rules. 'As a matter of fact,' he says, 'you're a great deal older than I was expecting and frankly a lot uglier.'

There's a flash of a grin, but so quick he can't be sure. 'How disappointing for you.'

She crosses her legs.

'Disappointment has become something of a hazard in this job.'

'In that case should we maybe dispense with the . . . uh . . . well . . . whatever, and get down to business?' She pulls a black file from her knapsack.

'Fine by me,' Rory shuffles through the paperwork in his hand. 'I've done a bit of work on the list you sent in and so far, of the people you requested, the Roxmeres have turned us down.'

'Pity.' She draws a line through their name.

'Balmoral is a little unlikely, as you might have guessed. Blenheim's a definite no.' He looks up, 'Where on earth did you get this list from?'

'Why. What's wrong with it?'

'You don't think you set your expectations just a little high?'

'I was told you could get a foot through the door.'

'Well, yes, some doors and it depends whose foot. Most of these people would rather have red hot needles poked in their eyes than be filmed.'

'Maybe so . . . but we have twenty million viewers and that kind of advertising you can't buy.'

'Hmm.' He looks at her closely, 'OK, well Hartingdon is actually not on our books, but I've called them — they might be interested.'

'Wait a minute, you missed one.' She frowns. 'Page four?'

'Hartingdon is page four.'

'Bevan is my page four.' She turns the papers to show him a photocopy of a newspaper article. A couple standing on the steps of an imposing eighteenth-century house. 'The Earl of Bevan? The queen's cousin?'

Before Rory is forced to respond, Benj provides a handy diversion by pushing through the door with a large tray. He's lost weight, Benj has. When he walks his trousers flap against his bony shins as if they're hanging on a washing line.

'Morning,' he says cheerfully. 'Coffee?' He positions a cup in front of Rory and a mug in front of the girl. 'One espresso and one Americano.' He utters Americano with great flourish, as if he were announcing the name of a Broadway musical. 'Benjamin,' he introduces himself.

'Maggie,' she says. 'Hi.'

Benj perches on the edge of the desk. 'Do carry on,' he says graciously, wrapping his grandfather's checked overcoat around him. Like most drunks, Benj is permanently cold.

'So, Bevan . . . cousin of the queen,' The girl turns back to Rory, 'famously beautiful house.'

'Er, right, Bevan,' Rory interrupts, 'actually Bevan is not a possibility because the house is,' he pauses, 'well as a matter of fact the house is—'

'Closed,' Benj says.

'Closed . . . right,' Rory repeats gratefully. 'Exactly. Thank you. The house is closed.'

'Couldn't we set something up with the Earl? From what I hear, he's some character.'

'Some character . . . Is that what they say?' he mutters.

'Yes, what do you reckon? Can you fix something up?'

'No.'

She blinks at him.

'The fact is,' Rory casts around, 'he's not . . . look the Earl is not—'

'There,' Benj says.

She looks from one to the other.

'The Earl's not there,' Rory repeats slowly, 'because he and his wife have gone—'

'Mad,' Benj says simply.

'What?' the girl says. 'Both of them?'

Rory glares at Benj.

'Both of them,' Benj ignores him. 'Mad as baboons.' He

hugs his arms round himself as if in a strait jacket and makes a gormless face.

Maggie Munroe starts packing away her things. 'Look,' she says, exasperation creeping into her voice, 'I don't have a lot of it, but you guys clearly need more time.'

'I'm sorry.' Rory shovels the last of the bread and butter pudding into his mouth and follows her through to the main office. 'The truth is one or two people *have* let me down recently.' He sends a draconian look back at Benj before wrenching open the door. 'But I'll deliver everything to you tomorrow. I promise.'

Outside the rain has stopped. A tiny ray of sun shines up the wet tops of the buildings. 'To your hotel,' he adds. His feet are turning blue on the wet pavement. 'Deal?'

But the girl is distracted by something. 'Jesus,' she says, apparently revolted, 'I wouldn't want your neighbours.' Rory inclines his head. Suspended by the neck, two dead birds are spinning slowly at the end of a rope attached to the door frame of the house next door. This, as it happens, is the other half of the mews building, where Rory lives. The pigeons, shot at the weekend, have been hanging for a couple of days and Rory wonders whether they are ready for plucking.

'January's a dismal month,' he suggests. 'Perhaps they were depressed.'

'Excuse me?'

'Look.' Rory drops the empty foil container in the bin. 'I'm truly sorry for the delay, I hope we don't seem too unprofessional.'

'Well,' the girl considers him, 'you didn't know I was coming, you haven't got my itinerary, you're wearing a skirt printed with,' she peers closer, 'some kind of rodent, and you've been eating something I wouldn't allow in my apartment, let alone my stomach. I can't imagine why I might have that impression.' Then she smiles prettily and sashays off leaving Rory staring after her, clutching his damp towel, looking not unlike a disgraced Roman legionnaire stripped of his shield.

Benj sits at his desk eating stem ginger.

'Fat lot of help you were,' Rory says, swiping the jar from him and digging out a chunk.

'I thought we didn't do "fly on the wall",' Benj says.

'We do this time.' Rory licks his dripping fingers then retrieves his trousers from the radiator.

'Why?'

'Rich flies.'

'How much?'

'Plenty much.' Rory rubs his thumb and forefinger together.

'Goodee.' Benj screws the lid back on the jar. 'In that case what's your problem with Bevan? Why can't they be normal clients like any others?'

'Because, as you so subtly put it earlier, they're not really very normal are they?'

'So,' Benj says, 'none of our clients are normal.' He leaves the ringing telephone for Alison. 'Presumably you've checked out the luscious Miss Munroe, and it's not like they couldn't do with the cash?'

Alison murmurs something then puts her hand over the receiver. 'Rory?' she says tentatively.

'You're actually suggesting putting them in front of a camera,' Rory says.

'Why not?'

'You don't think that might be just a tiny bit foolish?'

'Rory?' Alison tries again.

'What you have to understand, Rory, is that the kind of Americans we deal with love the aristocracy,' Benj says. 'They can't help themselves, it's a sort of compulsion to be impressed by breeding and culture, I mean the word "lord" is so dazzling to them they can't see the woods for the trees as it were. If I were you, I'd take any money you can get for Bevan.'

'Rory,' Alison interrupts timidly.

'What?' he snaps and takes the receiver she's holding out to him.

'You've always been a little over-sensitive about Bevan,' Benj continues oblivious to the darkening look on his cousin's face.

'After all, how embarrassing could it be?'

The definition of a waste of time must surely be getting people repeatedly out of trouble. As Rory noses the Rover onto the dual carriageway he feels like he's being regularly screwed out of time and energy. The police hadn't been specific on the phone but they didn't need to be. Their tone was familiar enough.

There isn't much traffic on the M1 and he finds himself close to the exit for Stockton on Tees roughly three hours later. A flashing sign over the bridge announces the reduction of the speed limit to 20 miles an hour. Cars have slowed to a crawl. Rory's thoughts turn instead to the girl. OK so she might have been a witch but she'd had a smile that serious face hadn't prepared him for. When she'd grinned it had been wide and wicked, like someone had just told her an unbelievably dirty joke. Then he rounds the bend and all thoughts of her disappear. A line of bollards cordon off the slow lane in which, to Rory's growing apprehension, he sees three cars welded together in a mess of disfigured metal. Angry drivers stand beside the vehicles, gesticulating furiously to policemen who, in turn, are taking notes. Ahead, an RAC truck turns through the gap in the bollards. Rory follows suit. A policemen shoves his hand in front of the windscreen. Rory gives his name and the name of the detective he spoke to earlier. The bollards are moved aside and a quarter of a mile further on Rory parks the Rover next to a service truck. Slamming the door shut, he notices that the bank to his left has been torn up, the bushes on the top flattened to reveal a ploughed field where a dozen uniformed men from the Motorway Services Department are milling around. Two more policemen stand on the edge of the hard shoulder, charting their progress and barking unintelligibly into walkie-talkies.

'So what ploughed? Don't know which crop. Mud with weeds looks like. Well stand by. Who? Oh he's here, is he? Where?'

'Excuse me?' Rory says.

'Got him. Yes. Now.' The policeman turns to face him. 'You're the gentleman my superior spoke to earlier?'

Rory nods.

'I see,' the policeman says. His colleague stares out over

the field across which the MSD are now tramping, arms linked like Morris dancers.

'Let me see if I have this correct, sir,' the first policeman says. 'This *thing* that has caused a multiple pile up on the motorway – this *creature* that has wasted four hours of police time, not to mention head-butted two members of the emergency services, belongs to your *clients* and is moreover being kept in their grounds for its *milk*?'

'Well yes,' Rory concedes, 'although not so much milk apparently, more . . . er . . .' he breaks off. The men in the field have started running. Rory and the policemen stare mesmerized as the large shaggy head of an American buffalo careers into view over the ridge. Panicked, the men split as the creature gallops through their ranks and charges towards the mangled hedge. Its pursuers, abandoning all attempts to maintain their line, resort to chasing after it in ragged chaos.

'As I was saying, not so much milk,' Rory says and does some brutal coughing. 'Cheese. Mozzarella cheese to be more accurate.' He can already visualize the headlines. *Saintly widowed mother mauled by buffalo, Siamese twins brain damaged by single kick. Handicapped busload of refugees . . .* Christ. He does a quick spot check. No bodies, no ambulances, and so far, thank the Lord, no press. Damage by the creature should be covered by Bevan's third party insurance, in the unlikely event of it being paid up to date.

The second policeman is looking sceptical. 'Is mozzarella cheese not traditionally made from the milk of the *water buffalo* rather than the American buffalo, sir?'

Rory digests this. Quite honestly he has never considered

whether mozzarella came from an American buffalo, a giraffe or was grown on trees.

'I'm sure that is technically correct, yes,' he says carefully. He looks into the faces of the two men and gives up.

'The thing is . . . it's actually rather hard to explain.' The expression on both policemen's' faces remains politely enquiring. 'My clients, themselves, are also . . . a little hard to explain.'

'And your *clients* would be, sir?' The second policeman who we shall now refer to as PC Fuckface, gazes at Rory with a faux deferentialism that makes Rory want to punch him in the kidneys.

'Alistair and Audrey Bevan,' Rory says. Thinking that by not giving their full name there is a chance, a tiny, insignificant, one-in-a-million chance that these two bastard pigs won't inform the press. A chance that next week will not have to be spent fending off journalists, that he will not tomorrow read the dread headlines in the *Sun*, but a chance that promptly dies a death with the knowing looks the police are busy exchanging. The first policeman carefully puts his pencil and notebook away. PC Fuckface itches a leg with his baton. 'That would be the Earl and Countess of Bevan, would it, sir?'

Rory is impotently furious at the large bold font of 'sir', but he's again diverted by the noise of thundering hooves. The buffalo, looking more pleased with itself than it has any right to, appears over the hedge. The policemen take a step back. The creature gazes down as if contemplating the wisdom of such a long jump – but it's a pause too long. There's a crack. The buffalo looks round in mild surprise and more than a little reproach at the emergency services, whose ranks have now swelled to twenty men, one of whom is hastily reloading his stun gun.

'As I was saying, sir,' says PC Fuckface. 'If the Earl and Countess are unable to keep their . . . er . . . little business ventures under control, they are very likely, next time, to find themselves behind bars.'

There's a screech of tyres as two vans side swerve the bollards. The press have arrived. Rory watches with loathing as men jump out trailing wires, cabling and a video camera which they point at the bank with feverish excitement. And now we can see why. A late-middle-aged lady in gumboots and tweed skirt has appeared on the scene. Positioning herself between the stun gun and the buffalo she calmly slips a leash over its head then leads the newly docile creature off over the ploughed fields. Rory turns back to the police. 'Do me a favour,' he says wearily, 'why don't you just arrest them now.'

maggie

When I was born the doctor's big joke was to tell my parents that I looked like a savage. My eyes were black, my face purple. Oh yes, the midwife had agreed, I'd come out whooping and hollering, all but carrying a tomahawk. The midwives were prone to laughing at the doctor's jokes because they thought he was pretty cute. My parents just thought he was a bigot. My colouring came as no surprise to them. My mother's great grandmother was Native American, a Kiowa who married a farmer from Oklahoma and with my sticking out cheekbones and black hair, I had obviously inherited her blood. As a child I loved to show off about my maternal ancestors, less interested in my father's more pedestrian Irish roots. When everyone else was hooked on Eloise and Stuart Little, my mother was busy reading me *Bury My Heart at Wounded Knee*. At school I argued the case for the Indians like the whole of their race depended on me.

I guess I should explain. As a child I was subjected to a degree of political conditioning. If I told you I had seedless grapes snatched from my hands because exploited Mexicans had been forced to pick them you might get the picture.

No weekend was complete without a protest outside City Hall and I went to my first anti-Vietnam march on Dad's shoulders, a sort of variation on a take-your-daughter-to-work day. Our photograph ended up in the *New York Post*. The next afternoon when a friend came over to play she asked me what a draft-dodging hippy was. My mother was incensed and quoted from Art Buchwald's column in the *Washington Post*. 'Do you realize,' she said, 'that with the amount of money required to kill each Vietcong, you could fly him first class to America, buy him a Cadillac, a membership to the most expensive country club in Connecticut – you could turn him into a bona fide capitalist and it would still be cheaper.' OK so that may not be entirely accurate paraphrasing, but I was only four years old at the time.

'Doesn't matter what you do with your life,' Mom finished up, 'so long as you make a difference.'

I was thinking about this as I walked into the Cadogan Hotel following my appointment at the locations agency. The truth was I was pretty pissed. I stood on the squared-stone floor of the lobby looking around for Wolf and Dwight, watching the receptionists behind the front desk swipe credit cards and deal with enquiries. It was a nice hotel, friendly and welcoming with heavy curtains and deep fabric covered chairs. The clientele were mostly tourists, American from the look of them, sixty/seventy-year-old ladies holding Burberry umbrellas and booklets of theatre reviews, their short grey hair under baseball caps. It was all very white and polite, all very *comfortable*. I didn't want comfortable. I wanted to chase stories that meant something, it was like Jay said – I *was* happy in the trenches with my Uzi. Instead I'd been sent to cover a goddamn tea party.

Dwight and Wolf weren't in the lobby, or the breakfast room. When I rapped against their door upstairs, I heard the sound of joint snoring and felt better. I knew every peak and trough of that particular concerto. Dwight and Wolf were my crew, my crack team. I'd been on assignment with them both many times and Wolf in particular had become a real friend. We first met while I was working on the film for my degree. Political corruption was the subject of choice and it was, as I bored anyone foolish enough to listen, going to be so lid-blowing that American politics would reform itself overnight. Somehow I'd been granted permission to follow a New York senator with a dubious reputation, filming him going about his business, fly on the wall style. After two days trailing him from the Oak Bar to the Rackets Club to the Plaza, he finally had to attend some trifling matter of government in his office but this meeting had only just begun when the building was stormed by a ABC news team headed up by the infamous Philip Grigson. Grigson was a reporter I'd always admired but he turned out to be a real asshole, ordering both his crew and me around in an overloud voice. Some story had obviously broken but whatever it turned out to be, I was as determined to get it as he was. Things soon got ugly. Philip kept shoving huge furry microphones into my shot, trying to queer my pitch. I put enormous radio mikes on everybody in the room claiming them as mine. It was pretty academic because as soon as the senator's press aide arrived the whole lot of us were thrown out, but it was my wire that was pinned to the senator's righteous bosom and I prayed he'd fall for the oldest trick in the book, forget he was miked up.

And hallelujah he did.

Philip, his crew, my 'sound recordist', a friend from college and I were all hanging around outside the office. I was trying to act cool, my lens pointed carelessly at the floor, because as long as I was getting sound, and I was – it didn't matter what I had on film. I could run it over footage of a duck marrying a Great Dane in a Mormon ceremony if that's what it took, but Philip's enormous cameraman, taking up most of the bench next to me noticed my red record button was lit up. 'Hey,' he said accusingly.

Philip stopped pacing the corridor and looked up suspiciously. My heart was in my mouth. The senator was being accused of a gross misuse of funds, but if this giant exposed me, I would definitely be thrown out of the building. The cameraman looked at Philip, then back to me. 'Your lens could do with a polish,' he said and passed me a cloth which I used to cover the record button just as Philip walked over.

It was his voice that really made me notice him. Wolf has a beautiful voice, like oil running over pebbles. I don't know what his parents were thinking calling him Wolf, he should be named Bear. Even with the curve at the top of his back, the cameraman's permanent stoop, he's six foot three and broad with it. He doesn't walk so much as *lumber*.

Later that week, I bought him a coffee. He told me he disliked Philip intensely but was too lazy or, I thought privately, too stoned to do anything about it. When I went to work for *Newsline*, I tracked him down.

The noise inside the crew's bedroom reached a crescendo. Wolf might have a beautiful voice, but he had a real ugly snore. I decided to leave the boys to sleep, they were jet lagged and besides, now we had an extra day in hand. The door opened opposite and a breakfast trolley was pushed out. I was just snitching a piece of leftover toast when it opened again and this time a man in a towelling robe deposited a handful of eggy Kleenex onto the dirty plates.

'Morning,' I said, embarrassed to be caught.

The man sighed deeply, dug into the pocket of his robe and stretched across the trolley.

'Oh.' I looked down at the couple of pound coins in my hand. 'Thanks a lot.' As he shut the door hurriedly, I looked down at my T-shirt and army trousers. If I was going to infiltrate the upper classes, I really had to get myself a more subtle uniform.

daniel

If you were fortunate enough to be given a helicopter tour of some of England's more green and pleasant lands, chances are you'd be impressed by the approach to the Bevan Estate. Flying deep into the county of Yorkshire you eventually dip into a valley whose stone- and bracken-covered hills mark the boundary of the grounds. Descending over woods and parklands you can follow the curves of the river until you eventually spot the house, built in the seventeenth century from stone quarried locally. With its annexes, wings and turrets, you might suppose you were about to land on one of England's statelier homes run by an immense hierarchy of staff. Circling the north-east side of the house you might also imagine that one of the more eccentric members of the family, perhaps nursing a passion for hybrid architecture, had whimsically added a folly of darker stone – or was it some kind of unusual walled garden? By now you might conceivably be confused by the morass of greenery in the centre of this folly, and as you draw in closer you might question why much of its stonework seems to be missing, why corners don't meet in the traditional manner and why height levels are so worryingly haphazard.

Possibly it would have struck you by now that something was terribly wrong. What you've been admiring is not a folly at all, but an integral part of the house, the east wing. Except its roof has caved in, while its smoke-blackened walls have crumbled and pigeons, constantly circling its perimeter, spend their days depositing guano on anything that remains between them and the ground. In short the place is a ruin.

Rory, however, approaches Bevan via the more conventional route of its drive. Despite slowing to the sign-posted 5 miles per hour at the pillared entrance, the next couple of miles must be negotiated with extreme caution. Numerous switchbacks are layered with stones so lethal you might be forgiven for thinking they had been hand sharpened to render maximum damage to tyres. Gaping potholes are filled with muddied rainwater and just when you feel it is safe to speed up to a whopping 6 miles an hour your exhaust is nobbled by random sleeping policeman built to discourage local drivers from practising their rally racing skills using Bevan as a short cut from the railway station to the village of Skimpton.

As he draws up to the house Rory notices some recent state-of-the-art repairs. Guttering, eroded to splitting point has been spliced together with twine and wire. An old wooden tennis racquet has been nailed over the drains to catch leaves. Alistair and Audrey Bevan, roused by the noise of wheels on gravel, hurry out. Alistair is a bluff man of seventy-five dressed in corduroys and a checked Vyella shirt which carries the faintest smell of mothballs. Audrey wears her usual uniform of tweedy skirt covered by a sleeveless padded jacket, zipped up over a long sleeved version of the same garment. Alistair is also wearing a padded jacket, but his is new, ordered as a nod to modern times from a farming catalogue to which he subscribes. They are accompanied by a vast grey setter, all tangled hair and elastic strings of saliva, which bounds down the steps in front of them.

'Get down, Lurch,' Rory thunders as the dog makes its leap. Setters are a neurotic breed, attracted to the person who pays them the least attention, so Lurch merely slobbers a little more industriously before throwing himself into a grateful heap on top of Rory's boots.

'Mrs Emery claims Lurch has been worrying the sheep,' Audrey says. 'She had the nerve to ring up and get quite snippy on the phone but Lurch has never been interested in sheep.'

'Besides he was locked in the outside room all day,' Alistair says. 'Bloody woman, must have been somebody else's dog.'

'Or maybe it was somebody else's buffalo,' Rory says.

Alistair takes off his glasses and wipes them on his cardigan. Audrey examines the mud on her gardening gloves.

'Don't you think it might have been sensible,' Rory says, 'after the oyster bed fiasco, following the surprise failure of the stone-polishing business, to run the *Genius of Mozzarella* by me first?'

'We didn't want to bother you, Robert,' Audrey pats his arm, 'You have enough on your plate already,' she adds soothingly.

'Would have all been perfectly fine,' Alistair says, 'it's just that we failed to take one or two little extra expenses into consideration.'

'This stuff came out of its nose,' Audrey explains, 'bright

green, absolutely beastly, we could see he wasn't at all well, poor old thing.'

'Then what with the vet's bills, the general anaesthetic . . .' but Alistair, catching the expression on Rory's face, loses momentum.

'You see, Robert,' Audrey says confidingly, 'buffalo are not really indigenous to the north of England you know.'

Rory feels the familiar quicksand of nonsense sucking at his feet.

'You are aware that mozzarella comes from the water buffalo and not the American buffalo, aren't you?' he says.

This trump card leaves them silenced.

Rory presses his advantage. 'Well what arrangements have you made to get rid of it?'

'Get rid of it?' Alistair says astonished.

'Well yes, surely—'

'Don't be ridiculous, Robert,' Alistair says testily, 'Your mother's grown far too fond of it.'

Alistair and Audrey would do rather well in prison Rory muses as he wanders up the path to the church. There's something about the ingenuous that makes them indestructible. A favourite story about our mother proves this point. Before getting married she'd travelled to Boston to see friends. At the airport she'd taken a taxi as instructed but discovered halfway through the journey that she'd misplaced her purse. The driver unceremoniously abandoned her in *Bonfire of the Vanities* territory – and there she'd stood, a white woman with her sensible shoes, headscarf and neatly strapped luggage, waiting patiently for help to come along

— which it soon did in the form of a purple limousine bursting with Puerto Ricans, flick knives wedged between their teeth . . .

'You los', baby?' they'd drawled. 'You wanna lift?'

'How thoughtful of you,' Audrey said.

She furnished them with her friends' address and the car sped off. History doesn't relate as to the conversation en route, though I've always had this vision of her, in an identical though possibly shorter skirt than today, squashed between the sweaty vests of her rescuers, uttering such gems as, 'You seem like a nice young man,' and 'What do *you* do for a living?'

When the car cruised to a stop in front of a deserted warehouse, Audrey looked out the window and remarked, 'But this is not at all where my friends live.'

'Sowhat, Lady?'

'Well,' she'd said severely, 'They'd be most awfully upset if I were late for dinner.'

The Puerto Ricans were so taken aback by this apparent lack of concern regarding her forthcoming rape and brutal murder that they promptly drove her to the address she'd given and firmly refused a tip.

From time to time Rory strokes Lurch's head as the dog trots by his side. Above their heads, rooks are screaming and cawing, the spiky pods of their nests lodged in the leafless boughs of the sycamores. The sky rumbles with an approaching storm. The path narrows and mud squelches under his feet. It's wet. Again. Grey, wet and warm. Not that I approve of Rory's disinterest in the English countryside but global warming really has seen an end to decent weather. Newspapers are apt to quote statistics about average temperatures remaining the same, but God knows, seasons used to know how to behave themselves. Winters were cold, summers were hot. There were Christmases when the countryside froze. You can't conceive how beautiful Bevan is in the snow. That moment when you turned into the front drive was like stepping through the back of the cupboard into *The Lion, the Witch and the Wardrobe*. The magic kingdom of Bevan, preserved in ice, ignored by road gritters, untouched by the outside world. There are so many memories here, so many of them good. We used to toboggan down this bank off the church walk. We built a launching pad at the top. We'd start screaming, end crashing, wind caught in our throats. God but we were brilliant too. Headfirst, sitting, backwards, kneeling, crouching, we'd steer straight for obstacles, the bigger the better. Rory blinking back tears of fear because we were the Bevan Boys Daring Double Act. The fearless undisputed champions of the sled. And then there were the summers — when the air was thick and hazy with the smell of roses and burnt hay, when the heat drugged you, when you could only just muster enough energy to collapse on the lawn or lie in the boat listening to the water slap against the bottom.

As he walks alongside the wall, Rory touches the velvety edges of emerald moss on the stone. I will him to peel it off, to remember how it feels — as satisfactory as a scab off the knee — Christ, how can Rory not think about these things? If he were to stop right now, if he were to just *try*, he might hear the drone of the hornets, he would remember clipping sweet peas into a basket, remember licking their sticky dew off his finger. He would remember crawling under the strawberry net in the kitchen garden — but Rory doesn't stop and he doesn't remember. Rory doesn't do nostalgia at the moment.

The avenue before the church was once a topiary of yews planted by my great-grandmother's gardener, Bindey. Bindey was a hunchback and famous locally for his ability to hold the largest number of clothes pegs in one hand, winning first prize at the village fête for thirty years running. He was a splendid character, almost a distillation of old England really and he used to fuss over the yew trees as if they were the batch of unruly children he'd failed to conceive with his wife. Mrs Bindey worked in the house and Bindey was inconsolable when she died. Up until that point the bushes had always been the best-tended things on the Estate. Now they've been left to grow into bouffant affros, but when we were children they were clipped into precise shapes, peacocks and pheasants, hollowed out in the centre, some large enough to hide in.

'Seen the boys, Bindey?' Great-Grandpa would ask.

'No sir,' Bindey would lean on his shears, 'given you the slip have they?'

My great-grandfather was a passionate gardener. He spent all his time in the potting sheds and greenhouses. He walked the grounds with his stick every morning checking for frost damage. A gentle man, he reserved most of his aggression for the deer that ate the bark off his trees. He smoked sixty cigarettes a day and nicotine had streaked the skin yellow on his fingers. When he talked, he had to interrupt himself to cough. He refused to accept that there was any connection between his cough and the amount he smoked: 'It's a little cold I've picked up,' he would say, or 'The pollen count is high.' One winter, he became very bad. The doctor told him he had a clear choice – give up smoking or die of emphysema. Great-Grandpa listened quietly. As soon as the doctor left, he went to the gardening shed and smoked ten cigarettes in a row. Two years later he was dead.

Rory stands now before the headstone in the churchyard. The flowers from his previous visit have drooped tiredly over the edge of the jar as if, having realized the impossibility of being decorative any longer, they might as well take a well-earned rest. I've been wondering lately about this custom of leaving flowers on graves. Why not something more interesting? Photographs or favourite foods for instance. An apple and game pie from Paxton & Whitfield, or even potted shrimps would go down nicely but Rory has picked me some early crocuses. He props them up in the jar and whistles for Lurch who is conscientiously digging up Mrs Bindey a few rows away.

On his way back to the house he meets Alistair trudging up the hill, his walking stick making soft plops in the mud. Since Rory's arrival he's drunk a half bottle of whisky but this does not make him completely unaware of his son's disapproval. Awkward in each other's company neither speak till they reach the car.

'Are you coming down this weekend?' Alistair asks.

'Probably not, Pa.'

'Right then.' Alistair is a little disappointed, but at the same time, a little relieved.

Rory's got the engine started and is crunching gears into reverse when there's a knock on the window. Alistair's face looms comically close.

Rory rolls down the window. 'Quick,' Alistair says, 'before your mother sees.'

From behind his back he hoists an item which at first glance resembles a tree stump but on closer inspection turns out to be the waste paper basket from the South bedroom. It's about a foot and a half high and made from a scooped-out rhinoceros hoof. There are no words to describe the depths of its hideousness.

Alistair glances anxiously towards the drive. 'Take it up to London, could you?'

'Dad, keep it, it's worthless.'

'You know, I do believe that old urn has got a crack.' Alistair squints towards the pillar by the back drive where the urn has sat, cracked, since 1971.

'Dad, honestly, you might as well put it back.' Rory doesn't begrudge Alistair's selective deafness, believing it to be one of the great perks of old age.

'Nonsense,' Alistair says stoutly. 'If Sotheby's got a couple of hundred for that moose's head this'll definitely be worth a little something.'

Rory knows this is a fight he will not win. He hears Lurch barking. Audrey, on the home-stretch of her afternoon walk, will appear any minute around the bend in the drive.

Sighing heavily, he pings the lock on the boot.

The pigeons are still swinging from their makeshift gallows when Rory arrives back at Connelly Mews. He unhooks the string and drops the birds into the rhino bin before humping them up the stairs and into his flat where he casts helplessly around for an available corner.

In the home decorating style favoured by our mother, things do not get thrown away. The verbs *to jettison* or *to discard* are against her religion, which decrees that objects, irrespective of size and state of repair were invented to be accumulated. In fact it would be fair to say that Audrey does not officially acknowledge the concept of mess.

Take the kitchen worktop at Bevan. At any given time you might find the following: a selection of chipped porcelain items, a damp sock, a dozen virtually empty jars with accompanying fungus of marmalade and chutney beneath their lids, one dead animal. Amongst these larger objects nestle old coins, (shillings, farthings) matchboxes, a nob of rancid butter, tiny exotic-looking shells, shreds of paper with illegible, though vital telephone numbers and inky pen tops – all of which are welded together by that special sticky paste made from dust, cooking grease and decomposed flies found exclusively in large English houses left uncleaned for twenty years. On top of all of this there would be the normal debris from daily food preparation. It's a wonder we didn't both die of E-coli as children.

As a result, Rory has always kept his flat white and gloriously possession free – at least until now. Lately ghosts from Bevan have begun taking up residence here. These days there's scarcely room to move amongst the plaster busts, stuffed birds and varying Dutch watercolours. On the table by the sofa sits the vase Rory sold for three hundred pounds and in the corner stands the card table that a private dealer from Cheltenham bought only last month. Those moose antlers, hanging on the wall and currently making themselves useful as a tie rack, recently fetched four hundred pounds at Sotheby's. Except they didn't, any of

them. It's a game Rory and Alistair play. A humiliation-free
method of inter-family money laundering. See, this is what
happens with our parents, you nail your foot to the ground,
then spend the next twenty years trying to gnaw it off
again.

Rory gives the bin a considered kick. It's not beyond the
realms of possibility that the chief of the Zulus once urinated
in it during a full moon and it's an irreplaceable African
artefact that by rights should be attracting millions of visitors
in the British Museum. 'Who would have believed it,' Rory
will be able to say to the newspapers, 'and to think, we
just kept rubbish in it.'

maggie

'Now let's see,' Dwight said, 'An earl is more important than a marquess, but a lord is more important than a sir . . .'

It was early evening and we were propping up the hotel bar having a drink. Dwight, my sound recordist, was a spry little man from Brooklyn prone to name dropping, preppy clothes and the occasional aggressive outburst. He was reading the copy of *Burke's Peerage* I'd purloined from Massey and acting like he was thrilled to be this close to a title, even if it was only on the printed page.

'Look. It's like poker,' I told him.

'How's that?' The barman, with whom I'd been flirting madly, was one of those Australian boys with a cherubic smile who was probably happier tossing sheep than shaking cocktails. He poured another shot of Jack Daniel's into my glass.

'Well see, a marchioness beats a viscount, which beats a sir. A full house of lords over earls is better than a couple of honourables – providing of course they aren't a pair of queens. A straight flush is better than a hot flush, but a royal flush,' I downed the bourbon in one, 'a royal flush scoops the board every time.'

The barman shook his head admiringly. 'I've never been able to get the hang of those.'

'Oh it's one of the few skills I'm really proud of.'

'Let's not forget baton twirling,' said Wolf. He emptied a bunch of photos out of a brown envelope. 'For you. Arrived Fed-Ex,' he raised one shaggy eyebrow, 'executive suggestions.'

I flicked through them quickly. English tourist scenes, even including one of the changing of the guard. 'Hmm, I think I might just manage to recognize the queen without a visual aid.' I dropped them into the bin behind the bar.

'Interested in the royal family are you?' The barman slid over a dish of monkey nuts.

'Why?' I asked, 'you friendly with them?'

'If I was, would I be working my hairy arse off in a bar?'

'I don't know. You could be their token peasant friend.'

'Poor Queenie,' the barman said. 'A nice lady with a bum job.'

'Yeah, poor Queenie,' Wolf said. 'Try to think of her as a downtrodden little woman who needs rescuing from her dysfunctional family . . .'

'I'll try,' I grinned, 'but it won't be easy.'

'Bishops, marquesses' younger sons, earls' elder sons, viscounts of England, Scotland then Great Britain . . . this is amazing,' Dwight said. 'It says here, one family can have up to ten different titles . . . ten!'

'Disgraceful, where's the guillotine when you need it.'

I swivelled my stool. It took me a second to realize that the man who'd spoken was Rory from Stately Locations. He looked different. He was dressed for a start. Black pants, grey turtleneck and heavy-soled boots. He had a deep frown line in the middle of his forehead which didn't dissolve when he smiled.

'Would you a like another whisky?' he asked.

'Bourbon? Sure, great, thanks.'

In his office I'd put him around late thirties. But there something really boyish about him. When he moved to the bar stool, I noticed his limbs were so loose they seemed attached to one another by holes and string.

I introduced the crew. 'Wolf, Dwight, this is Rory . . .?'

'Jones,' he said.

The three of them shook hands and I watched Rory Jones, like everybody else who's ever come across Wolf, trying to deconstruct his nationalities feature by feature. Wolf, a Japanese, Jewish American, is positively bizarre looking. Every feature he has is contradicted by another – a long ponytail at the back, a bald forehead at the front, the nose and the heavy skin of his Jewish father but the delicate almond eyes of his mother.

'Drink?' Wolf asked Rory.

'I don't, thanks.'

I was going to be facetious and say – what, never? Then I realized that 'don't', coupled with 'drink' always did mean never.

'So are we all set?' I said instead.

He undid a bulging envelope. 'We're all set. The good news is that the Duke of Roxmere has changed his mind. He's opening his house to the public next spring so this is a good time to get him. Also, if things go well, it will be easier for me to get you in elsewhere.'

'Fantastic.' This was a real scoop.

Researchers at *Newsline* had come up with the following: Roxmere family came from one of the most obscurantist sections of the English nobility. He was a diehard conservative who'd written several papers lamenting the loss of power and prestige of the aristocracy. He believed that the Empire's gravest error was to place political power in the hands of the lower classes. Thinking about Jay's sound bite, he seemed like a great candidate for snobbery.

Rory unpinned the envelope. 'Start with this. Map. Explanation of the house. History of the house. History of the family. Plenty of pomp and circumstance for you at Roxmere, dozens of servants, hundreds of staircases, wonderful pictures and . . . well, anyway, they're expecting us for lunch tomorrow.'

'Us?' I caught Wolf's eye. 'Oh no, there must be some mistake.'

'No mistake,' Rory said cheerfully. 'That's our job, read our brochure. We accompany people.'

'Well,' I said doubtfully, 'we work alone.'

He looked at me carefully. 'I don't think you quite understand. My clients are deeply distrustful of . . . er . . . *journalists*.'

'No problem,' Wolf said. 'Maggie's entirely used to that.'

'Plus the language in these places can be a little . . . oblique.'

'Oh I'm sure I can manage without an interpreter.'

'The point is,' Rory went on, 'it's a lot easier than you might imagine to put your foot in it.'

'So you're suggesting we "*Americans*" should be on best behaviour.' I was kidding, trying to keep things light.

'I'm simply suggesting that these people can require a little subtle *handling*.'

'You have my word. I won't snap my bubblegum between courses.'

His frown line only deepened. 'I think you're missing the point.'

I wasn't missing the point at all. The last thing we needed was somebody breathing over our shoulder.

'You're right,' I said. 'I'm sorry.'

'Fine,' he relaxed.

'Maybe it would be better for both of us if we found someone else to work with.'

I was startled by the flash of real anger behind his eyes. For a moment I thought he was going to tell us to go to hell, but I'd seen his offices; I had no idea what the English paid to film shampoo commercials in manor houses but I imagined it wasn't all that much.

He backed down. I could tell he didn't like it one bit but he covered it well. He secured the envelope with its metal pin. 'I'm sure you'll be fine,' he said. 'Good luck.' He shook hands with Dwight and Wolf. Then he put the envelope on the bar and walked out.

At the door he turned on his heel. 'Just one small word of advice.' The smile was back, lurking behind his eyes and for some reason it made me nervous, 'Be nice to all pets and for God's sake . . . don't be late for meals.'

'You look like you slept in the back of a truck,' Dwight said to me the following morning.

'Uhuh?'

'Want me to drive?'

'No thanks.'

'Because you know, if you're tired I'm very happy to drive.' He peered anxiously at the verge of the road. Dwight is a terrible passenger, always sucking in nervous intakes of breath and ostentatiously folding away side mirrors, but then I'm not much better myself. I'm visually dyslexic, I pretend to like to drive, but the real story is I have the greatest trouble reading maps. Not just maps either, architectural plans, Lego instructions. It's the reason I never did ballet. I always pirouetted anti-clockwise.

'I'm good thanks.' Really though I was tired. Unable to sleep, I'd spent half the night talking to Jay. 'I'm going to send you a screen saver with little computerized sheep leaping fences,' he yawned.

'Yeah right, you can't even work a computer.'

'I'll have one of the young people in my office see to it,' he said loftily.

'Sometimes a person can be tired without even knowing,' Dwight ventured.

I hit the brake. 'Dwight, Jesus, if you feel more comfortable driving, just say so.'

'I would feel more comfortable driving,' he said meekly.

I pulled the van over and we changed places without another word.

'Who would you rather sleep with, Wolf?' asked Dwight, 'Oprah or Joan Rivers?'

'Joan,' Wolf said, 'Oprah would be too preachy.'

'Hillary Clinton or Cherie Blair?'

'Cherry who?'

Dwight's teeth were small and very stubby and he ran his tongue over them now as he looked at Wolf suspiciously. He had always been confused by Wolf's stir-fry genealogy, figuring it made him frighteningly unpredictable.

'The British prime minister's wife.'

'Is she cute?' Wolf had graduated summa cum laude from Yale with degrees in political studies and socio economics. He knew exactly who Cherie Blair was. Wolf was rarely mean to anyone but he was mean to Dwight, referring to him as Smallboy behind his back.

'No, but Hillary's no peach either.'

'Oh please, she's a babe,' Wolf said. 'What's more she's the First Babe.'

I wound down the window of our rented van. The English countryside smelt of wet tarmac. 'Lunch was what time?'

'One o'clock sharp,' Wolf said.

'Time now?' I turned the map the other way round.

'One o'clock sharp.'

'What!' Dwight exclaimed. A passing signpost read Stourton on the Water.

'Godammit, Maggie. We've been through here. We've been going round in circles.'

For some reason, definitely one other than sartorial, Dwight had chosen to wear a necktie in the style of an English Rake. He tugged distractedly at the jaunty piece of silk as though it were choking him. 'I told you we should have left earlier. I told you.' His baby face scrunched up.

I looked at him apprehensively. The last thing I needed was Dwight going off at the deep end.

When I first worked for *Newsline*, Wolf and I had been researching a story about funding for schools. In a small town in Mississippi we witnessed a peculiar episode. We were in a hardware store buying batteries, standing in the queue behind some guy at the checkout. When he pushed a packet of shoelaces over the counter, the lady with 'Honey' pinned to her bosom said, 'That'll be thirty-nine cents and do you have a Slavens Value card, sir?' whereupon this man began shouting at the top of his lungs, 'You fuck ass over-weight nigger scumbag, your fat black face makes me want to PUKE,' before calmly handing over his dollar and strolling out of the store. Wolf and I stared after him. It wasn't so much his behaviour that stunned us but the lack of reaction from everyone else. I mean this was the land of fried catfish and baby alligators, a town where the ghost of the Ku Klux Klan had not entirely been exorcized. Apart from us, and you couldn't really count Wolf, he was the only other white person we'd seen. Honey just shrugged. He was a local she told us. He was sick and couldn't help himself. 'He jest opens that mouth of his,' she said, shaking her head solemnly, 'and out pours all the filth o'the world.'

Turned out he had Tourette's syndrome and Wolf and I figured that in any situation that involved transport, punctuality or paperwork, Dwight displayed minor symptoms of this same disease. Everyone in *Newsline* had a story about him. He was once arrested on landing because he'd kept up a tireless commentary throughout a flight about the plane crashing. Another time he'd been caught hyperventilating by the colour copy machine because he couldn't find his passport. The first assignment I flew with him he'd nearly come to blows with an air stewardess.

'What do you mean the hand baggage allowance is only twelve kilograms,' he'd demanded at check in.

'Civil Aviation Authority tests have shown, sir, that if a bag falls from the overhead locker and it's under twelve kilos, then it's safe.'

'Oh yeah, what's the baggage allowance in premium class then?'

'Fifteen kilos, sir,' said the poor girl, beginning to sweat.

'You're telling me it takes twelve kilos to hurt a man in coach but fifteen kilos to hurt a premium class passenger?' he'd yelled, 'What — they got better quality heads or something?'

He jest opens that mouth o' his and out pours all the filth o' the world. I wanted to apologize to her.

On the plus side, he was one of the best sound recordists in the business and indispensable for paperwork. He had a traffic cop approach to minutiae, in that once he started writing a ticket, he had to finish it. Didn't matter what it was: labelling of films, the spelling of interviewees' names, routes, maps, plane tickets, gas receipts. Dwight was meticulous.

Besides it was my fault. I should have rung Stately Locations for directions, but Rory Jones's parting shot had been issued as a challenge, not friendly advice, and like a moth I was now sizzling on the burning light bulb. Not only were we late for lunch, we were also lost. We'd hit this town a full hour earlier and it wasn't even much of a town, more like a piece of hived-off countryside criss-crossed by electricity pylons, gas stations, bypasses, round-abouts, the design of which all seemed pretty haphazard. Even the telephone boxes looked like they'd been acciden-tally dropped from an aircraft and lodged randomly in the mud. It was thoroughly depressing. A man in a cloth cap was sitting at the bus stop. He looked like he was prepared to wait for several years.

'Pardon me,' Dwight quickly wound down his window, 'the quickest way to Bedlington?'

'Well now,' the old man scratched his head, 'it's a good question. Let me see . . .' the regional accent curling his tongue made him barely decipherable. 'You go straight on about a quarter of a mile until you reach the field of corn. There's a turning just after the field, hidden by a bank on the right-hand side, mind you don't take it. Rather, take the fork after Frogsfarm, past the King and Custard, over the humped-back bridge, sharp right at the scarecrow, through a small hamlet then . . .'

Fidgeting like a live prawn on a griddle, Dwight ran out of patience. Muttering profanities, he rolled up the window and shot off leaving the local staring after us.

Dwight pulled up the van in the next turning.

'You drive, I'll map read,' he said and again we changed places.

In the back seat, Wolf lit a joint.

An hour later an enormous set of gates flashed by.

'Back, back!' Dwight yelled.

I rammed the gears into reverse, charged through the

gates and there, through the drizzle, was Jane Austen's England. Rich, lush countryside, deer wandering through immaculate parklands, which rolled down soft green banks towards a river. In the distance, a house loomed, terrifyingly grand.

'Whoah,' breathed Wolf. 'Magnificent.'

I stared through the windscreen. I knew houses like this existed but this was something else. It wasn't a house, more like twenty houses built one on top of another.

'Come on,' said Dwight feverishly. '*Come on.*'

DANGER. CATTLE GRIDS. DEAD SLOW.

The significance of this sign entered my consciousness way too late. The car hit the grids doing fifty. Dwight's head cracked against the roof, Wolf's arm smashed against my shoulder, but as we hurtled up the other side of the grids I was aware of something else – a wild flash of colour, the sickening thud of a body. I yanked at the handbrake. The van went into a circular skid then came to a halt on the soft verge.

Dwight was swearing, Wolf groaning, I was white with fear. There was blood on the windscreen. I felt faint as the reality sank in. I'd injured, or worse killed, a human being. Possibly even a child. Robotically I reached for the key and cut the engine. My hands trembled as I wrenched open the door. I walked unsteadily round to the front of the car but what I'd hit was not, thank God, a human, but a peacock. A beautiful, magnificently multicoloured peacock.

'Oh, dear God,' I said, flooded with relief.

The peacock lay on the road, tail fanned out defensively, emitting weird sounds from its throat.

'This is really extremely bad karma, Maggie,' Wolf said. He peered at the bird. 'Is it dead?'

'Of course it's not dead.' Dwight rubbed his forehead where a small egg was forming. 'Who do you think's making all that noise.'

'I thought that was Maggie,' Wolf said.

One of the peacock's legs was broken. It used the other to push itself away from us. A dark stain of blood discoloured the green of its feathers and seeped onto the road.

'Poor thing, look,' I knelt down. 'It's in pain, we've got to help it. Dwight, pick it up.'

'Are you kidding?' Dwight said. 'What if it bites? You pick it up.' He peered closer.

'How can it bite? I've practically killed the poor thing.'

'It's got a mean look to it.'

'I'll do it,' Wolf bent down and clumsily gathered the peacock in his arms. Quick as a flash the bird struck.

'Jesus!' Wolf jumped back clutching his mouth. Blood dripped down his chin.

'I know what we're supposed to do,' Dwight said. 'We're supposed to put it out of its misery.'

'Gee, let's give it a Tylenol' Wolf said.

'No, we're supposed to put it down. I read it somewhere. It's the kind thing to do.'

'Are you crazy?' I said. 'You want to *murder* it?' What was the deal with peacocks? Were they wild? Vermin? Good luck, bad omens, family pets? I could only pray this one didn't have a name and a sobbing child attached to it.

'We could wring its neck.' The peacock blinked its eye accusingly at Dwight.

'Great, and what if someone sees us?' I said.

'Who's gonna see us in a place like this?'

Wolf's lip was beginning to swell. He looked around the deserted parklands. 'Sherlock fucking Holmes,' he said sourly, 'that's who.'

We stood at the foot of the steps. From the top, a group of people were making their way down to us. An ancient man in a butler's uniform. Two elderly women, one in a smart floral outfit, the other in trousers and a sweater. A few steps behind them walked a priest.

There are rules in this business. My God they're pretty basic but you need to follow them if you want people to talk to you, because whatever preconceptions you might have of them, you can bet they'll have a worse one of you. So let's be clear: first impressions are paramount.

The group reached us. Like two warring parties on a tentative and possibly doomed peace mission we stood before each other. I had a sudden flash of who we were. We were the enemy. We were the Americans; the miners, ranchers, the soldiers who'd come to encroach upon the native's ground and steal their heritage, we were invading the Roxmeres' privacy and questioning their right to their land. My clothes were spotted with blood, Wolf, with his dishevelled ponytail and swollen lip resembled a demented Sioux tracker, Dwight with his absurd necktie looked like a private from F Troop.

The butler turned and signalled. At the top of the stone steps, silhouetted against the sky, flanks of servants appeared. We were badly outnumbered. Hell, if I'd had a white flag this would have been the time to wave it. The servants swarmed down the steps, formed a circle around the van and began unloading suitcases and equipment.

'What are these people called again?' Wolf muttered.

'Roxmere,' I hissed.

'Title?'

'Leave it to me,' Dwight said, and before I could stop him advanced unctuously on the floral lady, taking her hand and pressing his lips to her liver-spotted skin.

'Profound apologies Your . . . er . . .' he cast around wildly, '. . . your Liege.'

'Oh dear me no.' The floral lady squirmed uncomfortably. She stepped aside. 'This is Her Grace, the Duchess of Roxmere.'

The second lady stared incredulously at the peacock in my arms.

There was little hope for a treaty – only surrender. I held out the peacock. As a peace-offering it was surely ill-conceived.

'It just ran straight out in front of me,' I heard myself saying, 'there was no way I could have stopped in time.'

The Duchess looked from me to the peacock then back again. *Enough of these obsequious and false avowals of friendship.*

'In fact, not that I want to cast the first stone or anything, but I don't think it can have been looking,' I added weakly. Behind me, Wolf groaned as if to say, *Duchess, I am ashamed to have sworn allegiance to these Americans.*

To add to our woes, a grizzled little dog had appeared

from nowhere and began leaping at the terrified peacock in frenzied excitement.

'I feel awful,' I shouted at the Duchess over the chaos. 'I really truly am very sorry.'

I will punish those who have washed their hands in innocent blood said She Who Wears Rubber Boots, or maybe she just said, 'Take care of it would you, Father John,' because I found myself putting the peacock gently into the priest's extended arms, 'but you know,' I babbled, 'with the proper care and assistance – a long period of convalescence, I'm quite sure it will make nothing less than an absolute and complete recovery.'

At which point the priest snapped the bird's neck.

Jesus Christ was not only the Son of God. He was also of a very good family on his mother's side.

— Seventeenth-century French bishop

daniel

Rory parks the Rover on a bay in Irving Street, behind
Leicester Square. The parking meter is out of order earning
it a good kicking followed by a stream of abuse while Rory
scrounges around the car for a pen and scrap of paper to
leave a note. By the time he presses the entry buzzer to the
Beefsteak club he is steaming with irritation.

He gives his name to the doorman and moments later
the Maître d', a large gentleman experiencing no small
difficulty fitting into a pair of velvet britches, hurries
towards him.

'Good afternoon, sir.'

'Afternoon, George.'

'Thank you for coming, sir,' he says leading Rory through
to the club's inner sanctum. Rory neither knows this man
well, nor is a member of this establishment, but all staff
who work at the Beefsteak club are called George so as not
to humiliate the memory-impaired peers who do belong
here. That something as archaic as a gentleman's club still
exists is anathema to most people including my brother.
Personally I like to think of them more as a harmless form
of petting zoo where remnants of our species are kept alive

by a soothing mixture of familiarity, tradition and stodgy food – and frankly, if a group of old codgers find it comforting to sit around reading *The Field*, boring each other senseless with anecdotes, repeated ad nauseam, better they should do so in a controlled environment.

'He's in here, sir,' George says pushing open a heavy pair of doors, 'But I have to warn you that his father's only just left.' He withdraws discreetly.

Like its occupants, the air in this room belongs to 1920. No amount of spit and polish can exorcize its staleness. Rory passes an old man slumped into an easy chair smoking a cigar and reading the *Racing Post*. On his feet are a pair of velvet slippers embroidered with Mallard ducks in flight. Rory can barely hold his exasperation in check. What the hell was Benj doing here forty years too soon?

Anger fades as he rounds the corner. Benj sits in the seat below the bay window, a pyramid of cigarette ash in front of him. He's been crying, that much is obvious. His eyes are red and the sadness in them goes deep, tunnelling back to his childhood, to the interminable days of loneliness. Rory doesn't know how to mend the gaping holes in Benj's life but he's damned if he's going to allow him to fill them with alcohol. Benj glances up from the tumbler of neat gin in front of him. He looks shell-shocked. His eyes drop from Rory's face to the table. They both look at the glass. Then before Rory can stop him, Benj snatches up the tumbler and gulps down the clear liquid within.

maggie

My clothes had been unpacked for me and laid out in the Chrysanthemum bedroom, even my underwear had been folded neatly and put into drawers. It was all a little unnerving. I walked round barely daring to touch the fine fabrics and beautiful old furniture. The curtains were made of a flowery chintz (chrysanthemums?) and the four-poster bed was dressed, top, bottom and sides, with ruched skirts made of the same print. I tried to imagine sleeping in it with Jay but decided it would be like having sex inside a giant Kleenex box.

In the en-suite bathroom an old-fashioned set of hairbrush, comb, and clothes brush, all with ivory handles, was laid out on a glass shelf. On a table next to them a hairdryer looked like it might be on loan from a museum exhibition of twentieth-century inventions. Through the window, on the lawn outside, a skinny little girl was playing with her rabbit. There was something so self-contained about her that I fetched my camera off the bed. She had a ritual going: she would pick up the rabbit, stroke it, then let it go. The rabbit would hop two paces, then turn round as if to check, this far OK with you? Whereupon the little girl would pick it up stroke it and release it in a different direction. I wondered who she belonged to.

Along the corridor, in his appointed bedroom, Dwight was preening himself in front of a large gilt mirror. 'The Right Honourable Dwight,' he intoned, 'Dwight, peer of the realm, Viscount Dwight . . . Dwight . . .' he puffed out his chest and saluted . . . '*Heir . . . to the throne.*' He jumped as I opened the door. His bedroom was even more extravagant than mine with flocked wallpaper and a wonderful bed whose walnut headboard was intricately carved with fruit and birds. At the foot of the bed a lacquer box stood open on a table. Set into its velvet was a seal, a stick of red wax and an ink pad. Dwight touched the pad gingerly and held up a blue finger to show me.

'Excuse me, sir, madam?' As the butler appeared, Dwight closed the inkpad guiltily pretending to examine the wallpaper instead. 'Laura Ashley?' he ventured, running a hand over its elaborate surface.

'Eighteenth-century Chinese, sir,' the butler corrected gently, 'and of course, quite priceless.'

Downstairs, in a small anteroom, a reserved man of around fifty was waiting to greet us. Dwight, apparently recovered from his earlier gaffe stepped forwards without hesitation. 'Ah, Your Grace,' he said smoothly, 'a very good afternoon to you.'

The man looked faintly embarrassed. 'I'm His Grace's agent Glenville,' he returned Dwight's enthusiastic handshake limply. 'His Grace has asked me to put myself at your disposal.'

Behind me Wolf sighed.

'See, the way we work,' I told Glenville, 'there's no prep-aration, no set-up, it's all purely observational, behavioural, fly-on-the-wall if you like.' We were moving through one imposing room to another. All around us servants busied themselves with chores. In the State dining room, a line of men stood shoeless on a long table, polishing its surface, feet bound in soft chamois leather. In the Green drawing room another man at the top of a ladder was painstakingly cleaning dust from the cut crystal of a chandelier with a toothbrush.

Truth is, it was frustrating. Visually these were great scenes but Glenville wouldn't allow us to film. One excuse followed another. There was a problem with the insurance, the lighting might damage ancient tapestries, His Grace had not sanctioned that the staff be questioned. Finally Wolf was allowed to set up the camera in a never-ending corridor of family portraits. Glenville, all blushes and unnatural hand movements, began narrating in a stiff museum guide voice. 'The first Duke of Roxmere married the eldest daughter of the Beaufort family whose ancestors of course were descended from the——'

We needn't have wasted the film. It was hopelessly dull footage but I didn't want to risk offending him.

'Am I going too fast for you?' Glenville said.

God forbid. 'No, no, you're doing great.' Then I noticed something. To our left was a door to the wing of the house we'd been informed was private. 'Are you getting this, Wolf?' I shot him a look with a subliminal order attached.

'Now you mention it, I could use re-shooting the portraits from the beginning,' he said, eyes skimming over the no entry sign.

We had only a day and a half at Roxmere — fine if you're shooting a documentary, say, and have set up shots on a previous visit but with *Newsline* you shoot and scout simultaneously so you can't afford to get stuck with dead wood in front of the camera. As the only member of the crew without a proper job, as Wolf was fond of telling me, it fell to me to charm, waylay and flatter the dead wood so that those real villains, sound and visuals, could go about their work of finding something interesting to film.

I managed to get Glenville all the way to the Duke's library before he noticed the crew were still absent without leave. He looked anxiously to the door. 'I fear your colleagues may have got lost.'

I was happily sure of it.

'They're probably sneaking a beer break,' I said and Glenville looked reassured. The Duke's private library was a small square room lined in bookshelves. Glenville moved aside a pair of library steps and took down a slim volume.

'This might interest you. Dates back to the Magna Carta. Been in the family for generations.'

The door opened behind us and the butler walked in carrying the squirming terrier. 'Message for you, sir.' He released the dog which scampered off to its basket under a low table.

Glenville folded the note. 'I'll be back shortly, if you don't mind waiting here. Though if I could possibly draw your attention to . . .' He gestured to a discreet no smoking sign propped against the mantelpiece.

'And could I please impress on madam the importance of not, under any circumstances, letting the dog out,' the butler added. 'Little Timmy does tend to hunt.'

The dog glared from its basket, resentful of my role as temporary jailer, but it was no bad prison even for a dog. On a writing desk stood an eclectic array of objects: iron statues of political figures; a freakish miniature chihuahua in a bell jar; a dried hand on a stand, property of, its plaque informed, the Marquis de Sade. The dog soon settled into a routine of rasping snores and atomic smells. I turned my attention back to the bookcase. A volume of *A Midsummer Night's Dream* caught my eye. I took it down. Illustrated by Arthur Rackham, each plate was covered in delicate tissue paper. I carried it to a chair and opening the window for my cigarette smoke, settled down, soon too engrossed in goblins and fairies to worry about what the boys were up to.

Not that they lost much time in telling me later. After splitting off, Dwight and Wolf had found themselves in a vast ballroom. Though empty of furniture, Chinese urns, over-sized candlesticks and decorative dragon vases had been arranged slalom-style on the floor and the skinny girl I'd seen earlier was Rollerblading round them, a look of determination on her pale features. When I studied the footage later, I noticed that there was something else Wolf had caught on film, an expression of a freedom but a freedom tinged with wistfulness – almost as if she suspected fate was hunched right around the corner waiting to kick the wings from her heels.

She turned and glided towards the camera. 'I'm Artemis,' she said. 'Who are you?'

The crew introduced themselves.

'You don't look like a Wolf, do you eat girls?'

'Only ones dressed in red,' Wolf said.

She pointed her chin thoughtfully at her red skirt then back towards camera. 'Methinks you're an NQOSD.' She took a crushed packet of cigarettes from her pocket and placed one languidly in her mouth.

'A what?' Wolf said.

'Not Quite Our Sort Dear,' she cocked her head to one side. 'Or maybe you're an LMCM.'

'Is that a good thing?'

'Good heavens, no. It means Lower Middle-Class Monster.'

'How can you be lower and middle at the same time?'

The little girl looked thoughtful, then, puzzled herself, did a figure of eight backwards and pirouetted off still holding the unlit cigarette.

daniel

'*Learn to cook. Catch a crook. Win a war then write a book about it . . . I could paint a Mona Lisa . . .*' Benj sings tunelessly as Rory, reeling under his weight, pushes him up the staircase. He roots around in the hem of Benj's overcoat. Benj's keys are attached to a plastic model of Kitchener's head which barks, 'YOUR FRONT DOOR NEEDS YOU' as Rory inserts them into the lock.

'*I could be another Caesar. Compose an oratorio that was sublime . . .*'

'Alternately you could just try turning up for a full day's work for a change,' Rory says sarcastically.

'*The world's not shut, on my genius butt . . . I just don't have . . . the time.*'

'Work,' Rory struggles to turn the key, 'surely you remember — that strenuous activity where you go to the office . . . sometimes for as long as five whole days consecutively?'

'Nope.' Benj tries to focus, 'Sorry, doesn't ring a bell.'

Rory kicks the door open.

Pimlico is a dead-end residential spot of London at the best of times but Benj's flat, inherited from a great-aunt, is

in one of those Victorian mansion blocks that old people
invest in when they get fussed about being mugged at night.
The small windows make it dark enough but the addition
of floor-to-ceiling wood panelling transforms it to suicidally
depressing.

Rory brews up strong coffee and forces it down Benj's
throat. Shortly afterwards Benj makes a dash for the bathroom. On the ledge of the bath five Action Men in
camouflage gear sit watching him in affable silence as he
vomits. Rory watches him from the safer distance of the
doorway. Rory feels like an alcoholic by proxy, Alistair and
Audrey, myself, now Benj. *We're the generation that can kick
it.* Today he's less sure. He wants to shake Benj till his nose
bleeds. Go on! Puke your guts out, hope it hurts, hope it
lasts for hours. In this moment he hates Benj. Selfish little
prick. Why is it his responsibility anyway? He toys with
walking away, but he won't – not just because Benj is family
and Rory loves him but because in the complicated debit and
credit system he uses for measuring his own guilt, Rory
still believes he owes big time.

maggie

While the boys were filming Artemis, I continued reading until the clock on the table chimed loudly. I closed the book quickly. Where the hell were Dwight and Wolf? Then my eyes dropped to the basket under the table. Empty. 'Little Timmy' was gone. But how? The door was still shut.

I ran to the open window. Cloud had settled low over the valley. It was dusk but across the lawn and next to an elaborate Victorian monument, I could just make out a bush shaking violently. I stuck my fingers in my mouth and gave it all I had. My screeching whistle brought the dog crawling out from under the bush. It streaked towards the window but before I could snatch it up, veered sharply away and disappeared.

Moments later there was a scratching against the door. I wrenched it open. The terrier stood on the threshold wagging its tail. In its mouth was a muddy object which it dropped at my feet.

Gross. A dead rabbit. I peered closer then froze. Around the rabbit's neck and under layers of drying blood was a pink collar with a silver heart-shaped tag.

'Oh no,' I said faintly. 'Please, God, no.'

*

'What the hell?' Wolf said, walking into my bathroom.

'Don't say a *word*.' I squeezed another dollop of the shampoo onto the bloodied fur.

'Jesus, Maggie are you insane? What are you some kind of animal psycho?'

'I was supposed to stop the dog hunting, but it escaped.' I scrubbed at the fur with the ivory-handled nail-brush. 'I panicked.'

'So what? It's not like you chased the bunny and killed it yourself,' he said.

I switched on the hairdryer.

'Unless you did.'

'Did what?' I shouted.

'Chase it and kill it yourself.'

'For pity's sake, Wolf, this isn't a joke.' I switched the hairdryer off. 'You know we were specifically told to be nice to the pets.' I thrust the bunny into his hands and fixed the collar around its neck. 'There,' I brushed the fur flat with the hairbrush.

'Looks much better now.'

Then I caught his eye and we both collapsed in helpless giggles. Wolf recovered first.

'So where's the rabbit hutch?'

'Oh god.' I wiped tears from my eyes. 'The what?'

'It's apartment . . . you know, its place of residence before it was murdered?'

'I don't know.'

'Well you can't just leave it lying around.'

'Maybe they'll think it died of a heart attack.'

'Then let itself out of its cage and came up to the house

for tea? I don't think so. C'mon', he grabbed my hand, 'let's get moving.'

The hutch consisted of two cages, one empty, the other locked. Inside the locked cage a brown and white rabbit hopped around, pathetically grateful at its companions return. I propped the dead bunny against the straw. 'Kind of cute, no?' I said.

'Tail's missing, Maggie.'

I turned the rabbit and positioned its back against the cage. 'There, looks quite life-like, don't you think?'

'Notwithstanding rigor mortis,' Wolf said supportively.

'Truly beautiful place you have here.' Next to the Duchess, Dwight perched on the edge of his upholstered stool in the drawing room and sipped his tea, little finger crooked expertly. 'Did I mention that I love chintz?' he continued, 'Joan, my wife, also loves chintz, we have drapes very similar to these ones in Brooklyn. My mother was a big floral fan, quite the anglophile, would you believe. I myself was nearly named after one of your kings.'

'Tell me, my dear,' the priest said to me, 'did you see that splendid winter flowering cherry in the garden?'

I couldn't answer. Rooted to my own chair. Somewhere in the house a child was sobbing.

'As I was saying,' Dwight persevered with our hostess, 'there's a department store right round the corner from us, sells beautiful florals – could be they do mail order.' He leant forward conspiratorially. 'You know something, Duchess? I think you and I have the same taste.' He winked.

The Duchess's social smile barely shifted. She rang the small bell on the tea trolley summoning the old butler. 'What *is* Artemis doing, Simmonds?'

'She's a little upset, Your Grace.'

I could hardly bring myself to look at Wolf.

'Do tell her to pull herself together and come into tea.'

Artemis sloped in and sat on the fireguard snivelling furiously.

'Artemis?'

The girl turned her back on her mother. Her thin chest heaved with sobs.

'What *is* the matter with her, Simmonds?' The Duchess looked helplessly at the girl. I felt sick. I'd never had a proper pet, but boy, do I remember wanting one. The rabbit had been this child's only friend, the one bit of warmth and affection she'd known –

'I do believe, Your Grace,' said Simmonds, 'that Master Beckham and his wife Miss Posh are rumoured to be parting company.'

Artemis burst into fresh wails.

'Artemis, darling,' the Duchess tried valiantly, 'it is awfully sad, of course, but I do believe . . . er . . . Oasis will be a much stronger group because of it.' Artemis threw her a withering look and retreated to the fireplace.

As I allowed myself to breathe again the door opened and a tall patrician man with a hooked nose and defined cheekbones padded into the room wearing scarlet knee-high socks.

'Ah, Hereward, here you—'

'Quite extraordinary,' the Duke interrupted his wife. 'My dear I must tell you. Dear Flopsy, who as you know expired the day before yesterday and was laid to rest,' he glanced at Artemis, 'with all due ceremony of course, has now been found back in her hutch and, what's more,' the Duke continued agitatedly, 'she's clean as a bloody whistle. *Clean as a bloody whistle!*'

Into the very long silence that followed somebody eventually spoke.

'A rabbit resurrection,' said the vicar. 'Heavens above, how very unusual.'

daniel

In the sitting room, Benj struggles to lever himself onto the sofa, but misjudging the distance lands flat on his back instead.

'I am a drunk,' he says mournfully.

'I had noticed.' Rory lies on the floor next to Benj and both stare vacantly up at the ceiling.

'You know something, Rory,' Benj says eventually. 'You've simply got to get a grip.'

'I know.'

'Because whilst I, at least, am a happy and on the whole amusing drunk, you, my friend, have become a boring frustrated son of a bitch.'

'You're right.' Rory sighs. Above him is a glass chandelier that Benj inherited along with the flat. Were it to fall right now, Rory wonders, would he be quick enough to roll to safety? Just how good were his reflexes these days? He moves out of range.

'For goodness sake get a job you like,' Benj says.

'Had one, if you remember.'

'Well get it back.'

'And my parents?'

'They can look after themselves, they're *grown-ups* for goodness sake.'

'As you very well know,' Rory says grimly, 'they are not.'

Benj grunts at this.

'You're lucky,' Rory says, 'your parents are cold, unemotional, uptight . . . reasonably normal in fact.'

'And they spoke to me for the first time ever when I was twelve.'

'Well, my mother has an extremely large quadruped.'

'You know,' Benj says, 'recently I asked my mother if I was breast-fed as a child.'

'And were you?'

'I don't know. She told me to mind my own business.'

Benj's childhood. So superficially perfect. So seriously sick. Benj's mother had not touched him as a boy, not even as a baby. I'd been shocked when he'd admitted it. 'I don't think it ever occurred to my mother to kiss me,' he'd said. 'She did hug me once – although she'd just tripped over the carpet divider, so that might have been an accident.' Benj's mother disliked physical contact of any kind. His father disliked emotional contact of any kind. It was a winning combination for an only child.

'I take it you haven't introduced your father to the notion of selling Bevan then,' Benj changes tack.

It's Rory's turn to grunt. Idly he scans Benj's bookshelves. All the C.S. Lewis books, three copies of *Sword in the Stone*, hardback editions of *Mungo* and *Zulu Dawn*. It strikes him that Benj has got lost trying to find a childhood that never even existed.

'He's simply got to be practical,' Benj says. 'Can't you make him understand?'

'Inflicting any kind of self-knowledge on my father at his age is tantamount to abuse of the elderly,' Rory says, 'and besides, Daniel would never have given up Bevan.'

This gets a sharp look from Benj. 'Well if you're opting for a life sentence at Bevan, at least make sure it's not solitary. Find a girl you like.'

'Had one.'

'Find another.'

'Aren't any.'

'Aren't any left you mean.'

'Don't think for a single second I'm going to take a lecture on women from you lying down.' Rory puts his hands under his head.

'Strikes me you've taken precious little lying down since Daniel died.'

'Coming from you, Casanova.'

'True, but then at least I have a good excuse.'

'Which is?'

'Which is, women absolutely terrify me,' Benj says simply. He sits up and hunts in his pockets for cigarettes, retrieving the lighter from under the carpet. 'God, but we're a pair of fuck-ups aren't we.'

'Yes, that we are.' Rory sits up as well and leans against the sofa. 'Why are we by the way?' His mobile is ringing for the umpteenth time and finally he answers it. Alison, beside herself with joy at finding a legitimate excuse for calling him after work hours, has already left four messages.

As Rory listens to them, a resigned look on his face, Benj draws thoughtfully on his cigarette. 'Well in my case my father was a fuck-up, his father before him was a fuck-up, my grandfather's father was also a bit of a fuck-up. You know, you just inherit it, along with the death duties and the ugly furniture.'

maggie

When I opened the door of the Chrysanthemum bedroom, Rory Jones was standing outside. I shouldn't have been surprised. I knew why he'd come. He looked at me, clearly irritated, and I wondered whether I should scamper off to a basket under the table like little Timmy.

'Skirt at the dry-cleaners?' I walked over to the fireplace.

'I only wear it for best.'

I could feel his eyes on my back and turned to face him. 'Look it probably sounds a little worse than it was.'

'Oh?' His eyebrows shot up. 'How exactly might it have been worse? I know I told you to be nice to the pets but surely the shampoo and set was just a tad over the top?' His tone was bitingly sarcastic. 'From now on I really can't have you sniffing around any more houses, unaccompanied, as it were.'

'Like we're not housebroken or something,' I said lightly. The fact was my ass was in a sling. Without him I would have to either abort or start fresh and I guess we both knew it.

'Here's the situation,' he said. 'We've banked your cheque. I think you'll find it's non-refundable. So, given the circumstances, you'll have to let me know if you wish to continue or not. Of course you don't have to decide till morning.' He opened the door. 'Assuming you can manage till morning that is.' His tone was angry but I could swear he was laughing at me.

'Believe me,' I said politely, though it was all I could do not to level him with a punch, 'I can manage.'

I tried Jay's number again on my cellphone then snapped it shut. 'What is the point of a boyfriend if you can never get hold of him?'

'It's a time consuming job saving the world.' Wolf was lying on his bed smoking a joint.

'Well, you know something, at least it's a worthwhile one.'

'Mr Jones really got under your skin, huh?'

I grunted. OK fine, it was a great moment of payback so I shouldn't have begrudged it, but God knows he needn't have looked quite so smug.

I flopped on the bed and rested my head on Wolf's legs. 'What are we doing here Wolf?' Nothing about this story was gelling and I had only myself to blame. I felt overtired, felt like I could do with a good cry, sex, a holiday. More than anything I could have done with seeing Jay.

The last time I'd been on 'holiday' was when I'd joined Jay in Sierra Leone. It was a mistake for both of us. I had wanted to understand what his life was about, and when I got there I understood. It was about sanitation, clean water, funding. It was about lobbying a sluggish UN. It was an endless, thankless task and I was in the way – just one person more for him to organize. 'This is not your reality,' he'd said more than once. But the point was, it was *his* reality and I didn't belong in it.

'You know exactly what you're doing,' Wolf said. 'You just blew it, that's all.'

I grinned. 'You could at least make a minimal effort to cheer me up.'

He passed me the joint, and we smoked it in silence. 'Remember in Anchorage,' he said finally, 'when we were doing the stolen land story, that time when you tried to get in with the tribe elder and you agreed that me and Dwight would do that ice bonding thing and we had to squat in a deep hole naked with the Inuit guy with the mackerel breath and Dwight ended up losing feeling in the tip of his—'

'I remember.'

'That almost seems like fun now.'

I put my head on his chest and he combed my hair through with his fingers. I really loved him a lot.

'Are you happy?' he asked.

'I think so.' I was startled by the question. 'Are you?'

'How can you tell?'

'I don't know, but I can tell you what keeps me awake at night,' I said. 'What if you believe you're driving on a main road, one that takes you to a capital city, let's say, but you're wrong – all along you're on a parallel road but it's smaller, less interesting, it's going nowhere and the worst thing is – these two roads never converge?'

He thought for a while. 'At least there'd be no tolls to pay.'

I laughed and took another hit of the joint. Wolf always

had the strongest grass. You could chart his progress round a party by the line of monosyllabic glassy-eyed victims in his wake. 'One more before I go back to my room,' I squeaked in a helium Micky Mouse voice. 'How do I get back to my room anyway?'

I woke needing a pee. My left arm was numb. Wolf was asleep. His hair, loosed from its ponytail, was spread over one cheek. He looked like the bearded lady, on leave from the circus.

The corridor was dark. I tripped over the carpet then turned my ankle negotiating the steps to the bathroom. As I opened the door something brushed against my face – I yelped, thinking it was a spider but it was only the string from the light. I pulled it but no light came on, instead a bar heater above the mirror glowed red. It gave off just enough light to confirm that there was no toilet in this bathroom, just a bath and a sink. It took another ten minutes not to find where the toilet was located and arrive back where I started. If I hadn't been quite so stoned, I might have chanced the journey to my own bathroom, more than a thousand stubbed toes away – instead I eyed the sink. Oh well . . . I'd certainly peed in stranger places than this . . .

Dwight told me afterwards it sounded like a bomb exploding. He'd shot upright in bed. The blackness in his room was thick as tar and just as impenetrable but the noise had been too loud to ignore. He searched in vain for the switch on his table lamp, then, pulling back the covers, took a tentative step into the abyss. Hands extended to feel his way around the room, he found a cold surface to lean on. His hands pressed on something damp and soft. A face towel. That meant he was at the basin, which meant a ninety degree turn to the door. He took one giant step forwards and slammed into the wall. Befuddled and now in pain he felt with his hands round the wall until he found the light switch. His eyes had difficulty adjusting, because even when he'd switched it on his hands looked so dark. He shook his head stupidly. Then something caught his eye. The lid of the antique ink pad was up. He looked at his fingers, took a horrified step back. Around the room, indelibly printed onto the priceless eighteenth-century Chinese wallpaper, were the inky blue imprints of his hands.

Comedy cut to the bathroom. As silly accidents go I have long since cornered the market. Once, at school, I took a basketball so cleanly to the centre of my forehead it knocked me onto the floor and cracked open the back of my head. The double egg forced me to sleep on my side for a month. In Mexico, Wolf turned our jeep, a goat lethargically crossing the dirt road mistaken for a child. That time it was a telephone pole that cracked my head open. I have sliced my calf on a picture hook, got a black eye from a flying lens cap, a fractured ankle tripping over a *Dictionary of Erotica* at university but I had never heard of anyone being clobbered whilst actually peeing. At first I thought I had slipped off the sink and fallen to the floor, then I realized the sink had slipped off the wall and fallen onto me. I lay semi-naked covered in rubble, T-shirt hiked up, wondering whether things were broken; important things like my head for instance, because the whole thing seemed so funny, but then the lights snapped on, the dust cleared and Rory Jones stepped into the doorway.

The stately homes of England, how beautiful they stand,
To prove the upper classes have still the upper hand.
. . .
The stately homes of England we proudly represent,
We only keep them up for Americans to rent.

— Noel Coward

maggie

I got hooked on watching people at Rock'n'Roll concerts.

You could say that my dad, Mike, was one of the founders of modern rock'n'roll stage lighting. He was a bona fide hippy and proud of it — he still has a *Sergeant Pepper* outfit somewhere in the back of his closet. He avoided being drafted by claiming to be homosexual, a good wheeze at the time you might think, but he's spent a disproportionate amount of effort since trying to access his papers through the Freedom of Information Act to see whether this boyhood lie is still following him around. Every time his credit card is turned down, his bags searched at the airport, his mail is late — it's always the same, truth is he's a little paranoid.

Dad was at the Thanksgiving dinner when Arlo Guthrie wrote 'Alice's Restaurant' and was famous, before he married my mother, for his sexual exploits with various female rock divas who wished to be well lit.

My parents met in Haight Ashbury where my mother was making a documentary called *Love is Dead* about the decline and fall of the hippies and Dad was mounting the farewell concert of Jefferson Airplane. He was beautiful, laid back and stoned, but Mom was fierce. She prised him away from Grace Slick and marched him back to New York.

They were all set to make love not war and sure as hell not babies. My mother could organize a protest of 400 people standing on her head, but she couldn't organize a plumber or decent contraception. Even after the shock of my arrival, parental duties were fulfilled as an afterthought. I got new pants when old ones had shrunk to my knees. I had to walk around barefoot before either of them noticed I needed a larger shoe size and theirs were always the two empty seats at the school play. It wasn't that they were mean, they just never signed on for the whole stroller-pushing PTA parent thing. They never let me need them as a child and they don't need me now and I guess I'm the stronger for it. Still, it meant we never established much of a sense of family. Instead my life was slotted into their agenda. I didn't mind. I was happy trailing my mother's causes, and if Mom was away and Dad had a concert out of the city, he'd just pluck me out of school and take me right along with him.

Concerts were a blast. 'Just stay still and watch,' my father would instruct – which I would until, out of the blue, some huge man would hoist me up saying, 'This is no place for a little prawn like you,' and whip electrical cables onto the spot where'd I'd been sitting before stashing me like Raggedy Anne in a new place from where the whole scene would shift and change. Minutes later somebody else would come along. 'You shouldn't be here,' and again I'd be relocated. I became brilliant at being where I shouldn't. I was thinking about this the morning we set off. Being brilliant at being in the wrong place. It's a strange skill to have.

It was a windy morning. People struggled with umbrellas. At a pedestrian crossing a woman's headscarf whipped over her face just as she stepped out. Startled, she withdrew to the curb as the traffic roared by.

A wedding party poured out from a Greek Orthodox church. Children in old men's suits and women in young girl's dresses. The bride's veil blew around her, engulfing her in a cloud of swirling net. In vain, guests tried to untangle her but she eventually cast off the veil, laughing as it sailed up to the sky, while children hopped and jumped to catch it.

'I'm sorry, did you say something?' I said.

'I said, you're not going to sulk the whole week, are you?' Rory Jones repeated. We were driving through the outskirts of London in his car, an old Rover. Wolf and Dwight were following us in the van. I could have ridden with them but I'd opted to ride with Rory out of – what? Who knows. It had to be either masochism or some kind of reverse pride.

His comment was especially annoying as I hadn't been sulking at all, I was thinking how much I liked the expression on the Greek bride's face as she watched her veil spinning into orbit, like she was symbolically freeing herself from the prison of single life. It was a nice moment. One I would have liked to have had on film, but Rory had caught me with my pants down – quite literally. The joke was on me and he'd lost no opportunity to rub salt in the wound.

In the Stately Locations office that morning, he'd rung our next appointment to confirm.

'No, no need to have second thoughts, Lady Harcourt,' he'd said. 'Not *all* American women are brash, vulgar and distasteful,' he caught my eye and grinned. 'No, no, I'm quite sure you'll like her . . . yes, yes, very polite, charming, yes, yes, marvellous with animals.' He'd put his hand over the receiver. 'You do *do* charming don't you?'

To hell with him anyway. Maybe having him come along might not be a disaster after all. It passed responsibility for his clients directly to him – and he'd better be up for the ride because from now on, the way I figured it, these clients, whoever they were, were firmly in my sight line.

'The thing is,' he said, 'if you don't talk, I'll have to. I mean, after all, it's a question of manners.'

I continued flicking through the itinerary, around ten houses in all.

'It's my English upbringing,' Rory said. 'No matter how obstreperous or dull the person sitting next to you is, you must engage them in conversation.'

I doodled a hangman onto the back of the envelope. A man with a coronet hanging by the neck.

'Funny business to be in for someone who's not interested in people,' he added.

'I'm interested in people.' Goaded, I took out a cigarette and lit it. 'Talking to people is my job.' My matches had a picture of Roosevelt on the front and had arrived by FedEx that morning at the hotel. Jay collected presidential matches, thought they were very kitsch. It amused him to send them to me from time to time. The idea of the FedEx office trying to find a small enough box to pack them in amused him even more.

'What the hell is it?' the FedEx man would ask as he signed over the miniature package.

'I'm afraid it's the president's head,' I would reply solemnly.

Jay also collected president stories. Apropos nothing he might say, 'you know Lyndon Johnson once replied to something Jimmy Greenfield said with, "You dare to ask the leader of the Western world a chicken-shit question like that?" '

'Who's Jimmy Greenfield?' I'd say and get his 'oh-the-cultural-desert-that-is-youth' look for my trouble.

Rory was eyeing me from the driver's seat.

'What?'

'You know that thing in movies?' he said. 'When two people meet for the first time, spot each other across a crowded room and fall instantly, passionately, hopelessly in love?'

I looked at him.

'Well,' he said, 'I'd say quite the opposite thing has happened here wouldn't you?'

I stared out the window. Damned if I was going to let him see me smile.

'Nice day.'

'Beautiful,' he agreed, ignoring the sarcasm.

'It's true what they say. It really does rain *all the time* in this country.' I gave up fiddling with the car's dials.

'It's only been a couple of days.' Rory said, 'I'm sure it's been known to rain two days running in New York.'

'Yeah, but it's different rain.'

'How's that?'

'Less wet for a start.' I sipped my gas station coffee in its plastic cup. The world outside the window was grey, the sky dulled by cloud so thick you could have spread it on a bagel. Black crows circled in the boughs of leafless trees. 'Jesus,' I shuddered. 'I mean, no wonder you Brits are so repressed.'

'Ah, here we go – and this based on what? Your extensive experience of . . . ah yes . . . one family?'

'Come on, anybody would have felt uncomfortable in that place, I mean, even the butler knew more about that little girl than her mother. The woman didn't have a trace of warmth.'

'She was being polite.'

'She was totally inhibited.'

'I'd say reserved.'

'Try archaic.'

'A little old fashioned.'

'Uptight.'

'Shy.'

'They're just privileged with no purpose.'

'Oh yawn,' said Rory, 'that old aristocracy versus meritocracy chestnut. Your problem is you're incapable of seeing past the house and title—'

'Oh right, like you people aren't a little over preoccupied with blue blood and class?'

'As if *your* people don't have an overriding need to believe in Camelot.'

'Forget the Roxmeres, this isn't about one family – as a race you're cold, no passion.'

'The English don't consider it gentlemanly to have passion.'

'Oh – a little lame don't you think?'

'Well of course we have passion. It's just that we don't get quite all our emotions from those self-help books.'

'What emotions are you talking about? You send your kids to boarding school before they can walk.'

'Well, better the world of beatings and buggery than having them settle junior high school disputes with Uzis.'

I opened my mouth to say something then clamped it shut again.

'Oh my God,' he said, 'you're laughing, it's a miracle, alert the national press.' He paused. 'Why are you laughing by the way?'

'I don't know, you sounded just like my mother.' My mother, like everyone else in America, had long been obsessed with high-school shootings and was on the committee of Women Against Guns.

'Right wing blames it on the media, left wing blames it on the availability of guns.' I'd heard it a million times, 'be careful who you diss in school, honey,' she used to tell me, and by the way this was the full extent of her teenage advice, 'cos if they know anyone who even looks eighteen they can go down to their local Woolworths, buy a shotgun and blow you away.'

'So the question is,' Rory said, 'will your broadly objective views on the English be serving as the basis for your film?'

'Hey,' I said loftily, 'I'm just making polite conversation. I film what I see.'

'Oh and what's that?'

'What's what?'

'Well you're not exactly the "oh-gee-that-accent-makes-me-go-weak-at-the-knees, wasn't-princess-Di-a-saint" type of big-haired gushing American that we at Stately Locations have come to love and cherish.'

'Why have you got it in for journalists so badly?'

'Because they're unscrupulous and intrusive and they ride roughshod over people's feelings.'

I eyed him. 'Funny business to be in for someone who doesn't like talking to the press.'

He broke into a grin. 'Touché . . . It's a long story.'

'Which you're not going to tell me sometime?'

'Correct.'

'Even if I ask really nicely?'

'Are you always this nosy?'

'Being nosy is my job.'

'You must get a lot of doors slammed in your face.'

'Yeah, but the trick is to be on the right side of the door.'

'And you achieve this how?'

'My charm, naturally.'

'Of course,' he said. 'Your charm. How very unobservant of me.'

See here's the thing. You pick and choose who you work with on most assignments and you're careful, because the relationship between a crew can get precarious at the best of times. How much you all need each others' skill is carefully balanced. But people like Rory, the accidental TV tourist, can be a liability. You need them, so you put up with them. Once in a while you get the clever ones who think you might need more than a guide, a driver, an interpreter, whoever it is they've signed on as, and in those situations the only thing you can do is keep as far away as possible, stay professional and on the whole they're pretty easy to ignore. Or not, as it turned out . . .

The Harcourts lived in a breathtakingly pretty Georgian house south of the Wiltshire Downs. The moment they invited us in, had the tea fetched and eagerly began telling us the history of the place: grade II listed, twelve bedrooms, epitomizing the era's architectural details, pedimented columned entrance porch, well-stocked lake and flight ponds etc. etc. etc., I knew that the sooner we left the better. There was nothing wrong with them as such. The Harcourts failed us by being essentially nice decent people, and nice decent people just don't make good television. I took the opportunity to waylay Rory's suspicions by behaving beautifully. Rory took the opportunity to rub my nose in it by telling endless scatological anecdotes. 'Did you know the King of France used to go to the loo every morning and he would have all his ministers around him to discuss the doings of the country. I mean how many people can hold meetings in the middle of having a crap?' then even going so far as to present me, in the evening, with a map he'd drawn of the house's interior, with arrows marking the route from the living room to my bedroom and with every toilet highlighted by red stars.

We pleaded schedule nightmares to the Harcourts and planned to leave the next morning.

'So what do you do when you're not working?' Rory Jones asked me over breakfast. We were standing in front of a sideboard laden with silver dishes. There were tomato halves (fried), pork sausages (fried), bacon (fried), mushrooms (fried), triangles of bread (fried) and eggs (scrambled).

'Oh, you know,' I said airily, 'see friends, read, eat out . . . uh . . . see friends.'

'You said that already.'

'What already?'

'You said "see friends" twice.'

'Oh. Well the first ones are different to the second ones,' I said, defensively. Then I thought about the day I was offered the job on *Newsline*. I'd wanted to celebrate with someone but I hadn't known who to call. Eventually I got hold of Marnie, my oldest girlfriend and probably the sweetest person I know.

'Yay, Maggie,' she'd said, 'triple yay, the fruits of your labour − or labours of your fruit, can't remember which − are finally being realized. You are a goddess, of course you should come over, we'll crack some champagne.'

When she opened the door she was holding a tiny baby on one hip. I just stared and stared. I hadn't even known she was married.

'I know what you think I am,' I said to Rory.

'What?' He bit into the fried bread. Grease dripped down his chin.

'You're thinking work-obsessed, politically correct, lefty liberal New York neurotic feminist.'

'Oh no,' he slapped his hand to his cheek in pantomime horror, 'you're not a feminist are you?'

You don't know the half of it, I wanted to say. At my college, Welsley, people didn't burn their bras and dance around the Maypole because they considered the Maypole to be a phallic symbol, so instead they dug a hole and danced around the May*hole* . . .

Later in the car he asked, 'So what about boyfriends?'

'What about them?'

'Do you have one?'

'I hate the word boyfriend.' My hand closed over the cellphone in my pocket.

'I see.' He swung the car into the fast lane of the highway, 'What about dogs?'

'What about them?'

'Do you have one?'

'No.'

'Cat?'

'No.'

'What about a gerbil?'

'Nope.'

'Canary? Potted plant?'

'I'm not sure I want to stop long enough to have anything land on me.'

'OK, fine, commendably independent but where do you
have to be at Christmas?'

'Nowhere, thank God.' Then I saw he was looking horrified. 'Your point being?'

'My point being – are you attached to anything apart
from that damned mobile phone?'

I switched the cell off. Jay had once surprised me by
claiming he didn't know how I felt about him. I admitted
I had never dared let my guard down in case he took aim
and fired.

'What are you so worried I'd hit?'

I told him he'd probably be aiming for my head, but
being a senior citizen, might miss and shoot me in the heart
by mistake.

'Think Charlton Heston,' he'd said dryly.

Rory was still waiting for an answer.

'I just did a story on child prostitution in Brazil.'

'Uh huh, that's nice.'

'Oh I suppose it's a new concept for you to care about
people you don't know,' I said hotly.

'Perhaps it's a new concept for you to actually know
people you care about,' Rory retorted.

'Ouch,' I said.

The problem was that Rory was not easy to ignore. He
was totally obnoxious and delighted in winding me up.
Everywhere we turned, there he was, self-importantly pointing out No Entry signs, frowning if I dared ask a question
he considered out of line.

'Why don't you just stop telling me how to do my job,' I had a meltdown after one particularly bad day.

'Well you're like a badly behaved dog,' he said, 'I don't want you going off like a loose cannon.'

'If that isn't a mixed metaphor, I don't know what is.'

'Getting off the leash then. Is that better?'

'I don't like being put in a box, if you put me in a box . . .'

'Kennel.'

'What?'

'Kennel would work better with my dog metaphor,' he said apologetically.

'Fine . . . if you try to put me in a *kennel*, I will try to get out.'

So we established an uneasy pattern. Rory would deliver us, either stay the whole visit or long enough to gauge whether we were going to make trouble, and if not, would tuck us into the bosom of the aristocracy before driving back to London. He puzzled me. He seemed almost openly contemptuous of what we were doing and I didn't understand why he was in a job he found so distasteful.

'Did you leave the maid a tip?' Dwight asked pulling his shirt cuff down under the new tweed jacket he was wearing. We were loading up the van, on the move again after a two-day shoot at a house in Oxfordshire.

'A few dollars,' Wolf said. He caught the look on Dwight's face. 'What? How much was I supposed to leave?'

'Rory said at least twenty pounds.'

'I wanted to tip her not fuck her,' Wolf said mildly.

Dwight's face turned pink. He flipped open his holdall.

'Hey,' I intervened quickly, 'let's take a look at the map, Dwight.' I put my hand on his arm, 'Where to next?'

Dwight pulled out his maps and methodically began checking houses against locations. 'Let's see . . . if it's Tuesday it must be . . .' he flicked through the Stately Locations list of houses, 'Bevan,' he read and looked up for confirmation.

'You must be looking at an old list,' Rory appeared over Dwight's shoulder and took the file from his hands. He tore out the sheet with the photograph of Bevan.

'Bevan is out of bounds.'

Our England is a garden, and such gardens are not made
By singing:— 'Oh how beautiful!' and sitting in the shade
While better men than we go out and start their working lives
At grubbing weeds from gravel paths with broken dinner knives.

— Rudyard Kipling

daniel

Audrey hangs the telephone back on the kitchen wall.

'What's more she's going to pay us!'

Alistair looks up from his plate. '*Cash* money?'

'Cash money,' Audrey repeats in a daze, 'two thousand pounds.'

She sounds incredulous, as well she might. The last time either of my parents saw a windfall this large was when they put five pounds to win on Sore in the Saddle, a 300—1 outsider running in the Grand National.

'Not Sore in the Saddle,' Alistair said when Audrey returned from the betting shop in Skimpton. 'Sawsally, you silly fool.' He examined the betting slip. 'If this Sore in the Saddle is 300—1, it's more likely a goat than a horse.' When the goat had romped in first, Alistair bought shares in a company that intended to reproduce old master paintings in Braille.

'Bound to make a fortune,' he remarked at the time.

'Just wait and see. Robert will be awfully pleased with us, you know.'

'Can't count on it, he's so bloody bolshy these days. Anyway, what do they want with us?' Alistair says, having just identified the flaw in this otherwise perfect plan. 'What are they filming?'

'You know . . . old houses . . . English grandeur . . .' Audrey says vaguely.

'There's nothing grand left here.'

'Never mind, we could always show them the cellar. Pretend it was used for medieval torture.'

'We'll lock them in the cellar if they're tiresome.'

'They'll expect servants.'

'We could always dress Grandpa up as a butler.'

'Oh don't be so silly,' Audrey says fondly. 'Besides, he's at the chess club for the day.'

Few people who stayed at Bevan realized that there were no staff. They assumed that in a house this size, despite the ruined wing, there would be at least one or two people and Audrey and Alistair never disillusioned them. Instead they did everything themselves and when guests left a little something, they simply pocketed it. Being tipped by friends and relations, most substantially better off than they were, had been something of an eye-opener.

'What'll we feed them?' asks Alistair.

'I'll think of something.'

'Talking of which, what is this, darling?' Alistair says curiously. The slab of meat on his plate is the standard grey that all meat becomes following my mother's infallible recipe for 'safe' cooking.

Once upon a time there'd been a cook at Bevan. Mrs Preston used to dish up proper old-fashioned English fare. Suet pudding; jugged hare; chicken croquettes; treacle tart; rice pudding, always with a thick skin; summer pudding; roast beef with Yorkshire pudding, soft in the centre, its edges curling and crispy. When Mrs Preston finally died, eighty-two and no change out of nineteen stone, Audrey, who'd scarcely boiled an egg in her entire life, decided she'd have to make do. Alistair shot for the pot, Audrey made the pies and thus began her fateful love affair with the deep freeze.

In the beginning, Rory and I tried bringing down emergency rations. Fresh bread, the smelliest of cheeses, cod's roe, smoked fish. Instead of feeding us, these things fulfilled my mother's seeming pact with God to keep a well-stocked freezer. In went the fresh food, out came the frozen pie, that dreadful, dreaded, stringy mystery-meat dish.

Audrey takes another bite, giving the matter some consideration. 'Found it at the bottom of the deep freeze,' she says. 'We could have the leftovers tomorrow. We'll just say it's grouse or pigeon, they'll never know the difference.'

'Is it not grouse or pigeon?' asks Alistair.

'No,' says Audrey, 'I think it's badger.'

Oh . . . Oh . . . Aaaaaaaargh. I bloody well knew it.

'Frightfully good,' is all my father says.

maggie

Maybe it was the way he'd said it, maybe it was the expression on Rory's face — too set, too considered — or maybe the reason why this house had become compulsory viewing was because we'd been warned off. For the second time that trip. Bevan. The name had come up again and again. The only reason I'd added it to the original *Newsline* list was because the morning I arrived at the Cadogan Hotel, I'd found myself eavesdropping on two old ladies who were breakfasting at the table next to mine.

I'd noticed them because they looked like sisters, one with white hair coiled up in bun, the other's neatly waved over her ears but dressed identically in pleated skirts, shirts, cardigans and pearls.

'Always was of course. Even as a little boy.'

'Do you remember at picnics, his mother, old Lady Bevan—'

'The one with the dreadful Catholic hair?' One kept interrupting the other.

'That's right, she always made the butler sit twenty feet away with jam smeared on his head to keep the wasps off the food.'

'Wasn't she the one that kept a lion?'

'Indeed, bit the arm off the customs official at Heathrow.'

They were both amazed when I confessed I had never heard of Bevan. 'Oh my dear, but you must have. It's one of the great English houses.'

Judging from it's two-mile-long drive, however, there was no way you'd know it. The road was in a terrible state of neglect, the surface all torn up and pockmarked by giant craters of muddy water. In contrast, young trees on either side were painstakingly fenced out in small wooden crates and in the parklands beyond, a tractor stood stationary while activity in the form of several figures with chainsaws hummed around it.

'So how did you swing this by Rory?' Wolf asked.

'I didn't. I told him we were taking a "personal day". I don't think he knew what that was,' I grinned, 'but I must admit, he looked pretty embarrassed.'

'Aren't these the people that are supposed to be in the nut house?' Dwight said.

'Yeah. What was the deal with that anyway?' Wolf added.

'Beats me.' The drive had looped on itself and I could now see what was going on next to the tractor. An immense bonfire was in the process of being built. Shaped like a witch's hat it was already a good 12 feet high. Alongside it, several men were laying into a fallen tree with saws and axes then heaving branches up to another guy on the bonfire's summit.

'Beats me too . . .' Dwight stomped on the brake as sheep wandered across the road. More sheep were dotted around and a buffalo was grazing amongst the trees. Jesus, a *what*? I did an enormous double take.

'Because they sounded perfectly normal on the phone,' Dwight finished.

daniel

Upstairs in the first-floor corridor, Alistair rifles through Nanny's handbag. He gives it a quick sniff.

'What *are* you doing?' Audrey hisses.

'Smelling it.'

'What on earth for?'

'I don't know,' says Alistair much struck. 'Comfort I suppose.'

'Well be quick,' Audrey beseeches him, 'or we'll be caught.'

'Check the door then.'

Audrey peers through the keyhole of Nanny's bedroom as Alistair extracts a clip purse from her bag. 'One bottle of whisky, or should we risk enough for two?'

Audrey glances plaintively at the bulging purse. 'Why is Nanny so much better off than we are?'

'Because in fifty odd years,' Alistair folds the twenty-pound note into his pocket, 'Nanny has only ever spent her wages on Basildon Bond writing paper and blue hats from the Army and Navy store. She's probably amassed a small fortune by now.'

'Do you think she keeps accounts?' Audrey says. And

she might well be worried. When Nanny discovered Rory and I had stolen a pack of Wrigley's gum from the milkman's float there'd been hell to pay. I think our poor mother was more traumatized than we were by the dire threats of Borstal that followed. She has a sudden flash of us standing, knees grimy, heads hanging, and at the memory her eyes cloud.

'Shhh,' says Alistair.

'What?'

'Hear that?'

'What?'

'Car.'

'No.'

'Yes, listen.'

'What?'

'*Will* you be quiet,' he says creeping to the window. 'It's *them*. They're *here*.'

Out of habit Audrey breathes the smoke out of the window. Alistair made her give up when they were first married and she never lost the habit of hiding it from him. She can hear him below. 'Well done, well done, directions all right?' She leans out of the window. Good God, look at the equipment they were carrying. The girl was in front with the two men behind. One of the men was Chinese or Japanese, but enormous! A Buddha! The girl was younger than she'd imagined. Dark, pretty, but dressed in the sort of ubiquitous army gear of the young. She herself had never taken much care with her appearance. You couldn't very well grow up vain in Ireland. In the sixties when she moved to London, she felt horribly out of place. Her legs were too stocky for miniskirts. When she'd cut her hair short she hadn't looked gamine or pixieish at all — in fact, not long after it had grown out, Alistair told her she'd looked like Henry VIII.

She grinds out the butt on the window sill noticing that the rhododendron bushes need cutting back — and wonders how she will ever manage without Bindey, finally retired aged eighty-nine. Damn, the telephone wire has come loose. She stretches out her hand, gets a finger to the black cabling and prods it back into a crack in the brickwork. But she's leant out too far. Her hand slips, she loses balance and in an instant I see she will fall.

It's only a half landing, but I'm terrified it will break her hip. Instead her beloved rhododendrons envelop her in their prickly centre. 'Bugger,' she says with feeling. She touches the long tear in her stockings. 'Bloody bugger.'

'Ah, here's Audrey now,' says my father, rounding the corner just in time to see his wife pick her way out of a bush pulling twigs from her hair. Audrey strides purposefully towards the group trying not to limp. 'Well done, well done,' she says with a beatific smile, 'Directions all right?'

Alistair thinks they're very odd. He's never clapped eyes on a group of people less well equipped for the English country-side. Only the shortish one has brought his own boots but is, bizarrely, dressed straight out of the pages of a Jeeves novel. The girl is wearing gym shoes and a thin coat whilst the Buddha sports a pair of sandals with socks. They seem nice enough, however, so he gives them a tour during which they film the wine cellar, significant only for its lack of wine, the May bedroom, significant for the suicide of a jilted chambermaid who hung herself with my great great-grandmothers pearls. Then they film the dairy where there are no longer cows to milk just as there are no horses to ride in the stableyard.

My father relates the full history of the house for the camera and is gratified that Miss Monroe shows so much interest in his endeavours to keep it afloat.

'But what were you hoping to do with these?' She plucks a smooth pebble from a tray by the stone-polishing machine.

'Make them into toys,' Alistair says vaguely, 'arts and crafts, pebble dogs, birds, that sort of thing . . . made a whole family of rooks once but nobody was interested. People used to eat rook pie around here. They'd shoot the young peeping over the edge of their nests with an air gun. Thought to be a great country delicacy at one time . . . caught some young boys at it the other day as it happened, gave them a frightful rocket.'

At one point he asks whether she has met his son Robert, and I look forward to a potentially interesting moment. Though it can't be legitimately classed as six degrees of separation it is a spectacularly fine piece of irony that she's here, quite oblivious of the connection, and at some point the shit must inevitably hit the fan, as it were, but not right now − because when the question is asked, the entire crew is distracted, quite understandably, by their attempts to frame the buffalo in shot and Maggie treats the question in much the same way as being asked by a London cabby whether she'd ever come across his first cousin who lived in Delaware.

They're now in the old laboratory where my father is showing them the Heath Robinson contraption of pipes, funnels, bowls, milk and muslins he has erected. The Americans stare into a vat of some indescribably repellent gunk, which sits underneath to catch the drips.

'From the buffalo milk,' Alistair explains. 'Oddly enough *this* milk, when left to curdle, turns into an interesting cottage cheese texture which when mixed with . . .?' He turns to Miss Monroe.

'Chives?' she hazards gamely.

'No, no . . .'

'Pepper? Honey?'

'No, no, you're entirely on quite the wrong track. Sand! Here try some,' he passes Maggie a spoonful which she sniffs suspiciously.

'Go on,' he says, 'be brave.'

'Sand,' she repeats faintly, raising the spoon to her lips. 'And you eat this on . . .?'

'Don't be silly.' he snatches the plastic spoon from her, 'you can't eat sand, good Lord, *the milk* is against every EEC health regulation ever dreamt up.' He smears the contents of the spoon on his cheek with one finger. 'It's for face packs! You see the mozzarella was not a great success,' he confides and is deep into a colourful description of the creature's medical problems when Maggie interrupts him.

'But surely mozzarella doesn't come from the American buffalo?'

'Quite right, good for you. Water buffalo's the one you really want.' He lowers his voice conspiratorially 'got one of those on order as a matter of fact.'

But Maggie is now wearing an expression of exhausted confusion as if she'd been asked to memorize the 3,000 components of a nuclear warhead.

'Something wrong?' asks my father.

'No, not at all,' she says puzzled, 'it's just that I was wondering . . . well . . . are you sure it's a water buffalo? Isn't it an Italian buffalo you need?'

maggie

Another reason I love living in New York is the fact that it's a functional city. Obviously not in the psychological sense — I mean as a collection of people we're as psychotically challenged as anyone else — but in a practical sense, New York functions like nowhere else on earth. Everybody *does* something, provides some service, everyone, everything, has a purpose. The Bowery, for example, where I live, is not just a residential area, it's also the stainless steel headquarters of the city. For five blocks square all you can buy anywhere is kitchen equipment. Industrial stuff mostly: stoves, hoods, griddles, broilers as big as my sofa all hoisted onto the sidewalks by the guys who run the shops. In winter you see them standing outside clapping their hands for warmth and chatting to locals, blowing hot air out of their mouths. From my window their breath looks like cooking steam. I keep telling them they should cook on their stoves, sell a little chicken noodle soup to warm the souls of passers-by.

Outside stainless steel, you get plumbing. Sprayed on shop fronts are enticing offers. Ball caps! Filigree end scrolls! 45-inch elbows! The exclamation marks making them sound like new and exciting sex toys. Lighting lives beyond the plumbing and then you get to the thrift shops of SoHo – it's as I said – everything has a purpose whether it's buying, selling or recycling. One man's trash is another man's treasure. Nothing stays around long enough to gather dust.

This was not the case with Bevan. The house was extraordinary and tragic and unlike any place I had ever come across. Rooms led one to the other through panelled doors, each a degree colder than the previous; each in a progressively worse state of disrepair, boasting a different shade of gloom, a more marked degree of fade. Most depressing of all was the sheer quantity of useless *stuff* crammed high on every surface, but whether this stuff was tokens of love or just garbage, it was impossible to tell. Wolf slowly panned the camera over surfaces as we passed through. Newspapers, brittle and yellowing, piles of matchboxes, rusted hunting knives, old bits of guns, shelves of dried-up magazines – you had to struggle to get your head round it – if in another part of the world human tissue was being cloned and emails were flying through space, what were people doing living this way in the twenty-first century? Why did they need this house? Why not sell up? Was it fear or stubbornness or just plain stupidity.

The Earl conducted the entire tour in his dirty boots, insisting we did the same. So we tramped through leaving our own streaks of mud and I imagined them melting into the general brownness of the floor, gluing together the fray of the carpet, hardening in holes left by woodworm. As the house merged together into the murky colours of neglect I

began to feel wildly claustrophobic. I longed for the empti-
ness of my loft, for its clean, uncluttered space. I wanted
to lie on the floorboards with nothing better to do than
listen to the whirr of sewing machines immediately below
in the Chinese sweatshop and wonder at the irony of the
twenty-seven immigrants who spend their miserable days
sweating, running up tracksuits in which others will run in
order to sweat for pleasure.

Still, the Earl himself was pure *Newsline* Gold. Apart
from who he was (cousin of the queen, peer of the realm,
with one of the oldest family seats in Britain and God
only knew how many titles) he surely epitomized the point-
lessness of the aristocracy. He was a total anachronism,
a twenty-first-century dinosaur, and I wanted to get him to
admit it on camera.

'Well, since the House of Lords has lost most of its
hereditary peers,' I asked, 'what relevance has the aristocracy in today's Britain?'

'Absolutely none.'

I was a little wrong-footed by such frankness.

'Er, so . . . what would you say was left of the so-called
"playing fields of Eton".'

'Bugger all,' he replied in much the same tone of voice.
Wolf caught my eye and winked. I floundered on. 'Um, well
if that's true . . . what would you say your role was now?'

He took pity on me. 'If you're suggesting we have
outlived our usefulness,' he said gently, 'I would have to
agree with you, we are, in the words of the Duke of
Devonshire, "a spent force".'

'Do you think that the hereditary peers should have been
expelled from the House of Lords?'

'It was entirely undemocratic, so I understood, of course, but in a curious way the system worked very well.'

'You don't think people should be chosen for that position on merit.'

'Just because a man has risen to the top of his profession through drive and ambition does not necessarily make him a suitable public servant. Indeed there may well come a day when a man whose sense of public duty is motivated purely by his obligation to society will be sorely missed.'

I told him this sounded like a warning, and he agreed perhaps it was. When I quoted him Lloyd George's 'by what right are 10,000 people owners of the soil in this country and the rest of us trespassers in the land of our birth', he said, 'Oh but you see I'm not really the owner of the soil. I am a keeper of the soil, and in answer to your earlier question my "role" now is no more than guardian, curator of this house if you like. The only thing we're expected to do is keep things going for the next generation.'

'Expected by whom?'

'Good question,' he said.

I liked him. He made no attempt to wriggle out of tough questions and his wasn't the practised seductiveness people sometimes turned on for the camera. The Earl was totally genuine.

'Was there ever anything you wanted to do?' I asked him curiously.

He frowned and I realized he hadn't understood the question.

'You know, when you were young?'

'You mean what did I want to be when I grew up?'

I nodded. He thought for a while then he said, 'Yes. Not the eldest son.'

daniel

There is an image people have of alcoholic parents. It's an image that conjures up violence, wife beating, child abuse, self-destruction, family secrets, broken childhoods and it's not a pretty picture.

Benj's father is an alcoholic like this, effete, sneering, racist, sexist. When we were boys, home from school, he would hold court at the dining table demanding everyone's attention as his poisonous diatribe flowed against the world. He was certainly amusing, but amusing at everybody else's expense and the drunker he got the meaner he became. During those interminable meals, he would unaccountably cease from holding anecdotally forth, turn to Benj and rasp, 'Your turn to say something clever, Benjamin,' and a terrible silence would fall. If Benj failed to amuse the assembled company, his father would accuse him of being unspeakably dull and send him to eat in another room while guests and relations shifted uncomfortably in their chairs.

We were lucky. Our parents were not like that. We were also fortunate — or rather Alistair and Audrey were fortunate — in that they were entirely complicit in their drinking. If this had the result of closing them off from us, at least they were not closed off from each other. Our childhood was not overshadowed by cruelty or violence, it was instead governed by lack of focus, near misses, and yes, of course, there were family secrets. Our childhood was defined by omissions, places we didn't go, conversations we couldn't have, cousins we were no longer allowed to see.

But family secrets were not our biggest problem in those days. Our immediate task was to stuff our thumbs in the leaking dyke. Our most pressing concern was damage limitation – to keep the smouldering embers off the carpet, to lift my mother back into her chair, and always, always to prevent others from knowing. Then there was Alistair and Audrey's propensity for foot in mouth, their talent for causing embarrassment by simply being themselves. It wasn't just contained at home; it followed us to school. Cheques were bounced, forms were left unfilled. Rory and I, standing with our trunks at the school gates, forgotten and uncollected at the end of term. Our skill became the cover-up, the manufacturing of excuses. There are no places to hide from extreme behaviour. You deal with it by adopting extremes yourself.

Rory succeeded no better than I did in the impossible task of attracting our parents' attention and keeping it. What tools can you develop to turn the beam of somebody's spotlight onto you? 'Dad, I'm an alcoholic, a drug addict, Dad, perhaps you haven't noticed, but I'm actually black.' This is where our paths began to split. Rory retreated, I attacked. We embraced different religions. Rory drank the water, I took care of the wine. To me it's so simple. You drink, snort, take pills, it's only ever about trying to find a place where you can be happy – but here is the nub, I suppose, of Rory's resentment. Double abandonment. First by them, then by me. He does not forgive my parents for who I turned out to be; his tragedy is he can't accept that I would never dream of blaming them in the first place.

Something happens to a man when he realizes he has no choice, when he realizes he's lost a freedom he never had any rights to. Something drains out of him. It doesn't matter how big your Estate, how tall your trees, how smartly dressed your gardeners — nothing can compensate a human being for feeling absolutely worthless. I often wondered who or what my father dreamed of becoming when he was young, but he once told me in an unguarded moment that the day he inherited Bevan it felt as though his life was over before it had begun. But Alistair was an optimist. He loved Bevan. To him it was an enchanted land beyond whose boundaries the outside world barely existed — and Bevan, when he inherited it, had not seemed like the impossible task it does today.

Alistair didn't care if the house wasn't grand, he didn't care if it wasn't warm — as long as it functioned, and it did. The decay was gentle but probably not on a dissimilar time schedule to his own. Then came the fire. It decimated the east wing and nobody was sure how it had started. Maybe it was faulty wiring, maybe Alistair had been sloshed before it began. Certainly he was a lot more sloshed after they'd finished clearing away those great piles of blackened ash and bricks.

A year after the fire, the estate was ravaged by Dutch elm disease. It was 1976. Britain lost more than twenty million trees, thousands of which were on our land. Elms are one of the most romantic of trees, their apple-core silhouettes responsible for much of this country's graceful landscape. Dead elm was primarily used for coffins but there was such a glut you had to pay to have them taken away. Alistair, along with every other poor sod, was swindled blind by the timber merchants who claimed there was no market for the wood. The drive at Bevan had been lined with elms. Four hundred full grown trees, 100 feet high, 200 years old. Alistair refused to cut them down, thought they might survive. He spent a small fortune injecting them, but it didn't work. When they died, Alistair cut them down himself, every single one. Ten years of bonfires, maybe fifteen. I can see Bindey, grasping one side of the double-handed saw. I can see my father shirtless, sweating, leaning on the axe. I can still remember his face as he watched those trees fall. Over two centuries of growth and majesty reduced to stumps and I think it was the first time I ever saw a grown man cry.

maggie

Nanny, as the Earl and his wife called her, was a tiny, white-haired woman of extreme old age. She sat in front of the television, feet resting on a petit point stool. She presented a neat figure in tartan skirt and green cable cardigan. A cameo brooch pinned to the neck of her blouse kept in place, not just the peter pan collar, but also the strands of wrinkled skin that stretched from her throat to her chin and swayed gently as she spoke.

'I do watch *Friends*, yes, dear,' she said. 'I don't always understand the jokes but I do like to see nice young people enjoying themselves.' She poured another cup of tea and held it out to Wolf.

The old lady's quarters were a virtual shrine to the royal family. Walls were decorated with framed tea towels of the queen mother, and the engagement of Charles and Diana. The mantelpiece was home to a dozen or so commemorative mugs and there were even pictures of the two little princes, Harry and William, in silver frames. The other thing about the room was that, unlike the rest of the house, it was warm – in fact not warm, *boiling*. Wolf poured with sweat as he angled the camera through the door to Nanny's bedroom, picking out the headboard of her single bed. A large old-fashioned watch was pinned to its oyster-coloured satin and a bottle of lemon barley water stood on the bedside table.

'And you've been Nanny to all the family?' I asked her. I was about to pass out with the heat but the old lady was unruffled.

'I was employed by Master Alistair's mother, aye,' Nanny, like the Earl, maintained perfect composure in front of the camera. My bet was this was because she couldn't see it. She was ninety-five years old and held an incredible scorn for old people, proudly telling us of her disgust at younger generations taking to their beds.

'Nothing makes Nanny happier than doling out meals on wheels to decrepit pensioners twenty years her junior,' said the Earl wryly.

'I've kept myself busy, dear, and that's why I'm so healthy today.'

She was shocked when I asked her if she was resentful always living in somebody else's house. 'I've been in service all my life,' she said. 'My father was a policeman. As a family, we have *always* been of use.' She prided herself on never turning out a bad child, dismissing the notion of bad genes as nonsense. 'Bad breeding is cured by good upbringing,' she announced emphatically, 'not that his lordship wasn't a rascal because he was, I can tell you, eighteen years I wiped his nose,' she glanced fondly in the Earl's direction, then rapped, 'Alistair, must I tell you again not to lean against the fireguard.' She turned back to camera without missing a beat. 'As I was saying, Alistair was my pet, then after he was married there were the boys and now . . . well and now there's just the baby left,' her face softened, 'but he himself needs quite some looking after,' she sniffed. '*Quite* a handful let me assure you.'

'How old is the baby?' I asked, totally confused.

'Thirty-eight and bright as a button too. Poor boy leads a terrible rackety life down in the city, never one to eat properly . . . much too thin, just like yourself.' She felt her hands towards the tea tray, 'if you're no' drinking tea, then will you take a glass of milk?'

'No thanks very much I don't like—'

'Now,' she said briskly, 'I don't approve of dieters or vomiters. Lady Diana, may God rest her poor soul, was a vomiter . . . but in my opinion it's a wicked waste of good food. Alistair?'

The Earl poured milk into the cup she was holding towards him, 'Nanny knows best,' he said with heavy irony. Removing a baby beaker which obscurely had been clipped to his jacket ever since we arrived, he added a dose of whatever was inside before handing it to me with a wink.

Brandy from the smell of it. The Earl had the look of an alcoholic. His skin was rough, his face heavy and jowled, but although he continually took swigs from the beaker, he never seemed to get all that drunk. Plus he was in good shape, striding ahead of us all afternoon, pointing his walking stick at trees he'd planted giving us both Latin and English names and describing them as if they were fine wines. 'Now that's a *Fraxinus excelsior* "Jaspidea", little like your common ash but goes a wonderful buffer yellow in the autumn, over there is a full-bodied *Fraxinus mariesii*, ravishing flowers, white, like feathery smoke . . . left of the oak is a rather perky little *Coculus trilobus* from the somewhat risqué-sounding family of Menispermaceae.' But as the day wore on his attention began to stray and I detected a faint slur to his words.

Downstairs in the drawing room, he poured us all shots of neat Scotch from a decanter. From his pocket he produced a straw which he stuck in his own glass. It was one of those curly plastic things Toys R Us sell as Christmas stocking fillers.

'Uh . . . what's the significance of the straw?' I couldn't help asking. I watched fascinated as the golden liquid rose through its bends like oil in a pipeline.

'This?' He picked it up. 'Simple really. Question of economy. Alcohol reaches your bloodstream quicker when drunk through a straw.'

I had no idea what he was talking about.

'A higher level of inebriation can be achieved through less alcohol,' he explained patiently. 'Saves money. As I said. A simple question of economy.'

'A simple question of economy,' Wolf pointed the camera at Dwight. 'Tell us, your Earlyship,' he mimicked my voice. 'Is it the drink or the bad genes that make you a candidate for the funny farm?'

'Survival of the weirdest, dear boy,' Dwight said in his best English accent, 'Although five hundred years of sleeping with my sister sure helped.'

'Are you boys taking the piss by any chance?' I murmured. We were through for the day, and reluctantly packing up. I would have happily stayed longer but Rory had been adamant about not messing around any more of his clients so we were committed to meeting him at Stately Locations early the next morning. I had my back to the crew, checking out titles on the shelf. Bevan's library was nothing like as distinguished as Roxmere's but there were some lovely old books. An illustrated complete works of Shakespeare, the imprint on its spine rubbed almost bare. A navy cloth-bound copy of Milton's *Paradise Lost*, which I pulled out.

'These people are awesome, Maggie,' Wolf said. 'We couldn't have invented better.'

'*From morn to noon he fell, from noon to dewy eve, a summer's day; and with the setting sun dropped from the zenith like a falling star.*' I closed the book and tried to ease it back into the shelf but it wouldn't fit. The books on either side had closed ranks as though relieved at the extra space, but it wasn't a question of width, something else was blocking it from behind. I stood on the chair to investigate. Another thinner book had slipped from the shelf above and wedged itself in the way. I prised it loose and wiped the dust from the cover with my sleeve. It was a volume of Nietzsche – its title, *The Birth of Tragedy* engraved in gold. A piece of paper fluttered out. I stooped down and picked it off the floor. In fact it was a photograph, a barely legible pencil mark on the back dating it as 1938. I turned it over and suddenly felt the hairs on my arm rise. The photograph was of a group of children with their nanny, a man and a large Alsatian dog standing in front of a mountain chalet. It could have been any family holiday snap: Italy, Switzerland maybe. It could have been a scene straight out of the *Sound of Music*. Except it wasn't – the man in the picture was Adolf Hitler.

I turned it over and over disbelievingly.

'What's wrong, Maggie?'

I handed it to Wolf and fumbled to the front of the Nietzsche book.

Wolf read over my shoulder.

'*To my good English friend, Viscount Lytton-Jones, in memoriam of a most successful visit, Herman Goebbels.*'

'Holy shit!' he said.

I stared at it, stunned. 'Holy shit is right.'

'Drive safely.' Alistair Bevan seized my hand and pumped it. I thanked him, worrying some gravel under the toe of my sneaker. 'It's been really interesting.' I looked at the house, looked at the open door of the van, at the Earl's wife smiling at us in her misshapen tweed skirt, friendly, trusting.

'You know what,' I said, 'I think I left my cell in the library.'

I'd just got the book tucked down my pants and my shirt over the top when the old lady walked in. 'Found it,' I said.

'Well done.' She answered politely, though I could swear she could barely see me, let alone the cell I was waving in the air.

I passed through the door she was holding open. 'Nanny?' I hesitated, '. . . I meant to ask earlier . . . who is Viscount Lytton-Jones?'

She was quiet for a minute and I held my breath. Uncovering the vague snobbishness and eccentricity of the aristocracy was one thing, uncovering a Nazi collaboration was something else entirely. 'He died tragically,' she said finally. When she raised her eyes there was something fierce in their watery blue depths. 'I wouldn't mention it if I were you. It still causes the family a great deal of pain.'

As soon as Wolf steered the van out through the gates he turned on me. 'Show and Tell, Maggie,' he said, and I eased the photograph from my pocket.

'And just what do you intend to do with that?'

I didn't know, but I knew what the photo meant. Alistair, Con, William, Dinah, Robert. The names of the five children were written in pencil on the back. Viscount Lytton-Jones was Alistair Bevan's father. There was a story there, even if he was dead. It was just a question of finding it.

My mother once said that as a documentarian it was her job to shine the light into those dark corners where injustice was taking place because if you don't know what's happening, it doesn't affect your life, and if things don't affect your life, you do nothing to change them. There were crimes being committed all over the world, there were dirty secrets in every corner . . .

Back at the Cadogan Hotel I called *Newsline*. Bevan, potentially, was a very dirty little secret indeed but Alan's direct line didn't get me through to him and it took forty minutes of back-to-back talking to robots, literally, before the system found him.

'You better have something really good up your sleeve,' he said.

'I do.'

'Keep me in the loop and make sure you get everything for your original brief.'

'I will.'

Wolf waited till I'd hung up.

'So what are you going to do?' he asked for the second time and when I didn't answer he handed the photograph back to me. 'Tread carefully, Maggie,' he said. 'Whatever this means, it's probably not their finest hour.'

daniel

Maggie and her crew do not turn up at Stately Locations at the appointed time following their 'personal' day so Rory leaves the address with Alison and treats Benj to brunch in Yo Sushi round the corner, where plates of food are plucked like startled commuters from a moving conveyor belt. When Benj blurs his eyes, he imagines the accompanying clear soup bowls are shot glasses of gin. To distract himself from this taboo image he asks Rory when he first discovered Alistair and Audrey drank.

Rory tells him it was the time he nearly drowned.

I remember our mother then. She was never beautiful as such, but very striking. Strong features, thick dark hair. 'She was a great swimmer,' Rory tells Benj. 'She could have swum for England.' She'd grown up in Ireland and learnt to swim in the loughs and the sea. At Bevan she used to swim in the lake most days even in cold weather, cutting across the water, from jetty to boathouse, sleek as an otter in her thick rubber swimming cap.

The water was damn cold in that lake. Pike nibbled your feet and slunk around the jetty where there were only a few painful steps before the ground disappeared to nothing and the water became ten degrees colder.

Rory had only just learnt to swim when I announced we would steal the boat to go fishing. It was mid August and a hot, hot summer. We'd had a picnic and both Ma and Pa were drinking from the coffee flask. Coffee was a big thing for our parents. They took it with them whenever they left the house, once even driving the 10 miles back to Bevan because the flask had been forgotten. After coffee they fell asleep lying side by side on the tartan picnic blanket.

The boathouse smelt musty as we tossed the anchor in the boat and jumped down after it. Rory balanced his feet on either side to steady the boat as I eased it through the reeds and bulrushes, out into the bright sunlight.

'There's a Babar story like this,' Rory reminds Benj. 'Celeste and Babar give birth to triplets, Alexander, Flora and Pom, then embark on a series of fantastically irresponsible outings which these days would have social services rushing to fill out foster home forms.' He picks a Californian roll apart with his chopsticks. 'First they allow Arthur, who's, what, three or fours years old, to take Pom for a walk, but Arthur, who's rightly pissed off to be presented with not one but three sibling rivals pushes the pram over the cliff. Next, Celeste, who's gone berserk from breast-feeding triplets, gives the new-born Flora a rattle to suck whereupon she chokes. Finally Babar and Celeste go for a picnic and drink themselves insensible, leaving the toddlers to play by the lake. I mean everybody knows you don't let small elephants play by water,' Rory says, '*everybody* knows,' he trails off.

'And sure enough,' Benj says quietly, 'Alexander sneaks out in the boat and falls in.'

Rory caught the fishing rod in the weeds and gave it a yank. I lost the oars and Rory fell backwards. He thinks of Alexander as he sinks through the water. It's deeper and much colder in the middle of the lake and Rory can't get himself horizontal. The blackness of the water pulls at his legs. The crocodile swims towards Alexander and Rory worries about the pike. If they were a foot long at the jetty then imagine how big they are out in the middle. He's a lot more scared of being bitten than drowning.

He splutters up and down, down and up but just as his vision blurs to milky he sees Audrey powering towards him, her short hair capless. How she'd spotted him all the way from the bank, I've no idea. Just in time Babar throws the boat anchor into the throat of the crocodile. Just in time Rory feels himself plucked from the lake like a bobbing apple from a water keg. Crouched in the still drifting boat, I never saw such determination and purpose in my mother and I never would again.

'On the bank she gave me mouth to mouth,' Rory said, 'and in her mouth I tasted coffee.' He'd smelt it too on her breath as she'd hauled him back to shore. It was *her* smell, cosy and familiar. It clung to her like a scent and neither of us had ever found it unpleasant. She smelt of it in the morning and it was even stronger in the evening when she kissed us goodnight.

The next morning, Rory walked into the library. Mrs Bindey was on her hands and knees picking broken glass off the carpet. He handed her the top to the crystal decanter which had rolled to the doorway. The whole room reeked of coffee and he said so. Mrs Bindey straightened up and stared at him.

That was the day he discovered what whisky was.

'In retrospect, Babar was a latent homosexual,' Rory says.

'He most certainly was not.' Benj is incensed at this outing of his hero.

'He had an unhealthy preoccupation with his spats.'

'He was happily married to Celeste.' Benj takes a plastic dog turd from his pocket, puts it on an empty chicken yakitori plate and returns it to the moving conveyer.

'It's not normal for elephants to be that pernickety about their footwear.'

'He was the king of the elephants, he doesn't go by normal elephant rules.'

'Celeste had Munchausen's syndrome, Arthur was a retard and as for the Old Lady . . .'

Benj laughs. 'My father's convinced I'm a latent homosexual.'

'Are you?' Rory asks idly. He can see the crew's van mounting the kerb of the pavement outside.

'I have no idea,' Benj says. 'Maybe one of these days I'll be lucky enough to find out.'

News is part of our communal experience. News is a public service. I believe that good journalism, good television can make our world a better, fairer place.

— Christiane Amanpour

maggie

Sir Harding Montague was a wiry, extremely articulate man who enunciated his words in a voice unsettlingly lacking in peaks or troughs. He reminded me forcibly of a toad and, like the South American version of the species, when you squeezed him poison leaked from every pore of his skin.

Waverley, his Estate, was a gothic miracle of a house in the county of Suffolk. *Newsline* researchers had turned it up before Christmas. It hadn't been on the Stately Locations books, but Sir Montague had jumped at the idea of 'expenses' and Rory had grudgingly orchestrated a deal.

Montague had quite a reputation. He was notorious for his affairs with other women while his wife had quietly and discreetly died from cancer. He'd held a government position under Edward Heath, but had been fired when caught, 'in flagrante', as Rory put it, with a senior minister's wife. Montague's own description of the lady who had cost him his career was, 'Labia like an elephant's trunk . . . had to be careful or it would snatch things off the table when you weren't looking.' This dazzling imagery had made Dwight choke. Montague was an appalling character; snobbish, misogynistic, racist, and he took obvious delight in discomfiting us. 'I don't like that man,' Montague said, once he'd made sure Dwight was within earshot. 'I don't like his shoes.'

'Actually that makes two of us,' I agreed. Dwight's inexplicable transmogrification into an English gent was continuing unabated. For Montague's opening gambit — a show of Waverley's grounds, Dwight had worn a new pair of brown brogues, which Wolf gleefully later reported gave him terrible blisters.

The afternoon we arrived, we were able, by sheer good fortune, to film a fox hunt. It was everything we could have hoped for. The red coats, the sherry, the baleful howling of the hounds as they were given a whiff of fox. We even got the anti-hunt protesters, and Montague's hysterically funny dealings with them. Rory was totally against us filming and spent an hour on the telephone trying to talk Sir Montague out of it, but Montague clearly relished the controversy and Rory, having driven straight back to London soon after delivering us, was 200 miles away.

When he reappeared the following day he was still angry.

'The hunting issue is highly inflammatory, as you're well aware, so if you're going to include it you need to understand it.'

I had been about to make the same point myself, but the lecturing tone of his voice got to me. 'What was it one of your poets, Oscar Wilde or someone, called it? The unspeakable in pursuit of the uneatable? Yeah . . .' I said smugly, 'That was it.'

'Actually,' he said, 'it was Shaw—'

'Are you trying to say that you're pro fox hunting?'

'That's not the point—'

'Well I mean you either are or you aren't, right?'

'I'm pro fox hunting and I'm pro the fox.'

'My people might call that sitting on the fence.'

'I can tell you what I'm not pro,' he said, 'and that's the trumpeting lines of hideous sanctimonious do-gooders like yourself, ignoring the wishes of people in the countryside . . .'

'I suppose you're up for clubbing seals too.'

'. . . who feel they can dictate to their "intellectual" inferiors, ignoring the fact that everyone in a democracy has a free choice.'

'And why not eat a little dolphin in your tuna salad?'

'Before you start preaching to me,' he said furiously, 'perhaps you should be obliged, in between bites of your steak sandwich, to watch lambs and cows being butchered in an abattoir. Did you know that when cows smell the blood of their own species they start screaming in panic?'

He was insufferably pompous. 'Hey, I film what I see,' I yelled at his retreating back.

We didn't see him for the rest of the day, which was unusual, given his fondness for frowning and spluttering during interviews. We were talking to Montague in his dressing room where he had requested to be filmed, back-lit and coiled on his bed in a hilariously opulent velvet dressing gown.

'What would you say was the purpose of the aristocracy?' I pitched him the routine question.

'To be the elite of course, to maintain the hierarchies of wealth and rank, to set an example.'

'How to be illiberal and redundant?' I was hoping to goad him into a full-scale rant.

Sir Montague put out a claw-like finger and tapped my knee. 'Ah, you want to play the socialist agitator do you, pussykins? Incite the masses to riot and revolution? Well I'd like to suggest that you're motivated by nothing more glorious than social envy.'

I was happy to ignore the pussykins. Unlike the other two shoots we'd been on since Bevan, Montague was prime material and I didn't want to risk him drying up.

'You're suggesting that my motive for making this film is to, what?' I said. 'Exorcise my own inferiority as an American?'

'Of course. We have culture, you have *Star Trek*. Tradition is the law we live by – tradition in your country is that revolting little children's habit of begging for sweets at Halloween.'

'Yeah, and you Brits are damn lucky we saved your butts or you'd all be singing "Deutschland Deutschland über alles" right about now,' I shot back.

He gave a cackle of laughter. 'I think you'll find that some Brits are *still* singing "Deutschland Deutschland über alles".' he said.

'What do you mean?' I sobered up quickly.

Despite my bullish optimism on the phone to Alan, I'd got no further on the Bevan story. The evening we'd returned to London, I'd sat up half the night browsing the Internet, systematically entering names and subjects; World War Two, Fascism, the royal family. I'd stumbled across a few relevant pieces; a headline in a 1948 newspaper with an accompanying picture, 'Aristocratic sisters pose in front of marching Nazis.' A lot of information about the British Union of Fascists; endless articles on Edward and Mrs Simpson.

The boys had been no help at all.

'What do we actually know about the English royal family?' I'd asked over room-service burgers.

'Well, even I know they're *all* a bunch of Germans,' Wolf said. 'Look, it says here that Lord Mountbatten changed his name to Mountbatten from Battenburg.'

'Why?' said Dwight. 'Was he Jewish?'

'You know,' Wolf salted his fries, 'I bet poor Nietzsche got a really bad rap because Goebbels admired him so much.'

The truth was Wolf had lost interest. With the Viscount dead he didn't think there was a story to pursue and though I badly wanted to find one, I was beginning to think he was right. Even Simon Brannigan, my BBC contact, had been dubious. 'It was well-known that members of the aristocracy saw positive virtue in fascist regimes,' he said. 'Hitler had acquaintances in some very influential circles. The problem is families and friends have always closed ranks . . . there's tremendous class loyalty. There have never been names.'

I mean, it was frustrating. I had a name, but I couldn't give it to anyone nor could I find any threads of a story to tie up to it.

I looked at Montague. His remark had been completely unguarded and I wondered how far he'd let himself be pushed.

'Isn't it true,' I said carefully, 'that certain members of the aristocracy were involved with—' but that was as far as I got. His hand snaked out and grasped my wrist.

'My dear,' he said, 'there are several reasons why you would be particularly ill advised to follow this line of questioning further.' I was startled. His tone was measured but there had been steel in that grip.

I couldn't concentrate on the rest of the interview. As soon as we wrapped it up I switched on my laptop upstairs and read through every note I'd made. The morning after Bevan, I'd blown off our early start at Stately Locations and instead raced off to a historical bookshop in the Strand where I'd found books on the fascist Oswald Mosley, the BUF and the Mitford sisters. Now I took them out of my suitcase and searched through their indexes and bibliographies looking for inspiration. One of them, *British Fascism*, had been written by a historian, a Professor Lunn, who I now noticed from the blurb on the inside cover, lived in London. After Montague we were scheduled to shoot background footage of the House of Lords back in London so on whim I rang information and to my utter surprise Lunn's number was listed. My luck held out because when I dialled the number a soft, cultured voice picked up on the first ring.

'Professor Lunn?' I asked.

'For reasons that escape me,' Rory said walking into the room a few minutes later, 'Your company is required at dinner.'

I snapped my cell shut guiltily. 'Don't people knock on doors in your country?'

'Been doing your homework?'

'Just looking up the genetic factor that makes Englishmen

so obnoxious.' I shut down the computer and slid it forwards to cover the address Professor Lunn had dictated.

'Well, tomorrow's project is to find ten more things about the English you really dislike,' he said grimly, 'and don't worry, you can be sure I'll be working equally hard in the opposite direction.'

Professor Lunn's house was in Bloomsbury. Oppressively dark, dusty and book-laden it seemed the typical lair of an academic. Physically speaking, Lunn the professor was straight out of central casting. Woolly, bearded, a hint of a shuffle. Opera was booming from behind the closed door when I rang the bell and once inside I nearly gagged on the air quality. He sat me down formally in front of a desk covered in overflowing ashtrays, and I expected a lot of good-natured preambling, but luckily he got straight to the point.

'If I understood correctly you're interested in the connection between pre-war Germany and the aristocracy,' he said, squeezing a roll-up between his thumb and forefinger.

'That's right.'

'In that case allow me give you the clipboard version,' he lit the cigarette. 'The prime minister of England, Chamberlain it was at the time, thought England was ill-prepared for war . . . there was the famous debate at the Oxford Union.'

'This house will not fight for king and country.' I'd actually found and read the transcript on the Internet.

'That's right,' the professor nodded approvingly. 'Word of this inevitably found its way to Hitler who therefore believed that he could take England without a fight,' he paused to allow ash to drop into the china saucer on his desk. 'These were the days when Edward and Mrs Simpson were an item. No doubt you've seen one of the many films,' he added, faintly disdainful.

I nodded.

'Edward was under the impression he could have a morganatic marriage, that he could be king, although she would never be queen. When it was made clear to him this was not the case, he was forced to renounce the throne. It is well documented that he met with Hitler's people in Portugal and the assumption was quite simply that Hitler offered him a deal. Edward would help Hitler get England and in return he would be put back on the throne complete with Mrs Simpson – as a puppet king to be sure, but still . . .'

'But after the First World War,' I said, 'how could he think of doing such a thing?'

'Those who do not learn the lessons of history are doomed to repeat them,' Lunn quoted.

'And there were others involved?'

'There would have to have been. People inside England, influential but "safe" people who Edward was in touch with. Help on the inside.'

'And who is safer and more on the inside than Viscount Lytton-Jones?' Wolf said. We were still mulling it over days later, 'You can see how it might happen, Edward calls his favourite cousin and arranges for him to come and visit his nice new friend in Germany.' He hoisted the camera onto the stand and screwed it down. The Bancrofts, whose house we were currently invading, sat on their couch and stared fearfully into the black depths of the lens. 'Bring the family, nursemaid and kids, why not? All very kosher.'

'Exactly, though *kosher* might not be the tip-top choice of word to use when weekending with Nazis,' I added.

I'd asked Lunn why nothing had ever been written about these cohorts.

'Because it was hushed up,' Lunn said simply. 'In those days the aristocracy had the money and power to hush anything up. The royals knew of course, but it was a family affair. No washing of dirty linen in public etc. You must understand – the idea that a member of the royal family had collaborated was *unthinkable* and by the time it might have come out . . . well . . . England had already declared war on Germany.'

'But keeping it quiet. It's an amazing abuse of power. Dealing with Hitler, I'm sorry but these people were out-and-out traitors.'

'Nobody ever knew exactly who was involved,' said Lunn, 'and besides, this all happened nearly seventy years ago, they're probably all long since dead.'

'Yes, I'm sure you're right,' I said resigned, 'but if they weren't . . .?'

'. . . Then it would be an even bigger scandal than Ted Turner having a sex change.' Dwight uncoiled the wire of his microphone and blew a ball of fluff from its head.

'That wasn't exactly the way he put it, but . . .'

'So what now?' Wolf asked.

'If all the players are dead,' I said grudgingly, 'nothing I guess. Without a warm body, it's just old news.'

daniel

Poor Lord Bancroft, born on a Monday, packed off to the nursery Tuesday, prep school Wednesday, Eton, Thursday, Friday to Oxford, where he graduated with a respectable 2.1. Saturday he enrolled in the army. Sunday entered the bank, then on Monday he inherited the family home by which time, like Solomon Grundy, he was already dead.

Thank God the house was of manageable size as long as he was conservative with his money. And Lord Bancroft was nothing if not conservative. A truly sober fellow, in the non-alcoholic sense of the word, he lived a quiet life; a few friends, a spot of shooting, the odd weekend party. But he'd never ridden on a motorbike, travelled with a backpack, had outdoor sex, or sex anywhere for that matter except in bed with the lights firmly off. He'd never eaten in a Thai restaurant, stayed up all night, had a take-away, watched an American sitcom. He'd never used a mobile, worked a fax, turned on a video or taped a show. He might have enjoyed many of these activities but they belonged to a different world, a world that didn't understand him, didn't particularly want him, a world of which he was thoroughly scared.

He met his wife at a point-to-point. They had interests

in common; gardening, country living. Their life stretched before them as cosy and predictable as a cup of Earl Grey . . .

Lloyds seized everything they had, bar the house and contents. Lord Bancroft took it on the chin, but his world shrank a little further. Money grew tight. Eventually he let his faithful butler go. Mr Nieve surprised him by opening up shop in a town, 30 miles away, selling antiques. He offered to work one day a fortnight for which Lord Bancroft was grateful.

It was a few months later when Lady Bancroft first noticed something.

'Have you seen my earrings, darling? The ones your mother gave me?'

'You wore them only the other night,' he reassured her, 'I remember it quite distinctly.'

But Lady Bancroft was meticulous with her belongings. She had a jewellery box lined in velvet in which she kept everything that was precious to her. She was sure she'd put them back.

One day the wicker seat on the dining-room chair wore through. The set was eighteenth-century English – six spares were kept in the cellar and only used when the table was extended for special occasions. In the cellar Lord Bancroft found only four. He rang Mr Nieve. 'I think you'll find there were only ever four, sir,' Mr Nieve said smoothly. The matter was dropped.

On it went, a pair of hunting boots, a vase, surprisingly valuable, or had it been broken a while back? The awful spectre of Alzheimer's crossed both their minds. They began keeping incidents from each other, but finally the inevitable happened. Lady Bancroft's brother came from America to visit. Lady Bancroft's Boston-bred sister-in-law liked nothing better than picking up antiques in English country towns. She returned, late Saturday afternoon, excited to be in possession of a pair of beautiful dining room chairs . . .

maggie

'The butler had been stealing from them!'

'He stocked his shop straight from their house,' Rory had said.

'And they never suspected?'

'Did they strike you as the type that would?'

The answer to that had so far been an emphatic no. Now I looked over to where Dwight was feeding the microphone under Lord Bancroft's sweater. Despite Rory's build-up, I couldn't think of a single question to ask them. After the prospect of Bevan and a real story, anything even approaching *Newsline*'s original brief seemed about as fresh as over-warmed takeout.

'These people are like waxworks,' I hissed to Wolf. 'Look at them, are they even alive? I mean how the hell are we going to make this interesting?'

'Ask them about their sex life,' Wolf said.

'Ask them about their sex life? Why, that's just brilliant.'

'Why not.' Rory appeared in the doorway, 'Go on, ask them. I dare you.'

'You dare me?'

'Why, can't you handle it?'

'This should be interesting.' Wolf sighed.

Most people are painfully self-conscious when you film them. They make a little joke, play to the camera, poke fun at themselves and Bancroft was no anomaly. He looked as if he'd rather have a tooth pulled than answer the question I'd asked him.

'Frightfully bad form,' he faltered, 'not the sort of thing one talks about at all,' and I felt bad. He was too uptight to give up much but at least he was willing. The question had been a cheap shot for a laugh and I wish I hadn't let myself been goaded into taking Rory's dare. 'You can kick me out any time, you know.' I told him, genuinely hoping he might, 'I really won't be offended.'

Lord Bancroft sighed ponderously. 'Well, my dear, you have to understand that for a certain class of Englishman, sex, as such, is not stumbled upon until much later on in life. Boarding school, the army, the bank. For Americans I'm sure it's as commonplace as going to supermarket – "recreational" I've heard you young people call it, but I don't believe I actually encountered a creature of the opposite sex before the age of twenty-five.'

'Oh come on, Lord Bancroft, surely you had one of those nannies?' I tried to jolly him along.

'Ah indeed I did,' he said.

'Scary things your British nannies, they beat you with a wooden spoon, make you eat cod liver oil and don't they tell you that you go blind if . . .' From the doorway, Rory groaned and shook his head. I fluttered my eyelashes demurely at him.

'As a matter of fact,' said Lord Bancroft, and suddenly I realized that something interesting was about to happen. Self-consciousness can be exhausting and in the end it's invariably easier to relax. The harder people find it to talk about themselves the more revealing the moment of total capitulation can be and as a reporter you learn to look out for it because get this moment on tape and you've hit the jackpot. As Lord Bancroft lost himself in some memory, his every muscle seemed to loosen up and when he sighed it was like the final breath going out of a dying body. Wolf saw it too and he zoomed in close on his face.

'. . . it was my twelfth birthday,' Lord Bancroft wasn't looking at the camera any more, but straight through it, back to some forgotten picture of his childhood, 'I was just recovering from the flu, if I remember correctly. No, no, she never beat me, dear Nanny, in fact . . . well, in fact . . . she . . .'

'She . . . yes? She . . .' I prompted.

'She seduced me.'

There was a stunned silence. Lady Bancroft turned to her husband, aghast. Rory's jaw dropped.

I was shocked. I hadn't been waiting for a moment of revelation, just a moment of . . . I don't know, *intimacy* maybe, or television intimacy at least. 'That's terrible,' I said, praying he'd go on. There was a pregnant silence.

'No, no, no,' Lord Bancroft said finally, 'Not so terrible . . .' another agonizing pause. 'In actual fact, I quite enjoyed it. You see,' he said cautiously, as though testing

whether the thin ice he was already skating on might carry
a little more weight, 'personally I'm rather partial to sex.'

'You are?' Lady Bancroft turned sharply.

Wolf quickly pulled back to include her in the frame.

'Yes, my dear,' Lord Bancroft turned to her. 'I'm terribly
sorry, but I'm afraid I am.'

She lowered her gaze but when she raised it again, there
was a flash in those pale green eyes. 'Well' she said crossly,
'You really might have told me because . . . so am I.'

'Cut.' I said.

Rory and Dwight were playing tennis on the Bancrofts'
woefully unmaintained court. Rory was serving and I had
to laugh. No American would be seen dead on a tennis
court without the appropriate Nike shoes and Aggassi-
sponsored Head racquet that Dwight was scampering around
with. Rory was wearing faded shorts, a striped woolly scarf
and, despite the cold, a mildewed pair of sneakers with no
socks. His wooden racket was old and warped but he might
have been playing with a frying pan for all the difference it
made. He was a natural athlete, serving balls with absolute
precision at poor hapless Dwight, who sent one after the
other into orbit before Rory eventually dispatched him to
poke around in a field of nettles outside the court to retrieve
them.

'Ah, Maggie Monroe,' Rory caught sight of me, 'the
woman that brought tantric sex to the upper class—'

But somehow I just wasn't in the mood for it.

'You know what, I dare *you* to say something nice for a
change.'

Rory looked at me quizzically, then stuck his finger through the wire.

'What's that?'

'Truce?'

I hesitated then linked my finger with his.

'Truce,' I said and shook it.

'So I couldn't help looking at them after the interview and wondering . . .'

'What?'

'Well how they go about it.'

'*It* being sex?'

'What else?'

'You're thinking he has to make a noise like a capercaillie and she must respond like a terrified hen pheasant?'

'It's that whole politeness thing . . . go ahead, darling . . . no, I shouldn't really . . . oh go on, treat yourself, you come first . . . no, I insist . . . after you, my dear.'

'Thanks to you,' Rory said, 'now they're more likely be mounting each other neighing like warthogs.'

I burst out laughing. 'OK, so whose turn?'

'Mine unfortunately.'

'OK, truth or dare?'

For the first time since embarking on this oddball journey, Rory and I had managed to spend two hours in the car together without exchanging a single snitty remark. We'd come off the highway a while back and were now beetling through a series of small country lanes. A strong northerly wind was sending needles of rain across the windscreen of the Rover.

'I'm not up to another dare from you.'

'So truth then. Tell me one personal thing about your life.'

'Uh . . . name three birds of prey,' he said. 'How about we play that instead?'

'Coward.'

'Well what do you want to know?'

'I don't know. Anything . . . brothers . . . sisters, where you went to school. What do your parents do for example?'

'Uh . . . they're retired.'

'And before?'

'Unemployed.'

'They're retired from being unemployed?'

'See that?' Rory wound his window down.

'What?'

'Over there, church.'

The red herring was so obvious it might as well have been wearing a false beard.

'That heap of old stone you mean?' Actually it was beautiful. Tall and elegant, the church was built of honey-coloured brick.

'That is one of the few remaining sixteenth-century churches in England.'

'No kidding?' I said. Rory back-pedalled every time he came close to talking about himself so I was becoming an expert on ruined monuments of the English countryside.

'In 1537 Cromwell ordered the church to be plundered then burnt. When his soldiers came over the hill, Lord Haven, who owned the estate, set fire to his own house. The soldiers thought it was the church burning and so they left it standing. It has survived to this day.'

'Fascinating,' I executed a giant yawn.

'The sincerity of your sarcasm is impressive.'

'No, really,' I folded my jacket under my head and closed my eyes, but like all other personal fragments I'd wheedled out of him, I stored away the unemployed/retired family comment like a credit note to be redeemed later.

Rory Jones' car was a wreck. Stylish, sure, but mechanically a piece of junk — and it died on us without warning. Wolf and Dwight were ahead of us in the van, so no help there and the steep banks on either side of the road were too high to get a signal on my cell. We pushed the Rover onto the grass and waited for someone to come along and rescue us.

'Why do you drive around in something that doesn't work properly?' I pulled the collar up on my coat.

'I like old cars, they're romantic.'

'How can it be romantic to be standing in the rain waiting for a pick-up truck?'

'The English have a very strange definition of romantic. You wouldn't understand.'

'Try me.'

'Oh I don't know,' he sighed, 'extreme discomfort is romantic, crazy ideas are romantic, insane optimism is romantic, noble hopelessness is romantic — oh for Goodness sake, what is it now?'

'What?' I said.

'You've got that irritating face on again.'

'What irritating face?'

'Sort of smug, knowing incredulity.'

There was this great stand-up routine Bob Newhart did in the sixties, you probably remember it. Sir Walter Raleigh calls from America to try to sell the head of the West Indies Company on the idea of tobacco and this guy is not exactly convinced. 'It's a kind of leaf . . .? Uhuh . . . Let me get this straight Walt, you put *leaves* in your mouth? . . . and you do what? *You set fire to them?* What can I say, Walt, don't call us, we'll call you.'

Bob Newhart, Lenny Bruce, Mort Sahl, these were all names I grew up with. When Jay found a signed copy of Mort Sahl's 'Iconaclast' in my loft, he said, 'Aha . . . when satire and America coincided for the first and only time to my certain knowledge.' Jay claimed that Mort Sahl's tragedy was that he was brilliant with Eisenhower, but when Kennedy came in he was so happy that he ran out of material.

Anyway, every time Rory started with his how to be English lessons I'd say, 'Let me get this straight. What age are your children sent away to boarding school? Seven????????' Then he'd drop in something about these little seven year olds being made to fag and I'd say, 'Yeah, sure I knew it all along.' He'd say, 'No, no it's a kind of slavery of younger boys to older boys.'

'Uhuh?' I'd say. 'Well don't call us, we'll call you,' then give him my Bob Newhart face just to see how crazy I could make him.

'What can I say,' I shrugged helplessly, 'I feel it's my duty to more fully understand your people.'

'Well *my* people feel they have to romanticize trials and tribulations in order to accept them. Once they're accepted, we can have a nice cup of tea and forget all about them.'

'Aha, as in a nice cup of tea solves everything?'

'Exactly, as in when the Second World War was announced over the radio there was a power cut over the entire country because tens of millions of people rushed from their armchairs to boil the kettle for a nice cup of tea.'

'That's a great story. Is that true?'

'Perfectly true − war, by the way,' Rory added, 'being the embodiment of romanticism for the English, combining as it does discomfort, hopelessness, crazy ideas *and* insane optimism.'

War again. I couldn't get away from it. Not long after we started seeing each other I asked Jay whether he considered himself a war junkie. I'd spent most of the evening in his flat reading articles he'd written for Doctors without Borders. The articles were brutal but nothing to what being there must have been like. I wanted to understand what took him back time and time again. He'd been angry at the question. He took his coffee into the bedroom and didn't come back. I didn't know what to do. We hadn't known each other long enough to have laid down rules of engagement. I ended up staying because I had no idea how to leave. I fell asleep in his leather armchair and woke to find him removing the coffee cup from my hand.

'I'm sorry. I didn't mean to sound flip,' I told him.

'You're just young enough to think that love makes the world go round, Maggie,' he said heavily. 'Well it doesn't.'

'What does make the world go round then?' I knew what he would say; hate, war, grief, pain. Maybe he saw it in my face because he laughed. 'I don't know, kiddo . . . Pepsi probably. Could be Pepsi makes the world go round.'

He said he didn't like the word junkie, but was prepared to admit to being a recidivist. He told me war and danger held a hypnotic lure for him, and that for most people who got involved this was also true – until they burnt out. Most people in Jay's line of work burnt out a lot quicker than he did, so I wondered then, where were the scars from Jay's wars? Where was the blood?

My mother had two great theories. The first was her Scotch tape theory. She liked to mend things with it. This applied to everything. If it was broke it got Scotch taped. Items that were badly damaged got the double Scotch tape treatment; anything unScotch-tapable just got thrown away. It became a good joke for my father when I started dating.

'Is it Scotch-tapable?' he'd ask, finding me in tears over a boyfriend.

'I don't think so,' I'd sniffle.

'So throw him away.'

My mother's other theory was the blood. As a little girl, whenever I fell down and started bawling my mother would say, 'Is it bleeding?' as I presented her with my wound. 'Because if it's not bleeding it's OK.' Blood was her sole criterion for concern. No blood meant no crying allowed. This trick, believe it or not, worked until the day a neighbour's dog was hit by a car right outside our front door. Dad and I joined the small crowd that gathered. After a while the dog was pronounced dead. I looked for blood but there was none. That evening I asked my father what the dog had died of. 'Internal injuries,' he replied and this had profoundly scared me.

I had told Jay about my mother's blood theory and he

thought it very funny. He remembered it that night in his apartment.

'I'm not going to die from internal injuries if that's what you're worried about.' He laughed when he said it, but for some reason it made me want to cry.

'Now I come to think of it,' Rory was saying, 'your obsessive and rather tragic preoccupation with the repressed British and their stiff upper lips is simply an extension of this form of romanticism.'

'Oh,' I smiled, 'how do you work that one out?'

Rory pulled an old paper bag from the side pocket of the car and smoothed it against the bonnet. 'I'll make you a graph.'

Jay had sounded exhausted the last time I'd spoken to him. I asked him how he was and he said, 'Well behaved in many a doctor's office,' but I heard the tension tighten every word. We had one last gap coming up in the filming schedule, only a couple of days away. When Jay told me being in Bosnia made dealing with mudslides in Northern Pakistan seem like a stroll in the park, I told him he needed a break. We agreed to meet in Paris.

'Please do me the courtesy of paying attention,' Rory was saying. He'd drawn a circle on the paper bag, 'Extreme discomfort equals romantic equals insane optimism (because we believe a cup of tea will make everything all right) equals we bear with fortitude equals a stiff upper lip – ergo you think we're repressed.'

'Ergo?'

'Latin, ergo equals therefore.'

'Ergo,' I looked at the empty road, the broken-down car, the rain slicking his hair flat to his forehead and began laughing. 'You know, maybe it's not that all Englishman are hopelessly romantic, I think it could just be you.'

'What do you mean by "netting the sea"? Could you be a bit more specific?'

'Fishing,' Rory said, 'as in the deliberate trapping of the denizens of the deep.' He hauled a tangle of netting from the back of the Land Rover he'd borrowed.

'Fishing, as in poor harmless creatures flip-flopping around before they die a horrible painful death?'

Rory shook his head. 'Where does this appalling PC attitude come from? You wear leather, you pig out on steak.'

'Pig out on a steak – surely another very unfortunate mixed animal metaph—'

'Besides who was it who killed two beloved family pets in one afternoon?'

'That was accidental death—'

'And do you not eat fish?'

'Of course, I eat fish, I just think that whole hook in mouth thing is icky.'

'What's your preferred method of slaughter then? Shoot them with a rifle, electrocution? Or you could just question them to death perhaps?'

'Jesus,' Wolf rolled his eyes. 'Don't tempt her.'

A few gulls wheeled over the sea, squawking some unidentifiable warning to each other as we slid down the dunes. A group of tiny birds bowed their heads against the wind. Their legs, skinny as toothpicks, were mirrored on the wet sand. 'Dotterel,' Rory said, barely glancing at them.

It was a beautiful afternoon, sunny, crisp, the sky darkening to orange as dusk approached. By the time we'd had the Rover towed to our next pit stop, it had been too late to start filming. 'Netting the sea' had been Rory's alternative form of entertainment.

'For your next "how to be English lesson",' he announced, 'you have to be cold and wet for two hours without once complaining.'

'Oh God no,' I'd said, 'anything but that.'

We trudged along the beach. 'It's dead low tide,' Rory shouted over his shoulder. 'Perfect timing.' He turned and walked backwards, leaning against the wind.

'This can't be legal,' Dwight muttered. He looked apprehensively down the length of the deserted beach. Dwight was strictly a dry-dock boy, viewing the sea like some sixteenth-century Bruegel painting, dark, oily and filled with all kinds of scary monsters.

'It's highly illegal,' Rory said, 'but great fun. Sure you don't want to try?'

'Positive,' I said. 'I'll film.'

'Make a base over there.' Rory pointed at a small bay of rocks. 'You'll get some shelter. 'Take my coat if you're cold.'

'I'm fine, thanks.' But holding onto the camera, my hands were stiff as baseball mitts. He draped his coat over my shoulders. 'Keep this dry for me, would you?' He pulled it together under my chin and I was uncomfortably aware of his touch.

'This is what?' I said breezily, 'the North Sea? Famous for its oil rigs and freezing temperatures?'

'As opposed to − say the Pacific, famous for its balmy waters and palm trees?' Rory pulled off his boots and slung them towards me. 'Look after these too could you?' He rolled up his pant legs, picked up the wooden pole at the end of the net and stepped over a low breaker. He forged on as if walking fully clothed into the sea was normal and he was just running a little late for an appointment with King Canute. When the net was taut he stopped, waist high in water.

'Wolf, you come in halfway,' he shouted, 'and tell Lady Bracknell over there, he'd better stay on the break-line.'

Only then did I catch sight of Dwight's outfit glowing underneath the oilskin jacket he'd borrowed. Some sort of knickerbocker thing in garish check tweed cinched in at the knee. He saw me staring and had the grace to look faintly embarrassed.

'My grandfather's,' he said defensively.

'Oh yeah, sure they are, Smallboy.' Wolf stepped gingerly into the soapy water. I saw the shock of the temperature hit him. Resolutely he pushed on, waves breaking below his waist. Rory motioned for him to stop. Wolf groped in his shirt pocket for a half smoked joint and jabbed it into his mouth. He got a match to it and took a long hit.

From somewhere a cloud had snuck up on us. It was now starting to rain and I had to laugh. If this was Rory's attempt at bonding with his American brothers, it was going to backfire badly. Dwight and Wolf looked the very picture of horrified urbanites. I know my crew and let me tell you, ground cement runs in their veins. Besides, from the way he was pulling at his crotch, I guessed that Dwight's pants were already shrinking painfully. The rain soon became relentless. Water seeped through the coat, through both sweaters I'd put on and I could feel it cold on my skin. I kept the three boys in the viewfinder as they moved forwards, parallel to the beach. Dwight was still hovering on the break-line, dolefully clutching his corner of the net.

'They swim out into the shallows to feed,' Rory yelled, 'they'll come back in when the tide turns.' He wiped spray off his face with his shoulder. 'When I say now, pull the net round as hard as you can.'

I ran along the water's edge to keep up. The weather had cleared for an instant to reveal the sun, dipped low in the sky. Gallantly it tried to hang on but eventually yielded, slipping into the ocean as if the effort of suspending itself all day had finally proved too exhausting.

'Now,' Rory bellowed. He curled the net in a high arc. 'Dwight you bloody great poof . . . bring it in closer.'

Cautiously Dwight inched himself out to sea. A wave broke over the tops of his rubber boots. He looked over at Wolf, desperate for a little empathy, but Wolf had problems of his own. Puzzled he stared at the water. His enormous body jerked, he looked shocked, like he'd had his leg bitten off by a hammerhead but hadn't yet taken in how serious a problem that might be.

I watched in amazement as a smile broke over his face. He hollered something then gripped the net and whooped with delight. I panned round to Dwight, waist high in water. His face was flushed with excitement. Rory, holding the two sides of the net aloft, struck out for shore. I couldn't believe it. Laughing and shouting the three boys dragged the net in then collapsed, panting on the sand. Rory was first up. He hauled the net to safety from the advancing tide then peeled back its four sodden corners. Inside was a squirming mass of silver. He turned towards the camera and made an elaborate bow grinning from ear to ear. For a moment he was captive in my sights. He was Mandras from *Captain Corelli*, and his catch was for me and me alone. I found myself looking at him much longer than the image warranted, protected by the camera's clinical lack of emotion. With his fisherman's jumper, bare legs underneath rolled-up trousers and his black hair blowing in the wind, he looked twelve years old. I wanted to pull the camera down to film the fish but I couldn't. I was held by Rory's face and then it struck me why. I felt my heart beat. It was just the one thud, but it was loud enough to make me freeze-frame the image in my head. There was nothing in his face, nothing except pure joy of the moment.

They fuck you up, your mum and dad
They don't mean to, but they do.
They fill you with the faults they had
And add some extra, just for you.

— Philip Larkin

daniel

During the next break in filming when Maggie heads to
Paris, Rory drives to Bevan. In the hall he breathes in the
musty smell of the house and knots his scarf round the throat
of the Chinese Buddha on the stone table. It's Friday evening
so as he pushes through the swing doors to the kitchen it
occurs to him that this week he could have been on that
dig in Turkey. He could be squatting on his haunches and
feeling the hot sand sifting through his fingers. He could
even be flirting with that lithesome interpreter with the
buck teeth from Fez – or maybe he could have talked
Maggie into blowing out whatever business she was supposed
to be taking care of and dragged her along with him . . .

'Darling, how lovely,' says Audrey unwrapping the fresh
bread he has brought from the deli. She puts it straight into
the deep freeze and removes a frozen loaf of Mother's Pride
for dinner.

Rory has renewed his monthly promise to himself. Tonight
he will talk to Alistair about selling Bevan.

But after dinner, Nanny retires upstairs, Grandpa listens

to the radio in his bedroom, Alistair watches the ten o'clock news and Audrey falls asleep, her feet on top of Lurch. Rory bunks out and instead sits in Alistair's study and tackles the pile of unopened mail. He's appalled by how bad the situation has become. Alistair has always displayed ostrich tendencies when it comes to financial obligations but these days it's not just bills he ignores, it's all letters from polling cards to farm notices. Correspondophobia is what he suffers from — in my opinion, a perfectly rational fear of any document that arrives in a brown envelope.

When Rory first tackled the finances of Bevan he was optimistic that careful planning and economizing would make a difference. He soon realized he might as well stand over the loo and ritually flush down wads of notes with the Queen's head on. Bevan is a house that *eats* money. It's as if the architect, as a devilish experiment, set out to see just how uncost-effective he could possibly make it. A local paper once wrote an article on Bevan simply quoting statistics. They reported a staggering 240 doors, 75 of which led directly outside. Multiplying the cumulative draught by the average winter temperature, they'd come up with one hell of a heating bill.

So this is the Herculean task Rory has inherited. And it's not a task meant to be completed, simply carried on. Even for someone who signs up for it, this job can wear you down until you have no passion left to burn. If you don't sign up for it you might as well chain yourself to the rock and, like Prometheus, wait for that great eagle of frustration and futility to peck your liver out day after day.

Since the accident, Rory has had a choice to make. The same choice I had to make a few years ago and one, at the time, he fought me tooth and nail on. What was the point of keeping Bevan, he argued — if our parents were cold and tired, if they couldn't cope and their backs hurt, if they never took a holiday, didn't want friends to stay, if they had no fun, no bloody fun at all — but what I couldn't drive through his thick head was that if you took them away from Bevan, made them live in a cottage, dwarfed by their possessions, no trees to plant, no clearing to be done in the lake-field, no bonfires to be built, no head scratching about the latest damage to the drains in Bindey's cottage — then they wouldn't be our parents any more, because Bevan is in every breath they take. They cannot exist as separate entities and to force them to do so would be to expose them, to turn them into shadows of their former selves. Rather than being acceptable eccentrics, they'd just be two tragic septuagenarians clashing empty bottles at each other in drunken cheer. Besides, the point of keeping Bevan is that it deserves to remain standing. *Keep the house going for future generations.* You look after your inheritance. You protect the land. That's what primogeniture is all about. And OK, I didn't like it when it was my job, and now it's Rory's, he likes it even less, but decayed, putrid, atrophying though they might be, houses like Bevan are important. Tradition *is* important. If Rory gives up on Bevan, he'd bloody well better understand what's at stake.

But I don't want any favours from my brother. Saturday morning when he takes a walk with Alistair and tries to raise the subject I watch as crippling guilt and misplaced loyalty push him once again into a decision his heart is not in. Well you can stop that Rory, don't bloody lay this thing on my head. Why is it the custom to canonize the dead in the false memory of the living? I wasn't such a great brother half the time, so don't make out that I was some kind of hero, I was crap the last few years. And if you want proof? Remember that beautiful girl with tiger eyes? The one you were sniffing around for ages. The one who was sacked the very first day from her big Opportunity Knocks job, who cried those plaintive little tears on your shoulder? Well know this – I was the one who slept with her.

maggie

I'd been really excited at the prospect of two days in Paris, but when it came to it there was a problem finding a decent room. There was an Internet convention and every hotel in the city was booked. Eventually the concierge from the Cadogan found a room and I took it blind. When I arrived in Paris and walked into the bedroom with its sanitine coverings and general air of beige, I remembered the conversation about the English's warped sense of the romantic. Rory had claimed his ideal hotel in Paris was not the George V but a plain boarding house; a brass bed with an agonizing dip in its centre and an old crone stumping up the stairs with a bowl of steaming black coffee in the morning.

I mean there was nothing wrong with this room apart from it being identical to every other mediocre hotel room in the world. It was the coffee machine that got me − the brown plastic filter machine that stood on the dressing table next to paper packs of sugar and decaf coffee − part of the world's nod to the convenience-seeking Americans. I have been in some real polyester palaces in my time, some swanky hotels too. Extremes are great, but middle of the road? This one just depressed the life out of me.

Several hours later, I found just what I was looking for in the sixteenth quarter. The room was huge and old fashioned with peeling wallpaper and brass fittings. The bathroom had damp in one corner and a couple of the black and white tiles were broken – but there were no pastels, no coffee machine and of course, I realized too late, no CNN for Jay.

'Interesting choice,' he said when he arrived.

Drugged by an afternoon nap, I watched him groggily as he looked round the room.

'Tell me the truth,' he sat on the bed, 'am I too old and out of touch to appreciate that this is a hip hotel?'

'I'm really sorry.'

He laughed and kissed me. 'Did you know that when you're cranky your upper lip gets shorter?'

'Does it?'

'Yes it does.'

'Is it short now?'

'It's retracted almost entirely into your nose.' He kissed me again. 'Oh look here it comes, that's better.'

I laughed but he was right, I was cranky. The room wasn't romantic at all. It was damp and cold. Jay was sweet though. In the spirit of spontaneous bookings we chanced a family-run Italian restaurant he knew. It was only six o'clock when we sat down to eat but even so the restaurant was full. I was amazed by how attentive the service was until Jay, who couldn't keep a straight face any longer, admitted the owners were identical twins.

'So how is snobbery, debauchery and lunacy coming along?' he asked.

I began giving him a suitably witty account, but he soon interrupted.

'And who is this Rory character?'

'Oh just a guy, you know, the agent for the houses.' Saying it though, I felt the same guilt you get walking through the green light at customs when you have something to declare.

'Have you slept with him yet?'

'Give me another day or two.' I picked up the lamb bone and sucked out the marrow.

Jealousy was a relatively uncharted territory for us. I once asked Jay about all the nights he was away.

'Are you getting bourgeois on me, Kiddo?' he'd replied. When he saw this wasn't the answer I was looking for, he said. 'You're asking me whether I am *faithful* to you?' as if this was too high-schooly an attitude for him to dignify with a reply, 'You know what I feel about you.'

I thought the reply ambiguous, so I didn't push it further.

'He's been driving us around, a guide sort of, anyway, don't worry . . . he's just a baby.' I stopped.

Something in Jay's face flickered, but he didn't miss a beat.

'How many months is this baby?'

'A little over four-hundred and fifty would be my guess.'

I watched him as he reversed the calculation. Age was one of the few things I think he was frightened of.

He asked me once what my father missed most about being young.

'I don't know.' I still thought of my father as being young. At sixty-five he had become a sort of guru and consultant to stage lighting designers and could be found telling tales of the good old days when Dylan and Baez were king and queen and when tuning in and turning on was still a middle-class luxury.

I was about to answer 'excitement' but thought better of it. Instead I said, 'His ponytail I guess.'

Jay nodded. 'As good an answer as any.'

After we left the identical twins restaurant, Jay told me he might have to go back to Sierra Leone. He told me he didn't want to but I thought I could hear something else in his voice. We walked for a while. The moon shone on the curves of the cobblestones, black and polished. I heard the sound of a piano being played. We stood still as the notes tumbled out of a window above us, beautiful and melancholy.

'Listen,' I said. 'It could almost be Rubinstein.' I wanted him to kiss me then, just to have a cheesy moment in a narrow street in Paris.

'It ain't though.' Jay turned his coat collar up. I knew he wanted to go back to the hotel so meanly I made him walk on.

I think I needed something in Paris to inspire us. I tried to imagine us living there, just another pair of lovers, shopping for bread in the market, bargaining with crotchety dealers for the tin toys that, for some obscure reason, Jay loved to collect. But it wasn't to be.

On the next street corner Jay stopped and hunched his shoulders around a cough. I thought it looked deliberate, like he was trying to keep it quiet. The cost of a cough could be a bullet, I thought melodramatically. I waved down a cab.

Back in our brass bed with its dip in the centre, Jay reached for his paper and I felt my upper lip shortening. I knew I wanted more out of the evening but I couldn't isolate exactly what.

'What is this revisionist trash they're endlessly spouting?' Jay was shaking his head. It wasn't a question that required an answer and though he went on to explain what had enraged him – something in local government – all I heard was nationalism, fascism, interventionism on an eternal loop.

'Can we not talk politics for once?' I horrified myself by saying.

He turned to look at me. 'OK,' he said evenly, 'what shall we talk about?'

'I don't know.' His tone had made me feel five years old. 'Something light. Something *fluffy*.'

'I'm sorry, Maggie, I don't do Martha Stewart.'

I should have laughed but I couldn't. I curled up, away from him. I heard the rustle of newspapers being opened, but I don't think he was reading because I didn't hear the pages turning. After a while he put his fingers through my hair and rubbed my scalp gently.

'Please turn round,' he said. And I did. Blotting the dampness on my cheeks on the pillow first.

'Do you have any idea how lucky we are? Our relation-ship is made up of perfect free-standing moments . . . we get to travel light, no baggage, duty-free.' He put his arms around me and kissed the top of my head. Then he read me excerpts from the *Washington Post* in his Truman Capote voice which he did so brilliantly I laughed till my stomach ached.

'So Duchess of Roxmere, or the barmaid?' Wolf asked.

'Neither,' Dwight said.

'You can't have neither.'

'Suicide then.'

'You can't have suicide, you have to choose.'

'I'm telling you, neither.'

'My rules.'

'Sorry,' Dwight was outraged, 'my dick.'

We were having a pub lunch in a small village in Somerset. We'd unloaded our equipment and settled into Stamford, whose owner, the deeply conservative Duke of Normouth, more or less owned the county. His son Miles was due to arrive that night with a weekend party of younger guests. As this was the last house on the Stately Locations itinerary and as we seemed to have filmed nothing but middle-aged couples we'd decided to stay on.

Rory returned from the bar clutching bottles of coke and beer. 'What about you, Rory?' Wolf said. 'Who'd you'd sleep with – the barmaid, or the Duchess of Roxmere?'

'The Duchess is a client, so it would have to be the barmaid, who oddly enough,' he craned his head to give her a closer look, 'is rather sexy – in a terrifying sort of way.'

'OK,' Wolf said, 'now the barmaid or . . .' he looked around, but apart from the odd gnarled local the pub was deserted. His eye settled on me, 'Maggie!'

'Hey leave me out of this.'

'Hmmm.' Rory made a big show of chewing it over. I was about to protest again but Wolf put his hand over mine.

'American girls don't really find English men attractive.' Rory said.

'Oh and you know this because?'

'Ruined by their mothers, emotionally castrated, and ultimately gay.' These were my own words he was quoting back to me and to my disgust I felt my face redden up. 'I'm not saying Maggie's not passable looking but who wants to be put under the microscope and dissected?'

'Like I said,' I played for indifference. 'No passion.'

'We have passion. We just don't talk about it. You're not going to find an Englishman who'll declare himself on the first date.'

'Well why not?'

'Because an Englishman is obliged to play the game. He must follow the rules. To ask you out is to declare a romantic interest. To declare a romantic interest is to expose himself. In order to avoid that horror he is forced to insult you.'

'Insult you?'

'Yes, it's how an Englishman courts.'

'Oh,' I said faintly.

'First he must embarrass himself horribly, then it's advisable to highlight his own worst faults, finally it's important to be as rude as possible to the girl he longs to marry.'

'Jesus,' I said, 'no wonder you weirdos sleep with your dogs and take your wives for walks in the countryside.'

*

En route back to Stamford I asked him whether he followed his own rules.

'Of course.'

'So you insult all the girls you like.'

'I have a Ph.D. in verbal abuse.'

'And have you found this successful?'

'Actually I got as far as the proposal stage.'

'You're *married*?' It hadn't even occurred to me.

'Actually. No.'

I felt stupidly glad. 'Uh, divorced?'

'She left before the wedding.'

'*Before* the wedding?'

'She didn't take to the weather.'

'Jeez, where'd she been living all her life,' I matched his flippant tone, 'down a rabbit hole?'

'Rome.'

I tried conjuring up a picture of Rory sauntering through the Colosseum with a dark-eyed Italian girl but for some reason I kept superimposing my own image in her place.

'So . . . uh . . . what was she like?'

Rory's look said, *Enough of these tiresome questions.*

'Come on,' I wheedled, 'I'm just making conversation.'

'Why don't you just shine a bright light in my eyes?'

'Oh I see, you're a little uptight about this.'

'Not a *little* uptight. I am *very* uptight.'

'OK I'm sorry,' I relented. 'End of interview, I swear.'

The Rover hummed in neutral, stationary in front of a level crossing. The arm of the barrier was down. We waited . . . and we waited some more.

'So was she pretty?'

He ignored me.

'C'mon, tell me if she was pretty at least.'

'There's the train now.' Over to Rory's right, white smoke was rising through the trees.

'Are not Italian girls usually pretty?' I mused.

A muscle was working in his cheek.

'Was she smart? Funny? Did she have enormous breasts?' The train drew into the station.

'I mean you never know, she could have regretted dumping you. She could be pining for you, obsessing over you. She could even be stalking you, waiting for just that right moment to strike.' I peered through the window. 'If your ex-girlfriend's a psycho, I really need to know what she looks like . . . for my own self-protection if nothing else.'

I stole a look at him. He was laughing.

'Wait. Over there,' I pointed, 'is that her?' A woman had clambered off the train. Fifty years old or so, she strutted along the platform wearing the tightest of red suits. She had peroxide hair, orange make-up and impossible white stilettos.

Rory peered through the windscreen. 'Are you quite mad?' he said regretfully. 'You think I'd let someone like that go?' He gripped the steering wheel forcefully, 'I'd be a *fool*.'

I was laughing. He turned to me and his grin was huge and so was mine. Then like someone else entirely was pulling our strings we leant into each other and I knew that in a nanosecond we would be kissing. My whole body fizzed with how good that would be.

I pulled back abruptly. What the hell was I thinking?

*

Stella arrived with the rest of the house party. She was an artist of some kind. That she and Rory knew each other was obvious. When she walked into the drawing room she draped her arms around his neck and pressed her body against his. She kissed him on the mouth then watched his face as he talked.

She must have asked him what he was doing because they both glanced in my direction and she nodded, swinging a small sheepskin handbag fastened with a horn button. Her eyes said, *Watch it toots, this one's mine.* She had long dark hair which waved in the right places and despite her height, tiny elfin ears. Everything about the way she moved said waif, coltish, gamine. You could almost see her pheromones flying through the air, and even they were designer.

For the last three weeks we'd been filming our various aristocrats without the hindrance of guests and, as with any small group of people, you establish a familiarity that everyone becomes comfortable with. Now surrounded by these interlopers with their expensive bohemian clothes, jobs in theatre, art and fashion, it struck me again how little I belonged here. They were Wonder Women and I was Danger Mouse.

Looking at these girls and myself, we were different creatures altogether. Stella, for instance, was stick thin, I'm skinny too, but it was as though her limbs had been carved from a different category of tree to mine. I couldn't stop looking at her, so I could hardly blame Rory for doing the same. I hid behind Wolf and Dwight, shrubs from my own forest, until a gong proclaimed dinner. I worked on automatic pilot, Wolf and Dwight moved about the table with the camera, I asked questions, listened to answers, but all the time aware that I was watching Stella watching Rory.

Ever since the moment at the train crossing, things had changed. I felt knocked off centre, no longer sure how to look at Rory, unable to remember how I'd treated him the day before or even two hours earlier. This unwelcome feeling of unease and desire had crept up on me, self-inflated in my head and like a sleeping bag I couldn't roll it up tightly enough to stow it away. I don't know if he was aware of it, but I was. Very aware. Much too aware.

After dinner, the men drank port and the women congregated in the drawing room. All the girls smoked, but Stella was the one I sought out to ask for a light.

'Of course,' she said politely.

I told her I'd once heard this great urban myth. Some girl from LA had gone to stay with her fiancé in England in an incredibly grand house party like this one. The girl had been nervous and lit up a cigarette before dessert. The Duchess or whoever it was stood up abruptly and rung the bell for the servants.

' "The American appears to believe the meal is at an end," the Duchess had said and remained standing. Everybody was forced to stop eating and leave the room. Unreal huh?'

'That was my mother,' Stella said quietly.

We had been warned there would be after-dinner games. 'Kick the pot' was to be played in the pitch dark – which meant we wouldn't be able to film. We reached a compromise. There would be just enough light to film but not enough to ruin the tension. That tension could exist in a game of hide and seek played by adults was news to me but I kept quiet and listened while the guests downed brandies and rules were explained.

'The point of the game is for HE to catch and identify all the players. HE may identify players by touch, or trick players into identifying themselves. If HE identifies a player wrongly, that player is free to go.'

I went into a huddle with Wolf to work out shots. I hadn't yet figured out this English obsession with games, but my best guess was that it was their way of opting out of talking to each other so when Rory passed I chirruped, 'The lengths you people go to to avoid intimacy.'

'You think so?' he grabbed my hand and pulled me into the circle of guests. 'Then time you came in from the sidelines for a change.'

Straws were drawn for He and it was Rory who pulled the short one out. He began counting and we all scurried off. Within seconds the house was silent except for a stealthy footstep or creak of a door as hiding places were found and abandoned. 'One hundred,' Rory yelled, 'ready or not, here I come.'

Soon the game was being played in earnest. Behind a curtain, curled up on a wide window sill in an upstairs room I waited, feeling more than a little foolish. I thought of Jay and of what an absurd parallel we were making. He was in a country where people were playing their own after-dark games of hide and seek for real. I tried to imagine what he was doing at that moment. Having a beer with a

NATO rep in some motel, or discussing fundamentalism with an over-eager first-time journalist. At a pinch he could be playing bridge – a game he loved and claimed an addict could find a fix for in any country – but one thing was for sure, he would not be playing 'kick the pot' in the middle of the English countryside with a bunch of junked-up ex-public schoolboys. It was almost shaming, then, how much I was enjoying it.

The stillness in the house was punctuated by the occasional scuffle as someone was cornered, and ongoing wails from imprisoned Hoorays. Good-natured warnings were howled from the prisoners' den. 'Do not attempt rescue. HE is sitting on the pot. Get off the bloody pot you filthy cheat.'

Finally, after a prolonged silence, I heard footsteps powering down the stairs and a blood-curdling scream of, 'Pot's Out!' There was a roar from freed prisoners. A fellow guest burst by me, panting heavily. I could dimly make out his shape as he squeezed himself into an oversized umbrella stand. My legs were badly cramped, I had to move, it was now or never. I crept stealthily along the corridor. 'Pot's in,' someone shouted. Feet again thundered up the stairs like HVO troops on the rampage. More shouting. Chaos, then it was all quiet on the western front. I was out in the open – sorely in need of a hiding place. I dropped to my knees by the wall. Ha! I would fight and die a soldier's death but the wall I was leaning against gave way. I reached out with my hand. It wasn't a wall, but a tall heavy screen. Perfect. I slipped behind and forced my breathing under control. Enveloped by the darkness and silence, I soon lost track of time and place. My ears tuned to every noise, however insignificant, analysing it for danger. It was really unnerving just how real the game felt. The sense of being hunted was genuinely creepy. I could have been the last Christian on the run from Islamic killers. The hairs on my arm rose as I heard a creak. I froze then felt a stab of real fear. I peered between the hinges of the screen, but through the blackness saw nothing. I relaxed but then moments later, there it was again. Somebody was heading my way. My heart drummed. I shrank against the wall, trying not to breathe. It was hot. My shirt was damp with sweat – with a terrible jolt I realized that the screen was being peeled back, panel by panel.

'Aha,' said a voice softly.

The pads of Rory's fingertips touched the side of my head, moved slowly down my face then round the back of my neck. I said nothing, I would not talk and give myself away but the game Rory was playing was breaching every rule in the Geneva Convention. His fingers found the edge of my T-shirt, brushed against my rib cage. I was barely breathing, running out of oxygen, running out of resolve. My face was burning. When he kissed me it was like a ghost kissing a ghost because I couldn't see him and I certainly couldn't recognize myself. I slid down the wall, his grip tightened on my shoulders then let go – and suddenly, abruptly – I was alone.

Stella needed a lift to London. We'd finished packing the equipment into the van after breakfast when she came down the steps with her suede bag and threw it into the trunk of the Rover.

'You don't mind do you, Rory?'

Rory glanced at me.

'No problem,' I said mechanically, 'there's plenty of room with the crew.'

And suddenly it was all over. There Rory was, shaking Wolf's hand. 'I'm sorry I won't be around over the weekend,' and it was only then I remembered he'd warned us — right at the start — of another commitment. 'Parents' anniversary,' he now explained, and gave Wolf a pained look.

'No problem, man,' Wolf clapped him on the back. 'Come to New York sometime. Anytime. I'll take you to a Rangers game.'

I stood a short distance away, eyes itchy from the dust of a sleepless night. After 'kick the pot' had petered out everyone had drifted around, talking, swilling brandy round glasses. Stella had ensnared Rory on a couch built for two. She kicked off her kitten heels and curled her legs up underneath her. She twirled her hair around her little finger as she meowed.

I went to bed.

Rory caught my arm halfway up the stairs. 'Maggie . . . don't go . . . the night is still young . . . we could, er, let's see . . . do a thousand-piece puzzle . . . read *War and Peace* out loud, alternatively . . .'

'Rory. I don't think I should.'

'Should . . .' he said carefully, 'for such a small and uninspiring word, "should" has so many tiresome implications.'

'Yes it does.'

'Why?' he demanded. 'Because you're a lefty liberal

New York feminist and I'm a sexist, emotionally castrated Englishman?'

'Something like that.'

'Minor problems.'

'Rory?' We both turned.

Stella was at the foot of the stairs smoking a cigarette. Property rights were printed all over her face.

And now it was too late. The morning after the night that never was.

'Call me of course if you need anything urgently, otherwise . . .' Rory was standing in front of me, 'otherwise, good luck . . . and, er, send me a tape, if you remember.'

'Sure.' I stuck out my hand and, painfully aware of Dwight and Wolf hovering, said my professional thank yous. Rory climbed into his car. I busied myself with equipment shuffling as the engine of the Rover fired up. He hooted the horn.

'Bye,' I said and gave a mock salute of sorts.

'Bye-bye,' Stella called out of the window. She waved gaily as Rory drove out of my life.

daniel

Talk about spineless. What the hell is he thinking? Actually, that I can tell you. He's thinking why, oh why does he specialize in flighty foreign girls. He's thinking hopeless, no future, not even as a temporary refuge because, for certain whacky reasons of principle, Rory believes it's wrong to use people to stop up the holes in your soul. In other words he's retreating behind those stuffy Anglo Saxon sensibilities of honour and fairplay. If it had been me, I'd have tossed Stella out of the window and given Maggie a damn good shagging but seduction is an oblique art and Rory has never fully been aware quite how to practise it to its greatest effect. Once I accused him of having an old-fashioned attitude to women. He told me he was sick of having to compensate for my behaviour. It was true, I had a tendency to drop girlfriends at his feet like roadkill, sweet bloodied doves with their feathers all sticky and matted and proudly say, 'Now look what I've done.'

Back in London, Rory mopes on the sofa in Benj's flat whilst Benj, Pimlico's resident gastronomic genius, prepares him a 'snack.' Carefully positioned on the kitchen worktop stands a jar of sandwich spread, a bottle of salad cream and a pork pie. Benj cuts slices of Mother's Pride into triangles, spreads them with butter, then places them on the dusty blow heater to harden. Those of you who were sent to that great institution known as the British boarding school will recognize these Red Cross items. The rest of you unfortunate enough to have been kept at home, fed with your mother's home cooking, unable to experience either the pleasures of pedophiliac gym teachers or the rigorous beatings of assorted sadomasochistic masters will not appreciate why boarding school is to thank for England being a nation reduced to rapture by Marmite on toast.

'God I miss it sometimes,' Benj says. He smears sandwich spread on the bread and balances a wedge of pork pie on top. 'Great food, parental escape.'

He takes a bite. 'Frankly, school was everything a boy could want.'

'A little short on female company perhaps.'

'You are surely forgetting the twin marvels of matron's bosoms.'

'Thankfully I am.'

'For years after I left I used to ring sick bay just to imagine those vast mammary glands rubbing against each other as Matron ran to answer the phone.' Benj looks dreamy.

'No doubt she's still single,' Rory says dryly. 'Why don't you give her a call.'

'Talking of single women,' Benj passes over a morsel, 'how was your jaunt with the fragrant Miss Munroe?'

'It had its moments.'

'She boil anybody else's rabbit?'

'Actually,' Rory says, 'she showed remarkable restraint.'

'Was Miles's sister in residence?'

'I saw her.'

'Did you sleep with her?'

'Are you insane?' Rory nearly chokes on his pork pie.

'Why, what's wrong? She's nice, well . . . when I say nice what I mean is, she's available, she's handsome—'

'Quite. I'd be more inclined to feed her a sugar lump than sleep with her.'

'And Stella?' Benj says slyly.

'Stella.' Rory sighs. 'Stella should come with an "emotional vacuum" warning round her neck.'

Benj snorts. 'You're getting ridiculously hard to please in your old age.'

'As a matter of fact,' Rory says moodily, 'that's not strictly true.'

maggie

'*Madrid.*' Wolf reads out loud from a copy of the *Week* magazine in my bedroom, '*Jose Astoreka set a new world record by crushing thirty walnuts between his buttocks in fifty-seven seconds.*' He chuckles. '*Dortmund. A top German surgeon was fined four thousand pounds for making his patients do Hitler salutes. Claims that he was trying to improve their shoulder mobility was thrown out of court.*'

Dwight picked up another reel of film and checked its code against his list. 'Half of these are labelled wrong, Wolf.' He scratched out a number and corrected it with a resigned sigh.

'*Seattle. Lovelorn woman is accused of eating twenty red roses in a flower shop.*'

'Is the Duke of Normouth also Baron Normouth?' Dwight was poring over the wedge of notes that Massey had provided us with, pedantically checking the spelling and titles against the film's labels.

I pressed my knuckles into my temples. The drive to London had been long and snagged with thick traffic. I'd been silent the whole journey nursing a wall-to-wall headache.

'What about Bevan?' Dwight looked up, 'Seventh or the eighth Earl?'

'Who cares.' Wolf threw the magazine onto the bed. 'Let's go eat.'

'Here we go,' Dwight flicked the page. 'Bevan, Eighth Earl of, Alistair Joclyn, Jesus, look at the amount of other names he has, Ramsay, also Danby, Reevesdale, Lytton-Jones. Oh wait, here we go, Viscount Lytton-Jones, Daniel, deceased 1999 . . .' He squinted at the page. 'Hang on, Maggie. This is weird, Viscount Lytton-Jones was Alistair Bevan's father, right?'

'Mmmm.'

'But he can't be.'

'Why not?' Idly I picked up Wolf's discarded magazine.

'Because it says here he was born in 1961.'

'Let me see that,' I snatched the piece of paper from him and scanned down the tiny print, 'Viscount Lytton-Jones. Daniel, born 1961 . . . Wolf he's right . . .' The silly poker rhyme I'd invented to remember the hierarchy of titles came back to me. 'Dwight, when is a viscount not a viscount?'

'When he becomes an earl,' Dwight said promptly.

'On his father's death . . . exactly! That's it, we're not looking for a viscount at all.

'But we have an earl – Alistair Bevan is the earl.'

'Yes, but don't you see? That photograph was taken in 1938 when our traitor was still a young man – at that time it's conceivable his father *and* grandfather were still alive.'

'She's babbling,' Wolf said.

'No, she's right,' Dwight's face was pink with excitement. 'When one generation dies, everyone inherits the next title up. If the grandfather and father both died *after* that photo was taken, the viscount would have moved up two rungs – he'd be a marquess or a duke or something—'

Danby, Marquess of Danby . . . got it,' I stabbed at the page with my finger. 'Issue: Alistair, Con, Dinah, William, Robert.'

'Born 1904.' Dwight read over my shoulder. 'I cannot believe we didn't check this before.'

'And died?' I hardly dared breathe.

'Not died.' Dwight stabbed at the spot with his finger.

'Not died as in . . . not dead?' Wolf was now peering over my other shoulder.

'Not died as in alive,' Dwight said.

'Holy Toledo,' I turned and stared at them both, 'a warm body.'

daniel

'But where did you meet her?' Benj asks puzzled.

'In the country.'

'Perfect! See? Daniel was naturally attracted to the hare in the race, but you, Rory, will end up with the tortoise – of course a tortoise who's got enormous style and flair. Just think of the advantages. Country girls are tough, they're used to the weather, it's what I've always thought you needed – a nice solid English girl.'

'She's not English.'

Benj digests this.

'Perhaps Scottish then?'

Rory shakes his head.

'Er, Welsh would have to be my third choice.'

Rory just grunts at him.

Benj clatters the plates into the sink. 'Tell me it's not the bloody American.'

'It's the bloody American.'

'Terrific, Rory. Your brother dies, your fiancée runs screaming when you inherit the coldest house in England, you've been in a foul temper ever since, and now,' he draws breath, '*now* you go falling for the perfectly formed Miss

Munroe, whose advantages as far as I can see are . . .' he taps off on his fingers, 'a) not overly fond of this country, b) not overly fond of the people and c) not at all fond of the weather for that matter, so it's fortunate really that you're absolutely free from all responsibility to follow her when she leaves on?'

'Monday,' Rory says sulkily.

'Thank you, yes, Monday, in two days' time. For?'

'New York,' Rory mutters.

'Where, by the way, she also *lives.*' Benj runs out of steam. 'Christ, Rory, shag her if you must, but if you had an ounce of feeling for your friends you'd forget all about her.'

'I've kissed her.'

'What!' Outraged, Benj drops his cigarette.

'I've kissed her,' Rory repeats mutinously.

'And what else, might I enquire?' Benj stamps on the smouldering carpet.

'And nothing else. I just kissed her, all right. I wanted to kiss her and I'm thinking I'd quite like to kiss her again.'

Benj sinks onto the sofa. 'Bloody hell.' He shakes another cigarette from the pack directly into his mouth, 'Go home, Rory, I beg you,' he mumbles. 'Go straight home and take a cold shower before you do yourself some serious damage.'

From up here the light changes in London are sublime exercise in kinetic art. Brake lights, headlights, traffic lights all vie for supremacy as the four million cars that make up the giant toy cars of London streets weave their way through each other – and it seems a miracle given the sheer volume of traffic that so few of them actually bump and collide. In Sloane Square, where incidentally I did once bump and collide my moped, destroying much of the charming Victorian municipal fountain in the square's centre whilst *oh dear me, Judge, severely under the influence*, the lights have just completed another circuit from red to orange to green. Cars, jettisoning exhaust from their backsides, surge forth, breaking right and left around that comforting bastion of mediocrity, the Peter Jones department store.

All cars except one, that is.

The Rover remains resolutely at a standstill. Inside Rory sits motionless.

It doesn't take a genius to see that pushing things further with Maggie is a bad idea. It's not simply that everything Benj says is true, there's also the fact that Rory doesn't wholly trust her, all those nagging doubts he has conveniently pushed aside in the last few weeks. Who knows what draws him so strongly to this girl but let's just say on their first meeting he suffered something of a *coup de foudre*. Love is the drug, as they say, or maybe love will be Rory's drug of choice because when he thinks about Maggie he feels, well, literally sick – and he hasn't felt that good about anybody in a very long time. So he's running scared. He had decided to take Benj's advice and go home, maybe even ring Stella for the full emotion-free fuck experience. Now as he grips the steering wheel, the traffic continues to split around him. Ignoring the hooting of horns and the gnashing of roadrage teeth, he wrestles the Rover's clutch into reverse and performs a neat U-turn.

maggie

Wolf and Dwight hit the town. My guess was dinner, lap dancing and a friendly brothel. They made a big effort not to look relieved when I told them I wasn't coming but I was grateful to them anyway. I should have felt excited about the Bevan story being back on track but instead I felt confused and uneasy. I was glad to be on my own. It was only while I was swiping the card through my bedroom's security box that I realized Jay might be waiting inside. For the first time I disliked the uncertainty of it, then hated myself for feeling that way.

Alone in my room I tried twisting my hair round my finger Stella style, but I just felt silly. 'Rory,' I meowed. Then cut myself off. What a loser. The message light was flashing on the phone. I felt elated as I dialled nine to access voicemail then dashed when a voice announced my dry cleaning was ready. Finally I stood under the shower and let the water run over my head at full pressure but I knew that Rory was unfinished business and I'd go crazy if I didn't do something about it.

The operator informed me with some sympathy that there were 139 R. Jones in the central London area and

did I not have an actual address? Of course I didn't have an
address. I had no idea about his life, let alone where he
lived or what might happen if I showed up on his doorstep.
Would he offer me a Coke? Glass of wine? A tequila
slammer? Would he invite me in to sit on a sofa? Or a
beanbag? While he leapt up and put on some – Jesus, what?
what? The Mamas and the Papas? Puff Daddy? Verdi's greatest hits? I knew *nothing* about him. Fretfully I read through
the leather-bound file of hotel services cover to cover. Then
I read them through again in Spanish, French and German.
After that I ordered a club sandwich. It appeared in a
miraculously short time because when I heard the knock, I
was still sitting in my underwear clutching the soggy bath
towel to my knees. I wrapped it round my waist and opened
the door but there was no trolley waiting for me, no smiling
waiter holding a pen and a room service bill. Instead, in
the corridor outside, arms crossed casually, Rory Jones was
leaning against the yellow wallpaper.

'This is *the* famous chippie of north London,' Rory said.
'People come for *miles* to this place. Look.' He pointed to
the queue of people stamping their feet in the cold outside.
Inside, the fish and chip shop was decorated with tiles of
sea life and lit with brilliant gaudy striplights. The front
counter thronged with people holding out their hands for
warm newspaper parcels of takeout. In the seating area it
was hot and steamy in contrast to the freeze creeping over
the city. 'Unbelievably for England,' Rory had said as we
parked the Rover, 'it's actually going to snow.'
Flakes dropped silently past the window, blurring from

white to blue to pink as they floated across the strobed restaurant sign. The smell of batter was overpowering, the feeling of goodwill overwhelming, and at that moment there was no place else on earth I would rather have been.

'I used to have a fish you know,' I told Rory between mouthfuls.

'Really,' he said. 'Barracuda?'

'A little tropical thing.' In fact what I'd wanted was a sister. When that idea was shot down, I'd begged for a dog. The fish was a compromise. My father took me to the pet shop on West 67th Street. My heart was set on something exotic and colourful. We were directed to the tropical tank where the fish swam around like neon sweets – striped peppermints and rock candy with fins. I couldn't choose between them, then I saw this creature under the plastic shipwreck at the bottom of the tank. It looked so persecuted with its sad bulbous eyes. It was on special offer for two dollars.

'It was so cute, all black and velvety. I named it Magic Johnson . . . you know after the basketball player, but my parents told me it was racist.'

'It was?'

'I never really worked it out either.' I sighed. 'My parents are . . . well . . . it was always something; Vietnam, the plight of the Idaho potato pickers, support Lesbian Mothers.'

'My mother wouldn't know what to do with a lesbian. "Darling," ' he mimics, ' "Do peel this magnificent lesbian and pop it into the fruit salad." '

I laughed. 'You an only child as well?'

'Brother . . . one.'

'Yeah? Older . . . younger?'

'Daniel was a year older.'

I picked up on the tense straight away. 'Rory . . . Oh God . . . I'm so sorry.'

'Yes,' he said. He turned away, seemed to steady himself then turned back and said casually, 'Ah well, let's face it — as tragedies go, there are a lot worse.'

I was shocked by his tone. *Oh no*, I thought, *no blood here, just terrible internal injuries.*

But he'd already begun talking.

'Number one bereavement hot spot is losing a child. Two is a wife or a husband — although there must be a qualifying factor of youth and major heart-wrenching element such as victim was mother/father of twins or died after a long period of suffering. Next we have losing a fiancée which scores extra points because of 'blighted life' syndrome. Your parents dying doesn't cut the mustard if you're over the age of twenty-five — it's not tragedy if it's not before its time — and losing a sibling if they're under twenty is definitely considered losing a child for the parents, see category number one. After all those we move onto losing a sibling *over* twenty, in which case parents and other siblings get equal billing rights. Rock bottom on the list you get losing the sibling who's not a child, who's well over twenty — but neither a husband, nor a father, not anybody's fiancé, and then when of course that person is naturally self-destructive . . .' He broke off, put his head in his hands. 'I'm sorry.'

'It's OK, you should talk about it.' I put my hand on his arm but he shook it off angrily.

'I don't want to fucking talk about it.'

After a second or two he said, 'He liked to drink. One

night he got into an argument with a bus.' Rory's voice had
a shrug in it. 'He lost . . . I lost him.'

I twisted the napkin in my lap. 'What was he like?'

'Oh you know, charming, clever, funny, wicked. Everybody adored him. I did everything he told me to, of course.'

'You adored him too, huh?'

'Naaa, he was just a lot bigger than me.'

I smiled.

'When we were small he was always in trouble, *we* were
always in trouble. Then he'd hide in the linen cupboard and
I'd get the blame.'

'The linen cupboard?'

'English word for the only warm room in the house —
in our house to be more specific. We used to take our
books, stay there for hours curled up on the shelf.'

'God, I can't imagine. You must really miss him.'

'You know,' Rory picked up the vinegar bottle and
absently twisted its top. 'I still shout at him for scratching
my car when he hasn't borrowed it. I get irritated when he
leaves the top off the toothpaste, then I remember it wasn't
him, and I still celebrate his birthday every year even though
he will never get any older.'

I looked down at my shredded napkin, moved beyond
anything.

'Of course,' he said brightly, 'he was also a right bastard.
Nicked all my clothes and most of my girlfriends. Never
even considered giving either back.'

I listened to him as he talked on and I breathed easier.
The internal injuries weren't fatal. He might still be bleeding
heavily but I reckoned he'd pull through.

*

We walked to the car. Snow was settling in a milky film on the sidewalk. 'You know if all British institutions are as delicious as fish and chips, I might have to change my opinion of your people.'

'Oh?' Rory raised his eyebrows. 'Do you still need that much persuading?'

'Why? You think you're all so loveable?'

'Actually, yes, I think on the whole the British are pretty nice people.'

'*Nice* . . . Oh sure, just ask an Irishman.' I broke off. Rory was scowling at me.

'If there's one thing I can't stand it's that facile American attitude that the IRA are just romantic freedom fighters on a jihad . . . they're nothing but a bunch of murderous thugs.'

'Whoah, I'm sorry.' I'd been teasing, nothing more.

'Maybe you just had too much vinegar with your chips.' Rory said nastily.

'Maybe I did,' I said, stung.

'Maybe I should take you home.'

'I guess maybe you should,' I said stubbornly.

There was silence in the car.

'You're not going to sulk the whole journey are you?' I said eventually. Rory looked at me suspiciously.

'Because if you are, I'm going to have to talk . . . I mean haven't you heard, it's a question of manners.'

He laughed. 'OK, OK, OK, I'm sorry. Now do you want to see something I'm really passionate about?'

*

He parked the Rover in front of an arched stone entrance next to a security box. Rory knocked on the window. The guard inside was old and had a grizzled crew cut. He turned reluctantly from his miniature television to the hatch.

Rory handed him a twenty-pound note.

'You're a very sick gentleman Mr Rory.' He rubbed the money between dry fingers.

'Thank you, John.'

He ushered us through the hut and out the other side.

'Where are we?' I asked.

'Highgate Cemetery. Your parents would love it. Karl Marx is buried here.'

I gazed round in wonder. The whole world suddenly looked like it had been sprinkled with icing sugar. Snow had settled everywhere – it powdered the topside of red berries. It lay like a chalky overscore on the stone of gothic chapels and was piled into the crevices of gargoyles' mouths.

'We're in Narnia!' I said.

Rory squeezed my hand. 'This is the west side, the wild-west side. Normally people aren't allowed in here.'

'Except us.' I looked down at my hand in Rory's and tried not to think of it as the betrayal it was.

'Tonight we are exceptionally abnormal people.'

We wandered along the path, Rory pointing out sleeping stone lions, obelisks, headstones with funky engravings.

'Look,' he stopped in front of a tomb with an enormous effigy of a dog carved on top.

' "Tom Sayers," ' I read the inscription, ' "last of the bare-fisted fighters." '

'The dog was the chief mourner at Tom's funeral. Not a popular fellow it seems.'

He knelt beside another grave and swept the snow off with his arm. 'Look at this.' It was a cheap headstone, all the more poignant when compared with the elaborate splendour of its neighbours. A woman who had died in the plague was buried with her seven children.

'Shit,' I heard myself saying softly, and I looked at it for a long time.

We walked on. Snow continued to fall heavily. A fox stopped and stared at us from the middle of a pathway, his front paw raised questioningly. I was dazzled and in awe and I told Rory so.

'They say that in a place this beautiful, the disappointment of death is softened,' he said wistfully.

'How come you know so much about it?'

'I did some work here once.'

'Grave robber?'

'Archaeological work.'

'What do you mean?' I said curiously.

'I worked for the V and A . . . still do occasionally, when not squiring unhousetrained Americans round the country.'

'Whoah, wait a minute. You're an *archaeologist*?'

'Don't ask.' He gave a bitter laugh, 'Let's just say I got waylaid by family business. What? Now you hate archaeologists?'

'Oh no, nothing like that.' I'd been wringing my hands, trying to jump-start circulation. 'Bit cold that's all.' I pressed them under my armpits.

'We should have brought gloves . . . stupid of me.'

'Oh wait,' I said, struck by the brilliance of this notion.

I patted the gloves in the inside pocket of my coat. But when I tried to undo the buttons, my fingers were about as dextrous as raw sausages. I held them up helplessly.

'They don't seem to work.'

Rory took hold of my coat lapels. 'Cold hands, that's bad.' He pushed the first button through the buttonhole. 'Could lead to frostbite.' He undid the second.

'Frostbite's bad.' I couldn't drag my eyes from his.

'Very bad,' he whispered, 'before you know it your fingers turn green, drop off into the snow one by one—'

'Surely that's leprosy,' I said.

We kissed. His hands were inside my coat, wrapped round my back. Snowflakes dissolved against my burning face.

'Look at you. What a mess. Your ponytail's all over the place, your cheeks are red, you look like one of the wild things.' He pulled me to him. 'A wild thing from the wild side.' We kissed again.

'Give me your hands.' Obediently I stuck them out.

'Rory . . . I.' All evening I'd been wondering what to say.

'What?' He began putting on my gloves for me.

'Nothing . . . hey you know, just don't think I don't do this all the time.'

'What? Kiss Englishmen?'

'Every time I'm in a graveyard, sure.'

'OK.' He kissed me again and I knew I couldn't say it. Figured instead Jay was my problem and I would confront it later, when things were different, when my head wasn't dazzled by snow, when my heart had stopped buzzing, when my − wait a second, why was my heart buzzing?

'Your phone's ringing.'

'Leave it,' I said shakily, but he was already feeling for it under my coat.

'Seems rude not to get it while I'm here.'

'Hey stop that . . .'

'Stop what?'

'That,' I whispered.

'Just trying to give you a hand.'

'I hate to put you to so much trouble.'

'Believe me,' he said, 'it's my pleasure.'

I swayed against him. His hands found bare skin.

'Rory, uh . . .'

The cell buzzed so violently I jumped. Rory plucked it out of the breast pocket of my coat. 'You're absolutely right,' he said, mock surprised. 'It was here all the time.'

It continued to vibrate in his hand. 'What's more it appears to be rather sexually excited. No wonder you're so attached to the damn thing.'

I laughed and made a grab for it, but it slipped from my woollied hands onto the ground. Rory dove for it. Pushed me down. Rolled me over in the snow. I squirmed and broke free, he grabbed my leg, pulled me back, I kicked him.

'Christ, you fight dirty.' He pinned me to the ground. I stopped struggling. 'Come home with me, Maggie. Now, tomorrow, come up to my parents for the weekend.' I lay on the snow, grinning, nodding my head. Of course I would come. And I didn't care about Jay, I didn't care about anything much until I remembered.

'Oh Jesus,' I sat up abruptly. 'I can't.'

'What do you mean you can't?'

'I can't.'

'Why not?'

'I've got an interview.'

'An *interview*? I thought you'd finished. With whom?'
Sheer instinct kept my mouth shut.

'Can't you cancel it?'

'I can't, it's really important.'

'Wait a minute,' he joked, 'what could possibly be more
important than spending a whole weekend with me and my
adorable family?'

I was silent.

'Ouch,' he said and his eyes had grown wary.

Inside my hotel room the phone was ringing. 'I've just had
a call from Washington,' Jay said, 'I think I could get to
you by Sunday, so at least we could fly home together.'

Wherever he was calling from the reception was bad.
'Where have you been hiding the last week?' I could only
just hear his voice through the crackle. 'I've been leaving
messages.'

'I've tried to get hold of you too,' I said lamely, but Jay
was far too savvy.

'I'll see you Sunday.'

'Yes.' There was a pause.

'I have wanted to be with you,' he said heavily.

I hesitated. 'Me too.'

I couldn't sleep. Thoughts crowded and turned in my mind
like colliding planets. Finally I took the comforter off the

bed and opened the doors to the terrace. It was a desolately beautiful night. There was a half-moon, a dense stillness despite the icy wind which swayed the leafless branches of trees. Hunched up, I stared out over the railing. At two a.m. in New York, the city would be sleeping with its eyes open and its heart beating. People would be talking, fighting, eating, fucking. But London was truly asleep.

I felt lonely, out of sync with where I was, with who I was. A stranger to myself. I struggled for a little perspective but I was appalled at how much grey area Rory had introduced into the black and white of my objective. I cursed myself for committing the most heinous of crimes. Never get involved. Never. This . . . *thing* with Rory, whatever it was, had no foundations, no future, it made no sense. Jay made sense. Getting this story made sense.

The middle of the night is a dangerous time to put your life in order. As minutes concertina, hours spin away and the possibility of sleep recedes ever further, it's easy to make a pact with any devil who's on hand. Forget the sentimental soliloquy, I had no choice but to chase this story. I would get it and pump it for all it was worth and then I would get the hell out of England.

Three dirty Germans crossed the Rhine, *parlez vous* —
Three dirty Germans crossed the Rhine, *parlez vous* —
Three dirty Germans crossed the Rhine,
Fucking the women and drinking the wine,
Inky pinky, *parlez vous.*

— Bawdy trench song

daniel

Where had Grandpa been when she was up before? Surely there all the time? In the house, in his bedroom – sitting in his green wing-backed chair listening to his Beethoven and books on tapes. No, wait, I remember now, he'd been out for the day somewhere, but it doesn't matter. All I can tell you is that when my father picked up the telephone to find Maggie Monroe on the other end, it took him less than fifteen seconds to confirm that the Marquess of Danby was alive and well and living at Bevan. As soon as she asked the question, you might have thought my father would smell a rat. However there is no one less Machiavellian, thus he is incapable of recognizing the telltale signs in anyone else. Besides it's thrown into the conversation casually enough and when she goes on to tell him whatever fib she's invented about needing more footage, he's happy for her to return to Bevan. Moreover, unaware that all sorts of gaskets are about to blow, he insists that this time she and the crew spend the night.

It's not that he's pathologically naïve. It's just that he's lived with this particular family secret for sixty-odd years and hasn't thought about it for thirty. Within his circle of acquaintances there are plenty of skeletons in many a prominent closet. The baby in the bathwater, Lucan, the Beast of Glamys. There are countless stories of incest and bad behaviour about which our family, like many others, have closed ranks. It would never occur to my father that hushing up a scandal was an abuse of power and class. He considers it a matter of loyalty. He's as likely to betray family or friends as – let's say – be made Chancellor of the Exchequer. Despite the scorn universally heaped upon it this is one of the plus sides to old school tie nepotism.

As a child my father had played with his royal cousins. He could vividly remember having to be on time for every meal. After the 'unpleasantness', as his mother had called it, he never saw them again. He has no shame about his father's role in the scandal. Everyone knew that Edward was weak and had flaws but Grandpa had loved him and the idea of him being exiled was the worst possible thing he could have imagined. Home and hearth are what make the English function. My father believes, as Rory and I do, as my grandfather does, that it is right to make sacrifices for those you love. He understands, too, that there exists a time before any war when the spy, the ally and the enemy are indistinguishable from one another.

So when Maggie and her crew turn up, his overriding concern is simply one of temperature – that they be warm for the bonfire that evening. After giving them mugs of Nescafé, he herds them into the cloakroom and is rifling through the dozens of mismatched boots and coats that hang by the gun cupboard when Grandpa himself pushes through the outside door.

'Ah, here's my father now,' Alistair says.

And Maggie exchanges a look with her crew.

Grandpa, as is customary, is dressed in full military outfit. His trousers are beautifully pressed by Nanny, and he wears a jacket buttoned over a shirt and tie, all in the same khaki brown. A leather strap is fastened diagonally over one shoulder. His boots are polished and three medals are pinned in vertical symmetry down the length of his chest.

'Just landed, just landed,' he announces to no one in particular. He puts one foot in the bootpull and leans stiffly against the wall for balance.

'Any action?' He peers beadily around the cloakroom.

'Good journey, Pa?' enquires my father.

'Little bumpy,' Grandpa says. 'Otherwise, a damn good bit of flying.'

He notices the presence of strangers and his eyes light up. 'Prisoners of war?' he asks hopefully.

maggie

The Marquess of Danby strode around the drawing room picking out various objects of interest for our inspection. Two grand pianos, surfaces muddled with sheet music faced each other across the room, and from underneath he pulled out a box of musical instruments: a ukulele, a mouth organ, a guitar, its guts snapped and curled, some cymbals and a tambourine. 'We all used to play in the old days,' he turned them over nostalgically in his hands, 'the girls painted beautifully, everyone danced. Once a troupe of Russian gymnasts came to stay, awfully limber they were.' He unlocked a display case and removed a pair of Chinese figurines from the glass shelves. 'See these?' The Marquess had pianist's hands, his fingers were long and tapered, but the knuckles were crudely distorted by age. 'Collected by my grandfather on his grand tour . . .'

I was about to make appropriate noises about their beauty when he added, 'Hideous aren't they? Always longed to smash them.'

'Why don't you then?'

'Perhaps I will one day.' He turned the two figures to face each other. 'Hello there charming little Oriental lady,'

he mimicked. 'What a very pretty fan you're carrying.'
He dipped the female figure in coquettish deference.
'Oh how kind you are Honourable Sir.' The pitch of his
voice changed to female, 'but not nearly as pretty as my
drawers.'

Wolf and Dwight caught my eye.

'Perhaps,' continued the old man, advancing the male
figure closer, 'If Honourable Lady could just lift her skirt
then Honourable War Lord can—' He broke off. 'Good
God,' he exclaimed in disgust as rain splattered against the
windows, 'this weather really makes you want to go to
Tahiti and horse about with one of those Wahinis like
whichever one of those painter fellows it was . . . Gauguin,
I think.'

'Why are you wearing a uniform?' I said.

'Plane crashed on the lawn once to great excitement,'
he looked out dreamily at the darkening sky. 'Kept Italian
prisoners here for a while. Nice bunch of fellows, good
with the tractor. My mother taught them to play Up Jenkins.
They don't teach young people about the war,' he said sadly,
'they just don't think it's important, I suppose,' his eyes
became fierce, 'but I think it's important, don't you?'

'Yes,' I said truthfully, 'I do.'

'Good girl.' He patted my shoulder clumsily. 'I have
rather good memorabilia you know – travelled all over
the place, the Japanese were awful,' he waved his hand in
Wolf's direction, 'Pearl Harbour – long before your day of
course. So many stories . . . but most people are no longer
interested in such things.'

'Try me,' I said.

'Where shall I start?' the Marquess said eagerly. He winked and like a spider casting out its sticky web, I smiled back encouragingly.

'With your trips to Germany before the war.'

daniel

My mother sits at the green baize card table, a large gin and tonic in her hand. She finishes off the last three clues of the *Telegraph* crossword while Nanny completes her weekly lottery ticket. Grandpa sleeps, head lolling against the winged edge of his favourite chair, his feet resting on the matted dreadlocks of Lurch's back.

A small bird, a starling, is flying round the room. Trapped, it bumps itself against the heavy damask curtains then flies in increasingly frenzied circles until Alistair unlocks the window latch and pulls down on the sash. The bird smells freedom in the cold air and makes its bid. Reluctantly Alistair closes the window after it.

'Sun's over the yardarm,' says Alistair, surveying the uniformly beige sky outside, 'so how about a drink?' He pours a glass of whisky from a decanter and hands it to Maggie.

He's worried his guests are bored and doesn't know what to do with them. He's also nervous about the imminent arrival of Rory and begins only now to question the balance of money against the wisdom of inviting a television crew actually to stay the night – however much they are prepared to pay for the pleasure.

'Now,' he says, 'how many for supper?' He begins counting heads, 'One, two, three of us . . . then there's you lot, four, five, six.' He whips the glasses off Grandpa's nose then casually holds them to Grandpa's open mouth. 'Seven,' he announces, apparently satisfied from an inspection of the lens, that Grandpa is still alive. 'Seven for dinner is that right? Oh, and Robert,' he says, 'with Robert that makes eight.'

maggie

We sat on the twin beds up in Wolf's bedroom and studiously avoided eye contact.

'And you're sure you got it?' I asked.

'Quite sure.' Wolf nodded his big head.

'His reaction and the photograph in the same shot?'

'It's all there, Maggie.'

'Good,' I said, 'great.'

'Well, you wanted a story,' Wolf looked at me, 'and now you've got one.'

'I did, didn't I.' I scraped the toe of my shoe against the floor, 'which you know . . . is great, so, um, high five and all that.'

'Yeah, high five, crack open the champagne, let's smoke a cigar,' Wolf said.

Now it was Dwight's turn to look accusingly at me, 'But . . .'

'But what?' I snarled.

'He's so . . .'

'Sweet.' I finished it for him. 'Yeah, I know.' I sighed, rubbing the goosebumps on my arms. 'Hey, life's a bitch, right?' But a quote of Don Hewitt's, creator of *60 Minutes* kept popping unbidden into my head. 'The public's right to know doesn't translate into the media's obligation to broadcast.' The Marquess and his family were not the only people I'd found myself liking over the last few weeks. I didn't know what to think any more. Were the English aristocracy a class that deserved to be wiped out or an eccentric but splendid remnant of a tribe under threat? For some reason I remembered a story Alan once told me. Why, I don't know, because it was hardly a parallel – the son of a friend of his, a young soldier had been in Bosnia only forty-eight hours before he was sent into a building. The Serbs inside were taken by surprise. This boy, terrified, shot wildly around the room, killing everyone. He'd run into the kitchen to find another soldier facing him. The man had no gun. Instead he held a crumpled picture of his child and pushed it into the boy's face with shaking fingers. Overcome with guilt and horror at what he'd already done, the boy let him go. In the basement of that building they'd found three girls, dead, covered in ejaculate. The boy had gone after the Serb, found him and shot him dead. 'Try people fairly,' Alan said, 'then you needn't shed tears for them.' The Marquess of Danby might be a sweet old man now but he was also a Nazi sympathizer and a traitor.

Dwight and Wolf were still looking at me. I shivered, 'Jesus,' I dragged myself to my feet, 'I'm going to find a sweater before I die.'

The gunshots came moments after I'd left the room. I headed towards the noise, along a corridor, up a staircase, through a passageway. There was another shot, this time

louder. At the end of the passageway was a closed door, a
faded picture nailed to it. It was a child's drawing of a skull
and crossbones – or what was left of it. Droplets of blood
were crayoned around the warning. 'Enter here at your
peril.'

I turned the key, took a step into the room and then
the floor just swallowed me up. My legs buckled and my
arm ripped against something sharp. A stinging pain, then
my feet made contact with something solid. When my eyes
acclimatized to the dark I realized I'd fallen through the
floorboards to a half level below. Cautiously I hoisted myself
back up to the floor and sat down, dabbing at my bleeding
forearm and looking around. In this part of the house there
could be no pretence at normal living. Wallpaper hung off
the walls in great brownish curls. It was bitterly cold, but
not hard to see why. The room had shadows of furniture
but the walls beyond them ended in disjointed brickwork –
there was no roof. Birds wheeled and squawked in the night
sky above. I craned my neck up but there was another crack
from a gun and something thudded onto the floor close to
where I was sitting. 'Hey,' I yelled. From the other side of
the ruin a man stepped out. He lowered his gun, the scanty
light from the moon caught his face and I stopped breathing.

'Maggie,' he said. 'Maggie! You're here, you came, I
don't believe it!' He hurried across the room.

I didn't get it. Didn't even come close. 'What are you
doing here?' I clutched at my arm as the memory of Rory
appearing bootfaced at Roxmere came back to me. 'Oh no,
they didn't send for you did they?'

He stopped. 'No, they didn't send for me.'

And still I didn't get it.

'Then why are you here?'

He gave me a measured look, then he opened the gun and dropped the cartridges into his hand.

'I live here, Maggie.'

I stared at him stupidly. Then, like live wires crossing, snippets of information began sparking through my brain. *Pop,* Rory's determination for us not to come to Bevan. *Pop,* Massey reading from Burke's peerage, *eldest son recently deceased. Pop,* Rory in the fish and chip restaurant, *he had a fight with a bus, he lost, I lost him.* Nanny saying, *there's only the baby left now.* Oh for Christ's sake, Rory's agency contacts, the foot through all those doors. Robert, Rory for short, was the 38-year-old baby. I didn't want it to be true but it seemed so obvious. A radish could have put it together quicker than I had.

'Your last name's different . . . that's why I didn't get it, Bevan's the . . .'

'Title . . . one of them. The family name is Lytton-Jones. I dropped the Lytton. It does tend to confuse.'

'So the Viscount Lytton-Jones who died tragically—'

'Was my brother. Daniel.'

For some reason I just felt angry. 'All that time . . . All those things I said to you, and all the time you were . . . you were . . . well, one of them.'

'One of *them,*' he repeated flatly.

'But why didn't you tell me?'

'Wait a minute.' He took a step towards me. 'Who didn't tell whom? Why would you come here when I specifically told you not to?'

'Everyone told me this was one of the great houses,' I faltered, 'I was just doing my job.'

And only then did realization slam into me. My job . . .
my job. For crying out loud, how could I have been be so
stupid? I'd put the growing unease I'd felt over the last week
down to confusion over my feelings, down to guilt about
Jay, my lack of loyalty, spending too much time rooting
around in other people's lives, down to anything but its real
cause. 'Give them enough rope and they'll hang themselves,'
Jay had said. I thought of all the footage sitting in its neatly
marked reels back in our hotel room. I'd gone out of my
way to get the most controversial footage I could. Anything
I could make satirical or mocking. Leaving aside Rory's
grandfather, I hadn't a single frame I could possibly describe
as the puff piece I had sold Stately Locations and Rory on.

In this business, there's always a certain amount of
professional crapping on people, but you have to keep
some kind of integrity. You have to believe in some kind of
truth. My justification was that I believed something about
these people and I had sought out and found behaviour to
prove my point. But in the way witnesses at a murder trial
will have conflicting accounts of the same event, the truth is
mercurial. *'If there's more than one version of the truth, there
is no truth.'*

'Maggie, this is my family home for Christ's sake, and
you're a journalist.'

'Meaning what?' I turned on him defensively, 'I can't be
trusted?'

'Well can you? Why are you here? How long have you
been here? And just what have you filmed so far?'

I felt my face morph into a blank screen, incriminating
footage running all over it.

'My parents? My grandfather?'

'Your dad showed us around. We had tea with Nanny. Nanny made me drink milk. I haven't drunk milk since the fourth grade.' But even as I said it guilt flooded through me, because there is one thing I do know — however many different kinds of truth there are in this world, there is only one kind of lie — and that's a dirty one.

'You've seen how we work. We don't really set anything up. We don't tell people how to behave, we just film what we see.'

'So you keep telling me, Maggie,' he said tightly. 'But what exactly is it that you *do* see?'

I film what I see.

What a load of BS that is. The truth is angles and shadows. In an editing room the truth can be moulded and squeezed into whatever shape you want it to be. As a journalist, you are as responsible as your subject for how they appear on film.

The choices were clear — wing it, or run. It felt like two storm clouds had collided over my head but running is for sissies and whatever else you can say about me, I hope I ain't no sissy.

The look on Dwight's and Wolf's face was comical as Rory virtually marched me into the dining room. I smiled wryly at them and when Alistair Bevan looked puzzled and said, 'Oh so you have met Robert,' Rory said grimly, 'Yes, but it turns out we don't know each other all that well after all.'

At dinner, picking over the fragile bones of some bird on my plate I tried to imagine what it was like growing up in the lost splendour of that house. While Rory's grandfather regaled Wolf and Dwight with war stories using the salt and pepper as tanks, while Rory's parents drank and steadily became more removed, I watched, I opened my eyes and I tried to see. How Rory's mother surreptitiously pushed the heater closer our way when she thought we weren't looking. How only Wolf, Dwight and myself were offered a second helping. How Rory watched over his family so proprietarily, and God help me, I felt ashamed.

There had to be a way out of this mess but I couldn't see it. Whatever happened, I needed to talk to Rory before things got any worse – confession is a lot better than admission but it seemed I wasn't even to be allowed that luxury.

'We're so pleased you're all staying for the night this time,' Alistair said and I closed my eyes.

'*This time?*' Rory said. 'You've been here before?' he hissed. 'What exactly are you doing here again?'

'I was invited by your father.'

'That's not very likely is it?' and the biting sarcasm of his tone made me defensive.

'Well ask him if you don't believe me.'

But Rory's parents were unwrapping their anniversary gifts to one another. The packages were identical. A pair of police breathalysers. The Earl breathed into the tube then looked at the bag, eagerly awaiting the results. The indicator on the bag turned bright green; maximum over the limit.

'Marvellous,' Alistair said, 'they work!' He beamed at his wife. Rory's mother looked indulgent. Rory just looked exasperated.

'I *will* ask him,' he said, 'but in the meantime you don't film one more thing in my home.'

'Come on everyone,' Audrey pushed back her chair, 'let's light the bonfire.'

'And *don't* think we're finished with this conversation either.' Rory added.

In the parklands, standing in huddles around the bonfire, many of Bevan's old retainers and their families had ventured from cottages on the estate to celebrate the Earl's anniversary. The Earl greeted them all, some with a handshake, others with a rough hug. Everyone arranged themselves in a loose circle around the base of the bonfire as the farm manager's grandson, a thin sallow boy no more than sixteen, positioned himself at the top of the ladder and doused the 20-foot structure — looking more than ever like a witch's hat — with petrol. The ladder was taken away and the tractor driven a safe distance from the bonfire while Rory and Alistair walked around its edge, tossing more petrol from watering cans onto the hacked off branches and twisted boughs. When that job was done, they retreated fifty yards or so. The circle of onlookers moved outwards. A bow and arrow covered in a rag was produced. Alistair tested the tautness of string with a finger then handed it to Rory.

Rory pulled back his arm and took aim. Alistair held a match to the end of the arrow and Rory let fly. The burning cloth of the arrow cut through the darkness and buried itself into the hay piled around the brim of the hat. The bonfire whispered, crackled furtively, then to the cheers of the crowd, ignited with a sharp burst of light.

I stood alone, a short distance from Wolf and Dwight, mesmerized by the flames. Onlookers howled appreciation as burning sap caused the occasional explosion. Sparks zigzagged like miniature fireworks up into the night sky. Children ran around brandishing smouldering twigs like swords and it occurred to me that had this been America, there would have been safety ropes and warning signs posted and the occasion would have lost its charm. The heat from the fire was intense, I turned one cold cheek towards it then the other. The whole scene was so far removed from anything I'd ever been a part of and I wondered how it would feel to be there under any other circumstances rather than hostile. Someone put a mug of hot whisky into my hands and I accepted it dreamily, strangely in love with everything that was going on. Eventually the structure of the bonfire gave up on itself and collapsed in a heap of sparks. Children who'd been steadily creeping closer jumped back squealing with excitement and I came back to reality. I scanned the outlines of woolly hats and lumpy coats for Rory's rangy figure but he had gone.

Inside the house the sound of the piano led me to the drawing room. Rory and his father were playing a duet, one at each piano. It was a classical piece, which they played musically but very erratically. One after the other, chords jarred. I stayed hidden in the doorway and watched them.

'You're out of time, Rory,' Alistair shouted good-naturedly. But even with my non-musical ear, I could hear it was Alistair who didn't have the dexterity to keep up.

'Rubbish,' Rory shouted back. 'We're enormously talented.'

Alistair missed another chord. 'Goddamnit!' He crashed his hands onto the keys.

'Come on, Pa,' Rory said.

But his father stopped playing. 'It's no good,' he said, putting his hands into his lap. 'Too old.'

Rory went to sit next to his father. He picked up Alistair's hand and began rubbing his fingers with the bottom of his jumper, as if Alistair were a child who'd lost his mittens. I thought then of a proverb I'd once heard 'When a father helps the son, both laugh: When the son helps the father, both cry.'

'Not old,' Rory said. 'Just cold.'

They began the piece again, one hand each, laughing, making mistakes, teasing one another. I felt a stab of something unfamiliar. I guess it was envy but there was something else – I'd spent my whole life revelling in the fact that I didn't have to belong. Now whether I had any right to or not, I felt part of something and in a few days I was supposed to go home and betray them all. Nice one, Maggie.

I was no longer alone. Wolf stood behind me, camera raised. I blocked the lens then took the camera from him. Wolf looked at me, then to Rory and his father. He gently touched my cheek with his big hand and walked away.

Alistair and Rory were still playing. Every so often Alistair executed a fast whirly diddly movement. You could hear how good he must have been before arthritis had thickened his joints and bones.

'Who's going to look after your mother when I'm not around?' he shouted.

'Come on, Dad.'

'No, I'm serious.'

'Perhaps we can arrange something at auction.'

Alistair laughed but stopped playing. He put his hand on Rory's shoulder.

'Maybe,' he said, 'well . . . maybe when Daniel died,' he stopped short, as if he'd set himself a verbal mountain to climb but didn't know whether he'd brought the right equipment. Rory sat perfectly still.

Alistair took a deep breath, 'Well, maybe we should sell this house.'

Rory stared at his father, astonished.

'Yes, yes, I know,' Alistair said heavily, 'impossible, of course, absolutely impossible. Rory, I'm so sorry about everything.'

'It doesn't matter,' Rory said, and I could see he was struggling. 'Really, Dad, it doesn't matter.'

They looked at each other, a million words unsaid between them, then Alistair broke the spell with a snort. He grabbed his beaker from the side of the piano, removed the lid, poured the brandy down his throat, then turned back to the piano and broke into a solo of vigorous chopsticks.

I know cold. I have been cold in many places. I've slept on floors, in the back of pickups, I've slept under horse blankets on the frozen earth. The body is prepared to put up with all kinds of discomfort for all kinds of bullshit reasons, but this cold was different. This cold was ungodly.

It took all my will power to strip to my underwear. In the bathroom a sign on the toilet read 'No sharp yanks' which made me laugh until I understood that the reason the toilet didn't flush, sharp yanks or not, was because the water inside was *actually frozen*. I peered at it almost expecting to see miniature skaters in furry earmuffs gliding over its surface. The basin next to it was marbled brown with stains but at least there was a comforting dribble of water with which I brushed my teeth. This scanty hygiene routine chilled me to such a degree I put all my clothes back on, coat and socks included and was about to jump into bed when I noticed the electric heater in the fireplace. I flicked the switch and crouched expectantly in front of it. Nothing. On examination the cord led to the back of a dresser but it was too heavy to move. On my stomach I fumbled the plug towards the socket but it wouldn't go in. I looked at the plug in my hand – three square prongs, I looked at the socket in the wall – three round holes. The two were entirely sexually incompatible. I gave up. I got into bed trying to dispel the image of myself being found the next morning, stiff, dead, frozen as solid as a Good Humor popsicle.

daniel

Rory sits in Pa's office and works steadily through the mail. He slaps stamps onto twenty or so envelopes, flicking the bulb of the light to keep it going. He knows Maggie has gone to bed and wonders what she is thinking.

Leona said that Bevan reminded her of a mausoleum. She'd shivered when she said it. That was the second time he took her home. The first time she'd said Bevan was 'romantic', 'so pretty', 'like a castle in a storybook'. The cellar with its toads and chains was 'amazing'. Later it was as though she watched those chains being attached to Rory's ankle. It had been the day after the funeral and Rory suggested they took a walk. They'd got a quarter of the way down the drive before Leona looked sadly at the bottom of her camel trousers, lightly splattered with mud, and announced she'd try to do better next time. At supper she'd wrestled valiantly with the pheasant, but she'd stared at the bread sauce as though it was vomit. Rory promised she'd never have to live there, but she hadn't believed him.

Rory continues with his quest for fiscal law and order but his concentration is shot to pieces. Lethargic from boredom he slows to a crawl. He's finally admitting to himself that his motive for keeping Maggie from Bevan has shifted, it's never been the so called 'unpleasantness'. As with Alistair, our grandfather's secret has been so long buried, Rory doesn't even consider it, it's no longer to do with the threat of exposing the family to the derision of millions of viewers. That was his *excuse*. His *reason* is that increasingly he's finding it hard to see himself independently of Bevan and he knows full well that acceptance is nine tenths of defeat.

He imagines Maggie upstairs in bed, naked and pale against the bitter darkness of the room. He remembers the touch of her lips, the smoothness of her skin. He runs an imaginary finger along the line of her body, feels her ribs dipping into the curve of her waist. He traces his finger out over her hip, across her leg to the inside of her thigh, but his fantasy is somewhat moderated by the sure knowledge that Maggie naked and prone in a room in which the temperature barely reaches above freezing point even in summer, is highly improbable. The fire is gasping in the fireplace, the wood basket empty. In a burst of frustration, Rory picks up the remaining bills on the desk and shovels them into the grate.

maggie

This was crazy, I climbed out of bed. Somewhere in the house, there must be blankets. Blankets would be made of wool and right then wool was what I needed. I prowled the narrow corridors. A trunk in the upstairs hall looked hopeful but was full of antique Chinese baby clothes all beautifully wrapped in tissue paper. I opened a door into a room with a rocking horse in the corner. More of a nursery than a bedroom, the floor was stacked with boxes of broken toys and a line of silver cups sat on one of the bookshelves. The cups had been awarded for every kind of sport from running to cricket. I picked up a yellowing cutting of two teenage boys, their arms linked, tennis rackets raised. The heading read 'The Fabulous Bevan Boys'. I crept out. The room was too sad, too full of ghosts. How much of himself had Rory left behind in that nursery? Distracted, I opened the next door I came across and was mortified to find Alistair and Audrey inside, huddled up in bed. Alistair was wearing an overcoat over his pyjamas and reading out loud from a paperback. Audrey was laughing up at him. On their bedside tables instead of the standard Evian water stood two bottles of Famous Grouse Whisky.

'I'm so sorry,' I backed out hurriedly, 'I was just looking for a blanket.'

'Linen cupboard, dear,' Audrey called after me. 'Down the hall, over the half landing, right at the side table with the serpents' heads, second door on your left.'

It was less of a closet, more of a room. Heat blasted from the boiler in its corner. I can truthfully say I'd never felt so emotional about an inanimate object my entire life. I wrapped my arms around it, pressing my face to its hot dry surface.

'Hey there.'

I jumped. Rory's angular body was curled up between the slatted shelves, his head resting on a stack of paisley quilts.

'Rory! Jesus, you scared me.'

He swung his legs to the floor, dropping the book off his lap.

I retrieved it, mumbling something about hypothermia, lack of blankets, broken radiators and frozen fingertips.

'You're right,' he interrupted gently. 'It's not exactly Claridges.' He removed the book from my hand.

'I'm sorry.'

'Don't be, your fee will go towards repairing the central heating.'

'Rory, we should—'

'If you're thinking this is a good time to talk, it's—' he cut himself off. 'Look, you came for a blanket didn't you?'

He sifted through the shelves, forcing me back against the door. It swung open and a gust of icy air blew in. I leapt back inside, collided with Rory. Steadying me with one hand he reached slowly behind me for the handle.

'Best to keep it shut,' he said, pulling the door firmly to. 'Purely for health reasons of course.'

We stood close, swaying, not quite touching, until I felt myself start to burn round the edges.

He dropped my coat to the floor, ran his hands up under my T-shirt and in one swift movement hitched me onto the slatted shelf behind, hand resting lightly at the base of my spine as he unbuckled his jeans.

He pinned my wrists against the shelf, moving slowly inside me. My skin was slicked with sweat, the muscles on his shoulders shone under the light. I closed my eyes, but when I opened them again I caught him looking at me, and what I saw in his face wasn't what I expected. The exposure felt painful, confusing, so I closed my eyes again. I didn't want everything laid out so bare and raw in front of me, because what I'd seen in his face was anger.

'Look at the state of you.' Rory gently rubbed at the lines indented onto my skin by the shelf.

We were lying in a damp heap of tangled limbs and clothes on the floor. The ceiling blurred into focus above me. The cold, the heat, the sex all had a soporific effect. My whole body felt like it was slow cooking to sleep – just a small raw centre of emotion left.

'Look, I'm sorry,' he said curtly.

I felt my eyes slide away, but he held my face in his hands.

'No, I mean it. I'm sorry.'

'You looked straight through me. You scared me.'
'Maybe, but you've been scaring me for weeks.'
'That sounds bad.'
'It's bad in the only way that bad can be good,' he said.

Back in my bedroom I traced a finger over his eyelids.
'Don't sleep.'

'Uh oh,' he groaned. 'High maintenance. I knew it.'

'No, no, you're wrong,' I protested. 'I maintain myself.
I'm zero maintenance.'

'Of course you are, you're Maggie the Cat.'

I didn't recognize the reference.

'*Cat on a Hot Tin Roof*. Tennessee Williams. You're
Kipling's cat who walks by herself,' he said softly, 'and all
places are alike to you . . .'

I woke sometime near dawn. The night had washed out to
lavender and the air was chilled and still. Morning was
biding its time, waiting for the sun to come along and warm
it. Rory was wrapped around me, our bodies interlocked.

I lay awake, just wondering. When you tilt the axis of
your world even a fraction off centre, the degree of fallout
can be colossal. It's fatuous to make comparisons but I had
become so used to sex with the emotional contraception of
barriers and checkpoints, I'd become so good at sanding
down my expectations to match Jay's. Don't take much,
don't feel much, don't depend at all. Here with Rory there
was no future to consider, no rules to abide by, so the
strength of my feelings took me by surprise. I stayed awake

a long time, content, limp, slothful, dazed, I turned these unfamiliar words over in my head, all antonyms for my usual edgy self. It was as though somebody had pulled out a stopper and all the jumping beans had drained from my body. I felt like hurling them in the air and shouting hallelujah.

'The first earl had a penchant for little boys, the second liked nothing better than sleeping in all his wife's jewels . . .' Rory was propped up on one elbow, 'The third was scorned by his love, a pickled-onion heiress, and so became passionate about the plight of seagulls, and the fourth, my grandfather's grandfather, was sexually obsessed with the queen.'

'Oh please,' I laughed.

'Truly. He was endlessly writing her filthy letters, "I must report that I dream of you, Sire, naked and dripping as you emerge from your bubble-bath," . . . although in his younger days he liked to object at weddings.'

'Now I know you're making all this up.'

'Absolutely not. You know that moment when the vicar says, "Speak now or forever hold your peace?" For a time he was the scourge of every young bride in the north of England.'

'And you?'

'And me what?'

'What's your passion? Bevan?'

'God,' he said heavily, 'not really. Buildings, yes, graveyards, monuments, sites, stones, bones, anything old, crumbling, decaying.'

'But still, you gave up something you loved doing to keep *this* going?' I looked around the room. 'Why? For your father?'

'Don't sound so horrified. Have you never given up anything for somebody you loved?'

Jay had been married once. His wife was beautiful but highly strung. She loathed his job. For five years Jay followed her map, redrew his. It had broken up their marriage. Jay believed that if you loved someone, you shouldn't force them to give up something they were passionate about. Never make a career choice for someone else's reasons.

'Why would you ever put anyone in that position?' I said, but the words had sounded a lot more convincing coming out of Jay's mouth.

'Because love is selfish, Maggie. Love is *Top of the Pops*, number one emotion on the selfish chart. Love is a messy and inherently sad emotion, which is why so many people live in mortal terror of it.'

'So the one thing you're dedicating your life to preserving is the one thing that will prevent you from being happy?'

'Maybe, I don't know. All I do know is that I haven't done the thing yet that I'm most proud of.'

'Which is?'

'Who knows. Could be anything. Maybe I'll write a great song or save a kitten from drowning, maybe I will just preserve Bevan for my father . . . Look, I'm not sure I could possibly make you understand.'

'I sort of understand, I do. I think it's kind of noble . . . nutty but noble.'

'Which is, ironically, also our family motto.'

'It's not so bad — where I come from you'd be a real catch.'

'Where you come from any male who's single, can sit up and take nourishment is a real catch.'

I laughed. 'Well I hope at least you get an enormously important title as compensation.'

'Oh sure. Right up there between Master of the Horse and Companion to the Bath.'

'Oh boy.' I sighed.

'Oh boy, *sir*, to you.' He tipped me onto my stomach and slid down the bed.

Later he said, 'Surely it's unethical to sleep with your victims?'

'I consider it a perk. Anyway you're not my victim.'

'I am closely related to him.'

'I could always sleep with your father if that makes you more comfortable.' Classical music was coming from somewhere. I strained to hear it better.

'Don't be disgusting.' He pushed his leg between mine. Now, from somewhere else in the house, a telephone had begun ringing. 'Oh Christ,' Rory said resignedly. 'It's bound to be for me, Nanny will answer it, she'll come in, see I have an erection and there'll be hell to pay.'

I burst out laughing. 'The thirty-eight-year-old baby.'

'I don't think you'll find many babies with one of these,' he muttered, lowering himself on top of me.

'Does Nanny think you're not old enough to have sex?'

'Nanny believes you are *never* old enough to have sex.'

'Well she's not going to know you're in here.'

'Nanny knows everything,' he said darkly.

I assumed he was joking but as he said it, there was a sharp rapping on the door. I looked at him disbelievingly. He yanked the covers over our heads as I dissolved into helpless giggles. 'Quiet, wench,' he hissed. The door opened and small neat footsteps crossed the room. Rory clamped his hand firmly over my mouth.

'Your cousin Benjamin called with your office messages, Robert,' Nanny said. Rory inched his fingers up my thigh. I stifled a gasp. 'I've written them on a piece of paper,' Nanny continued, her tone of voice implying that young Benjamin had left a small dog poop in her hand rather than a note.

Rory's shoulders were heaving with silent laughter.

'Rory!' Nanny said warningly.

Rory stuck his hand out from under the bedclothes. 'Thank you, Nanny,' he said meekly.

daniel

Rory lies in bed, catatonic with goodwill towards the world. Next door Maggie is running a bath. The immersion heater flares on and off as she vainly adjusts the hot and cold taps. He's about to warn her about the scalding temperature of the water when there's a squeal. He nearly laughs out loud until he remembers it was at this point Leona started packing, remembers how he saw escape reflected in her eyes long before the train drew into Skimpton station.

'You know something,' Maggie shouts from the bathroom, 'I guess England's not so bad after all. I mean, two inches of hot water is really quite a luxury when you think about it.'

Rory stretches out contentedly. Benj's note scratches against his foot. He attempts to retrieve it with his toes, but it drops to the floor. He feels around under the bed but his fingertips brush against something else. Whatever it is, it doesn't have the putrid consistency of your average Neolithic Bevan lost property item so instead of recoiling in horror he closes his hand around it and finds himself pulling Wolf's camera onto the bed.

'So Nanny never married?' Maggie shouts from the bath-room. 'No steamy affairs with the local priest?'

'She was in love with a soldier. He died in the war.'

'Poor thing.'

Rory fiddles absent-mindedly with the controls. He powers on the camera and presses the rewind button. 'What did you say you got on film yesterday?' he asks and at the same time wishes he hadn't. In the bathroom, Maggie sits bolt upright. 'I told you,' she says warily, 'just background stuff.'

But Rory has already pressed the play button. There is no sound but the images are more than enough. As he fast-forwards and backtracks through footage from the last twenty-four hours, the viewfinder presents him with the all-too-familiar scenes from the Bevan comedy drama.

'Not even my grandfather?' he asks, watching Grandpa's puppet show with the Chinese figurines. Anger starts boiling in his head as he watches Alistair showing off the breathalyser he's preparing to wrap, Audrey sucking whisky through her curly-wurly straw and then finally there is Grandpa again, turning the knife over in his hand. As Rory stares, realization building, the camera zooms in close until there is nothing in the frame but Grandpa's thumb smoothing over and over the swastika embossed on the knife's handle and Rory's anger turns to cold hard fury.

'Rory.' Maggie stands in the doorway, she's thrown on her clothes without drying herself and water seeps through the thin cotton of her T-shirt like blood from an exit wound.

maggie

'God damn you to hell, Maggie,' he said softly. 'God damm
you.' I walked over and took the camera out of his hands.

I gave a sort of helpless shrug, but he was having none
of it. He grabbed me at the elbow and propelled me towards
the door. I struggled, but his grip only tightened. The music
we'd heard earlier became louder as Rory marched me
along the corridor, down the stairs and into his grandfather's
bedroom. The old man was sitting in his armchair, eyes
shut despite the ear-splitting volume of the music. On his
lap a photograph book was open and resting on top of a
tartan blanket.

'Rory, please don't do this.'

'What do you see here, Maggie?' he demanded.

'It's not—'

'What little pigeonhole best fits your prejudice today.
Lunatic? Worthless peer? Nazi collaborator?'

'It's not like that—'

'You're damn right it's not like that. How dare you think
by filming you have *any* understanding?'

'Is that you, Alistair?' the old man yelled above the din.

I rubbed my forearm where Rory had held it. He turned

down the volume on the stereo and kissed his grandfather on the forehead. The Marquess's eyes flickered open. He felt for the book on his lap. Rory bent down to pick up a photograph that had fallen to the floor.

'Not lunch yet, is it?' the Marquess asked.

Rory shook his head. He tried to manoeuvre the photograph back into its mount but the Marquess took it from his hand.

'Know who this is, Rory?' The photo showed a young man in uniform standing erect and smiling.

'Cavendish,' Rory said gently.

'Yes,' the Marquess traced his finger across the browning image, 'Cavendish.'

He closed his eyes. I thought he had drifted off, but he started speaking. 'Knew he'd been shot because there was a hole in his head. There were brains coming out of the hole so I pushed them back inside.' He looked at Rory, 'Somehow I thought that might help, do you see?'

'I know,' Rory put his hand on the old man's shoulder.

'Carried him for ten miles,' the Marquess said, 'I suppose I knew he was dead, but I had to do something.' He touched the photograph dreamily, 'He was my friend, do you see?' He felt down the side of his chair and pulled out a pair of headphones.

Rory turned on me, 'As soon as war was declared, he fought, he was the first to realize he'd made a terrible mistake . . .'

'Rory. I was following a legitimate story,' I pleaded.

'*Legitimate*,' he practically spat the word. 'Christ, do you people realize or even care about the damage you do in your self-righteous pursuit of the truth? It would be hugely upsetting to my family, they would be hounded by the press. What *is* the point, just before he dies?'

'Rory you have to believe me, when I came here, I had no idea it was your family.'

He slammed his fist into the side of the chair. 'Don't you get it — it's always somebody's family. God, what an idiot I've been. I, of all people should have known better. In fact, what am I talking about?' He looked at me scathingly. 'I did know better.'

'Maybe you did,' I said, 'but I didn't, I really didn't, things have changed now—'

'Now what?' he said bitterly. 'Now that you screwed *every* member of the family?'

'Rory, that's not fair.'

'Oh don't tell me, last night you had an epiphany. How sweet.'

'You're not listening,' I said angrily.

He put his hands up, 'Spare me the bullshit, Maggie.'

'It isn't bullshit. It's the truth.'

'Well if that's the case, you should have no problem giving me the film.'

I stared at him. 'I can't,' I stammered.

'Won't you mean,' he stated flatly. 'Besides, you can't use it without the release forms.'

'Rory you can trust me.' I didn't know what else to say. I needed time and the tapes were my only hostages. 'You *have* to trust me.'

'Trust you!' he said and the scorn in his voice nearly made me walk. I wanted to get as far away from him, as far away from myself as possible. Rory made a visible effort to keep a hold on his temper.

'I won't sign the release forms, Maggie.'

And I thought, *Just when you think it can't get any worse.*

He was waiting for me to say something, to be the person he now knew I was. I badly wanted to disappoint him but it seems I couldn't.

'Your father signed them yesterday.'

He looked at me then like I was someone he didn't want to know any more.

'At the time my grandfather was acting out of a fierce sense of family, tradition and loyalty, three things you know absolutely nothing about, Maggie.'

It was like my brain had its eyes wide open but refused to let my mouth speak.

'I see,' he said. 'Well in that case, I suggest you take the money and run. Go on, get out.'

'I'm already gone.' I turned. Got to the door. Saw how easy it would be to walk straight through it. Turned back.

'Rory, I don't want to run, I always run.'

'Why are you telling me this?'

'I'm telling you this because, because if you were to ask me to stay . . .' My voice was so low I could barely hear it, '. . . I would stay.'

He looked at me steadily.

'Turn the bloody music thingy up would you, Robert,' Grandpa shouted from his chair. His headphones were still clamped over his ears.

'Maggie,' Rory said helplessly, 'every time I think I know who you are, you turn out to be someone else.'

'Please try to understand.'

He shook his head sadly but there was no softness left in his eyes. 'I really don't think that's possible,' he said.

daniel

If it were me, still lobbing pebbles into that waste-paper basket two hours after she'd left, I'd get off my arse and go after her, because what does it really matter? Why is it we're so good at allowing every petty, mean-spirited emotion to stand in the way of the bigger picture? Paper covers stone, stone blunts scissors, scissors cut paper. Round and round it goes. If I've learnt anything, it's that life really *is* too short — it wasn't just a tired old cliché after all. Too many times the things we get side-tracked by are no more than false trails. In the final reckoning the only emotions that truly hold water are the incontestable ones. So I will Rory to snap out of it, because let me tell you something: you can live in a broken home, you can play with a broken toy, but you cannot love with a broken heart.

And amazingly enough he does snap out of it. He stuffs his clothes into a suitcase, jumps in his car and I think, *Good God, this has a chance of ending well after all.*

Rory drives like Toad of Toad Hall, all horns and swerves and brakes. As he pulls up opposite the Cadogan Hotel, it occurs to him that in the last couple of hours he cannot remember turning right, left, on or off the motorway and wonders how the hell he got here. Now he wonders what the hell to do next. The narrow road he must cross to walk through that hotel entrance widens into a six-lane motorway. Maggie's film has held a mirror up to his own attitude and to confront her means he must first confront himself. He doesn't recognize any of this yet but I hope he will before too long, in the meantime he's stymied by indecision.

He knows one thing for sure, that when the moment comes he will not let her go.

Then the moment is upon him. And anybody who says God does not have perfect timing should watch this space because Maggie is walking down the steps of the hotel. She's pale and her hair is caught up in a rough pony-tail. She tips the doorman, who touches his cap and smiles. A porter wheels a trolley full of luggage down the ramp. Rory's out of the Rover, hand raised, mouth open to shout, when a tall man with a shock of grey hair lollops down the steps and catches up with her. He squeezes her arm, says something, teasing maybe, certainly flirtatious, because when she replies he laughs and kisses her – an easy kiss of possession.

Oh Rory. I see the look on his face, watch his arm drop, watch him shrink, climb back into himself, then into his car and drive off without a backward glance. And my heart aches for him.

Why was he born so beautiful?
Why was he born at all?
He's no bloody use to anyone,
He's no bloody use at all.

— Anonymous

maggie

Jay was tired. He fell asleep as soon as the plane took off and didn't wake until the pilot announced we were flying over New Jersey. I sat in the airless vacuum of my seat and stared blindly at the miniature screen in front of me.

Jay stirred only once. I looked at him. He was breathing with his mouth open and the deep worry crease between his eyes was even deeper than ever.

In the cab home I feigned a stomach bug.

'How about some treatment at the renowned Alder clinic?' Jay asked. I shook my head and he didn't push it. 'I've got to go to Washington for a few days,' he said, 'but when I get back let's try to grab a little time together.'

I nodded. 'That would be nice.'

When we got to the Bowery, Jay carried my suitcase into my building. I looked around at the industrial grey paint and graffiti. I was home. The last few weeks seemed surreal, only twenty-four hours earlier I had been in the middle of the English countryside telling a man I barely knew that I would stay if he wanted me to. What was surreal was that I had meant it.

'Talk to me, Maggie,' Jay said. 'Ever since Paris you've had this expression on your face.'

'Like what?'

'Like I've been auditioning for a part that you don't know how to tell me I haven't got.'

'Jay, can I ask you a question?'

'Is it multiple choice?'

'Why did you start seeing me, do you think?'

'Let me see now,' he started ticking off an imaginary checklist on his fingers.

'Jay, I'm serious.'

He pressed his knuckles into the crease of his frown. 'So we're going to have this discussion now.'

'I think so.'

He paid off the cab and we sat on the steps of the building. He took my hand and began separating the fingers.

'We believe in the same things, we want the same things from each other, you're independent, entirely low mainten-ance—'

'You make me sound like a package.'

'Didn't you just ask me to gift-wrap you?' he said lightly.

'The thing is, I don't think I can be a package any more.'

'Not even if you can have satin ribbon and hand-turned edges?'

He was hedging and we both knew it. These were the discussions we had agreed not to have. Our anti-nuptial contract.

'Was it because you didn't need me to need anything from you?'

He took off his glasses. 'It was because I didn't want to

take more from you than you could give,' he corrected gently.

'How does anyone know how much they're capable of giving?'

'Where is this coming from, Maggie, what's making you unhappy?'

'What if I wanted to give you *everything*.'

'You do give me everything . . . everything I want.'

'What if I wanted to give you more.'

'What "more" are we talking about here?' Jay asked.

'I don't know. A child?' As soon as the words were out of my mouth, I was almost paralysed with shock. Couldn't believe I'd said it. Didn't even know where it had come from.

He was quiet. 'You couldn't give me a child,' he said eventually.

'Am I that selfish?' My laugh sounded false.

He didn't reply.

'Because you don't want one?'

'Because I can't have one.'

I automatically thought, low-sperm count, weak swimmers. I thought adoption, baby from China, love in a Petri dish . . .

'I *won't* have children, Maggie. I can't.'

There was something in the way he said it which made my whole body go still.

'You never told me.'

He rubbed his eyes wearily. 'It's not the sort of thing you go round telling someone on a first date. "Hey, shall we go to dinner, and by the way I've had a vasectomy." '

'It's not funny.'

'No', he said. 'It's not funny. Why is this an issue all of a sudden? You told me you didn't want children.'

'I don't.' Jay had asked me once. I'd said no and he'd said good. I hadn't realized the question had an invisible 'ever' attached to it.

'What is this really about then, Maggie?'

I couldn't explain, wasn't sure myself. Maybe subconsciously I'd just used the one thing against Jay I knew he couldn't come back from. You can't extort commitment out of somebody, it's not a tangible thing to be handed over or promised.

'Look at me, Maggie.' He spread out his hands and they trembled a little. 'This isn't from drink, or because I'm an old fuck, there are things I have seen that will never leave me. Try to understand. What have I got to offer a child? What have I got to offer anyone?'

I didn't answer. In my head, the moment just crystallized into how differently we thought about the future.

'You're idealistic now, you'll be less idealistic in twenty years. Look around you, Maggie. The world isn't a particularly nice place. Love doesn't conquer everything.'

'I know, you told me, love doesn't make the world go round, Pepsi does.'

'Hate,' he said, 'rage, grief, greed, war – those are the things that make the world go around. Love just makes it all a little less painful.' His voice was harsh and I felt numb.

'Can we Scotch tape this?'

'I don't know.' I was crying.

'Don't give up on me, Maggie,' he breathed into my

damp hair and kissed me. 'Please, please don't give up on me,' but all I understood was that he'd given up on himself.

The oldest possession in my loft is an egg. When the stainless-steel boys delivered my fridge, the egg was already in it. For a long time it was the only thing in my fridge — save a few cans of SpaghettiOs for which I have a weakness (cold and preferably out of the tin). After a while there seemed no way of ridding myself of the egg without the risk of it breaking and the stench would have been apocalyptic. So for safety, I drew a face on it with a red felt marker and left it there. That was three years ago.

Staring into the fridge, standing on the bare boards of my kitchen I was struck by the spartan decor of my loft. It didn't look minimalist, it looked studenty, but after I had slept for a couple of hours at least it felt more like home. I opened one of the spaghetti cans and organized the videos from England in sequence in front of the television.

On *Newsline* you get the first edit. Initially you present the material as you want. If that doesn't wash, it becomes a question of give and take — more specifically they take and you try as hard as possible not to give. If you mess up totally Alan can and will put someone else onto it but this doesn't happen all that often. One of the great things about Alan is that once he hands out an assignment, he generally doesn't interfere in the creative process until you screen the finished product for him. Alan likes to be sure of coming to the material fresh and remaining objective enough to gauge whether the final story is solid in terms of content,

whether it makes for compelling viewing, and more cru-
cially whether it is a *'Newsline'* story.

Usually I get as much footage as I can then try to find
a route through the material after. I know that the end
result is a puzzle to which you have the key as long as you
are prepared to worry and jiggle the pieces enough. Working
for *Newsline* I learnt to edit in my head as I went along, but
in order to do this you need to keep a clear view of what
you want to say. And that was my problem. I no longer
knew what that was.

When you grow up with absolutes, there are good guys
and bad guys. There is the pure and simple truth and a
self-righteousness that goes with believing you're with the
angels on every issue, but let's face it, the truth is rarely
pure and it's never simple.

I rewound the tapes over and over again, looking at
the faces of the Bancrofts, Lady Roxmere, heard my own
indictments, *cold, repressed, snobbish*, remembered Rory's
retorts, *shy, scared, lonely.*

I paused on Montague. *'Some say inheriting a large house
is a cruel burden, but I say if you've got a family that's been in
possession of a house for a very long time you want to keep the
bloody thing going. I mean that's what primogeniture is all about.
It is the duty of the eldest son to keep the place intact.'*

'Bevan was my father's private war,' Rory had told me.
'The elms were his casualties. He's spent the last twenty-
five years planting trees. My father has earned the right to
his land.'

I freeze-framed on the Earl of Bevan himself. *'We are
dinosaurs. We have clung to tradition even though it has driven
us to bankruptcy but of course the knowledge that we are passing*

on a huge burden to our eldest child is less attractive than it used to be.'

My confusion meant that I had no idea where to start or end. The set of moral values with which I used to define right and wrong, fairness and decency, had been skewed. I had lost my ground rules, and with no ground rules I didn't feel safe enough to tell a story, and with no story, there would be no film. I finally pinpointed why this was such a scary admission – the implication being that if I'd got this project so wrong I had to question so many other judgements. I wondered about past programs I'd made, how passionately I'd felt about issues, how fairly I'd manoeuvred edits, manipulated questioning or back-to-backed two non-consecutive incidents to make a point. The film-maker can be as guilty of planting evidence as any bent cop. It's no fun shining a torch in your own eyes and, as I watched the tapes, I wondered how many people had been burnt by the flare of my unswerving certainty.

Dawn broke over the city, two, three, four times. Sun glinted off the fire escapes outside the window. The sewing machines whirred beneath my floor. When I ventured out to the deli to pick up some food I noticed that someone had painted a row of watermelons on the inside of the elevator. Everything was as it used to be yet nothing felt the same and time continued to run on and out.

On the fifth day, I made the mistake of picking up the phone without screening the call. Alan was on the other end. I bargained with him for a little more time. He knew, because I'd told him, exactly what story I had on tape and he thought what I was going to produce would be worth it, but I heard the warning in his voice. Not long after my stay of execution was granted I got into a crying fit and couldn't get out. When it was over, I thought that by rights, I should feel purged. Rory was a bug I caught in England, a particularly virulent one. Now I was rid of it. But it wasn't like that at all. Instead, never had I felt such a failure, both as a journalist and as a human being.

daniel

Rory's in a blue funk and I reckon if ever there was a time for a Dionysiac moment this would be it. If it were me, *exampli gratia*, I would be wallowing like a hippo in a river of alcohol by now but, as we've seen, Rory's made of sterner stuff. He does not succumb. Instead, curiously, he takes to cushion scattering with a vengeance, stripping bare the mews house in a burst of feverish energy. Even the moose head comes off the wall and gets chucked into the back of the car along with the rhino bin and Bevan's other artefacts of the past. When Rory delivers them home he gives no explanation for their return and Alistair does not ask for one.

Upstairs in the nursery he dumps everything on the floor. He has every intention of leaving them there without a backward glance, but he does give a backward glance and some bird charts stacked in the corner catch his eye. There are three of them, old and warped. Seabirds, Birds of Prey, Marsh Dwellers. When we were children we were given two pounds a chart to memorize them. Rory moves aside a stack of cardboard boxes and squats down.

'Greater Black-backed Gull, Gannet, Kittiwake,' he

closes his eyes and whispers. 'Arctic Skewer, Herring Gull, Little Tern.' He opens his eyes and sits down on the floor staring numbly at the posters. 'Latin name for wren?' he can hear Alistair asking. 'Troglodytes, Troglodytes, Troglodytes,' he hears my reply. You see, I want to point out to him – all the snippets of other people you absorb as a child will, one day, absorb you.

After a while Rory notices that one of the cardboard boxes he has moved is full of papers from my room. Hesitantly he sticks his hand into this lucky dip of memories. Out come letters, bills, photographs; Rory and me, mouths smeared with orange ice lollies. Another; I am dressed as Robin Hood and he, Maid Marion. A picture of my grandmother, holding the newborn Rory in his christening robe. Her bosom is so massive, he looks like a tiny brooch pinned to it. He unfurls a school photograph. There I am at the back, shockingly good looking even in the midst of spotty puberty, and there is Rory, one row, one year and, as yet, two undropped bollocks away. He crams the photos in his pocket and keeps digging.

I know he will find the map sooner or later and he does. He recognizes my handwriting and looks at the big envelope, undecided, before opening it.

There's a field at Bevan, to the far left of the farm road, which climbs a hill directly west then drops rather anticlimatically away leaving nothing more dramatic than a horizon of stunted fencing. I have always had a notion to plant a wood there quite from scratch and I thought it would be rather romantic to do this at the beginning of a new century. Everyone has their own idea of a legacy whether it's a book, a film or a child – it's not that I'm competitive but trees outlast most of them. 'The thing I am most proud of.' This was a silly game Rory and I used to play. Well, the Millennium wood was to have been it for me.

Most people when they design a wood draw it rectangular, but I wanted this one to be more interesting so I drew a shape at random. Bordered naturally on three sides by the paddock, the old orchard and the fox cover, I gave the fourth edge a curvaceous sweep which lent it a whimsical look. The idea was to create a wide ride running through the wood with statues and tree houses along the way, before eventually opening out into two clearings in the centre. The clearings would be planted with all sorts of odd and rare trees, 'Liquid Amber' and pear trees for example, both more usually associated with gardens than woods, then evergreens planted behind for a dark backdrop. I thought of putting a bench in the middle where one day mine or Rory's teenage boys might sit and catch a smoke. Rory turns the map over to cross-reference the tree plan on the other side. I'd chosen things that turn lovely colours; there was a red cedar or two, some *sorbus* for their berries – and a lot of ash which goes umber in the summer, a dried reddish haze in winter and does well in boggy ground like we have at Bevan.

My plan had been to enlist everyone's help; get the children up from the village, teach them about plants, give everyone who ever worked at Bevan a tree with their name on it . . . but look, I'm getting carried away by my own genius. Rory's not studying the map any more – he's staring at the floor, more and more anguished, his face all screwed up, then before you know it he's started crying and I see that the poor bastard is in a lot more trouble than I thought.

maggie

I opened the fridge and stood hopefully in front of it. All that was left was a can of clam chowder, a bottle of red wine with a corkscrew embedded in its top and, of course, the egg. I must throw out the egg. The egg was symbolic – a sign of something rotten in my life. As I heated the chowder I wondered how to achieve its eviction without breaking it. An egg carton seemed logical, but that meant buying more eggs and then what to do with the rest? They'd sit in the freezer for ever and my problem would have multiplied. Eventually I decided to wrap it in an old pair of briefs and put it – well not in the trash can, from where it could be traced back to me by angry neighbours, but somewhere safe, where it would be dealt with swiftly, where there were other competing putrid smells – a hospital for example. So that was the plan. Swaddle the egg in warm clothes and leave it at the hospital. No doubt when it was found dozens of depressed post-partum chickens all over New York would be questioned. *Please come forward, you obviously need help, you will receive sympathetic treatment.*

I'd still not edited my footage, hadn't even left the house for the last two days. Now I was definitely losing it. I took a walk. Though night, the cold bite was fading from the air. Winter would soon turn to spring. I headed west along Rivington Street, aware as I always am on returning home how different this place is to any other. People are loud and sharp, the air buzzes with tangible energy. It was after midnight but the streets were packed and lights were blazing. Even the traffic was snarled. When I hit Broadway I saw why. A car had crashed up on the pavement; its door jammed open against the kerb. It had knocked down a trash can and the pavement was decorated with the waste of city. There were the usual disco lights of cops and ambulances and the street was being cordoned off. I detoured into the all-night record store which was deserted save for a few music addicts patrolling the second-hand aisles. In world music I picked out some Cuban tapes I'd been meaning to get for ever. Heading downstairs to checkout, a man was pushing out of the classical section, a bunch of CDs in his arms. Music boomed through the glass door as I held it back for him and I stiffened. I know nothing about classical music, but this I recognized.

Beethoven's ninth symphony. The music Rory's grandfather had been playing at such ear-splitting volume that morning at Bevan. I bought it, feeling a little foolish. At home I slipped it out of the case and fast-forwarded to the passage I was looking for. It was a short piece of music, but very powerful. I don't know what it's supposed to be written about, but to me it seemed to be about courage, about death, pain and glory. I turned up the volume, played it loud. Opened all the windows and played it louder still until it had chased all the other stuff out of my head. Then everything was clear.

In the morning, I rang a contact of mine and arranged to rent a small editing suite with a technician thrown in. I headed downtown, the film packed tightly into two cardboard boxes. For the first time in a week I felt completely calm – OK so maybe there is no truth, but you've got to believe in something.

daniel

Benj's father dies. Suddenly and unexpectedly. He gets no chance to make his old man amends, no time for the usual last-minute pact with the living before he faces the dead – and a punishment, I believe, richly deserved as was his tumour in the stomach while we're on the subject of karma. One minute he has indigestion, the next they're slicing him open and there it is – the big C – nurtured on his internal river of bile, sprouting like watercress in and around every organ in his body. He doesn't survive the operation.

The effect on Benj is predictable. He disintegrates, regresses, ages, weeps, jumps a generation, celebrates and mourns all with varying degrees of confusion and guilt. At the funeral he stands by his mother in the church wearing a suit which looks like it has been made for a much fatter man. Benj maintains his composure for most of the service then walks unsteadily to the lectern brushing Rory's fingertips as he passes. As he stands up there, gazing out over a sea of expectantly mournful faces, I wonder whether he will go off at the deep end, take this opportunity for an exquisitely timed revenge – out his father for the emotional and physical abusing shit of a man that he was. Instead Benj delivers an address so touching, so wry, so fucking true, that it reduces most of the family to tears.

After the service Benj gets drunk and stays that way for a month. Rory makes no attempt to stop him, simply monitoring him closely, occasionally feeding him and when not delegating the job of babysitting him to Alison, sleeping on the sofa himself in Benj's sitting room. This is all quite good for Rory, leaving him little time for his other favoured pastime – obsessing about Maggie. When he does obsess about her, he still fails to appreciate the simplicity of the situation which is no more complicated than this: Maggie is attached to nothing and nobody while he is attached to everybody and everything. Instead he executes a competent job of convincing himself he's motivated by nothing more than pique. She had got under his skin in the same way that another driver stealing a parking place from under your nose leaves you with a seething murderous resentment wholly out of proportion with the crime. He is convinced these feelings will, given time, pass – but is not particularly surprised when they don't.

When Benj comes out of his stupor he makes an announcement. For the first time ever he feels in control. He feels all powerful and will take steps to change his life. He tells Rory that he knows he can achieve anything. Rory is mildly impressed until Benj adds that these accomplishments include the scaling of rooftops and soaring through the air unassisted by wires. 'Things are about to change,' Benj says, the frightening gleam of the converted in his eyes. 'We're in the dawning of a new era. Someone will have to lead the people and show them the light, that person could be me and I could be well paid for it.' At which juncture Rory checks him into the Priory clinic and goes back to work.

maggie

I have always had a secret passion for the Central Park zoo. The noise, the smell, the meeting of furtive lovers and chatterings of school kids exchanging baseball cards. When I was in third grade, my school organized a day trip there but my mom wouldn't sign the permission form. The rest of the class went and I was sent home early. Of course I knew my mother was right to disapprove of caged animals, but when other teenagers were smoking their first illicit cigarettes, I was rebelliously throwing bread at penguins.

Wolf was waiting for me at the entrance, leaning his considerable bulk against the railings. I bumped him.

'Hey.'

'Hey yourself.'

We wandered through the park. It was April now and during the time I'd spent editing, the cherry trees had blossomed. The Bowery, Little Italy, Chinatown were all ablaze with marigolds and pansies. I've noticed something amazing about New Yorkers. They'll steal the hub caps off your car and the spokes out of your bicycle wheels but they have the sensibility to leave the public flowers alone. They

want the city to smell and look nice while they pick over
its bones.

In the park, people were draped over benches, laid out
on the grass or leaning against trees reading books, pitching
into mitts and generally enjoying the first real warm sun
of the year. A frisbee came spinning our way. Wolf sent it
back, cutting low through the air.

'You know who you reminded me of when I first met
you?' I told him.

'Who?'

'Chief.'

'Chief?'

'The Indian in *One Flew Over the Cuckoo's Nest.*'

'Deaf and dumb?'

'I may have found it disconcerting how little you talked.'

'Did it ever occur to you I couldn't get a word in?'

I grinned. I was afraid to ask him so I didn't.

You hear of those screenings for Hollywood turkeys when
executives sit down for the first time and take a look at
where their dollars have gone. Apparently the air takes on
a certain quality as if the fumes of so much disappointment
actually pollute it. They say there's a smell. Well, of course
it wasn't quite like that after I showed the edit, but up on
the tenth floor of the *Newsline* building, there was definitely
a vibe – and it was not a good one. I guess I shouldn't have
been surprised. The CBS suits who had become a fixture
at *Newsline* wouldn't know a good story from a shoe shine.

Alan eased himself up and out of his chair, 'What happened to this hot story you were chasing?'

'It didn't pan out.'

'Aha.'

'It was a hot story, but the trail was cold.'

'I see. So this is the piece you're expecting us to run?'

I met his look squarely. 'This is the piece I'm handing in.'

Alan cleared his throat. 'This might be fine work, Maggie, but it's not the fine work I was expecting, in fact let's be clear, it's twice not what I was expecting. What happened to your original brief?'

'Yes.' One of the CBS execs had joined us. 'Where are the beautiful gardens, the pomp and circumstance, what about all that royal stuff we suggested you include?'

You could see why he was disappointed. I mean there was no sex, no celebrity, no ground-breaking scandal – but it was a good story, it was a touching story and I told him I thought people would want to watch it.

'But they're all so . . . well . . . so shabby these people,' the executive looked at the blank screen. 'The female demographic wants glamour, it wants something to aspire to. No one's interested in downtrodden.'

I reminded him that Lesley Stahl from *60 Minutes* once did a story about divorced wives living out of their cars in Beverly Hills. She shot it, loved it, but *60 Minutes* refused to air it. They said no one would be interested. She kicked and screamed and eventually got it shown. It had huge ratings. I told Alan I thought he should air my piece exactly the way it was and I kicked and screamed but it didn't do a lot of good. Alan listened throughout, but I could tell the argument was academic. It didn't matter whether he agreed with me or not. He wasn't running the show any longer.

'The material should go to someone else,' the executive said when I'd finished.

I looked down. My sneakers were covered in subway dust. I had a flash of Rory in his greying tennis shoes throwing the ball up in a perfect arc. If I handed the footage over to *Newsline*, ironically it would be edited according to my own original brief of snobbery, debauchery, lunacy. If I refused to hand it over, I would probably be fired. Alan put his hand on my shoulder, 'Everything you've got, Maggie, give it to either Ed or Neil today and we'll see what they can do with it.'

I nodded and Alan looked relieved.

I got out of there quick. Alan eviscerated by bean counters was something I never thought I'd see.

'Hungry?' Wolf asked.

'I could eat a horse.'

'Settle for a dog?'

At the stand he waved away my dollars. I didn't mean to look surprised. It's not that Wolf was ungenerous with money but small acts of chivalry had never been his style. He lathered on mustard and sauerkraut and handed me the frankfurter.

'A) you've quit,' he said, 'and will therefore soon be on welfare and B),' he soused his own bun in mustard, 'well . . . talk round the building is you damaged the tapes on purpose.'

'Well let's just say personally, professionally, technically, I've truly messed everything up.'

'Aha . . .there you go again,' Wolf said. 'As George Bush said to Geraldine Ferraro, "Snatching defeat out of the jaws of victory".' He grinned at me, a blob of mustard on the side of his mouth.

'Oh Chief . . . so you *did* like it?'

'Yeah well. I thought it had real heart.'

I didn't trust myself to speak. We sat down on a bench.

'Talk is they could sue you,' he said.

'They could.'

'But you don't think they will?'

'Naa, I don't think they'll bother.'

'So what are you going to do?'

I gave an elaborate sigh. 'I don't know. Nothing for a bit, see how that feels. Then look for another job, maybe think about doing that documentary we always talked about.'

'I meant about your love life,' he said.

When Jay returned from Washington he took me out to an Indian restaurant near his apartment. 'You're wearing a black hat,' he said. He touched the spark of electricity on my hair as I pulled off my beanie. 'Any chance there's a white one in your bag?'

We sat down awkwardly. One of Jay's president stories was when Reagan was woken in the middle of the night to make decisions on some knotty foreign problem he would ask, 'Do they have white hats or black hats?' before making a decision, turning over and going back to sleep. 'Just think,' I could hear Jay saying, 'the entire foreign policy and maybe the history of the world hung on what colour hat the baddies were wearing. Incredible.'

The food arrived and I watched it jumping and splattering on the plates in front of us as if it were too spicy even for itself. We both waited for one of us to have the courage to begin.

'I could have it reversed,' Jay said eventually, but I heard the *if you really wanted me to*, in his voice. I reminded him that you were never supposed to force someone into giving up something they believed in.

'It's a low blow to use a man's own bullshit against him.' He took my hand.

'You are not the real you when you're with me,' I said desperately.

'The real me?' He raised his eyebrows.

The thing was, Jay wasn't a recidivist. He was a war junkie. He needed to stand close to someone who was dying in order to feel alive – that was his addiction. I wanted to tell him I understood but I couldn't find the right words. 'I feel like time you spend with me is time taken out from being you,' I said. 'Your reality kicks in when you leave me in the morning. Well I can't just be your treat when the going gets rough.'

'I think that's a little unfair.' When I said nothing he added, 'Ain't no pot of gold at the end of the rainbow, kiddo.'

'Maybe there is, Jay, maybe I just need a different map to get to it.'

'Tell me about him,' was all he said.

When I finally got around to saying the name, he looked

up from his plate. 'Lytton-Jones? Wait a minute . . . is there a Daniel?'

'Yes,' I was amazed.

'I know him.'

'I don't believe it.'

'Yes, I do, well I don't know him exactly, but I met him. Ethiopia, I think it was. Very English, funny. He told me he took a homeopathic approach to drugs, i.e. anything that was plant-based was fine – heroin, marijuana, cocaine, "If God put it there it must be OK".' Jay chuckled. 'It really made me laugh at the time.' He was doing a piece for some English satirical magazine – I don't know how seriously he was actually taking it.'

'He's dead now.'

Jay nodded like this didn't surprise him.

When the cheque came he said, 'I feel like I've been run over.' He put fifty dollars on the plate. 'And so you leave me, bloodied by the side of the road.'

You feel run over, I thought. *While you're in hospital, look me up. I'll be on the women's ward across the corridor.*

I stretched over the table and kissed him on the cheek. He caught my hand. 'If that's your idea of a Band-Aid,' he said softly, 'I'm going to need a larger one.'

'I'm so sorry, Jay.'

He sighed. 'You know what we are, Maggie? Just two people maturing on a different schedule . . . I read that somewhere and I thought of us.' He took my hand and turned it over in his like he was examining it for signs of the future. 'Two people maturing on a different schedule –

at least that's the way my old man's pride is going to sell it to my young man's ego.'

'We've been together a long time now,' I told Wolf. 'I don't know, he's everything I always wanted. He's grown-up and decent, he's serious about things that really matter, he believes in the things I believe in, he's a really good guy, a good man. He has all the right heroes – God, he's virtually a hero himself and well . . . well the truth is I've finished it with Jay.'

'Actually I meant Rory.' Wolf wiped the ketchup from his mouth.

There was such an expression of tenderness in those heavy features I felt my face crumple. While I cried, Wolf ate the rest of my hot dog.

When I finished, he handed me the paper napkin.

'I have nothing to say to Rory.' I blew my nose

Wolf shook his head slowly. 'You see, this is why you will be great at making documentaries. You'll never have to worry about thinking up happy endings.'

I had no idea what he was talking about.

'You don't have to say anything to him, Maggie,' Wolf said, as though instructing a first year film student. '*Show* him.'

'What do you mean?'

'Send it.'

'The film?'

'Yes, of course the film.'

'What's the point, he hates me,' I said sulkily.

'Send it anyway,' Wolf said.

daniel

A few days before Benj's get out of jail card becomes valid Rory goes down with a bad case of flu. Its sheer spite takes him by surprise and he finds himself in bed with a high temperature watching a succession of Carole Lombard movies which he only partially manages to follow. When Benj appears on the doorstep, the event is notable only because for the first time in his life Benj is four shades less green than his cousin.

They lie sprawled on the floor, take-away menus scattered between them, watching *Miss Universe* on the telly. The mews house is bare and cold without the furniture. Rory misses the moose head; despite the obvious drawback of it being dead, the moose had actually been quite good company – a low maintenance virtual pet – and Rory quite often finds himself talking to its blank space on the wall, which has done little to improve his temper.

'And a number ten,' Benj says into the phone.

'Park or bif?' demands the voice on the other end.

'Which is it?' Benj is confused.

'That's why ask. Park of bif. Which you wan?'

Benj sighs, he has always assumed the point of numbered

menus is to avoid confusion of this sort but he's far too good-natured to say so.

'Rory,' Benj nudges him with his foot, 'see what number ten is would you?'

Rory grunts. On screen the Miss Universe candidates, holding their numbered placards, parade their teeth, bikinis, hopes and dreams across the stage.

'Rory! Number ten?'

'For fuck's sake . . . Miss Uruguay.'

'Oh thank you very much, so very helpful. Right, my friend would like one Miss Uruguay . . . yes with hot sauce . . .yes cash on delivery is fine. Yes, thank you too.'

'You're a real wag . . . a natural vaudevillian,' Rory says sourly as Benj hangs up the phone. 'I mean, are these witticisms spontaneous or do you practise them beforehand?'

'Sorry, I wasn't listening.' Benj is a little offended. Having traditionally been the recipient of efforts to raise the level of his own happiness rather than someone else's, he is ill trained for the job in hand.

'I was just wondering what kind of wit you were,' Rory says grouchily.

'Just your average halfwit.' Benj sighs again. He stares at the television. 'Hey, you know, I've got it. Stella's having a party in Suffolk this weekend. Some fantastic possibilities there.'

'Such as?'

'Wine, women, song.'

Rory doesn't bother to acknowledge this.

'Um . . . well,' Benj stumbles, 'women, girls . . . er, sex?'

Rory gives him a withering look.

'Sex!' Benj rallies. 'Come on, surely you remember. That strenuous activity where a woman puts her naked body at your disposal. Sometimes for as long as five whole minutes consecutively.'

'Sorry,' Rory says. 'Doesn't ring a bell.'

On screen Miss Chile is being crowned. She bursts into tears and adjusts her Grecian-style gown around her Brazilian-style boobs.

'Anyway, I'd better go home this weekend. I haven't been for months. My father has bought a seaweed-extracting machine.'

'But Bevan isn't by the sea.'

Yes,' Rory says wryly. 'Well spotted.'

maggie

The waxy orange flakes floated on top of the water. The fish's bulbous head quivered with excitement, his little mouth opening and shutting like, well, a fish, I supposed. He gobbled up the flakes. Wolf eyed me over the top of his *New York Times*.

'Another four weeks,' he said, 'and that fish'll be floating.' He stretched his feet out on the ottoman and flipped the page.

I grabbed the handykit off the table and dragged a chair over to the wall. Aimed the hammer at the nail. 'Shit.' The nail dropped, twisted, to the ground; I sucked my thumb.

'Still haven't heard anything, huh?' Wolf searched out the sports section. I glared at him then chose a larger nail from the metal box and executed a repeat performance. The picture was a little crooked, but it was good enough. The loft looked completely different furnished, though I couldn't decide whether better or worse – I kept tripping over things which I hadn't remembered buying, but once I'd tripped over them, turned out they were quite comfortable to lie on.

'Maggie?'

'You know something, Wolf, it's so much safer in life to be a cynic. Santa Claus, the infallibility of your parents, a believable religion – they all fall by the wayside sooner or later. We're told stories of monsters in the woods, then scolded for having nightmares. We're drip-fed fantasy then taught to be suspicious of anything that has no roots in reality so why, oh why are we still conditioned to believe in romantic love?'

Wolf grunted and went back to his reading.

I wrenched open the window. Manhattan was in the throes of a freak heatwave. It was so damn hot it steamed at night. The air hung over the city, hazy and polluted. Yesterday in Washington Square a girl tore off her shirt in protest. Both her nipples were multiple pierced and she had 'fuck me' tattooed across her belly button. Later in the day a large scantily clad Hawaiian reeled into me on the subway and asked, 'Have you ever been raped?' As opening gambits go I guess it left a lot to be desired. Luckily a group of Asians came aboard causing him to bellow, 'CHINKS!' every few seconds. The Asians just nodded their heads politely. God, New York in the spring. The city was lurching from 99 degrees to 49 on an hourly basis which was interesting as my internal emotional temperature had been doing roughly the same thing.

It took me days to post Rory the film. The problem was I didn't know what to put in the note. I tried flippant, casual, professional but none of them seemed right so in the end I just sent the film on its own, figuring that if it didn't say what I felt then nothing I could put on paper would help much anyway.

After I sealed the package, it sat on my desk for days.

Finally, Wolf came round one morning with bagels and juice. He saw it there, neatly addressed, and simply picked it up without saying a word and lumbered off to FedEx.

For a week I was on a high. Whatever Rory thought of the film at least a line of communication would be opened. After two weeks, I tracked the package and received confirmation that it had been delivered. I kept giving Rory new deadlines to get in touch and the weeks started to pile up on top of each other like unreturned library books. As soon as I realized he wasn't going to get in touch I tried to fill myself up with hate, hate, hate for the slimy boy germ that had exposed me to all this emotional garbage. Well to hell with him, at least I had tried.

'So just how much longer are you going to give him?' Wolf said.

Out of the window I watched the last of the trestle tables being carried through the doors of the building. The Chinese sweatshop below was closing, their lease up. They invited me to their goodbye party. I hadn't intended to go but at the last minute I changed my mind. Most of the racks had disappeared along with plastic bags, sewing machines, and accompanying loops of electrical cabling from the ceiling. The space looked completely different — well, not unlike what my loft used to look like. The centre of the floor had been chalked out as a dancing zone. I don't think I'd ever thought about the kind of dancing that Chinese tailors liked but these guys were into waltzing big time, beautiful old-fashioned tunes like the *Blue Danube*. I forked noodles off a paper plate and watched the seamstresses move dreamily through the airless room. I liked the party at first, assuming its mellow, drifting atmosphere was out of choice, then it occurred to me that it was because all these people had lost their livelihood and had no idea where their next pay cheque was coming from.

'I've been offered a job,' I told Wolf. A young NBC journalist working in Cambodia had committed suicide. Her papers had finally been found, along with her diary. The network wanted someone to retrace her journey and cover the MIA story at the same time. It was something I was really interested in doing it but I'd been finding excuses to put off the decision for as long as possible.

'You could come too now that you've quit and are on welfare.'

Wolf looked up questioningly.

'I already agreed to go,' I told him.

daniel

As soon as Bevan appears round a bend in the drive, Rory stops the Rover and gets out. From here the house is still magnificent. When he shuts his eyes he can conjure up the drive before the elms were cut down. Their replacements, limes and turkey oaks, stand nearly 15 feet high. One day, not in Rory's lifetime perhaps, but one day, the drive will look like it did when we were boys. The trees will outlive us all.

Spring is on its way. The buds are swelling on the horse chestnuts. The grass around my headstone has shot up to knee-high. Rory slings the dead flowers into the nettles then opens the plastic bag that he's brought with him from London. Inside is a photograph frame: a picture of a fantastically sexy girl wielding a whip – he leans it against the headstone. He crouches down and scrawls a message across the glass with a felt tip. 'Daniel, you fucker, thought you could do with a change.'

Rory waits for Alistair in the office where he reads the crumpled remains of the *Telegraph*. It's not that he's worried about getting the money back for the seaweed machine, it's just that it's so brain-damaging, the relentlessness of the whole thing. Trying to pre-empt Dad's financial gaffes is like trying to second guess the direction a frog will jump next. He reads a biographical account of Ted Hughes's marriage, occasionally, Eeyore-like, surveying the bulging pile on the desk, but old habits die hard. Furious with himself, he throws the *Telegraph* down and works the mail methodically until he hears a door slam and his name being shouted.

'Office,' he shouts back.

The buckles of Alistair's gumboots make a clicking noise as he walks down the hall.

'The fence to the old paddock needs replacing,' he says from the doorway, as though he'd seen his son at breakfast rather than nearly two months previously. 'Come take a look at it with me?'

'Dad, we need to talk.'

'And bring that farming catalogue, would you?' Alistair flutters his hand. 'Padded thingy near the bottom, could have something useful in it.'

Rory hands over the catalogue.

'Dad.'

'Deer have been a bloody nuisance this spring.' Alistair slices through the envelope with his letter opener. 'We're going to have to fence all the new trees as well.'

'Pa,' Rory says very quietly.

Nervous, Alistair fumbles with the envelope, dropping its contents to the floor.

Rory bends down, 'I need you to listen, please just for a minute——' then he breaks off. What he's handing his father is not a farming catalogue with its comforting photographs of ploughed fields and Massey Fergusons but a copy of a video with the words 'For your next bonfire' scrawled over a *Newsline* label.

'Something the matter, Rory?' Alistair queries innocently.

Rory is looking thunderous. He paces back and forth across the small room. Nanny, Grandpa, Ma and Pa sit in Nanny's room, all glued to the small screen.

'It's just that you seem a little ill at ease,' Alistair says, enjoying his son's discomfort hugely.

'I didn't particularly want you to see this,' Rory says through gritted teeth. 'I didn't particularly want *anyone* to see it for that matter.'

'Shame about the twenty million Americans then,' Alistair quips cheerfully. He turns his attention back to the television and gives a tremendous guffaw. He pats Nanny's knee.

'Oh Nanny, you have such screen presence, I've always thought so.'

Nanny looks deliciously pleased with herself. She carefully fingers another almond slice on the plate in front of her.

'Too bad our nice Miss Munroe wasn't around when Rory cut up the dining room curtains so he could dress like Julie Andrews in the *Sound of Music*,' Alistair says.

Audrey glances at Rory apprehensively.

'Remember, Nanny?' Alistair gently removes the remains of Nanny's paper napkin from her mouth.

'I do, yes indeed.'

Rory stops pacing and looks at the screen just in time to catch Alistair and Audrey sipping whisky through their curly-wurly straws. The shot cuts to Grandpa holding the Chinese figurines in his hands. Rory has already seen the sequence of this footage and is terrified of what's coming next. He thinks of the weeks ahead spent fending off journalists, his grandfather in the spotlight, his family humiliated and ridiculed.

'Right, we're not watching this any more.' He leaps up and attempts to switch off the television, cursing himself for not warning his father about Maggie.

Alistair grips his arm, 'Shut up and stop being a bore.'

'And do sit down,' Nanny commands.

On screen, Alistair is leaning on the dairy door, the baby beaker clipped to his dirty Barbour, painstakingly describing his recipe for buffalo face packs. The dread footage of Grandpa, or even any reference to it is not yet evident, nevertheless Rory can hardly bear to watch. His own commentary, rather than Maggie's, is running over the visuals so he cannot see that somehow she has achieved something rather remarkable. She has caught the eccentricity and yet the charm, she has shown the snobbery but also the sadness but as still no sign of Grandpa and his swastika knife appear on screen, Rory's relief gives way to other less noble emotions. Alistair looks closely at his son and quite correctly reads embarrassment hidden behind the scowl on his face.

And at that moment, something dawns on me — what Maggie must have known all along and Rory has singularly failed to understand — that however bizarre our parents' moral codes and way of life might seem to the rest of the world, they are perfectly ordinary to them. People can be happy with the way they're portrayed as long as you show them just the way they are and judging from my father's response Maggie has succeeded in doing just this.

'What a pompous twit you turned out to be, Rory,' Alistair says lightly. 'I rather thought we'd brought you up better than that.'

Rory looks wildly at him.

'I may not be the world's most successful businessman, but at least I try. In fact, your mother and I spend *all* our time trying to keep Bevan going for you.'

'For me?' Rory finally loses it. 'For *me*?' He jumps to his feet again. 'How can you say that. I hate this bloody house,' he howls.

'No,' Alistair shouts, '*I* hate this bloody house.'

'What are you *talking* about, Dad?' Rory's totally wrong-footed. 'What do you mean?'

'Exactly what I said. I hate this bloody house.'

'Dad, this is your home, this has always been your home.'

'Yes, it's my home,' Alistair says vehemently, 'but God knows it's no fun any more. Has it never occurred to you that we kept it going for Daniel, that we keep it going for *you*? For *your* children?'

This hits Rory low in the guts and winds him totally. 'But why did you never say anything?' he eventually manages.

'Oh, I don't know,' Alistair says wearily. 'I don't suppose you ever asked.'

In London, Rory shows the film to Benj. Five minutes aren't up before Benj is laughing his head off. He quickly apologizes and snaps opens another can of Coca Cola. When the credits finally roll, he says, 'So she didn't shop Grandpa after all . . . and how guilty out of ten do we feel?'

'All right, all right,' Rory says grudgingly, 'I suppose you think I should go after her.'

'Don't be ridiculous, she's completely unsuitable.' Benj helps himself to another slice of toast and cod's roe. 'You know these American women, they all insist on central heating.' He ignores the dirty look. 'Besides, you can't trust these foreign correspondents, she'd be off with a scud stud in the blink of an eye.'

This is too much for Rory's frayed nerves. 'Screw you,' he takes a swipe at his cousin. Benj ducks. 'That's not to say you shouldn't apologize though.' Benj calmly squeezes more lemon onto the cod's roe. 'You were, after all, particularly vile to her.'

'So you *are* saying I should call her then?' Rory says hopefully.

'Let's not exaggerate,' Benj says. 'A brief note would be more than adequate.'

To say what? Maggie had not sent a note. He'd taken the envelope out of the dustbin at Bevan and given it a good shaking. Why had she sent it? Professional courtesy? Where was the boyfriend and was he still around? Why had she sent it to Bevan and not to London? These questions are all irrelevant but serve as reasonably good excuses not to leave a message every time he calls and gets her answering machine. The fact is Maggie's film has made him think. She's reached a kind of truth he has been unwilling to face. She's presented his life to him, everything he stands for, and he's unsure how he feels about such painful exposure. He knows too that his anger is misdirected. The real culprits were around long before she appeared; himself, our father, me for copping out so spectacularly. *Is there anything else you ever wanted to be?* Maggie had asked. *Not the eldest son*, Pa had said. Rory feels a tightness like a rubber band around his heart and the pain sends him underground.

One night about a week later he has a dream. It's after the fire and he's sneaked up to the east wing. The forbidden east wing. He stands by the door, terrified by the blocked shapes of furniture shrouded in dust sheets. I am in the middle of the room wearing my games kit; shorts, an Aertex shirt and scuffed Clarks sandals. He watches me as I walk round in circles, humming the same tune over and over again. I smile at him, he smiles back. Then without warning the floorboards give way and I slip through. My arms are thrown out to him but he is rooted to the spot until the moment I disappear. Only then, as if magically released, is he able to rush to the hole. He looks down and sees me, he stretches out his arms but I am still falling. I will fall for ever.

He wakes up in a cold sweat. For a while he lies there, darkness encircling him, then, knowing sleep is impossible, goes to the kitchen for some water. He knocks against the drainer and saucepans clatter to the floor.

Saucepans clatter to the floor. Take the bike, Daniel, take the bike.

The Bevans are a careless family, we lose a lot of people. Alcohol, pills, guns, self-loathing, fear, weakness, guilt . . .

Saucepans clatter to the floor. And now I am there, back in the house. I am with him.

I pick up the pans and stack them one by one on the drainer.

'What's up?' says Rory, sleepy and crumpled from the doorway.

'I'm having a little problem sleeping.' I balance the last saucepan on top of the plate rack.

'It would help if you went to bed,' he says and I can tell how annoyed he is.

'How 'bout I borrow the car?'

'Again?' His tone is sarcastic. 'It's only just back from the body shop.'

'I need to go out.' I try to keep the alcohol from my voice, then I think, *Damn him – why the hell should I?*

'Go out. Where? It's four in the morning.'

'See a man about a dog. Ha.'

'You're drunk.' He takes the bottles from the dustbin. 'Christ, Daniel.'

'Tanked, tiddly, pissed, pie-eyed, bibulous, soused, shaken and stirred but not drunk, so what's new?'

'Daniel you promised.'

'Oh, my friend, be warned by me that Coca Cola, milk and tea are all the human frame requires and with that the wretched brother—'

'Daniel, just go to bed.'

'I want to go to Highgate. To the cemetery.'

'Well I'm not letting you take the car so you'll have to bloody well walk.'

'It's fifty degrees below zero!' I shout at him.

'Take the fucking bike then,' he shouts back.

Take the bike, Daniel, take the bike.
And he hurls the padlock keys at my feet.

In the back of the cupboard, behind the Domestos and the Ajax, Rory finds the bottle of whisky. He unscrews the lid and drinks it. The brown liquid slides down his throat like treacle.

He wakes about six hours later. He makes it to the loo just in time. When he surfaces again it's two o'clock in the afternoon and someone is beating a gong inside his head. He endures another bout of vomiting after the first coffee. After the fourth coffee he takes a cold shower and calls Maggie.

maggie

Ever since I worked for *Newsline* I have kept two packed suitcases in the closet by my front door. They're there for quick escapes. One is labelled hot, the other, cold. Inside the hot suitcase are three pairs of cotton combats, T-shirts, boots, and plenty of underwear. I searched the loft for some books to throw in as well. I always seem to take more books than clothes and leave them wherever they get finished. It's nice to drop a well-thumbed paperback in places you've been. It feels a little like carving your name onto a tree.

When the phone rang, I let the machine pick it up.

'I was going to hang up again, but . . .'

I recognized his voice immediately. Held the book tight in my hand.

'But then I wondered whether all those consecutive hang-ups might not seem a little creepy even by New York standards so—'

I grabbed at the portable under my bed.

'Christ, Maggie,' I heard the surprise in his voice, 'I didn't think . . . you're up early.'

A month ago I would have told him that I was up early a lot, that I wasn't sleeping too good, but, crouched on the floor I didn't know what to say. Even the simplest of sentences seemed beyond my power so I just said I was packing.

'You're going somewhere? When are you back?'

'Oh you know, this year, next year, sometime, never.'

'There was a long pause. 'Look I just called to say . . . well . . . how have you been?' His voice took on my own stilted tone.

'Fine . . . you?'

'Good . . . great.'

Wonderful. After three months of silence we were finally speaking, the way two people speak when they know a tree might fall on their head any second.

'Why did you call, Rory?' Three months was a long time. What was I hoping for? I had no idea, an apology? Some kind of acknowledgement that I was not the total bitch he thought. But there was nothing but silence down the end of the line.

'Rory, I'm leaving this evening. I'm going to Cambodia and . . .'

'I'm sorry,' he cut in, 'I'm obviously keeping you.'

'No, no, it's fine,' I trailed off and the conversation drifted even further out of reach.

'OK, well . . . it was nice to talk to you,' he said and I felt pride kicking in. I had got real efficient at not thinking about Rory these days. Keep tearing off the scab and it doesn't heal.

I dug my nails into my hand. 'Yeah, you too,' I said and hung up the phone.

daniel

In the white sunlight of late afternoon, amongst the usual limo hassling and police whistling of JFK airport, Rory throws his holdall into a yellow cab.

'Bowery, corner of Rivington Street,' Rory says, 'and please hurry.'

Maggie had said that her flight was *this evening*. It is now four o'clock. Four o'clock is afternoon. Five o'clock is still afternoon. Six is a hybrid hour, between afternoon and evening. Six is the earliest an evening can reasonably be expected to begin. *This evening* lasts until *tonight*. Seven is this evening, so is eight. Nine is pushing it. Ten o'clock is definitely tonight. Rory does his sums and reasons therefore that Maggie's flight is due to leave between six and ten o'clock, which means she would have to leave the house between three-thirty and seven-thirty giving him a four-hour window of opportunity – except judging by traffic it will probably be four-thirty before he arrives, knocking one pane out of his window. Still, three out of four is a 75 per cent chance, Ladbrokes would give him 3–1. If Maggie were a horse, these would be good odds. But hang on — Maggie didn't say *flying* this evening. She said *leaving*. That could mean leaving the *apartment* this evening which could mean flying *tonight*. This changes the odds considerably. Anything is possible.

As he presses the intercom on the outside of Maggie's building, noises from the real world penetrate his consciousness almost for the first time since he's left London. The air is warm and carries the smell of frying food. Sun gleams off the stainless steel of fridge doors and sink tops along the street. Traffic streams ceaselessly by. Then the door he's leaning against buzzes violently and he stumbles in.

maggie

'Two minutes,' I shouted at the intercom, 'Oh and could you please help me down with my bag?' I left the front door open, suitcase zipped shut in front of it and looked around quickly for my backpack. When, instead of the driver from Tel Aviv cars I'd been expecting, Rory bounded through the door, there was no way my mouth would open, let alone have words come out of it.

'Maggie,' he grabbed my arms. 'Look, tell them you're sick, tell them you're ill, tell them you've lost interest, lost a limb, tell them you can't write, can't film, can't function, tell them anything you like but just please, please, please, Maggie, I beg you, tell them you can't go.'

'Oh my God . . .'

'I mean it, tell them you're not going.'

'And then what?' I was still staring goofily at him.

'I don't know,' he said, 'then we will . . . well . . . we'll . . . uh . . . well obviously, you've got to come home with me. I mean . . . it's the village fête this weekend.'

I shook my head. 'Oh, Rory, why did you have to come now?'

'To stop you from going, of course. Cambodia's a horrible place, hot, wet – the food will be, well probably delicious,' he conceded, 'but you'll get hideously fat . . . wrinkled.'

I laughed, but my laughter nearly turned to tears. Rory pulled me closer.

'Stay. I'm asking you to stay.'

'All this time. You didn't even call—'

'Begging you to stay.'

The buzzer sounded. I looked to the door.

'It's too late, Rory.'

'Maggie, come on, of course it's not too late.'

'Everyone's waiting. I've got a job to do . . . responsibilities.'

'Fuck 'em.'

'*You* of all people.' I said, shocked.

The buzzer sounded again. 'That's my cab.' I pressed the intercom.

'And fuck your cab,' Rory said cheerfully.

'Tel Aviv cars,' scratched the voice.

Rory grabbed my hand. 'Look, I know I may not be even close to what you had in mind—'

'Rory don't.'

'And that probably scares you. I know it scares the hell out of me.'

But what I was scared of was how easy this could be. I felt completely split in two, but it seemed far safer taking my cues from my old self.

'It's too late, Rory.'

'Wasn't it Oscar Wilde who said something like, I will wait for you for ever . . . as long as you're not too long?'

But it just felt like a chastisement.

'You can't just turn up after three months and expect me to drop everything,' I said angrily.

'Maggie, I know I screwed up, I really did – more than you know, but . . . oh fuck it . . . look, the fact is . . . I need you.'

I heard everything I should in his voice but it didn't reach me. Instead I felt overwhelmed by panic, cornered, like I was in a big black box and gradually all the oxygen was being sucked out of it. How convenient it had been to blame Jay – but our relationship had danced as much to my tune as his. Now Rory has laid himself bare, what exactly was I prepared to give up for somebody I loved? Not enough it seemed. I snatched up my backpack. 'Well don't need me. I don't want anyone to need me.'

'Oh yes?' he said wildly. 'Well what about Magic Johnson 2. What's the poor little bastard going to do? Cook for himself?'

I looked round. My poor little fish was doing laps in its bowl on the table, its existence entirely forgotten. I picked it up and dumped it in Rory's arms. 'Present,' I said, then I turned and ran.

He caught up with me as I got into the cab. He was still holding the fish bowl. The water had slopped down the front of his pants.

'Damn it, Maggie, you're running again. It's a bad habit, you said so yourself.'

'Please,' I begged the driver. 'Just go.'

'Promise me, Maggie, when you get there, you'll stop

for a minute, just one minute, and think about whether I'm right.'

I shook my head helplessly. Forget the daydream, look at the two of us, our lives were mutually exclusive. Whatever future there might be would only ever play itself painfully out within the narrow lines we've both drawn around ourselves.

'Actually, let me revise that. One minute might be pushing it, so look, take two.' He got a better hold on the glass surface. 'I mean, who are we fooling here, take as much time as you like. Maggie, please . . .'

The cab jolted forwards with the surge of traffic and moved slowly off. I looked out the back window. Rory's mouth was opening and closing, but I couldn't hear what he was saying. Instead, I carefully focused on Magic Johnson 2, swimming around his bowl, getting smaller and smaller and smaller as the cab gathered speed. Thankfully we turned the corner, and the tears began to leak down my face. Outside in the street, the cherry trees shed blossom like confetti over the city.

daniel

'Two thousand for the weekend but for that you get to sleep in Churchill's bed.' Benj leans back in his chair and props his feet up on the desk. His tea, a boiled egg and a slice of toast, sits in front of him.

Since giving up alcohol, his appetite has become ferocious and the resulting half stone he's put on makes him look and feel well, at least he's assuming that this unusual feeling of energy is what people like to call 'well'. Above all he enjoys the programme and attends religiously. There is no semi-AA for Benj.

'No, no, my dear madam,' he says with exaggerated chivalry, 'It's extremely unlikely that Churchill, or indeed any surviving members of his family, will also be in it. But perhaps for an extra hundred or two I can tempt you with a glimpse of Queen Mary's bloody nightdress?'

Alison appears silently at his elbow and places a cup of tea beside the boiled egg. She notices the toast and without thinking, slices it into neat soldiers.

Rory walks out of his office clutching a leather holdall.

'Rory, stay here this weekend. We can, uh, uh, well . . . we'll take in a couple of reclamation centres . . . go see a

cemetery perhaps. Have our legs amputated, you know,'
Benj says weakly. 'Have some *fun* for a change.'

Rory laughs. 'It's the fête. I promised I'd go.'

Benj takes his feet off the desk in excitement. 'Oooh,
will they have whack the rat?'

'Why, do you want to come?' Rory asks hopefully.

Benj notices his toast. A great smile spreads across his
face. 'Actually,' he looks meaningfully at Alison. 'Perhaps
I'll stay.'

Alison blushes and fiddles with her hair.

In Skimpton, Rory passes signs for the village fête. On a
whim he parks the car near the train station, heads down
the slope, and crosses the railway track towards Bevan.
When Alistair was a boy, the train would stop at the bridge
to allow Grandpa to jump off with his suitcase. Rory scram-
bles up the bank to the park. A week of sun has finally
brought out the full glory of spring. The countryside has
metamorphosed from grey to green and it's the best that
England can ever look. Primroses and crocuses blanket the
ground, the chestnuts are nearly out, the park is full of
lambs. By the river the bulrushes are swelling, the weeping
willows thickening, herons are nesting. The giant sycamore
holds out its massive boughs over a tangled bed of wild
garlic plants, their damp pungent smell so comforting. Rory
absent-mindedly pulls on the frayed length of rope attached
to a branch some thirty foot up the tree, as boys, our means
of transport from one side of the brook to the other. The
wind feels warm against his face. A day like this he thinks,
one perfect day can keep you going for the rest of your life

— and there will always be one more perfect day. Rory sucks the air into his lungs, holds it there for a long time before expelling it and he remembers then what he has always known and so often denied — that Bevan is spectacularly beautiful, a magical place that will always be a part of him. He remembers what I used to tell him; that no matter how hard you try, there will always be something of the father in every son.

The house feels empty. Rory shuts the front door behind him and walks down the hall. Dust spins in the air as light, flooding through the dining room windows, refracts off the glass chandelier. Rory hears noises and opens the door to the drawing room. A stocky fellow in a suit is standing by the wall. He mutters something and a second man, grasping the end of a tape measure, rises off his knees and advances on Rory hesitantly.

'Afternoon,' he says, thrusting out his hand. 'John Fielding of Knight, Frank and Rutley.' He misinterprets Rory's look of astonishment for lack of brand recognition.

'Property Agents,' he explains, handing over his business card.

maggie

If your job is to poke around in others people's affairs, you have to understand that you're living a life of borrowed experiences. In your head you might store thousands of frames, fragments of other people's existence, but the memories these give you are transient. They're facsimiles, carbon copies of the real thing. And because there's no long-lasting emotion behind them, they too, like the ink on fax paper, end up fading with time. And after a while, it makes you wonder, it really does, what tangible moments your own life is actually made up of.

'OK, Maggie,' Wolf said patiently. 'One more time. Take it from the top.'

'Sure, ready,' I adjusted the expression on my face, tried to concentrate. 'In this painful period of er . . . uh . . . American history. Goddamnit,' I broke off again. I was making a real mess of it. From the moment we'd begun the MIA assignment I'd been subject to this helpless daydreaming.

'Try it again.'

I cleared my throat. 'At last some of the long-sought men Missing In Action will have their remains flown back to their loved ones who perhaps will find, er, closure . . . look, do I have to use the world closure,' I said crossly, 'I hate the word closure.'

'Not like you're looking for it yourself or anything,' Wolf said dryly.

I glowered at him. Took a huge breath, faced his camera, began again. 'At last some of the men long gong, glone, GONE . . . aaargh'

'Let's go get you some lunch,' Wolf was employing his most condescending voice.

There wasn't much to be had in the way of lunch in Phnom Penh. We'd been eating in the same small restaurant on the far side of town for days, but Wolf, impatient to get at his rice and boiled Pepsi, pulled me into a rat run through the town's back alleys. I followed sulkily in his wake, scuffing my boots on the cracked mud. As we reached the end of the alley he stopped abruptly and I bumped into his back.

'Ow.' I said belligerently.

'Look.'

'What?'

'Over there. Look.'

'Where?'

'He must have followed you.'

My breath caught in my throat. I scanned the busy street, but I could not find the face I was looking for in that bustling sea of people.

'There,' Wolf said, and I saw what he was looking at.

On the road facing us was a tattered billboard. Underneath the word 'Restaurant', written in both English and

Cambodian, was a picture of a fish. A black fish, one of those big ugly Chinese ones with bulbous eyes not unlike—

'Magic Johnson 2,' Wolf said. 'Ahhh, sweet. He must have swum all the way just to see you.'

'Wolf. You son of a bitch.'

Wolf retied the elastic on his ponytail. 'I'm sorry to say this, Maggie, but you're a real piece of work yourself.'

'Me?'

'Yeah, you. Fine, go ahead, die a wizened bitter old hag, see if I care.'

'Wait a minute,' I said defensively. 'Whose side are you on?'

'I'm on your side – at least I used to be, but you're stubborn and stupid so now I'm on my side – because anyone that's dumb enough to care about you including and especially me is liable to get an ulcer.'

I stared at the stupid black fish.

'You will go anywhere, attack anything, fight for any cause you think is important but someone actually needing you is more than you can handle.'

'Shut up, Wolf.'

'That's your problem, you're scared to death.'

'That is such bullshit,' I howled. 'I am not.'

'Yeah, you are. You're scared of all the things you want the most.'

'I'm not listening to this.' I stomped off.

I blinked back the tears for the second time that week. I guess when you get lost, it doesn't happen in one go. What happens is you take a series of wrong turnings so small it takes you a while to cotton on to the fact your life is not on the right track any more – well who's going to sit you down and tell you it's too late?

'Who would have thought, Maggie,' Wolf shouted after me. 'You are a goddamn sissy after all.'

daniel

Rory heads cross country towards the cricket pitch. In the distance he can hear the caterwaul of a Wall's ice-cream van. He knots his jumper round his waist and vaults the stile. How just like Pa, he shakes his head. How just like Pa to say nothing.

The fête is teeming with people. The air smells of sawdust. All the familiar stalls are up – coconut shies, bottle stands, guess the weight of the pig. Overturned crates are laden with jars of marmalade and chutneys. Rosie from the village shop is judging the gardens-in-a-tin competition and Bindey's nephew is laying out oversized turnips and marrows for inspection.

At whack the rat a gargantuan man Rory recognizes from the Skimpton darts team brings the heavy mallet down on the rat onto which, this year, somebody has actually bothered to sew a tail. The blow sends the rat scurrying up the pole. His supporters cheer then groan as it stops inches from the bell.

Rory wanders on. A bouncy castle seems to be this year's capitulation to the new century. Scores of grubby toddlers fall over each other in a sticky mess of mucus, tears and ice cream. By the middle of the pitch, the smell of sawdust has been overpowered by a stall frying onions and sausages. Rory sees Nanny holding court on the bingo stand then spots the sign behind her. *Donkey rides 50p.* Two bored donkeys graze mournfully on dandelions while next door to them a line of hysterically excited children and parents queue in front of a second sign. *Buffalo Rides £2.*

Audrey stands behind a long table trying to serve four people at once. The table is piled high with bits and pieces from the house. China, books, pictures, even the Buddha from the hall table is on it. As Rory walks over Alistair pops up from the boxes underneath the table, the moose head in his hands. He dumps it unceremoniously in front of a waiting customer.

'How much for the moose?' Rory elbows his way in.

'I'm bid six pounds by this kind lady.'

'I'll give you four.'

'Do you mind?' the woman says, a little annoyed.

'Ten pounds, not a penny less,' Alistair demands.

'Three,' says Rory.

'Ten,' the woman bids indignantly.

'Right, if that's the way you feel — two pounds fifty,' Rory grins at his father, 'and that's my final offer.'

'Have it for nothing,' Alistair says. 'After all, it belongs to you already.'

The woman finally understands what she's up against. She moves away, smiling faintly.

'On condition you take it away,' Alistair heaves the creature into Rory's arms.

Rory rests it on the table. He's about to open his mouth but Alistair is way ahead of him.

'Not now, Rory.'

'I've just come from Bevan.'

Alistair nods. 'Try to understand,' he says. 'I will miss my trees, I will miss the view over the park probably every day for the rest of my life, but I will survive. We, your mother and I *will* survive.'

'But, Pa—'

'We've had to come to terms with the death of our child,' Alistair says. 'What the hell does a house matter after that?'

Rory nods dumbly.

'So take the damn moose and go and find your grandfather.' Alistair puts his hand on Rory's shoulder and gives it a squeeze, 'You're actually a little in our way right now.'

Towards the end of the cricket pitch the stalls begin to peter out. Behind the tea tent on a patch of grass dotted with empty beer cans, two spotty teenagers are snogging for England. Rory rests the moose on the ground and skims the crowd for Grandpa. He sees the military jacket first, set neatly down on a hay bale outside a stall, then Grandpa marches out, shotgun in hand. He's transferred the medals to his shirt and they flash in the sun when he moves. Rory smiles.

Grandpa looks through the viewfinder of the gun. He makes an impatient gesture as if the sights are not up to scratch then puts the rifle to his shoulder and fires. There's a sound of shattered china.

'Ha!' Grandpa exclaims. 'Loader,' he bellows. An arm,

holding a second rifle, hastily appears from inside the tarpaulin.

As Grandpa merrily continues to obliterate the remainder of Bevan's legacy, Rory closes his eyes. The sun is warm against his forehead. He feels like he could chart his entire life through every fête past and for the first time ever, he feels like this is not a bad thing.

'Loader, where have you got to?' shouts Grandpa. 'Come out here at once and take a turn.' Rory opens his eyes and blinks into the sunlight.

maggie

Grandpa put his arms round me, levelling the rifle in my hands. 'Steady,' he warned, 'Line it up. Steady, *steady.*'

I closed one eye, squeezed against the trigger. The gun smashed painfully against my shoulder. On the bale, one of the Chinese figurines exploded.

'Oh, good girl!' Grandpa took the rifle from me and reloaded.

I saw Rory then, standing by the entrance of the tent, or rather leaning against the guy ropes, arms crossed. He'd seen me too, I could tell, and was watching us, a look on his face I couldn't read. I held my ground. I had come 6,000 miles, I had crossed another continent to be there, so I reckoned the next 40 yards were up to him.

He pushed himself off the ropes and ambled over. People between us sped up and blurred, then he was in front of me.

'So,' he said nonchalantly. 'Just landed?'

'Yeah.'

'Good journey?'

'A little bumpy,' I said, 'otherwise . . . a damn good bit of flying.'

He pulled me close. I could feel his heart pounding.

'Look,' I said. 'I just want to get one thing straight.'

'Yes?' His eyes narrowed suspiciously. 'And what might that be?'

'I'm not going to be one of those weird little women who make cucumber sandwiches and wear flowery hats. I'm not going to join the Women's Institute, or eat bread sauce, I won't share bath water with anyone except you and I will never and I mean never ever live in a house without adequate central heating.'

'Anything else?' he said mildly.

'Yes. I also want to point out . . . well . . . don't think that just because I've come here, I'm here for good or anything like that. It's like . . . I mean you do realize I have a job, or well I'm looking for a new job because it's not like I'm going to give up my work or . . .'

'Or your what?' he demanded.

'Well, my work . . .'

Rory broke into a grin and it was like I'd been waiting my whole life for someone to grin like that at me, 'Well that's a relief,' he said. 'Because following in a long-standing and proud family tradition, I am destined to remain seriously broke.'

daniel

The new owners of Bevan are businessmen. Developers with their eye on commuters from Stockton on Tees. Though not averse to the idea, they utterly fail to understand why Rory, having sold them the house and land, is spending no small percentage of the purchase price planting a wood for them. Needless to say they put it down to eccentricity.

I, of course, know better.

There are fifty shovels in the back of the tractor. The clearing teems with people. Rory has gathered them all together; everyone who has ever worked at Bevan, their families and grandchildren; the Skimpton cricket and darts team, Rosie from the local 7–11, even Doctor Banks from the village. Over the last few weeks most of Rory's clients from Stately Locations have also made the pilgrimage, the Bancrofts, the Harcourts, the Roxmeres, Benj, Alison, my mother, my father, Maggie. Rory methodically ticks them off a list, his list that has been appendaged to my map. They take their trees, carefully labelled in Latin and English, and one by one they plant my wood, and I am proud. I am really proud. Here's what I think, for what it's worth. The land does not belong to the new owners, just as it didn't belong to my father. The land does not belong to the ramblers, the twitchers, picnickers, prospectors, city weekenders, gypsies, Estate owners or farmers, it belongs to those who work it and are passionate about it.

It belongs to those who are prepared to put their soul into it.

Rory has moved off some way from the crowd. Overhead the air darkens, the weather changes fast and furious. Clouds hurtle through the sky. Rory stands in the clearing looking down the valley towards the house. He takes off his boots and the soil feels damp between his toes. He can smell the seed, smell the honeysuckle lifting off the breeze. He sees the woods, the park, the great oak tree bowed in the fox cover. He hears the sound the wind makes as it blows through the flowers of the horse chestnut. He feels the current in the earth, the rain on his skin. He sinks to his knees until the water has seeped through his clothes then he turns his face skywards and I see he's understood.

When Rory drives down the drive of Bevan for the last time, he will have Maggie in his car and the moose head strapped to the roof. God only knows where they think they're going but at least together they might have some fun getting there. As for me . . . well who knows? Bob Dylan said, 'I'll let you be in my dream if I can be in yours,' and I think that's a pretty good trade off. I still don't know where I am, but my hope is I'm only passing through. Meanwhile, finally, jealously, gratefully, tearfully, I can and damn well will raise an imaginary glass to my brother.

To say that the English aristocracy is a spent force is undeniable, but to say it is no longer of value is not necessarily the case. In the end it's family that counts. Our story, depending on who's telling it, is one of irreversible decline or, as I prefer to see it . . . a story of survival against the odds.

— Earl of Bevan

Acknowledgements

Hunting Unicorns originally began life as a screenplay embarked upon by my sister Susie and me as a way of threading together some of the humiliating fates suffered by those to whom the more staid traditions and values of the English are a complete anathema.

My thanks, therefore, to all those people who on hearing of the project flooded us with urban myths, embarrassing anecdotes and deliciously weird stories.

Apart from it being a revelation to discover just how many people had an Alistair or Audrey Bevan somewhere in their family tree, I loved all these stories because they really made me laugh – no bad thing when you find yourself locked into a room with an obstreperous computer. Those urban myths that found their way into *Hunting Unicorns*, namely the bunny, the basin, and the wallpaper, are silly enough but, believe me, fall way short of being the silliest.

My eternal thanks to all those friends who for one reason or another stopped me toppling over the edge whilst writing this book: Nan and Andy for Brooklyn and bagels. John and Emily for their tower of flies. Susie for tuna sandwiches. Carole for her wisdom and breakfasts at Balthazar, Sarah and Clare for their google wizardry and Mr Kipling's almond slices. Nanda for her tortillas and above all, Dave for the Barn.

Thanks also to the following for their invaluable help: Molly Dineen, Rebecca Frayn, Catherine Bailey, the London office of Médecins Sans Frontières, Charles Kidd of *Debrett's Peerage.*

DETROIT PUBLIC LIBRARY

3 5674 00584581 4

DETROIT PUBLIC LIBRARY

BROWSING LIBRARY
5201 Woodward
Detroit, MI 48202
DATE DUE

Cigarettes

CIGARETTES

A NOVEL

Harry Mathews

Weidenfeld & Nicolson
New York

C . 3

Portions of this novel first appeared in *Conjunctions* and *The Review of Contemporary Fiction.*

This work was supported by a grant from the National Endowment for the Arts.

Copyright © 1987 by Harry Mathews

All rights reserved. No reproduction of this book in whole or in part or in any form may be made without written authorization of the copyright owner.

Published by Weidenfeld & Nicolson, New York
A Division of Wheatland Corporation
10 East 53rd Street
New York, NY 10022

Published in Canada by General Publishing Company, Ltd.

Grateful acknowledgment is made for the following:

Excerpt from *Two Serious Ladies* by Jane Bowles. Copyright © 1966 by Jane Bowles. Reprinted by permission of Farrar, Straus & Giroux, Inc.

Excerpt from *Parade's End* by Ford Madox Ford. Copyright © 1950 by Alfred A. Knopf, Inc. Copyright renewed 1978. Reprinted by permission of the publisher.

Excerpt from *The Big Sleep* by Raymond Chandler. Copyright © 1939 by Raymond Chandler. Copyright renewed 1967 by Mrs. Helga Greene. Reprinted by permission of Alfred A. Knopf, Inc.

I'VE NEVER BEEN IN LOVE BEFORE by Frank Loesser from "Guys and Dolls." © 1950 by Frank Music Corp. © renewed 1978 by Frank Music Corp. International Copyright Secured. All Rights Reserved. Used by permission.

TAKE HIM by Richard Rodgers & Lorenz Hart
Copyright © 1951, 1952 by Chappell & Co., Inc.
Copyright renewed.
International Copyright Secured. All Rights Reserved. Used by permission.

Library of Congress Cataloging-in-Publication Data

Mathews, Harry, 1930–
    Cigarettes.

    I. Title.
PS3563.A8359C5   1987   813'.54   87-8174
ISBN 1-55584-092-2

Manufactured in the United States of America

Designed by Paul Chevannes

First Edition

10 9 8 7 6 5 4 3 2 1

BL   FEB 25 '88

In Memory of Georges Perec

Contents

"Let me tell you a story on the subject,"
said the Linnet.

"Is the story about me?" asked the Water-
rat. "If so, I will listen to it, for I am
extremely fond of fiction."

Oscar Wilde, "The Devoted Friend"

Cigarettes

Fourteen pairs of relationships kindle and
smolder in this novel about sex, intrigue and
greed in the art world of Greenwich Village
between 1936 and 1963.

Allan and Elizabeth

JULY 1963

"WHAT'S HE MEAN, 'I SUPPOSE YOU WANT AN EXPLANA-
tion'? He doesn't explain anything."

The gabled house loomed over us like a buzzard stuffed in
mid flight. People were still arriving. Through the lilac hedge
came the rustle of gravel smoothly compressed, and swinging
streaks of light that flashed beyond us along a pale bank of
Japanese dogwood, where a man in a white dinner jacket stood
inspecting Allan's letter with a penlight.

He passed the letter around. When it was my turn I read, in
another revolution of headlights, ". . . the state I was in—barely
seeing you when they were taking me away . . . Darkness,
blinding light . . . I couldn't manage a squeak." I too was
confused. Even dazzled by Elizabeth, could this be Allan?

I wanted to understand. I planned someday to write a book
about these people. I wanted the whole story.

After an absence of many years Elizabeth that day had come

3

back to town. A little after midnight she went to the "casino," as the last private gambling club was called. Allan was leaving. Having drunk too much and started a noisy argument, he was being politely bounced. He passed Elizabeth in the glare of the lobby. At the door he was told, "Next time, Mr. Ludlam, please keep it down. And watch yourself on the road."

"Thank you. Who *is* she?"

"Beats me."

Outside, the night was hot and starry. Allan started driving home, stopping on the way at the Spa City Diner. Maud would have long been asleep.

He had two cups of coffee, chatting with late-night customers. He wished he could visualize Elizabeth exactly. (He remembered the sparse whiteness of her clothes, the flurry of her red-gold hair.) He knew she had seen him; her ready acceptance of him in those circumstances made him wince.

Allan had cleverness, if not wisdom, and he prized it. He held the world and himself in contempt. Recently he had shown kindness to me when few others had. My best friend had died, and gossips had cruelly blamed me for it. "You're lucky," Allan told me, "learning young what bastards people are. 'People,' " he added, "includes me." He meant that befriending me made him no better than the others, only smarter. He mistrusted his own decency.

On his way home, passing the Adelphi, he saw a red-haired figure in white crossing the faintly lighted porch. He braked. Perhaps a minute passed while he recollected that he was a local worthy, that he had already demeaned himself, that he was still drunk. He parked his car and went into the hotel. On night duty he found Wally, who had known him for thirty years. Allan asked if it was too late for a nightcap. Wally said, hold the fort, he wouldn't be a minute.

The lobby looked empty. Allan stepped behind the front desk to examine in the open register the arrivals on this first day of

July. He stopped at a familiar name: Elizabeth H., the woman in the portrait Maud had just bought. He had met her once or twice, long ago. She might have been the one at the casino. Perhaps he had unconsciously recognized her—that would explain her effect on him. Hearing Wally returning, he noted her room number.

After a minute spent sipping his highball, Allan said he was going to the john. Out of sight, he entered the honeyed glow of the carpeted stair. On the third floor he turned right. He had no plans.

Behind one wall a pipe produced a spasmodic whine. Unless, Allan thought, a chipmunk was trapped in the old timbers; the sound struck him as animal. He counted door numbers until he reached Elizabeth's.

The whine was coming through that door. He pressed his ear to the wood. The voice was not a chipmunk's. Allan dropped to one knee and set his eye to the keyhole: Yale. The edges of the door lay snug in their jambs.

The high voice sang waveringly on, needling Allan like a stuck car horn. He tried the doors of the adjacent rooms. The one on the right opened, and he entered a dark bedroom where light from the street revealed an empty bed. Crossing the room, Allan raised the window and leaned out. A ledge a foot wide ran across the building at floor level. From the window at his left faint light was shining. Gripping the window frame, Allan lowered both feet onto the ledge and slid along it. Reaching the light, he was confronted by backlighted blue shepherdesses strutting in a monotony of willows. The curtains allowed his sight no chink. Again he heard the voice sustaining its reedy cantillation. In the lobby, when the woman had looked at him and then looked away, from the unbuttoned top of her dress one unhaltered breast had slipped and been tucked back smoothly into place. He had conceived her nakedness under the white cotton and the cinched broad belt buckled with golden snakes.

He looked down at the street—anyone there could see him—and began retracing his path. Downstairs, Wally waved him out into the fervent night. Allan was so astonished that if Maud had woken up when he came home, he might have told her everything that he had done.

In his letter, Allan wrote Elizabeth, "I kept wondering, was it really your room? Your voice? Who was with you? What exactly was he or she or they doing to you? I didn't want answers—I wanted *you*. I felt *deprived*."

Finding Elizabeth took him a week. He had many friends in that little town: some of them said they knew her; one of them had been asked to a party where she was expected. Allan went too.

The party was being given at a large house on Clinton Street, near the edge of town. Allan pointed out the woman from the casino across the lawn, and his friend confirmed his hunch: she was Elizabeth. Allan peremptorily declined to be introduced to her. Twenty minutes later he regretted his refusal. He had hoped to catch Elizabeth's attention; she had not even looked at him. He derided himself as foolish and incompetent. Two waterless drinks aggravated his helplessness.

Turning away from the crowded bar, where he had gone for a third helping, Allan found Elizabeth waiting behind him. He looked into her eyes as hard as he could. She did not recognize him. He was comforted that she hadn't remembered his disgrace, discouraged at having made no impression on her. He hoped, absurdly, that she would see at once that she already obsessed him. She smiled: "You look lost."

"I was. You're the reason I'm here." He had lost all assurance, so that what might have sounded impudent rang true.

Elizabeth slipped her arm into his. "Tell me what's up."

They moved out of the crowd. Hardly knowing what to say, he confessed his expulsion from the casino and his having seen her there, in some disarray. Elizabeth laughed: "At least *you* noticed." Allan's embarrassment attracted her more than the usual urbanities. "And now?"

Allan thought of the voice in the hotel and blushed again. "How about dinner? At the casino? You'll put me back in good standing."

"OK. But if we play, you'll have to stake me. I've got barely enough for bed and breakfast."

At the casino, after reserving a table, Allan bought five hundred dollars' worth of chips and gave half to Elizabeth, for which she kissed him on the cheek. They agreed on roulette.

Leaning over the seated players, Elizabeth bet all her chips on the first turn: a hundred and fifty dollars on black, the rest on 17. "Pure superstition," she told Allan. "It *never* comes up."

Quinze, impair, noir, et manque were announced. ("Close, at least," remarked Elizabeth.) A man yielded his seat. The croupier slid a hundred and fifty dollars towards her, neatly stacked.

Allan sat down across the table. He felt mildly irritated. He decided to ignore Elizabeth's play and concentrate on his own. Before betting, he kibbitzed a list of recent turns from a neighbor and watched six more himself. Allan liked roulette. It tested his self-control: he made himself bet at foreordained intervals and on numbers he had chosen statistically. He scored early that evening with a 6 *en plein* that put him ahead two hundred dollars. (He glanced at Elizabeth's chips: worth a thousand at least.)

He won another two hundred during the next half hour. He had more than doubled his stake, and their table was waiting: time to quit. An old man was sitting in Elizabeth's seat.

"Nice going."

As he turned, his nose grazed her breasts. "And you?"

"It was extremely exciting—close to two thou at one point. Shit!" She pointed to the wheel, where the white pellet was cruising in 17.

Allan's irritation returned. He was irritated with himself. He knew that Elizabeth would have played no differently with her own money; and she had cost him nothing, since he had made good her loss with his winnings. She was looking at him without remorse, almost with contentment. She did not care whether she lost or won, and that made him jealous. He hated losing. He could not help thinking of Maud. Elizabeth was beginning to frighten him.

She told him later, after slapping him hard in the face, "You bastard, stop holding back!" One of her legs was hooked behind his knees, the other encircled his hips.

In love, too, Allan exercised self-control. He took care to please first. Elizabeth preferred abandon—no "mine" or "yours," certainly no yours and then mine. For Allan, a woman's pleasure guaranteed his own. It was money in the bank.

Elizabeth nailed him: "I love the things you do to me, but let's not spend all night paying our dues. It's *you* I want." He started to explain. She laughed: "Look, I like being irresistible, too. Stop running things."

He agreed to try. Trying only discouraged him more and shriveled his purpose. Elizabeth understood how he felt. She began playing with him as with a child. In a while he somewhat forgot his predicament; and then when he too was playing she slapped him again, just hard enough to toughen his desire with sportive vindictiveness. He let go, and kept letting go, and as he did so, a high, eerie, familiar wail filled his head. He forgot himself, he forgot everything, except for one offstage, insidious question: Who's listening tonight?

The next day he wrote her a letter: "I suppose you want an explanation. . . ." He must by then have known that Elizabeth wasn't interested in explanations; he must have known that he had nothing to explain. He had urgently wanted to write her, and he had yielded to his impulse without realizing that it

sprang from something he hadn't told her and wished he had—
that he was married to Maud. He still did not mention Maud
in his letter. He told himself that a woman like Elizabeth
wouldn't care.

Elizabeth had learned about Maud with no help from Allan.
When he next saw her, she had changed. She had become more
interested in him, less so in "them." She had accepted her role
as a married man's lover.

They met late in the afternoon, two days after their first
encounter. When Allan acknowledged Maud's existence, Elizabeth insisted he talk about her. Once again he found himself
baffled. He berated himself for not admitting his marriage at
once. At their first meeting he had immediately suppressed the
urge—what was he to say, "You're the reason I'm here, and I'm
happily married"? At supper he had been afraid of displaying
his desire. He felt that warning Elizabeth about Maud would
seem as obvious as taking off his pants; and after that it was too
late.

In twenty-six years of marriage Allan had sometimes been
drawn to other women. He had never before loved two women
at the same time. He now felt compelled to keep them separate.
Telling Elizabeth about Maud, like the thought of telling Maud
about Elizabeth, made him afraid of losing one or even both of
them. Even in his private thoughts, pretending he had two
unconnected lives felt safer. (He was unexpectedly troubled by
the portrait Maud had bought: a painted "Elizabeth," chosen
and paid for by his wife, was waiting to be hung on a wall in
his house. Although Allan earned, as they say, "real money,"
he had always respected Maud's, augustly self-replenishing, as
the guarantor of their position. He did not love Maud for her
money; he had also never known her without it.)

He struggled with his novel passion. He could not understand Elizabeth's many kindnesses at their second meeting. She
struck him as all too obliging—eager for details about Maud,

fussing over a present ("My favorite demisemiprecious stone!"), agreeing to meet him whenever he could get free. Her docility suggested, illogically and inescapably, that he no longer mattered to her. If he had, she would have made more of a fuss. Had his silence concerning Maud brought this about? He must have disappointed her in other ways, too. When he asked her, she swore he hadn't.

They met several times during the rest of that week. To Allan's amazement, Maud made it easy for them. His stay-at-home wife started partying every day. Once he knew Maud's exact plans, he would notify Elizabeth and, later, drive to her hotel.

Sexual vacations begun in dalliance may become exhausting exercises in self-discovery or evasion. Allan had fallen in love, and hardly knew it, and labored vehemently to control what he refused to admit. Elizabeth did her best. Touched by his confusion, she wished he could like himself a little better, and she let her own liking for him express itself openly and attentively. Her compassion only put her further out of reach. Allan felt she was turning him into a fool. He had lost his script.

He had hoped that Elizabeth would fall desperately in love with him. That might restore his worth. He could then anticipate the pain of letting her go.

Allan consoled himself with their pleasure—hers, his—and resorted to it with growing fury. He grew pale beneath his tan. Elizabeth began to look at him with maternal concern.

A week passed. Their fifth meeting left him more disheartened than ever. He had gone to Elizabeth in unusually good humor. He had pleased himself by writing an effusive letter of thanks to a man who had helped him. He had reassured himself with propitiatory acts—changing into a striped mauve shirt she admired, going to the barber's, drinking only water at lunchtime.

He had hoped that when he entered her room she would fall into his arms. Instead, she gave him the quickest of kisses and a glance, not unkind, implying that men never looked more ridiculous than fresh from a barbershop. She sat him down on the couch to watch television: the sixth at Belmont. She followed the race like a child at a circus, with the kind of look he yearned to kindle in her eyes. At the finish she shrieked.

"You see," she explained, "he's a friend."

"The owner?"

"The horse." His name was Capital something. "I'm thirsty for gin-and-tonics."

They drank awhile, until Elizabeth at last embraced him. They undressed, bit by bit, caressingly; finally Allan went into her like a fist. She shrieked again, she started laughing, wrestling him like a happy ten-year-old grappling with a roommate. She pulled his hair and called him Capital something. She did nothing to conceal her happiness. He watched himself giving in, and gave in. Once again she was proving too good for him. More than good: the thing itself. Stratagem and skill would never get the better of her. She had nothing to lose. He lay under her feeling plundered.

She coddled him and kissed his mouth. He turned his head aside: "You don't know what I've been going through."

"I guess not. I've been having too much fun."

"You don't really care who I am. . . ."

"Let me think. This is Sunday, you must be—"

"You never even call me by my own name." The words shamed him. A nervous weariness was seeping through his body. Elizabeth looked down at him, perplexed. She felt motherly again—a step away from passion, as he might have noticed if he'd stayed awake.

They decided to take the next day off. Allan pleaded business; Elizabeth accepted his suggestion with an inward smile. She told him she would go riding at ten. He could reach her later if he wanted. She hugged him goodbye: "Goodbye, Allan—sweet Allan."

Allan hadn't lied. He had an appointment the following

morning, with a man whose trade was horses. They had a tricky deal to conclude, one that Allan expected would keep him late; but he was driving home before noon. Approaching his driveway, he stopped at the sight of a horse on the lawn, tethered to a birch tree and cropping the grass. He parked on the road and skirted the grounds to the back door of his house.

He let himself quietly into the pantry. From the front rooms came familiar voices: Maud's and Elizabeth's. Allan took off his shoes and tiptoed up the back stairs to his bedroom, where the voices did not carry. He thought: I'd better get this job finished. He picked up the phone to call the city. Through the dial tone he heard Maud speaking, her voice far away, then abruptly stilled. Someone else was using that particular downstairs extension.

He heard no click of a handset being replaced. Dialing his number, Allan said "I love you" into the speaker. His call was promptly answered.

Knowing that Elizabeth was listening, he felt a sickening need for her as he began stating his business. He wanted to be sick in her lap and be forgiven for it. After telling himself, hang up, go downstairs, talk to her, Maud or no Maud, he went on giving instructions.

He carefully repeated his words so that Elizabeth would remember them. He was making an arrangement that would reveal him as unscrupulous, even criminal. He wanted Elizabeth to understand that she did not know him at all, that he was more than the man she thought she knew. She would junk him for good, but with a certain astonishment, a certain respect.

He crept downstairs. The women's voices sounded louder. He listened from the hall:

". . . you still want that milktoast?"

"That's for me to decide!"

"It's him or the portrait. You can't have both!"

Each vehement declaration was followed by a silence as of

mythical personages raising high the boulders with which they would assail one another.

"You're disgusting!"

"It's my portrait, isn't it?"

"*Of* you—hardly yours!"

"Cut the crap, Mrs. Miniver. I need something to show for my week."

Allan gazed across the living hall to the front parlor. He stepped forward, then turned away, realizing how foolish he would look without his shoes. Elizabeth's words made him want to disembowel her, and at the same time want to cry. Through the library door he saw the still-unframed portrait resting against a wall. He remembered how light the painting had seemed for its size. Taking it from the library, he carried it out the back door.

Allan brought the portrait to the city that afternoon and stored it, wrapped in a sheet, in the back of his commuter's apartment. Leaving the house, he had planned to burn the painting; now he was unsure what to do with it. He did not know what to do with himself, either. He could not imagine speaking to Maud. The next morning, however, he felt a new concern for his wife, or at least for her opinion of him.

Allan's deal of the previous day required him to find supplementary insurance for a racehorse. The horse, a competent, veteran gelding, had come up lame after his last race. Because only one stablehand knew of this, the owner planned to subject the horse to a hard workout during which he would almost certainly break down. This would supply the pretext for destroying him. The owner aimed to collect all he could in insurance claims. He had been told that Allan might help.

As a partner in an established firm of insurance brokers, one that dealt chiefly with large businesses, Allan could not be expected to insure one horse. It might seem even less likely that he would help out a fraudulent small-town client. However,

Allan had already involved himself in much greater frauds than this. For years he had periodically swindled the insurance companies he usually represented so well.

He would have found it hard to provide a sensible explanation for this clandestine activity. It had begun in the late summer of 1938, when the hurricane that ravaged the northeastern United States swept through the site of an unfinished, undercapitalized housing project in Rhode Island. Allan was approached by its developers and their contractors with a discreet plea to rescue them from imminent bankruptcy. They suggested that he arrange to have them reimbursed for the damages they would have suffered if they had completed the project, as would have been the case if the construction schedule had been met. Allan realized that proving their claims unfounded would be a hard task for the best of inspectors, given the devastation wreaked by the hurricane in that part of the state. He found himself tempted hardly at all by the ten-percent commission, tempted considerably by outrageous wrongdoing: no one he knew or worked with would dare contemplate such a risk. He accepted it, got away with it, and became—like someone who audaciously tries a cocktail for breakfast and soon finds himself a chronic morning drinker—addicted to professional deceit.

Allan was now being asked to persuade a small insurance company to offer preferential terms to the owner of the doomed racehorse. This was why he had put through his call to the city. He made it clear on the phone that his own commission had been attended to.

The gelding was to be killed that week. Allan knew that in such a small town, with her love of racing and horses, Elizabeth was sure to hear of the event. She would then understand what his phone call had signified. However, he had forgotten about Maud. At the time it had not crossed his mind that in their screaming match Elizabeth might tell Maud what she had heard. Allan felt confident that after twenty-seven years Maud would not abandon him because of a week's infidelity; but she had no inkling of his other, devious business career, and this sordid affair might disgust her. He couldn't blame her if it did.

Allan also craved to be forgiven. That next morning, he called Maud a little before noon.

"A horse? Just a moment." Maud's voice faded: "Do you know about Allan's insuring a horse?" She spoke again into the phone: "We don't know a thing about it."

"We?"

"Elizabeth and I."

"Elizabeth . . . ?"

"Your Elizabeth."

"She's there?"

"I've invited her to stay." Allan kept silent. Maud added, "Keep in touch. Someday I might invite you to stay, too."

Oliver and Elizabeth

SUMMER 1936

THE TOWN LIES ON A LOW PLATEAU OF SCARCELY RE-
lieved flatness; its humid climate swings from fierce cold in
winter to fierce heat in summer; yet visitors have been coming
here for generations, to "take the waters" of its saline springs,
to attend the fashionable August meet, and to observe each
other. Though remote, the town has seen even its year-round
population grow as its safety and amenity make it more and
more attractive to prosperous big-city families. A thriving black
community, established years ago by seasonal waiters and stable grooms who decided to settle here, has helped give this small
and sheltered place a cosmopolitan air.

Twenty-seven years before Elizabeth's return, the town had
been chosen as the seat of a July political convention. One
evening early in the month a garden party was given on the
grounds of one of the twenty-room "cottages" on North Broadway. More than two hundred guests attended, dressed in pale

summer colors, all too much alike for anyone's comfort but their own, clustering in groups as irresistibly as starlings. Among them, one young man stood conspicuously apart and alone. He hadn't come back to the town in twelve summers, since he was ten.

He had enjoyed watching the noisy throng (whom would he meet? like? love?); nevertheless he decided, after a second glass of champagne, that he should either mix or leave. He saw a face he knew—a young woman he had once been introduced to. He went up to her. She looked blank.

"You don't remember me? Sorry—I don't know a single soul . . ."

"Not even me!" she exclaimed. He named their mutual friend. "You're Oliver! I'm Elizabeth Hea—"

"I recognized *you.*"

"Terrific. Say, I don't know anybody either, at least that I'd want to. Let's team up and take our pick." Before Oliver could state his doubts, Elizabeth had imprisoned his left arm. "You go first. How about the lady in blue—pretty nifty, wouldn't you say? Not too old for you?"

"Not at all. I like older women." He was a year or two younger than Elizabeth—an abyss to one fresh out of college.

"I *see*—and she's so spry for twenty-six! Excuse me," Elizabeth said to their prey, "this delightful young man whom I've known for ages and can vouch for his adorably low intentions is nuts about you, and shy, so I thought I'd do you both a favor. This"—her hand clenched Oliver's shrinking elbow—"this is Oliver Pruell."

The name briefly drew Maud's gaze: "I thought I remembered all the Pruells. . . ." Because Oliver did not seize the opening, Maud turned back to Elizabeth. She made a distracting go-between.

Elizabeth kept Oliver continually off balance, introducing him with statements like "I can't imagine what he sees in you, but he's dying to meet you." He was soon relishing the game: he met two post-debs, the governor's wife, and a hooker of terrifying beauty, while introducing Elizabeth to the judge, author, and athletes of her choice.

He became rapidly obsessed by Elizabeth herself. Meeting the hooker may have predisposed him. Even then, he continued to think of Elizabeth as "older" and so "too old for him," until, as he was leading her towards some outlandish hunk of a half-back, she nudged him, with complicity more than intimacy: he was standing right behind her, and he felt her buttocks press against his thighs, soft and muscular as a tongue. Caught in midsentence, he could barely play out his part.

Near the end of the evening, Elizabeth was accosted by a pawy young man impervious to her evasive chatter. Allan, a little drunk, would forget the incident. Oliver stuck to Elizabeth's side, not letting the other man's back or elbow evict him, until he went away. A grateful Elizabeth asked Oliver to take her home.

She was staying with friends nearby. She didn't suggest going someplace else, or ask him in, or sit with him on the veranda. She only kissed him on the cheek, as if to say, I like you, I trust you. This was not what he was looking for, but he dreaded being clumsy. She *was* older. He needed an invitation.

On her way in she said, "I'm going to the Meville Baths tomorrow. Join me? I'll be at the pavilion at a quarter of ten. Ask for cell number eighteen. It's supposed to be the nicest on your side." Oliver went home content.

Next morning at Meville Baths, a private venture specializing in mud (it was dignified as *fango,* in a bow to Battaglia in the Euganean Hills), guided by a debonair Negro in seersucker uniform, Oliver found awaiting him in Room 18 a tub of what looked like steaming shit. He was issued a hooded terry-cloth robe and a pile of towels, given instruction in mud use, and left alone. He gazed dubiously into the tub. What good to him was this last resort of gnarled rheumatics? Having undressed and draped a towel around his hips, he slumped onto a stool, raising his eyes longingly to the frosted bluish skylight.

He heard a scrape of metal and, looking around, saw a door by the bathtub open slightly. A coral-nailed foot slid through the interstice. The door swung open to reveal Elizabeth. She kept one hand behind her back and with the other held to her throat an unvoluminous towel which, dangling as she stepped into the room, uncovered symmetrical fragments of still-unmuddied, clothesless skin. Because a lady was entering the room, Oliver of course stood up. Elizabeth asked, "Care to tango in the fango?"

Oliver felt his own towel slipping. As he grasped it with both hands, Elizabeth smoothly sidearmed from behind her back a mudball the size of a Hand melon. It caught him fair between the eyes.

He stood there blinded, suffocating, naked. Elizabeth's snicker reached him from a distance. She had withdrawn to her own room. She hadn't closed the door between. Oliver gouged the gunk from his eyes and mouth, scooped copious handfuls from the tub, and strode after her, set on revenge.

Now wrapped in a bathrobe, Elizabeth was standing in her room by the far door. As he advanced, she told him, "Wait," and he obeyed. She then emitted a shriek of heartrending terror. Another shriek followed; he still didn't understand. Someone was running down the corridor. Oliver raised one mud-filled hand. Elizabeth, still wailing, stepped away from the door, which opened to admit a sturdy matron whose apprehensive expression changed rapidly to one of bewilderment and then outrage. Oliver hurriedly turned back towards his own room, only to find that Elizabeth had slipped behind him. Whimpering disconsolately, she now barred his way.

The matron was moving towards the tub. Oliver saw the alarm button dimpling the wall above it. With the cunning of a beast at bay, he kept his mouth shut, slapped a fistful of mud over the button, and bolted out the door and down the corridor of the ladies' section.

Chronometrically his flight lasted twenty seconds. He passed one customer with her attendant; another, unaccompanied, who did not notice him; and a cleaning woman trundling a cart full of woolly sticks. In imagined time his course approached infinity, and during it he met other figures less palpable and far more real: his father jubilant at having his worst fears justified, his mother chalk-white on the sickbed to which his disgrace had brought her, the foul-mouthed trusty on his chain gang. He experienced terminal revelations about man's fate and the nature of reality. He recognized truth as both absolute and incommunicable, time itself as irreversible and irrelevant. He verged on a mystical understanding of *caritas*.

A racket of flapping feet—his own—recalled his circumstances. He then entertained the clever thought that the women's rooms might all have rooms for men next to them. Doors between bolted only on women's side? Why not? Women, women never molest men, ha ha, only men women. Togetherness possible if OK with girls? Baths big lovenest? He tried the next door: open, room empty. Unbolted party door: open, room empty. Opened door to far corridor—nobody there, all chasing maniac on other side! Lucky Oliver! He cantered back to Room 18, where, shutting himself in, he squatted breathless on his heels.

He'd better keep moving. Wash first. He stepped up to the basin. More luck: from the mirror glared a mud-masked face that might have belonged to Al Jolson, or anyone. He had remained anonymous. His still-gasping mouth was opening in a grin of chiaroscuro dazzle when, from under his raised arms, two sharp-fingered hands began curving around his chest to tweak his nipples. He started to giggle. She made him fuck her in the tub.

Over lunch he asked her: Why not last night?

"Where? Front porch? Back seat? No-luggage hotel? We still," she added, "need a place to go. I think I know where. Doesn't your skin feel *mad?*"

They drove out to the village called Lake George. At first Mrs. Quilty acted hostile. She had long ago worked for Oliver's mother, and she told him, "You're no Mr. Ratchett, you're Oliver Pruell. Master Oliver, what a thing to ask!" Oliver prepared to flee.

Elizabeth said, "All the more reason to help us, Mrs. Quilty. I've never talked about you with Mrs. Pruell, but I'm sure she has nothing but praise, and Frederick Stockton recommended you in glowing terms—"

"It's a difficult time we're living in, that's what I say," Mrs. Quilty interrupted. "Hard saving money, what with the government takes it all in taxes, even keeping the house in repair, you have to start paying city prices to people, and when all is said and done, there's no respect anymore, no respect from the young anymore, no respect at all—someone my age, used to be young men would tip their hats, now you're lucky if they nod." Mrs. Quilty barely paused. "It's eighteen-fifty a week, in advance, if you please."

Elizabeth made Oliver try out the room at once. His qualms were forgotten.

He asked her, "Who's Frederick Stockton?"

"Your father must know him. He had an arrangement with Mrs. Quilty. He also introduced her to other gentlemen. Hence the righteous indignation. She was quite an artist, it seems. That's how she paid for the house. You shouldn't have let her put you down."

"If she ever told my mother—"

"She doesn't give a hoot about your mother. She just knows you do."

"So why did she bother?"

"To show who's on top. You're too vulnerable, sweetie. Listen: you can be the way people want you, or they can be the way you want *them.*"

"OK." Oliver pondered: "Even my mother?"

Elizabeth smiled: "I see what you mean. . . . Does she still keep a time clock on you?"

"No. But she thinks a lot about me."

"Sure. She's a mother."

"I never know *what* she's thinking about me anymore. I'd rather have you to come home to."

"You'd like me for a mother?"

"You bet I would."

"Not a chance, baby." She sank three nails into his perineum. "Love you like a mother? Even Mrs. Quilty knows better than that."

Oliver reddened. "Love?" Elizabeth gave him a noisy kiss. She trapped him with her knees and elbows. "Hey!" he complained. "Am I supposed to love you?"

"What do you think's going on?"

"I don't think anything. I don't know. I've been having a terrific time. I love this. . . ."

Elizabeth let him creep his way to the next question, which he voiced a little high:

"Do you love me?"

Arching her brows preposterously, Elizabeth replied, "Dunno. Been having such a terrific time. . . . Dumbbell." She licked his lips.

Oliver felt towards Elizabeth an enthusiastic curiosity as to what she might do next, and not just in bed.

He had "written" in college; now he wrote her poems. They fell sneakily between the erotic and the obscene. She read each one slowly back to him, making him squirm, asking for more.

At the end of the third week in July, Oliver received a letter from Louisa, the friend who had originally introduced them.

She quoted what Elizabeth had written about him: "My Oliver! So elegant, so smart, and what of it? That's what trust funds are for. He has something else that may redeem the greed of his forebears and the repulsive expense of his education: enough talent to scram. He's just written a sonnet about my derriere that's so good that I swear to (a) get it published and (b) go riding every day to make sure it still means what it says. . . ." Reading this, Oliver told himself something like: She thinks, therefore I am.

Elizabeth's comments also dismayed him. Had he no worth except as a writer-to-be? Would he have to scram? Oliver liked his comforts. More immediately, he felt sick at the thought that, if his poems were published, his mother and father might read them—a ridiculous fear, and a real one.

On an afternoon in mid-August Elizabeth suggested they go fishing on Lake Luzerne.

"I hate fishing."

"At least you'll find out what might have been." He had an inkling of what she meant: his father cajoling a trout fly through forbidding foliage.

"What are we fishing for?" he asked as he pushed off their skiff.

"Who knows. Middlemouth bass?"

They took turns rowing. Twice Oliver pulled up a round-eyed, rough-scaled perch, which smacked the metal bucket for a while. In the middle of the lake Elizabeth racked the oars.

The afternoon was gray and placid. They lay in the bottom of the boat. Oliver rested his head against the cushioned plank at the stern, Elizabeth tucked herself against his side, a cheek in the crook of his shoulder, one hand inside his open shirt. The water slapped the slowly turning boat with varying briskness.

He watched the boat's slow gyrations, the little waves accumulating to slap it gently. Over the lake from reed-lined shores came a mulchy scent. Water and hills wavered in diffuse

gray light. It was as if life had ended and he were dreaming a
recollection. He could not tell what he was feeling. His feelings
had turned into repetitions of waves and of the grayness that
almost did not change, under the bright low sky.

He let the boat drift. He had no place to go. He did not think,
except as part of the dreaming. Everything that had ever happened was only seeming, a seeming of having been dreamed, not
mattering, without matter. The boat rocked sleepily, turning
this way and that, providing his feelings, his thoughts, their
objects. For one moment quickly gone he tried to say what was
happening to him (maybe Hegel, maybe Heine; they didn't
matter either). He had nothing to grasp. He was surrounded
entirely by the dream of his being. He was surrounded by
nothing. He did not need anything outside himself, outside this
dream.

An hour passed. He gazed into the sky. The darkening grayness altered in the west. Above the silhouette of hills glowed
low, scalloped reefs of emberish red. "Nothing outside us
stays." Thought again subsided into the murk of woods and
water, the clouds in their moment of fire and extinction looked
to him like his own life being given shape, a hymn of pleasure
and melancholy.

To the east the sky had assumed a darker and more soothing
complexion: a slope of cool blue, or coal blue, the color that as
a child he used to call policeman blue. He thought of the uncle
the mention of whose name turned grown-ups silent, in disgrace, having squandered his money and his good marriage
with other women. He was living in a suburb of Cleveland with
a Mrs. Quilty. Blue, blue, policeman's blue. Oliver looked into
the darkness and felt a shudder of power, realizing that his life
belonged to him entirely, that there was no one else. He would
never know such happiness again. When Elizabeth woke up,
night had fallen.

Oliver's parents came back from Europe. He divided his time
agreeably between Elizabeth and the family house.

On the morning of the last Wednesday in August, Elizabeth took Oliver to the track, leading him through the stable area to a particular stall, where a handsome bay stallion glared out at them.

"Assured, by Sure Thing out of Little Acorn. And look." Elizabeth pointed to the local listings in the *Morning Telegraph:* Assured had been entered in a thousand-dollar claiming race that afternoon. "They must be nuts. We can't not buy him. It's the best bargain since Louisiana." She wasn't kidding.

Oliver began arguing with her: something was wrong with the animal, where would they find a thousand dollars, what would they do with a racehorse? Elizabeth: she'd seen Assured work two days earlier, they'd raid his piggy bank, they'd buy another horse so it wouldn't be lonely. "You're right about one thing, though. It *is* fishy. Let's ask your father."

Mr. Pruell was a member of the Association, which at that time ran the track. Since Oliver's adolescence he had become a mystery to his son, who hoped he would remain one as long as possible. Oliver had a plan, kept secret even from himself: he would become so triumphantly successful that Mr. Pruell's dragonlike nature would be disarmed before he could unleash it. The summer had fostered Oliver's confidence. Elizabeth had authenticated him. She now threatened to mix up parts of his life that had remained comfortably distinct.

He implored her not to consult his father. Elizabeth knew he had no reason to worry and told him so. He refused to accompany her. This childish stubbornness offended her.

Elizabeth saw, perhaps too easily, that Mr. Pruell liked her and loved his son. She phoned him, he invited her for noontime cocktails and listened to her story.

"He can't really be claimed, you see—it's just a race to keep him fit. All the same, I'll check." He called up the owner, then told her, "Yup. The genteel fix is in. You understand—we all know each other here, and in cases like this, it's hands off. You'll have to look for another horse."

"Another dream gone! Mr. Pruell, this morning in the cafeteria, over at the track, I heard a man talking about Assured—that's how I knew he was running. I don't think he's heard about your arrangement."

Mr. Pruell made several more calls, the last one advising Assured's owner to scratch him. "Good girl. There's some fellow from out of town—Jersey, I hear—"

"Me too."

"Not Jersey *City*, surely? I should have been told. You deserve the Juliette Low medal," Mr. Pruell fondly added. "Now, you stay for lunch, and I'll take you to the track—the owner wants to thank you in person. Where's my little boy?"

Oliver went to bars. "How's Elizabeth?" he was asked. No one in town had ever seen him without her. He skipped lunch. He arrived at the track before two and stood in the infield with rented binoculars. He soon spotted her in the clubhouse with his father and some other men. One of them, lanky and young, stuck close to Elizabeth, staring at her, talking to her whenever he could. Elizabeth did not notice Oliver. Assured did not run. He went to Mrs. Quilty's: no message.

That evening Oliver drove out to Riley's Lake House, where a good band was playing. He stopped at the bar. A group of young people came in, some of whom he knew. He took a seat at their table, next to the lanky man he had seen at the track. Oliver began talking to him. His name was Walter Trale. How did he like it here? He had come here to work. To work—at his age? Yes, he was already earning his living, as an animal painter. Oliver said he liked the way animals looked unpainted. Walter laughed and explained that he did portraits of favorite animals. He had just painted Assured. He had made thousands of dollars since he was fifteen. He would go to college anyway, starting next month—gee, next week. "Unless I drop everything."

At this, Oliver felt delectable foreboding. He leaned invitingly towards his companion. Walter confided, "There are moments, you know, when the doors fly open—no, you see there aren't any doors at all."

"Holy smoke, Walter. Tell me more."

"Once I fell in love with a circus elephant."

"Walter, you can't expect me to believe that."

"You know how kids get crushes, don't you? I was eight. I wanted a picture of him, so my mother took some snapshots. He came out looking like a bag of fog."

"Mmm."

"One night I had a dream about my elephant. It was as if he was on a screen, but he didn't look like a bag of fog, he was all there. So next morning I drew him the way he looked in my dream. I had my love souvenir, and in one night I'd learned how to draw animals. They say it's natural talent, but the only natural thing is I was crazy about that elephant."

"You know, I wouldn't tell that story to everybody you happen to meet."

"I just love animals—I've loved all kinds of animals since then. The funny part is that I could never draw people."

"Why? Don't you love people?"

"I never felt as though I didn't. Still, you can imagine, getting so much attention and money, spending all this time with these rich old guys and their wives—I wondered, am I some kind of fruitcake? So today I met this person."

"You mean, a *woman?*"

"It wasn't so much that she was beautiful, it was the way she moved. Her fingers and knees moved the same way her face did, or maybe it's the other way around. You understand what I mean?"

"Boy, do I!"

"I couldn't take my eyes off her. She could see I was going crazy looking at her—" Walter broke off. Oliver asked him what had happened next. "She was really nice. She's coming to pose for me tomorrow. I can't believe it."

Oliver could. He was starting to say, "Well, I have to take

a shit something awful," when the band boomed into "Stompin'
at the Savoy." They gestured goodbye in the din.

Oliver went back to Mrs. Quilty's. No messages. He sat in
their room. He hadn't called either; but he was the one who had
been left out. Events had taken place where his presence had
not been missed. Elizabeth and his father, Elizabeth and Walter
(her business, of course)—Elizabeth had revealed herself as a
kind of person he hadn't suspected: a right bitch.

Unfair? Had she treated *him* fairly? His weeks with her had
exhausted him. She had demanded so much. She kept wanting
him to change. Like buying a horse. She was insane to think he
could write.

She had given him a wonderful vacation. Now vacation time
was ending. Next week came Labor Day, when he must go back
to the city and find a job. But why not get the jump on everybody and do it now?

He was discouraged at the prospect of staying alone in the
city, until he realized he could call his friend Louisa. He could
then be the first to explain what had happened. She must know
other girls.

Oliver left a letter for Elizabeth with Mrs. Quilty. In it he
blamed himself for the day's events, although he did mention
"others you have met." He said he was not surprised that she
was leaving him. "While I benefited from being your lover, I
don't think I benefited you, because my character is entirely
inadequate. I'd never be able to keep up with you. . . ." He
should have written "down with you"—Elizabeth had pulled
him earthwards. Oliver resembled a balloonist, unable to steer,
able only to rise or sink, and now he went up, up—firing the
air in his mind until he floated once again among comforting
coal-blue pinnacles.

He left the next day. Elizabeth never answered his letter. In
December he received the latest issue of *The Presidio Papers,*
a little review published in San Francisco, containing three of

his poems. Such a magazine, he told himself, would never come into his parents' hands. He was wrong. When his father died, years later, Oliver discovered that throughout his life he had collected erotica old and new. He found *The Presidio Papers* in his collection.

Oliver and Pauline

SUMMER 1938

T WO YEARS LATER, AFTER GRADUATING FROM COLLEGE, Pauline Dunlap came to stay with Maud Ludlam, her sister, and Allan, the husband Maud had taken the summer before. Maud, who was six years older than Pauline, had acted as a kind of foster mother to her ever since their father had become a widower.

Their father had died that March, leaving his entire estate to his daughters. The orphaned sisters learned, in the weeks following his death, that the conditions of their inheritance were known only to themselves and their father's lawyers. No one else seemed aware that Mr. Dunlap had amassed a great deal less than the many millions attributed to him, or that, as a believer in primogeniture, he had bequeathed nine-tenths of his fortune to his elder daughter. Since Maud was now married, the sisters decided to keep these facts to themselves: Pauline might benefit from appearing as a conspicuous heiress.

Oliver, who had known Pauline in boyhood, rediscovered her early that summer. He had come up on vacation from the city, where he now worked in his father's office. Both he and Pauline knew at once who the other "was" (a Pruell, a Dunlap), they enjoyed meeting once again, and when, later, during the party that had reunited them, a thunderstorm caught them out of doors together, a complicity emerged. They had taken refuge under an immense copper beech when lightning transsected the night and revealed Pauline picking her nose. Oliver couldn't pretend he hadn't noticed: "So that's how you spend your free time."

Pauline waited for the thunder to rumble away. "I couldn't wait. It *is* a basic pleasure."

The shower ended. They walked back to the lighted house. Merely sprinkled, Pauline's elegance had not been impaired. Had Mainbocher or perhaps Rochas, Oliver wondered, clothed that well-turned young body? She wore a dime-size yellow diamond on one hand, chunky green stones around a wrist; and at her throat, hung from a velvet band, a sumptuous tear of a pearl lay pink against her skin. Even after the rain, her hair kept the neatness of its image in rotogravure, combed sleekly back from her rounded forehead, the snug curls behind her ears starred with real, unwilted cornflowers. Eyes pure white and blue looked at Oliver with moist glitter as she implored, "You won't tell?"

"Never—provided you have supper with me tomorrow. Otherwise . . ." Oh, tomorrow was impossible. But not the evening after.

They dined. He liked her enough to take her out again. He liked her because she trusted him so readily. She liked him because he was easy to trust. He had a hold on himself, the know-how of someone who has not just been to schools.

She less liked his stopping at the politer kind of caress. Oliver could not have said what inspired his punctilious reticence. He simply felt that he could not take advantage of such candor. His decorum may have expressed a fear of seducing someone rich: among other things, "trust" meant taking good care of people's money.

At one roadhouse supper he watched her nimbly shattering a lamb chop with the stainless-steel chopsticks she always carried. Her one-handed performance undermined the known laws of physics. Oliver asked, "How do you manage? You're better than any Chink."

"Oh, don't use that word! Did you see the newsreels? Families bombed out of house and home! I *long* to go there, to do *something*. They need help so badly."

"Are you being serious?"

"As far as I can tell."

"Then go. Join the Red Cross. Volunteer with the Quakers."

"Oh, no. I have to see for myself. *I* want to be the one who decides what to do."

"You can still go there—"

"I can't afford it."

"You're *not* serious, you see? You could hock half your jewels and rebuild Nanking."

"They're not mine. Not yet," she quickly added. Leaning forward, she momentously confided, "Not only do I pick my nose, I'm on an allowance till I'm twenty-five."

"And by then your charge accounts will be surging through five figures. . . ."

"Oh, Maud buys me my clothes. But not China." She ate some more chop. In a most endearing way, she looked through his eyes, right into him: "Why won't you sleep with me? Is it me or is it you? Should I try Tabu? Lifebuoy?"

He hesitated: "It will be your first time out, won't it?"

"I'd start with the second if I could."

"You're as svelte as the *V* in Veedol, but—"

"Don't tell me! Just, please, give it sometime your most

earnest consideration." He promised to do that. Pauline continued, "Maud's a dream, but of course I'd love a little independence—you know, my own dough?" She added, "What's the fun of owning a horse if you can't pay for its oats?"

He explored legal possibilities with her, none of them very promising. "Try Lady Luck."

"Oh, I love to gamble. But how? The market's dead as a doormouse. Anyway, you still need capital to get started."

"You like horses—"

"Don't tempt me! My roommate did work out a terrific technique for betting."

"See? Your worries are over."

Oliver was joking; not Pauline. For the next week she was inaccessible before sundown. She spent her days in the Association library, which kept a complete set of the *Morning Telegraph*. She used the paper's charts to verify and improve her roommate's system.

The system decreed that, to be playable, a horse must have won its last start over a distance no shorter than that of its forthcoming race. To this requirement Pauline added certain strict indicators of the jockey's form. According to her research, when jockey and horse satisfied her conditions, which she cleverly reduced to three algebraic equations, she could pick a winner every third race.

Her method had one disadvantage. It eliminated so many entries that she could only bet on one race in twenty, and when she turned from theory to practice, a week at the local track gave her two chances at best to venture her five dollars. She lost once, and won once, at nine to two. While strengthening her confidence, the results also made clear that earning seventeen-fifty a week would not transform her life.

"I think I'll peddle my charms instead," she told Oliver, "something I may do anyway if you don't get off your fanny and into mine."

"Chopsticks, that's *not* your way to talk."

"Wrong nickname, toots. The point is, so far my system's no answer to a virgin's prayer. I suppose I could raise the ante."

"May I point out that Ma Bell and a good book can put every track in the land within your greedy reach? You'd have eighty races a day to pick from instead of eight."

"Terrific, but where does one find a bookmaker?"

"Just ask me."

"You do get around."

"In this town? There's one under every rainspout."

Oliver began taking her bets. Play increased dramatically. Pauline became even more infatuated with the lure of mastering risk, and her system at first worked better than Oliver had expected. But soon she grew impatient again. Her hopes had risen higher, and her rewards had remained slim: hours of calculation and a dozen bets for a profit of seventy dollars. She wanted China.

One day Oliver brought her bad news: their bookmaker had not appeared, and they had missed a winner. As he anticipated, Pauline responded with more fright than anger: "If I can't stick to the rules, I'll be wiped out for certain."

Oliver by now had become irrevocably involved. He did not know why—certainly not to help. (Scarcely a hundred dollars was at stake.) It felt to him more like a kind of seduction, one in which he was playing a spidery, rather feminine role. When he took her money, his skin would prickle electrically, as though he were masterminding a conspiracy.

"You're right," he replied. "You have no reserves, and at this rate you never will. I've got an idea."

"Oh, hurry."

"There's something called a martingale. When you lose, you double your bet, and you go on doubling till you win. Then you recoup all your losses *and* you get paid off on a bigger stake."

"OK. So I bet five dollars and lose, and next time I rebet that five plus another five makes ten"—she had her pad and pencil out—"and I lose and bet five plus the fifteen is twenty—right, doubles every time—and twenty at three to one is sixty instead of fifteen, so: I'm ahead forty-five dollars instead of . . . five? Why have you been hoarding this wisdom?" Before he could answer: "Wait! What if I lose? I'd be out, um, thirty-five instead of fifteen—couldn't that get expensive?"

"You bet the thirty-five with your next five and get it back—eventually you're bound to win. You say you never have runs of more than three or four losses."

"I showed you my tables. I ran into some bad streaks, but they were few and far between."

Oliver knew better. No matter what the game, losing streaks come as surely as nightfall; and sooner or later every gambler discovers the martingale. Oliver watched her charm herself with its promise.

He himself found charm in her growing dependence. He thought of repeating the drama of the unplaced bet in order to replenish her confusion but, instead, simply warned her once or twice that his bookmaker was out of town. "The powers that be always seem to do their being elsewhere," she cried. Her impatience made her the liveliest company. She almost succeeded in unbuttoning his deliberate propriety.

After a week, events of themselves produced a crisis: Pauline had seven straight losses. The last one cost her three hundred and twenty dollars. She dreaded putting up twice that amount, dreaded not betting. Oliver offered to stake her. She refused as vehemently as she could—not vehemently enough, she knew, although not insincerely. Oliver remarked, "You sound as though you'd be doing *me* a favor."

To Pauline, this suggested a way out: "I'll make a deal with you. If I can't pay you back, I'll bequeath you my maidenhead. And you *have* to accept it."

"Pauline, you're a babe in the wood."

"To hell with it. I'll ask Maud."

The prospect of having her in his debt excited Oliver. "I consent. But I insist on choosing the place and time."

"Maybe. I'll give you a week's leeway. While 'cherry-ripe themselves do cry. . . .' The horse is Disrespect. And he's going to win. Then I'll rent a real man, you churl."

This cunning insurance contented Pauline. She found fresh hope in her future. Disrespect finished out of the money, however, and with the loss her confidence shriveled.

Pauline was overcome with unexpected, unappeasable shame. Oliver's reassurances left her cold: "Even *if* the money didn't matter, *I* do. I won't let you let me off. I'm not a silly little girl."

"I know. We should have opened a joint account, then it wouldn't have mattered." Oliver did not know what he meant by this badinage.

In spite of their agreement, Pauline's remorse quenched any thought of not paying the debt in cash. She decided to earn the money. Oliver was surprised and not very concerned. Whether Pauline paid him back or not, he was becoming the center of her life. Never before had he so dominated anyone.

As for the money, Oliver had little faith in any gambling system, certainly not in Pauline's. He had laid off none of her bets; she had had no bookmaker except himself. She owed him nothing—he was holding six hundred and thirty-five dollars that belonged to her.

Pauline asked Maud to help her find a job. Maud, unaware of Oliver's importance in her life, suggested his father, a good friend who, at this time, was busily reorganizing the Association, of which he had been elected president. He might well think of something for her to do.

Disconcerted at first, Pauline quickly convinced herself that Oliver presented no obstacle to her approaching Mr. Pruell. She called on him the next day. They did not talk about jobs. He had noticed more than Maud, and he knew how his son spent his evenings. He liked Pauline. When he took her into his study, it was he who made an appeal: "Are you in love with Oliver? I hope so. I need help."

"Help with *Oliver?*"

"It seems to me he's turned into another person. Until a year or so ago, he used to treat me like an old fart. He knew what life was all about, and I was the slave to business. Now he not only respects and trusts me, he's actually gone to work for me. I'm worried."

"Don't you think he's happy the way he is?"

"How can he be? When I was twenty, I wanted to be a writer too. But I had no gift for it, so I went to work and made money instead. Listen, my dear, from the start I had a notion that if I made a fortune it would be so a child of mine could lead any kind of life he wanted. Why should Oliver do what I've done all over again? If he wants to write, he should write."

"Are you sure that's what he wants? He's never breathed a word—"

"He has real talent. You look skeptical. Well, I haven't much to show you since he left college, only some poetry, and that"— he took *The Presidio Papers* from a locked drawer—"extremely off-color. Still, you're a big girl." He handed Pauline the review.

She read about ten lines, after which, despite her host's warning, the volume tumbled to the floor. Pauline turned very pink, from more than embarrassment.

"I'm an idiot, forgive me." Tactfully, Mr. Pruell did not even smile at her predicament. "You'll have to take my word for it. You know, fathers usually discourage this sort of thing."

"Who was she?"

"And before it slips my mind, don't tell Oliver about the poems. I'm supposed not to know."

Pauline promised. She would have promised Oliver's father anything.

"Cherry-ripe, remember?" she chided Oliver that evening.

"How could I forget? *You* seemed to have." He kissed her in the mouth. "Let's meet at Meville Baths at eleven."

"In the *baths?* In the *morning?*"

"Ask for Room Thirty-two."

Oliver knew the time had come. Pauline's fresh fervor hardly surprised him; it confirmed his belief that power sticks to those who disdain it.

Oliver made exuberant love to Pauline—his poetry come to life. After the baths, he enjoyed her in other unlikely and even more public places: a treehouse, a moonlit green on the golf course in Geyser Park, the bottom of a rowboat on Lake Luzerne. They also used his room at Mrs. Quilty's, spending long afternoons there. He did things with his mouth she had never dared imagine. He invented the ways she felt.

His exuberance was not feigned. In reenacting the things that Elizabeth had taught him, he made them his own: they became proofs of his mastery. He watched Pauline fall in love with him with heartfelt joy.

He knew she would want to marry him. He let her broach the subject and told her, "You live in a style I won't afford for years."

"I'll eat cereal three times a day. I'll save the box tops."

"That's just what I mean."

"I only want to live with you forever. It can't cost that much." Oliver shrugged. "I'll get a job."

"My beloved, qualified *men* are unemployed these days."

"I tell you, I know people."

"You're a swell girl, Pauline, but you've been schooled for a life of idleness. What would our friends say if I let you work? I'd hold down two jobs myself if I could, but there aren't enough hours in the day."

"Oh, I don't want you to work *more,* I don't want you to have to work at all—not in an office."

"What do you suggest I do—make book?"

Pauline took this for a possible pun: "Ask your father to help. He thinks I'm good for you."

"He *is* helping. I'm on the payroll."

"I bet he'd set you up."

"If I were on my own, I'd like to show what I can do by myself, not with *his* money." Pauline smiled. Where Oliver meant starting his own business, she envisioned late nights over a typewriter.

"There must be something we can do—*I* can do. Oh, why am I such a twerp?" Oliver kept very still: as if, holding a sure hand in a game of chance, he were waiting for his adversary to plunge. "If only . . . ," Pauline was saying, and Oliver did not budge; did not light his next cigarette.

Pauline had decided not to tell Oliver about her true expectations. She honestly believed the matter irrelevant: she'd always had enough money, and they would have enough. She saw nevertheless that, to be convinced, Oliver needed tangible prospects.

Maud wanted her to marry well. Maud had money to spare. Would she spare it? Why not? Oliver never knew what bitterness then came between the two sisters. Pauline had only told him that she would ask Maud to advance the date of her inheritance. Oliver accepted the lie and discounted it—wills could not so easily be changed. He did not care. In his own way, he was as indifferent to money as she was. He was getting what he most wanted: Pauline was committing to him everything she had.

Two days later, Pauline told him what she had obtained from Maud: her spending money would be doubled, their father's house in the city would be put in her name. Oliver was impressed. He maintained a show of reluctance for a day, then yielded, all too content to declare to the world that this lively, beautiful, sought-after young woman had preferred him to all others.

Mr. Pruell gave a party to announce their engagement. Maud did not attend; she was traveling in Europe. She did not even get back in time for the October wedding. Because of a war scare, her train out of Vienna had been canceled, and she missed her sailing. Oliver might have guessed at other reasons; he felt too happy to look for them. Like a driver who has found a shortcut on his daily route, like a soldier who has won an objective without bloodshed, like a writer who has made his point thriftily, he drew happiness from his own efficacy. At the engagement party he realized that the money he had kept from Pauline's seven bad bets covered the expenses of his courtship down to the last dinner and drink. He indulged himself by confessing this deceit to her.

"You're a cad and a bounder," she said, "putting me through that torture for nothing."

"But we still have the money!"

"And what if I'd won, huh?"

"You're delightful and adorable, but when it comes to practical matters, leave them to me."

A note of seriousness in his words affected Pauline: "I want to leave everything to you! A propos—how about a date in your treehouse?"

Oliver took her in his arms and nibbled her eyebrows. "Why don't we wait? Let's make our wedding night a second first time."

"You're kidding—no? OK, if you say so." For a moment she felt stifled by the dog-day weight of his benevolence. She wanted to put her hand on his cock, in front of his parents, in front of their friends. She only asked, "No more treehouse? No more Mrs. Quilty?"

Oliver smilingly shook his head. He would never make the mistake of confusing Pauline with Elizabeth, or her demands with his own needs. She belonged to his life to come, the life that now stretched ahead of him like a succession of well-ordered, discreetly lighted rooms: the marble-flagged entrance where Pauline in long gold dress stood waiting by the door; the upstairs drawing room furnished in Louis XV, with a few cushioned couches and armchairs covered in softest gray and beige, their ease set off against the evening-dress formality of a grand piano; a dining room whose mahogany table, almost black in candlelight, was surrounded by tuxedoed cronies smoking cigars and drinking port; the ground-floor den with its chesterfield sofa and chair, its desk full of secrets, its private telephone, a refuge in which to explore the solitude that gave a man of the world his most substantial pleasure. She belonged to a perspective that he could enter without the slightest qualm or effort. If he could claim little originality for this perspective, he nonetheless took pride in it as in a personal creation, perhaps because he felt so entirely its possessor.

Oliver's self-esteem did not lessen when he learned, much later, the facts of Pauline's inheritance. He never overtly reproached her, and in truth the revelation left him almost grateful. After all, it confirmed that he had the right to manage things, the right to show condescension and pity, the right to control.

Owen and Phoebe: I
SUMMER 1961–SUMMER 1963

Y EARS LATER, ON THE VERY JULY FIRST THAT ALLAN LUD-
lam discovered Elizabeth, and in the same town, Owen Lewison
instructed his bank in the city to settle a large sum of money
on his daughter, Phoebe, then on the eve of her twenty-first
birthday.

This was not the first time Owen had decided to endow his
daughter: two years earlier, he had told her that he was estab-
lishing a trust fund to provide her with an income of her own.

He had spoken to her on a day in mid-August, while they
were sitting outdoors in a shade of maples. Beyond the blurred
distances of steamy fields and hills squatted blue-tinged Adirondacks. Phoebe blushed through her damp tan.

"Poppa! What have I done—"

"Go on—you do everything wonderfully."

"You don't mean school? That doesn't even—"

"Oh, yes, it does. But this isn't a reward. I want you to learn
how to run your own life."

"Poppa, I plan to go to work—"

"Well, I *want* you to work."

"Then—"

"But with room to maneuver. So you can be choosy. So you won't be tempted straight off by some well-heeled john. Two hundred a month ought to help."

"That's fabulous, Poppa—"

"And with luck it'll grow."

"Poppa, what if—" She hesitated. "What if something special comes up—like buying a car? Not that I want to, but—"

"Ask me. It'll be a pleasure."

Owen explained that he would keep control of the capital: "That's what needs to do the growing. You do agree I can manage that best? You can see, too, that it would be a mistake to deplete it for something like a car."

Of course Phoebe agreed. She had already begun making a plan. Knowing that she would have money of her own was reviving a particular desire.

That spring she had attended an extracurricular lecture at her college. The students had invited as speaker the first long-haired young grown-up male she had ever seen. He wore boots and jeans with his suede jacket and string tie. He lived in the Rockies, and he spoke of their areas of unsullied wilderness. He spoke of the inroads being made in the wilderness by urban man. He spoke of the corruption in capitalist society, how it degraded whatever it touched, individuals included, out of its need to turn a profit. The wilderness, he said, encouraged individuals to remain simply themselves: it forced them to acquire a knowledge that proved incomparably useful for leading happy, self-sustaining lives. He had long held revolution as his political ideal, but he now saw that the time for revolution had not yet come. Until that time came, he recommended renouncing society. No one asked the speaker what, in the wilderness, people did with their evenings. Phoebe and her peers, usually so skeptical, accepted his precepts raptly.

Soon afterwards, in the city, she met a young man who fleshed out the lecturer's vision. He was to spend the coming year in New Mexico as a forest ranger. She had gasped her admiration, which had led him to suggest: Come along. Although he loomed golden and vast, Phoebe could not then even dream of such a prospect. Now she wrote to him: had he meant it? He phoned back to say he had.

When Phoebe announced that she was leaving college to help guard the timberlands of the southwest, Owen, who hadn't smoked in a decade, compulsively clutched an empty breast pocket. He considered himself swindled.

He knew enough to hide his feelings and dicker. He at first expressed only surprise, commenting that it seemed a foolish life for her to lead—she couldn't even do the work. Phoebe claimed she could; she'd been a star on pack trips, better than most men. (His own fault, he reflected—he'd raised her like a boy. Her brother had been the indoor child.) Perhaps. But why stop two years short of her B.A.? She replied that a diploma in art from a progressive college didn't have much pull these days—it could even be held against you. Owen asked: And the art itself? For ten years she had wanted to become a professional painter. (Owen could accept that possibility. He didn't expect his girl to go to law school, and everyone had pronounced her talent genuine. She should go on studying art. Afterwards she might grow out of it, or she might succeed. He imagined visits to her then, in the city. . . .) Art, said Phoebe, what's so great about art? "I'll be doing something real."

"Even Marx knew better than that—remember 'productive work'? Nothing very productive about staring at trees."

"Poppa, *you* said room to maneuver—"

"I meant, to get someplace in the world—the 'real' world. Not run away from it."

"You're taking the money back?"

Owen wanted to know more. "These 'friends' in New Mexico—do they include a boyfriend?"

"What are you so afraid of? I'm not spending my life there. He's not a boy, he's a man," Phoebe couldn't help adding.

Owen was afraid—not of what Phoebe imagined, but of being excluded. He sincerely wanted Phoebe's freedom and saw himself as part of it.

"You'll be junking the benefits of nineteen years. You're too bright for the forest primeval—"

"But it's what I *haven't* learned—"

"—and if you want to go off with a 'man,' say so, for Christ's sake."

Of course there was a man—someone to provide the excuse for change. Phoebe got herself stuck defending this man she hardly knew. She embarrassed herself; she made herself angry; she grubbed for justifications.

"As soon as I want something, you welch."

"Phoebe, I'd be irresponsible—"

"Bullshit, you want to run my—"

"—what's best for you. Please watch your language when you're talking to me."

"The best is what *you* . . . That's what the money's for—to depend even more—"

"Forget about New Mexico."

"Goodbye, Poppa." She left before she started crying. (How could this clever man act so dumb?)

Phoebe went walking for two hours. Back home, she made some long-distance calls, packed two bags, and caught an evening bus to the city.

She left before her mother came home: Phoebe called Louisa the next day to explain her decision. Later, she kept in touch with her, so that both her parents would always know that "she was all right." Eight months passed before Owen saw her again.

Phoebe never left the city: the prospect of life in the wilderness with a golden youth had quickly lost its allure. She stayed for a while with the family of a college friend. She realized that her first task was to earn a living. Her old painting teacher helped her find jobs as an artist's model; daring to pose in the nude gave her confidence. She proposed herself to several photographers, some of whom did fashion work, one of whom shrewdly distinguished, among her many attractions, her slim feet and ankles. He specialized in shoes. Four months after leaving home, Phoebe became a professional model from the knees down. A few well-paid hours a week supplied her needs.

While Phoebe was learning how to support herself, her teacher introduced her to several artists. Phoebe went to their shows, visited their studios, met them after work. Their lives appealed to her. They had not yet been uprooted by a booming market; the Cedar Bar was still a flourishing club. Their work filled her with a passion of emulation, not of any one manner, but rather of the zany dedication the various manners expressed. She began coveting a style of her own.

She did not imagine she knew anything. She was preparing herself for art school, hoping Hofmann would accept her, when she saw a show by a painter called Trale, someone her teacher had often mentioned. This small retrospective, his first in many years, was hung in a gallery on East Tenth Street. Phoebe spent an hour there on her first visit and went back the day after, and the day after that, to make sure that in Walter Trale she had "met her master." She decided to make him exactly that.

Owen would have admired her efficiency. She persuaded friends of friends to introduce her to Walter, and later to recommend her. She let him often be reminded of her, strolling past him at the Cedar, for instance, on de Kooning's obliging arm. When at last she called on him, with six drawings, decorously smudged into a semblance of originality, he found himself on her side from the start. He looked at the drawings, and at her, and accepted her request to become his apprentice. She would do his chores, model for him occasionally, and work under his guidance.

Walter lived in a loft building on Broadway and the corner

of Ninth Street; he found Phoebe a kitchenette studio on the floor below him. She settled into a new life. Walter took his role seriously. Between what he made her do for him and what he made her do for herself, she scarcely had time to display her feet.

On a warm, drizzling mid-April morning, two months after Phoebe moved in, Owen paid her a visit. She had told him to meet her at Walter's, where the door was never locked and he could just barge in; which is what he did, a little early, having made the unfamiliar trip to the lower East Side in less time than expected. He did not see Phoebe at first. Near the far end of the vast room, Walter Trale was sketching a nude model, and the sight of her compelled Owen's attention. The model was not sitting still: she was slowly turning under the painter's gaze, as though performing a slithery dance, lying, crouching, kneeling in turn, shifting from one position to the next with a slow-motion regularity that struck Owen as both impersonal and hypnotic. The woman was young: her skin glowed, her nipples showed a uniform pink. He caught a glimpse of pink lips amid the slidings of her thighs before the long hair fell away from her face, which revealed itself as Phoebe's.

Owen told himself, it's a setup. Seeing him, Phoebe said, "Oh, shit!" Walter put down his stick of charcoal, wiped blackened fingers on a white cloth, and held out a hand to his dazed visitor.

"Oh—Mr. Lewison! I guess this isn't what either of us planned. Sorry—just trying to get in one last drawing." Owen watched Phoebe's bottom disappear into the bedroom. Walter said, "She's a great model. She knows how to move."

"Is that so?"

Walter forged on: "She *really* knows how to move. Not just lying there, like a still life. You know, the French call a still life a *nature morte*—who wants a model to be a cadaver? Like they're supposed to play dead, and we pretend they're 'prob-

lems in form.' Talk about treating a woman like a thing! I mean,
why leave out the desire, the liveliness, if you're painting a
nude, you *can't* leave it out, it's probably the most real thing
there is—you remember Renoir, 'I paint with my penis'? So
when Phoebe"—Owen's upturned eyes reminded Walter of
Perugino's saints—"said, Let me try moving all the time, then
I could keep seeing the life in her, I said, OK, and it works. You
know, in a way it's not her I paint, it's her—"

"That's extremely interesting," Owen said as his daughter,
dressed, came back into the studio.

"She's a remarkable girl, in more ways than one," Walter
concluded. Owen took Phoebe out to lunch.

With her clothes on, Phoebe looked as radiant and unfamiliar to Owen as she had naked.

"Poppa," she told him when they were seated, "I want to say
something right away." Owen thought: bad news. "Your giving
me a hard time last summer was the best thing that ever happened to me. It made me learn what to do with my life."

"Hardly to my credit."

"Yes, it is. Taking the money back was great. I'm managing
to pay my own way. When you came into Walter's studio (isn't
he fab?) I realized that one good thing poppas can do is be
mean, sometimes. I love you for it. I do love you, Poppa. I hope
you approve of me a little."

"You're looking well." Owen made insinuations about her
private life. Phoebe said she was too busy for men (she meant,
one man).

"And your 'fab' friend?"

"He's *your* age, Poppa. Almost."

"Exactly."

A visit to Phoebe's studio nearly convinced him. The not-so-
big room, bright even on a wet day, reflected a committed life:
a thin couch, a chair, an armchair buried in laundry, in the
kitchen a table strewn with the debris of breakfast assuredly for

one. The walls were papered with drawings, gouaches, and unstretched oils; the floor, stacked along its edges with stretchers and rolled canvas and paper, was a labyrinth of paint cans open and shut. There were two easels, a large and a small, and by the window, with a swivel stool at either side, a ten-by-four expanse of thick plywood set on sawhorses, without a squinch free of professional clutter.

"Hey," Owen asked, wrinkling his nose at the turps, "you *live* here?"

Phoebe opened the window. Turning back, she found Owen examining the canvas on the larger easel. "Don't ask me, I'll tell you! It's been driving me bats. Ever since I got hooked on Walter, at that show in January, I've wanted to copy one of his paintings, except he wouldn't hear of it. I kept coming back at him, and one day he said, OK, you asked for it. What he's making me do isn't copying exactly. I have to get the same results the same *way* he did. He can tell—you know, if the stippling is done with a soft brush or a stiff brush, or the paint is laid down with a spoon handle instead of a spatula. Which direction his hand was going. What he drank the night before. . . . This was my favorite of all he'd ever done. An old thing—'A Portrait of Elizabeth.' "

"Elizabeth seems to have led a hard life."

"I've scraped it down four times already. I don't think I'll ever get it right. Each time I try, though, I get five hundred and fifty-three new ideas. If you see anything you like, Poppa, just ask for it."

From a pile on the table he picked a soft-pencil self-portrait. Phoebe's eyes looked bemusedly out of it into his, and, during the ensuing weeks, he looked back at them often, with a fascination made up of resentment, yearning, and uncertainty. He realized that he admired his daughter. The thought of seeing her again made him timid.

In those days Owen often came to the city without Louisa.

Calling Phoebe before one such visit, he offhandedly said, "I don't want to be bothering you. . . ." She answered, "You'd better had!" He offered to take her out for an evening. Where should he reserve a table? Would she like to see a play?

"Not much. Let's see how we feel. Whatever we do, I'll enjoy it. Come for a drink at my place. Maybe we'll just stay in and watch *Bonanza.*"

Owen had wanted to do as well by Phoebe as his own father had by him. His father, a hardworking small businessman, had had his career cut short by a fatal car accident during Owen's last year at Ann Arbor. Owen at twenty-one had found himself owner of a factory in Queens that supplied processed graphite to pencil manufacturers. Knowing little about the business, he agreed to run it: it was well organized, he knew he could learn quickly. A few months later a fire broke out in his stockroom, destroying the entire inventory and half the plant. Accountants urged him to collect the insurance and write off what was left of the factory. Doing so, he made a significant discovery.

Two companies of firemen had appeared during the fire. They had declined to do their job until Owen had the wit to offer them twenty-five dollars each (a week's wage at the time). A more experienced businessman might have known that this practice was common, but Owen was outraged; enough so to list this graft in his claims to the insurance company and thus symbolically denounce it. He expected no compensation. The claim was nevertheless paid.

From this windfall Owen drew a conclusion that eventually turned into a plan; this he submitted to an old friend about to graduate from Columbia Law School. The friend reacted favorably. Owen suggested they go into business together, using as their working capital the money he had collected from the fire.

Owen had realized that small businesses like his father's, low in reserves of capital and dependent on high productivity, were at the mercy of a single disaster. A delay in reimbursement by their insurers—his own had taken almost a year—could wipe them out. Such companies would hesitate to press ancillary claims that might postpone settlement. Owen proposed creating a service that would take over cases in which a natural disaster had crippled a business, reimbursing basic claims immediately, making its own profit by exploiting secondary liabilities covered by the insurance. The outcome of Owen's dealings with the fire department had suggested that such profits might be large.

Owen and his partner founded a company to supply such a service. They took great care in the choice of their first clients. They proved themselves industrious, clever, capable of rock-ribbed persistence, even lucky. Their venture was so successful that after five years their presence in a case often persuaded insurance companies to settle quickly rather than risk uncertain legal battles.

Owen prospered. His career brought him not only wealth but satisfaction: his initiative and ingenuity were constantly challenged; he felt that he was usefully serving small businesses and, later, businesses not so small. His success introduced him to the society of the traditionally well-to-do—bankers and professional men who set themselves higher than unassuming entrepreneurs like his father. Owen envied the confidence such people showed in their own distinction. Because he was both prosperous and amenable, they accepted him readily enough. Eventually he married a young lady who, although poorer than he, belonged to a venerable Philadelphia family.

Throughout their marriage Owen remained devoted to Louisa. She had soon given him what he most wanted of her: a child, and particularly a daughter. During her two pregnancies he looked forward so intensely to their outcome that by the time Phoebe was born she was already the focus of his desires.

Owen was relieved to have a girl. He could cultivate her happiness—his own happiness—without concern for the combative and methodical virtues required of males. He watched over her education in and out of school. He made sure she learned early how to swim and ride, and later how to ski and play tennis. He took her to the ballet to kindle wonder in her and then sent her to ballet school. At her first sign of interest, he exposed her to books, plays, and music; and to sustain her precocious artistic bent he kept her supplied with everything she might need, from clay and crayons at three to oils and acrylics at thirteen. He remained a consistently fond, demanding parent. Good-natured and smart, Phoebe thrived under his supervision. By the age of seventeen, the contentment she felt in herself shone out of her like whiteness out of snow. Owen rejoiced in his parental success. By then his work had lost much of its challenge—it had become a means less to achieve than to conserve. He began looking to Phoebe for surprising triumphs.

Ten months before, their quarrel and Phoebe's departure had bred furious disappointment in him. Now that they had made peace, he still did not understand her. She had thanked him with convincing sincerity for "being mean"—a strange conclusion to draw from his nineteen years' munificence.

He came to her studio at seven, a benign hour on this late June evening, when the hot, clear air was suffused with cinnamon incandescence. Phoebe had prepared chilled unshaken gimlets for him. What should they do? They drifted out into the never-ending dusk. She led him across town to a steak house off Greenwich Avenue, modish but not deafeningly so. From their table, Owen looked about warily. Here, at least, bohemia seemed ready to spare him.

A wine from the shores of Lake Trasimene, which he never had seen, nor would see, opened in his mind vistas of remembrance and expectancy. He had begun speaking to Phoebe about some incident in his past when a sturdy swaggering youth approached their table and cocked a hand in greeting: "Hi, Phoeb."

"My father, Owen. Harry."

"No shit!" Harry observed. "Listen, doll, Bob is blowin' at El Pueblo at ten. Thought you'd want to know." (Owen asked, "Blowing what?" Phoebe answered, "Horn.")

After dinner, with conscious benevolence, Owen said, "Why not?" They wandered around six corners to Sheridan Square. The near-dark sky flared with the refractions of fireworks upriver.

"It's a French horn," Owen disappointedly remarked, having savvily looked forward to trumpet or sax.

"That's life," Phoebe chuckled.

"Who's Bob?"

"Scott," Phoebe whispered. "And that's Woody Woodward on alto, Doc Irons on vibes, Poppa Jenks on drums"—three blacks and one white, all young, who at the stroke of ten filled the gloom of the Pueblo with a clangor so intricately sweet that Owen felt bewitched. A green smell spiced the air.

"They're very fine," he exclaimed.

Phoebe looked gratified. "They may join us after this set."

Owen felt a pang. He'd only conversed with Negroes who worked for him. How well did Phoebe know them?

She was explaining: "Walter's sort of their sponsor—at least, he got them this gig."

When, white-shirted and cool, the musicians sat down at their table, they paid no attention to Owen. A few customers, including Harry, came over to pay court. Otherwise they all sat together quietly and contentedly, as if after a long day they had settled on a veranda to watch the moon rise over cornfields, or Lake Trasimene.

At eleven-thirty Poppa Jenks drained his glass: "Owen!" Owen sat up like a schoolboy caught dozing. "Anything you'd like to hear?"

"Uh—'All the Things You Are'?" Owen hazarded.

"Right. Right?" he asked the others.

"What's that shift—"

"Down a major third. G to E flat, same as 'Long Ago.' " To Owen he added, "Mr. Kern was an attentive student of Schubert, and a thrifty one."

They returned to their instruments. A young man in tailored denims bent abruptly over Phoebe: "Fourteen West Eleventh. Domerich. *Vaut le détour.*" The musicians broke once more into their wry jubilation. The Kern ballad was disseminated in a bustle of counterpoint.

Afterwards, Owen again said, "Why not?" and they made their way eastward, in night now, deep but not dark: through ginkgo leaf, window-light stippled the sidewalks with pale orange. The air had scarcely cooled—only, by alleyways, mild gusts on face or nape suggested swipes of a celestial fan.

After half an hour at the party, Owen asked himself what, if anything, was happening. Something must be happening, because he wasn't bored. Phoebe had soon abandoned him—for his own sake, he knew: he would do better on his own. He stood near the bar and watched the other guests, many of whom were also watching. For a while a pickup combo—bass, piano, sax— played in a far room. What talk he heard sounded mostly small, a counterpart of the nudging and touching, friendly, not particularly sexual, that brought groups together and dispersed them. A California breeze was fluttering the Thai silk curtains. In this mildness a few isles of agitation survived: "Then he asked me, 'If I go to bed with you here, do I have to go to bed with you in New York?' and I told him, 'Sweetie pie, of course not!' " Owen failed to match a face to the melodious voice. He did not understand why he felt so much at ease among people whom he didn't know, who seemed no more concerned with one another than with him, who nevertheless acted neither hostile nor indifferent.

His impressions made more sense when the dancing started. The stereo came on like the summons to a Last Judgment where all would be saved. No one asked anybody to dance because nobody could hear. People danced or didn't. The notion of "couple" was dissipated in a free-for-all that spread across three rooms.

Owen loved dancing of every sort. Earlier that year, when the Twist had first appeared, he single-handedly imposed it on upstate gatherings still attuned to Xavier Cougat. Here the Twist had followed the Conga into oblivion; a new, less definable order reigned. Owen began reducing the apparently chaotic movements of those around him to a pattern he could imitate.

When he entered the arena, he found himself facing a woman, scarcely younger than he, who bore a compelling resemblance to Angela Lansbury and comported herself with stylish abandon. He tried to follow her lead and couldn't. She drew suddenly close to him—he thought she was going to kiss him—to shriekingly murmur in his ear, "Don't do *steps.*" He failed to grasp. . . . "No steps!" she insisted, leading him to the sidelines. "There aren't any rules. Just anchor one hip in space—make that your center, OK?—and let the rest go. Do what the music does—anything." She demonstrated. He tried. "*Any*thing!" she urged. "Shut your eyes and listen."

From time to time he stopped at an open window to cool off. He would then attempt, by smiles and gesticulations, to express to other bystanders his approval of the new culture. Once a young woman, as if to fortify his conversion, led him straight back into the action; once a young man. Owen's fear at the touch of that firm hand dissolved among the dancers.

He was progressing from exuberance towards fluency when Phoebe stopped him. In a quieter room she introduced him to Joey, a painter in his twenties with a problem she wanted Owen to consider: a fire in his studio, a landlord refusing to pay for repairs. Insurance? Not the right kind, according to the owner, who Joey thought was stalling in order to evict him. Owen told him to call his office the next morning and ask for Margy; he would phone her instructions. It occurred to him how easily he might extend his services to individuals so plainly in need of them.

The party was subsiding. Owen and Phoebe followed a gang of celebrants down the walnut banister, out onto Manahatta's stony pave. Arm in arm they headed west in search of a White Tower. Owen said, "Then I'll drop you home. I wish I felt sleepier."

"I see!" Phoebe turned them back towards Fifth Avenue. "You trust me?"

"With a vengeance."

She was hailing a cab. "Belmont, please. Service entrance."

"You want the hotel, lady, or the track?"

"The track. Take the bridge, please," she added. So they could see the dawn.

The not-quite dawn: the cab glided smoothly towards chalk dust cascading out of stars into eastern cloud-of-light. When they set down at the stables, Phoebe led the way to the cafeteria, which was half full and wide awake. They took coffee and Danish to a table at which five males were sitting, the youngest a diminutive adolescent black, the oldest a sixtyish Chicano. The group affably made room for Owen and Phoebe and went on with an earnest discussion of a horse called Capital Gain. ("By Venture Capital out of No Risk," Phoebe explained. "These people work for the McEwans.")

Walter Trale had kept friends from the days when he painted horses. He liked going to the track, and sometimes brought Phoebe along. She had met several owners, and because she knew horses, she had talked her way into the stable area and made friends there as well.

Pushing away his tray, one man said, "Let's try him out." All proceeded to the stables. Capital Gain was saddled and led forth. At the training track the young black was told, "Six furlongs, remember, and keep it tight. He may still hurt."

Dawn turned into day. When the horse pulled up at the end of the workout, the Chicano declared, "He's all right."

"He'll be up in six weeks," someone added. "Hey, Phoebe, want to walk a hot?"

The horse was huffing as it pranced sideways up to them. While a tall black held the bit, the exercise boy dismounted and handed Phoebe the reins. The horse turned a bulging eye on her, shaking his head like a wet-eared swimmer. Phoebe stood looking up at the head and spoke to it for a while before leading the animal towards the stables.

"Half an hour should do it," the man told her.

To Owen, his bare-legged and tight-skirted daughter looked alarmingly frail alongside the silver-gray stallion, three years old and foaming with power. Where had the others gone? He didn't say a word to her, he kept at a cautious distance; but when Capital Gain reappeared around a corner of the stable, Owen saw him jerk his head back without warning, pulling Phoebe off balance. As the reins went slack, the horse reared, wagging wicked forefeet above her head and whinnying huskily. Turning around, Phoebe held the bridle loose until the horse came down to earth and lowered his head. She stepped up to him and grabbed the reins closer to the bit, yanking them almost to the ground, holding them there with all her weight. The horse kicked and swerved and could not raise his head. A moment later, to Owen's horror, Phoebe with a stern cry of "You motherfucking" something-or-other began driving her small fist into the animal's neck. Soon after, she resumed her stroll, with the stallion again obediently in tow.

Near the end of Phoebe's stint, Capital Gain's owner arrived. Mr. McEwan had come to look at his horse. He was pleased to find him sound; pleased to see Phoebe, too. He invited her and Owen to the clubhouse for a second breakfast.

They ate a much bigger, better, and longer meal than their first: fruit, eggs, bacon, toast, buckwheat cakes, tall shining pots of coffee. They sat at their table for an hour and a half, in low eastern sunlight, in early-morning shade. At last Mr. McEwan left for work. He had behaved with perfunctoriness towards Owen, who realized that here he was no more and no less than his daughter's father, until Phoebe injected some helpful information into their talk. By the end of breakfast the men were chummily discussing business. Owen looked on Phoebe with freshened eyes.

The day had started hot and dry. The pair wandered across the track, where groundsmen readied the terrain for the afternoon and sparrows hopped about rare droppings. They bowed through a fence into the empty infield. They sat down on shaded grass. Fat robins policed the grounds; yarmulkaed chickadees pecked their way up thickset branches; beyond the linked pools, black cutouts of crows were pasted against yellow-green baize. A breeze carried vibrations of urban traffic and an occasional drone from the sky. Owen leaned his head on his knees.

Phoebe was poking him. "Poppa, stick around. It's nice out here." Owen grunted assent. His eyes would not stay open. "Don't forget Joey." He nodded, sighed, and sat up. Phoebe held out her hand: "Try some of this, Poppa."

"What is it?"

"Medical snuff. Poppa Jenks gave it to me—he endorses it one hundred per, and so does Freud."

"You're sure?"

"Just don't sneeze."

"Sort of like nasal Alka-Seltzer."

He sat in a phone booth with a diminishing column of dimes, chattering to his secretary like a telex as he transmitted, as fast as he could master it, the clear stream of ideas flowing through his consciousness. He solved the case of the thieving computer. He mitigated the death of the essential engineer. For Joey, he told Margy to check the insurance on the building, accuse

Joey's landlord of being criminally negligent, and point out that with Owen's help he could become an honest profiteer. "What do you mean, am I all right? On a day like this, who could *not* be all right?"

Phoebe had disappeared. He looked through the club rooms. On the terrace, Owen thought he might soon float away. The infield remained almost empty—one idle groundskeeper, another man standing immobile in the shadow of his Stetson.

"He should sell that hat to a developer." Phoebe was behind him, carrying a big paper bag.

In a clump of copper beeches by the stables, on a tablecloth spread on the ground, Phoebe set out lunch: two club sandwiches, four pears, a slab of rat cheese, a frosty thermos of martinis. They ate and drank.

From the stables came the bustle of nervous men and the stomping of hooves. The time for the first race was approaching. Owen felt pleasantly restless: "Let's go take a look."

"This is no time for camp followers," Phoebe told him. "We'd be in the way."

"Well, I feel like joining the party."

"They thought of that. You get to bet."

As they strolled back to the clubhouse, Phoebe said, "I'll go scout the field and meet you at the paddock." At her return she announced, "My Portrait in the sixth."

"My Portrait is a horse?"

"By Spitting Image out of My Business."

Preferring to "check the form," Owen bought a *Morning Telegraph* and through the afternoon studied it with the reverence of a Talmudic scholar. When they left, after six races, he had lost less than he might have. He had also paid Phoebe back for their lunch, and she had bet the money on My Portrait, who paid off at nine to two. She forced the winnings on him: "I did it for you. I never bet."

"You—Miss Spunk?"

Phoebe persuaded Owen to take the train back—the fastest way home, even if he dreaded an "awful crowd." Other early leavers entered their car. They seemed quiet—no beer-heads, no "youngsters." The last ones in had to stand, filling the aisle. The train started up with a jolt and a clang.

Owen soon regretted his forsaken taxi. He found himself hemmed in by bodies bulbous or emaciated, all clothed according to some perverse notion of unfunny clownishness, each swaying face stamped with metropolitan distrust. His gaze at last came to rest on a couple sitting across the car: neatly dressed, not bad looking, in their Latin way—he had caught a few words of Spanish. The man, who wore an open white shirt and beige slacks, had a slender body, dark, thin features, pepper-and-salt hair, and a black mustache. The woman, in a cotton print dress and white shoes, looked younger—pretty, a little coarse, perhaps, yet so amiable, her fine teeth flashingly set off by her black, brushed-out hair. The man's merry eyes caught Owen's at the moment Phoebe nudged him: "Just like us."

The man's eyes looked into his with cheerful indifference. Of course, a father and daughter. Like us: the man, therefore, "like me." Owen searched for feelings like his own in the alert face, whose nostrils flared ever so slightly as he stared. He thought: What signs do my feelings leave in my face?

He turned away to consider someone nearer: a man with florid swollen features, short strawy hair above a shaved pink nape, a heavy belly that bulged through a half-untucked Hawaiian shirt over low-belted pants of shiny plaid synthetic gabardine—And so on, thought Owen, ad nauseam. Why did he mind? His own body felt warm and stupefied. He noticed that the light outside the train windows had become detached from his perception of it; and he saw that a similar hallucinatory change was occurring in his neighbor. He was separating into disjunct entities—still a looming, monstrous straphanger, while his eyes belonged to another body, another space: through them shined light from afar. A disjunct light existed behind the appearance the man turned to the world. That slob body had become an empty vessel with autonomous light inside it—a Halloween pumpkin. The pumpkin grinned at him, as pumpkins should. Why? It was answering his own smile. All right. Owen extended his smile into a little nod, as if to say, Win some, lose some; or, Been quite a day. He lowered his gaze. The awful crowd—should he care? He shyly glanced at others near him: veterans of one summer afternoon, each encased in his rind, each accumulating incongruities, pains, shames, even signs of happiness, to conceal that uncanny light—their masks, their lives. Phoebe was snoozing on his shoulder.

From Penn Station she took Owen straight to Walter's. Walter was giving a dinner, to which she was inviting him: she was cook.

For a while they remained alone in his studio. Phoebe hustled in the kitchen. Owen stood in front of the northwest window, looking into a cherry-blossom sky festooned with jetliner trails. A molelike question was rummaging inside him: What is wrong with this? He ignored it and abandoned himself to the view of Jersey.

Walter arrived, then his guests—two women, two men. Each acted as lively and curious as a dog off its leash. Apparently they all led busy lives, in activities Owen could not recognize. What was, or were, sociolinguistics? Where was Essalen? Was a concrete poet a writer or a sculptor? Who was Theodore Huff? He was pleased to have discarded jacket and tie.

Phoebe made them all drinks (chilled gimlets for Owen). He did not know what to say to these people. They didn't mind. While he sensed that they were funny, the context of their wit and gossip escaped him. At last he mentally put his tie back on and asked them questions. They asked him questions in turn, and he told a little about himself. The others listened attentively. He succeeded in getting credit for helping Joey the painter.

Towards the end of the meal, after Walter had urged him to talk about his work, Owen revealed something Phoebe had never known:

". . . Neither of us had capital—just the insurance from the fire. But you're right: we needed more than that to expand. We might have raised enough money from the banks, but it would have been just enough—it would have meant being dependent on them for maybe ten or fifteen years. We talked about the problem for weeks, and gradually we agreed on a solution— actually, we backed into it, because it wasn't only risky, it was illegal. That was twenty-five years ago, and I haven't even *parked* illegally since then. This is what we did. There'd been an accident on the waterfront in New London. A tug banged up a wharf, pretty much wrecking it, and on top of that some gasoline drums spilled and set the whole thing on fire. The wharf belonged to a ferry company. It was a company with high operating costs and a low profit margin, so the owners were happy for us to take over their claims. We paid them right off what it was going to cost to rebuild the wharf. Normally we would have gone on and made our profit on secondary claims like losses due to interruption of service, damage to reputation, stuff like that. But we found out that the ferry people had taken out a policy for fire with one company and a policy for maritime damage with another company, and furthermore, even though the business was chartered in New London, because its services involved other places such as Long Island they'd used one insurance company in Connecticut and one in New York. So, since the wharf for all practical purposes had been wrecked twice over, once by the collision and once when it burned, what we did was press all the claims against *both* companies. I can tell you, we went through two very scary months. Once, inspectors from the two companies missed each other by minutes; and of course if they'd found us out, we'd have been through. But we got away with it. We cleared about a hundred thousand dollars—not enough to retire on, but that was still a lot of money in nineteen thirty-seven, and we felt a lot better set to take on the big boys. And that's what we did. We really buckled down. I don't know if I could work that hard anymore," Owen concluded. "Nowadays I do ninety percent of my business by phone."

A few seconds later he fell asleep. "Rack time, Poppa!" Phoebe shouted in his ear. Eventually she got him up and put him to bed in her studio. Their long day had ended.

When Owen woke up the next morning, he found a note from his daughter: she had "slept elsewhere"; he would find coffee, bread, butter, and eggs in the larder. She apologized for the evaporated milk: "I couldn't face shopping after the dishes." So she had gone back to Trale's place. Owen did not want breakfast. He missed his *Trib*.

Phoebe came in at ten. He warmed to her hug. She said to him, "Poppa, I've got to kick you out. This looks like a heavy day."

"A whole day without you? I don't think I can manage."

"It was fun, wasn't it? You keep right on playing without me."

"All right." He added morosely, "I really shot my mouth off last night."

Phoebe looked bewildered. "You were a smash."

"No kidding."

"Poppa, I just want to work. Why the soap opera?" Owen said nothing. "Want to meet for dinner?"

Owen said he'd see and put on his jacket. He felt hung over. Stepping out on peculiar lower Broadway, he looked forward to his office.

All day long, Owen talked to himself about Phoebe. She had downtown elegance, talent, and a passion for her work. She had friends low and high. She was attractive and smart. She had devoted herself to him without reserve. What more could a father want?

He wished she would demand the money he had promised her. Perhaps she could give him drawing lessons that he could pay her for. His irritation grew. He gave Joey's landlord a piece of his mind.

He imagined being old and widowed: Phoebe would take care of him. He would quietly watch her life out of the corner of his eye.

He wasn't old, he didn't need Phoebe looking after him. She had been cruel turning her back on him—you spend a hundred bucks, and next morning, see you later.

Remembering the bet on My Portrait, he silently begged her forgiveness. He called Phoebe to say he'd love to have dinner.

Phoebe that evening looked tired and worried. Some days, she told Owen, she felt she'd never make it. Her fingernails were caked, her hair bunchy, she wasn't wearing lipstick. Owen saw in these signs of trust a refusal to make an effort for his sake. She failed to suggest a next meeting.

He went on brooding about her. Something was wrong. Owen had become confused and didn't like it. Away from Phoebe, he thought wistfully of the night and day she'd given him. Why hadn't there been more? This first "why" soon led to others. Beyond all of them, "something must be wrong" lurked in a beckoning shade. If there was to be no more, why had Phoebe bothered with him? She had not merely been dutiful. Why had she led him on and then let him down? Allowing these questions to seem real planted a crystal of suspicion in Owen's mind, which crusted with cold like a pond in plunging frost.

He reviewed once again the time spent with Phoebe. He told himself that she had not chosen their activities accidentally. She had given him new experiences of new kinds of people: artists, jazzmen, stable hands, a "beautiful crowd." What did they all have in common? The answer came to Owen on a hot, windy afternoon at the corner of Madison Avenue and Forty-eighth Street. When the light turned green, he stepped back onto the curb to stare into a wickerwork-iron trash can. Phoebe had been making a fool of him.

She had been teaching him a lesson: these new people had nothing to do with him. Phoebe had lured him into enjoying activities and attitudes that belonged to her, not to him. She was telling him, If you like my life so much, what can yours be worth? The year before he had opposed her; she was taking her revenge. She was showing him who had been right and was still right.

Owen had found something clear and nasty to batten on. He disregarded the noticeable thrill of suspecting that his daughter had betrayed him; he only relished his relief at having an explanation. He enjoyed his discovery so much that his sentiments towards Phoebe brightened perceptibly.

Owen saw Phoebe twice in August and once in September. He tried to make their meetings altogether casual. To Phoebe he seemed determined to undo what they had shared, pointedly refusing a stroll down Third Avenue one hot night because of "all the people," not going to a party because dancing was "no fun anymore." Owen would have denied such intentions. He had so thoroughly become the mistreated father that he forgot all his once-happiest expectations. He was defending this identity "innocently."

Phoebe occasionally prodded him. When Owen declined having drinks at Walter's, saying, "Walter's OK, but you know I can't stand his friends," Phoebe asked, "Like Jack McEwan?" With whom Owen had recently dined.

Usually she accepted his comments docilely. Owen was therefore surprised to notice, after a time, an undisguised aloofness on her part. He had sometimes spoken frankly to her, he knew; didn't she pride herself on her broad-mindedness? Her coolness did not discourage him, but rather confirmed him in his role of responsible, misunderstood parent.

Something more preoccupying had strengthened his commitment to that role. In the course of the summer Phoebe gradually succumbed to what was first considered a mood, then a psychological state, and at last—much later—a disease. The condition revealed itself, slowly and relentlessly, in symptoms of fatigue, morbid emotionalism, and depression. During the following autumn and winter, two good doctors assured Owen that Phoebe was suffering from a type of neurasthenia. Influenced by his own passionate conviction, they attributed the source of her trouble to the irregular life she had been leading.

Whatever a child's age, her health remains a parent's prime concern. Owen found Phoebe the best doctors he could trust. Otherwise he kept to the background, reserving for himself the right to protect his daughter from the prime cause of her disorder—her wayward life. Wary of Phoebe's stubborn independence, he waited for an opportunity to intervene. One came late in December. Chronic insomnia had left Phoebe exhausted. Her resistance to infection had been sapped. When she caught the flu it turned into bronchitis, then pleurisy. She had to stop modeling; her money ran out. Having learned as much from her psychiatrist, Owen called up Phoebe and went to see her.

Her studio looked a mess; so did she—a frail, livid derelict. Owen made her some tea, chatted a while, then offered to resume the payments from the trust fund he had set up the previous year. It "was still there, waiting for her."

Phoebe began to cry. She cried like a six-year-old, with long, violent sobs. "I *am* tapped out. I thought you'd given up on me."

"That's nonsense."

"You've been very hard. I felt so close to you last spring, last June—it seems ages."

"I've been worried about you, that's all."

"I feel so awful. Sometimes I feel like I'm dying."

"You don't take care of yourself."

"I do. I go to the doctors and take all the pills, and it doesn't ever help, not for long."

"Tell me one thing. Are you still taking drugs?" Phoebe looked at him incredulously. "Can you honestly promise me you'll stop taking drugs?"

"You should ask Dr. Straub. He tries out a new one on me every week."

"Not that kind of drug—marijuana, amphetamines, cocaine . . ."

"Do you think I'm crazy? I mean I'd *have* to be nuts to, the way I feel."

"It's not you—it's your friends I worry about. Can't you just promise?"

"No sweat."

"Good. With your money you could take a good long rest and get really well again. How would you like a week in the Bahamas? Be my guest. If it's good enough for Jack and Mac, why not us? One other thing—" Owen neither paused nor altered his tone of voice, warm and urgent. Why should he hesitate? The sight of Phoebe had not only appalled him, it had mightily reinforced his disposition: he knew what was holding her here, what had to be given up. "I want you to go to a real art school. You haven't been making the kind of progress you should. I know Walter's a nice man, and I know how fond of him you are—I'm fond of him too. But he's not a good teacher." Owen thought that through her sunken cheeks he could see Phoebe's teeth. She said nothing. He concluded: "That's something I consider essential to your well-being. That's the first thing you have to do before we get you organized."

Phoebe glanced around the studio, its walls crowded with

work that Owen had ignored. Copious tears again flowed over her face and dripped off her chin. In a voice steady enough, only a little hoarse, she told him to get out.

"I know it's difficult," he replied, "and I know you're upset—"

"You are a bleeding asshole."

"—but sooner or later you've got to face the fact that you're unwell *and* unhappy. Think it over. Ask yourself why."

As he left, Owen thought: She's a very sick girl. He had done what he could. He was glad she was in good hands. Calling on her had depressed and somehow elated him. Phoebe's insults had provoked a warm rush of what he did not dare recognize as relief.

He phoned Dr. Straub to say how concerned he was. He would appreciate being kept informed.

During the ensuing months, Phoebe kept getting worse: depression, insomnia, feverishness. In late spring she was taken to a hospital with pneumonia. Her doctors refused to release her unless she allowed them to perform certain tests. These enabled her disorder to be identified as acute hyperthyroidism, also known as Graves's disease. Phoebe began a treatment with a drug called methyl thiouracil. Its initial effect proved slight. At the beginning of June she agreed to return to her family's house upstate, not because she wanted to, but because her mother's insistence and her own helplessness left her no choice. Ten weeks afterwards, her treatment, no doubt begun too late, was abandoned, and she consented to undergo a subtotal thyroidectomy at a nearby hospital, which she entered on the fifteenth of August.

At the time of Phoebe's earlier hospitalization, Owen's attitude towards her changed. He had plainly done her an injustice, and he knew better than to claim good intentions as an excuse. He had blamed Phoebe's condition on her behavior—a judgment that, as well as wronging her, encouraged the doctors he had chosen to persevere in their mistaken diagnosis. He told himself that she could never be expected to forgive or understand him. He must simply make what amends he could and pray that she would find a way to leave him in peace.

When she came home, he committed himself to a program of discreet and fervent atonement. He did whatever Phoebe asked of him without the least complaint. Owen's contrition was matched by Phoebe's contempt. As a condition of her return, she insisted that he move to the guest annex at the far end of the house. When she heard his voice, she often asked her mother to shut him up. Sometimes she summoned him to her bedside to supply new fuel for her scorn. ("What rich creeps did you insure this week?") Or she would demand things of him (such as reading *Two Serious Ladies* out loud to her; she wept at its beauties and raged at his boredom) as if he were a lackey whose career of swindle and rape had just been disclosed. Whenever he appeared she stared at him out of bulging, hateful eyes. When Owen came into possession of Walter's portrait of Elizabeth, he let her ridicule his motives for acquiring it and did not try to explain them. She was so outraged that the picture belonged to him that he had it sent up from the city to be hung in her room.

Phoebe's treatment of him comforted Owen. It allowed him to go on playing the dutiful, now penitent father. The role, hard and forthright, continued to reassure him. Owen dreaded above all the agitating uncertainty into which Phoebe had twice led him. Of course she still loomed dangerously in his future. How would she behave once she was cured? Most likely she would want to be reconciled with him. Her harshness towards him could become the pretext for excusing his own unfair behavior. Owen abhorred this possibility and preferred being punished. He longed for Phoebe to live her life and leave him out of it.

On July first, Owen settled a large amount of money on his daughter. Unlike the trust fund, this arrangement made Phoebe truly independent. She would have no further need of him. To outsiders, his gesture seemed generous; intimates saw in it an expression of remorse and hope. Owen claimed he was fulfilling a father's obligations. He could scarcely acknowledge his eagerness to escape from fatherhood altogether.

In late August, after her operation, Phoebe asked Owen to visit her in the hospital. He went to her late in the afternoon. In her room, the dark glow from the lowered blinds and drawn purple curtains revealed an emaciated shape.

Owen had not seen her awake since the operation. Phoebe's hair, cut short and flattened with sweat, looked like a skullcap on a skull. Her skin lay waxily over the bones of her face. Owen experienced fright, revulsion, a spasm of pity.

At first she said nothing as she gazed at him out of huge inexpressive eyes. She held out her hand. The thin hot hand gripped him hard. He didn't know what to do or say; he began sweating himself. She finally spoke, in high, almost whimpering tones: "You're my father. I feel awful. I don't know what's happening to me. I feel so awful I don't feel anything else. I can't talk much. You mustn't stay long. I do want you to know"—from a box at her side Phoebe pulled a Kleenex and spat into it—"I wanted you to know . . . something. It was when my feelings got wiped out I understood, I understood something about you and me. We've been playing a dumb game, both of us. We've been turning you into a shit. You can keep playing, that's all right, but not me. I plan to love you whatever you do."

Owen felt himself being gathered up into a wet, smothering shroud. He longed to scramble away from that room and his bony daughter. Her grip tightened. He cleared his throat: "Phoebe, you have to believe me, I've done everything I could to you."

He did not realize what he had said until she grinned: "Maybe, but I gave you a lot of help." She let his hand go. She shut her eyes, spreading wrinkles across her face. She looked like a crone. "I love you—ring that buzzer, will you? Please do it fast. Bye bye. Come back soon."

Owen hurried through the cooled corridors and lobby, out into the dank brightness that smelled of wet grass and decay. Tears simmered in his eyes. He had behaved so cruelly to Phoebe, so many times: how dare she love him? She had trapped him. She had had the last word.

Owen would have liked to cough up his feelings, as though he had breathed a beetle into his lungs. He could not identify his feelings. He got drunk. He woke up at three in the morning and wove fantasies of living under another name in a country he had never seen. He thought that he, or at least his life, had gone insane. He wished that Phoebe had never been born.

The Labor Day weekend passed. One afternoon Owen went into Phoebe's empty bedroom, where the portrait of Elizabeth, brought back from the hospital, had been set against a wall. Owen stared at it malevolently. He knew the woman in the painting all too well. Her masklike abstractness had made of her an unrelenting, unresponsive witness of his past mistakes and present helplessness.

He said aloud, "Up yours." He wished he had the nerve to piss on her. He spat on her instead and with his fingertips rubbed the spittle over her face. The paint felt slick and tough. Owen became deliciously aware of being alone in the house, as if the house belonged to someone else and he'd sneaked into it like a marauding boy.

By the window stood a table littered with Phoebe's makeup. Owen took an eyeliner pencil and with a grunt of satisfaction drew blue whiskers across Elizabeth's ivory-gold cheeks. Under the soft point the surface held firm. Encouraged, he picked up tubes of scarlet, purple, and orange-red lipstick. He bedizened the mouth and eyes with spots, stripes, and flourishes. Holding the three tubes in a cluster, he enclosed the entire head in a whorl of grease.

He felt better. He even laughed at himself. Through the window he looked across his lawn and the lawns of his neighbors into the dark woods nearby, warped here and there by clear vapor rising in hot, late-summer sun. He found a box of Kleenex and began erasing the mess he had made. Tissue after tissue fell to the floor blotted with the colors of Phoebe's mouth. He used a soapy washrag to remove the remaining traces.

Soap and water proved less than sufficient. The paler areas were still misted with purple or pink. To complete the task, he fetched a can of turpentine from the cellar, tore a clean shirt into rags, and began lightly rubbing away the last stains. He had finished cleaning one cheek and was proceeding to the eye above it when his rag caught on a crust of paint running along the rim of the eyeball. Burnt sienna surged into the eye's light ocher. He wiped it off as gently as he could; the ocher in turn spread into the nose. Owen swore. He went into the bathroom and came back with a toothbrush. Having dipped it in turpentine, he shook it out and rubbed it half dry on his sleeve. Leaning his elbow against the canvas, he started to slowly and scrupulously brush away the misplaced paint. His diligence was succeeding when a brown speck sprang from the elastic bristles and slid down the upright surface. Instinctively Owen jabbed at it with the cloth in his left hand, spreading a fresh blotch of softened paint beneath the injured eye.

Stepping back, Owen saw that he had inflicted serious damage. He wondered how to repair it. Half irritably, half jokingly, he told himself: I own the goddamn thing, I might as well enjoy it. With a turps-soaked rag in either hand, he vengefully attacked the painting. Soaking the pigments of the right eye, he smeared its colors across the fiery hair into the pale landscape above Elizabeth's head. The smear looked like a horn. Who ever saw a cow with one horn? He drew a second streak from the other eye. He drenched the mouth and blurred it into a haze of mauve. The rest of the face he obliterated with the orange of her hair.

Owen carried the painting, toothbrush, and turpentine down to the cellar. He used a chisel to loosen the tacks on the back of the stretcher before stripping away the canvas. He pulled the stretcher apart and sheared the canvas into ribbons, packing them into a burlap sack along with the rags and toothbrush. Outside the back door, he stuffed the sack into a garbage can underneath other refuse. He took the disassembled stretcher to the garage and with a hatchet split and chopped the wood into insignificant slivers, which he dumped on a pile of unstacked kindling behind the neighboring shed. He then retreated to his room to wash his face and hands.

Owen and Phoebe: II

1962-1963

W HEN OWEN TURNED AWAY FROM HER THE SUMMER BE-
fore, Phoebe could see what was happening; not why. Owen had
begun treating her as an enemy. What had she done to antago-
nize someone she so loved? She kept her patience, hoping that
if he did not end his hostility he would at least explain it. Later,
she turned cautious and, sometimes, hostile herself. Owen then
stared at her without surprise, as though looking at a curious
old photograph.

Phoebe had begun suffering from two misfortunes. First, for
several months she lost Louisa and Walter, either of whom
might have helped her. Second, her insidious disease con-
taminated both her life and her perception of it.

When the thyroid gland misfunctions, the effects are not felt
as symptoms. Depression and excitement, even indigestion, are
interpreted as private, "natural" experiences. Not until September did Phoebe consult a doctor—a general practitioner who

identified her trouble at once. She should, he said, be given the customary basal metabolism test; for that, he advised her to see a specialist in endocrine pathology. Owen recommended someone; she made an appointment; and her misfortune was then compounded by misdiagnosis.

Dr. Sevareid had an expert's insight: he had treated thousands of glandular disorders and could spot them at first glance. As soon as Phoebe walked into his office, he saw that she did not have thyroid disease. He told her so. Of course she should take the basal metabolism test—it could only prove him right. He forthwith introduced her to the nurse who administered it.

The test measured metabolic activity by recording the units of oxygen a patient consumed in a given time. In an adjoining room the nurse blocked Phoebe's ears and nose with rubber plugs and fitted a mask over her mouth. Through the mask she would breathe oxygen from a nearby cylinder; the plugs would restrict her oxygen intake to what the cylinder supplied.

After Phoebe had started breathing through the mask, the nurse went out of the room for about a minute and a half. When she returned, she checked the results on the monitor and was dismayed to find them abnormal—dismayed because she believed in her employer's flair as much as he did. During her absence, she said, one of the plugs must have worked loose and let in air. Since she could be fired for such negligence, she begged Phoebe not to tell the doctor she had left her alone.

She had no need to worry. Dr. Sevareid glanced at the results and remarked, "A little high, but nothing to write home about. You must have leaky ears."

Phoebe was pleased not to have to lie about the nurse and pleased not to have thyroid trouble. She was surprised to learn that she suffered from cardiac neurosis.

"Don't worry, your heart's OK—it's only a minor disorder of the nervous system."

Dr. Sevareid gave Phoebe what she craved: an authoritative

explanation of her unusual feelings. She never doubted his judgment. He could describe symptoms she had never even mentioned—her breathlessness, her blushes. When he asked her to hold out her hands, they trembled helplessly.

"You can see the condition is physically real, even if it has a psychogenic origin. It's what people used to call 'nerves.'" Phoebe blushed on cue. "You've probably been upset for a while about something or other, natural enough at your age—or *any* age." He smiled warmly and prescribed Miltown in moderate doses. If she didn't feel better within a month, she could always try psychotherapy.

The tranquilizer took the edge off Phoebe's anguish. But her spells of depression grew worse, with each passing day and night her angry heart beat faster, and she spent nights no less wakeful than before. She was perhaps most discouraged by the voice in her head. Originally no more than a murmur, it now grew into a merciless yammer, berating her with things she could hardly bear hearing—her own voice turned mean.

Phoebe named this voice her squawk box. She blamed it for making her heart pound, for keeping her awake at three in the morning, for rousing her every two hours when she slept. When, one day, she realized that she had begun talking back to the voice, she asked Dr. Sevareid for the name of a therapist. He advised her to speak to Owen. To Owen he confidentially recommended his colleague Dr. Straub.

Like Dr. Sevareid, Dr. Straub was experienced and honest. Phoebe could not know that to both doctors Owen had described her at length and in terms confirming his own prejudices. To Owen, that Phoebe was neurotic proved her way of life wrong and justified his mistrust of her. She had been mistaken from the start. He should have forced her to listen to him, forced her to stay home. Owen wanted her doctors to support these views, and he drew them a portrait of Phoebe that approached caricature: her life had lost all regularity, her friends belonged to the fringes of society, she took drugs, she indulged in sexual promiscuity.

Phoebe knew what Owen thought of her. Whenever she discussed her life with him, he remained earnestly uncomprehending. When she told him she had a hard time getting to sleep, he suggested she stop staying up so late. She disliked being given advice fit for children and detested his conviction that he understood her. She decided to keep silent in his presence. She said to her squawk box that explaining things to him was like trying to change a political party by joining it. Her squawk box scolded, *Baby, is that how you talk to the doctor? He'll tell you who wears the nuts in the family.* Phoebe: "You're so *cheap.*"

Phoebe inspired kindness in Dr. Straub, and she welcomed this kindness. She could not guess how pathetic Owen's description had made her appear. Dr. Straub had readily accepted the description because she came to him tagged with Dr. Sevareid's unimpeachable opinion, and he needed evidence that her neurosis had substance.

Phoebe herself supplied further evidence. Her feverish excitement provoked a sexual itch, and she masturbated frequently. She had no male friends that especially attracted her, and she was misguided in her choice of strangers, even at social gatherings (the only occasions where she dared approach them). She had three one-night stands that left her feeling degraded. When Dr. Straub learned of them, Owen's account of her seemed even more plausible.

Unaware of her disease, beset with disagreeable sensations, Phoebe concluded that she must simply be strange—perhaps truly neurotic. A sense of solitude invaded her, whether she was alone or not. She decided that the world was leaving her to herself; and because she did not make the easiest company, she wondered what else might comfort her. Since even the most ordinary experiences now took on unusual intensity, she began speculating that the world around her represented more than what she had heretofore seen in it; that life, and her life in particular, depended on a less visible, more abstract, more significant reality. Looking for manifestations of this idea, she found them in abundance: in the unwittingly expressive gestures of others, in the penetrating glances they gave her, in words that leapt at her from the humdrum contexts of what she heard and read.

Louisa, who saw Phoebe several times in November, was disheartened by her appearance, and even more by her obscure new way of speaking. Once, discussing Owen over the phone, Phoebe breathily said to her, "Darling Momma, how is it he can't understand? The bads, OK, but even when I'm ecstatic? I know that it's always just Nature working on my mind. So I feel it working on my mind—"

"Everyone has their ups and downs—"

"No. It's why can't *I* be a little voice in the big chorus? I'd settle for being a pocket thermometer."

"A thermometer?"

"You know, when the sun moved to the heart of the earth (it's still there, actually), anyone could feel it—even the Presidential Mediators."

"The who?"

"There's only one planet, Momma, whatever the astronomers say. You know what I call it?"

"No."

"An apple of love divine! By 'divine' I just mean a coherence of *apparently* contradictory vectors. That's what gives us a glimpse of the holy spirit. You know, the spirit of the hole? That's where the thermometer goes in. A joke, Momma."

"Oh—I see."

"Anyway, it's all the same, and it's *me.*"

Louisa apologized for not understanding her and asked for time to think about it. Soon, however, all Louisa's time would be devoted to her son, Lewis, and she would leave Phoebe to Owen—he had always "adored" her and had her best interests at heart.

The words *hole* and *Presidential Mediators* had drifted into Phoebe's speech from conversations with her squawk box. She had told it, "I'm just a worm in the Big Apple. . . ." *So, what did you see, huh?* "Cuter girls than me, I can tell you." *Cute boys, by the Lord. I know you—every boy's a cute one.* "No, they make me sad. They find a girl and lead her straight to the icehouse, to see what she'll be like when she's old. It's crazy." *You walk down the street and all you think about is love. You better keep your girlie hands to yourself, you little bitch.* "I do that all the time." *I don't mean that. It's the far slope I'm talking about.* "You mean the hill, with the convent of the Sacred Heart?" *Oh, you're the heart—the artichoke heart! Not the holy heart, because that wouldn't be a hill but a hole. . . .* Phoebe was stuck with this pun on *holy.* She pierced, she was pierced with the holes of her body. Through them she thought she might penetrate to the exalting light coursing through her.

In October, at the climax of the missiles crisis, the general fear affected Phoebe violently. With the danger gone, the abstract meaning she looked for in the world was briefly embodied in a heroic image of the President. She wrote him a letter:

If we admit that Nature works upon the mind, war is then a question of mind. I know that you know this. While the sun was floating up over Brooklyn this morning, I saw that you had mastered the coherence of contradictory vectors that alone gives us a glimpse of light, which some call love divine, since it harmoniously fuses races, nations, and religions in a peace that passes understanding. Because you have mastered this conflict, I feel as if stunned with love, like a bell in a wedding of angels. You have (not on purpose) decked out each corner of my heart with exquisite fiercely scented flowers. Nor, walking beside you, would I forget her, still and ever an adorable feminine apparition pursuing me and encouraging me like the spring breeze in her smile. That's how I've been cured of my regrets, in fact.

Squawk box said: *Don't bother him when he's so busy.* "OK, I'll send it to the Presidential Mediators. They'll know what's best."

Phoebe showed Walter her letter; he suggested she sleep on it. If she liked writing, he asked her, why not keep a working journal? A great idea, Phoebe replied. The letter read like gibberish when she next looked at it, and she put it away in a drawer, while her squawk box sniggered, *You still adore Him.* . . .

Phoebe saw Walter less and less. Priscilla had come into his life, looking after him, taking up his time. Phoebe inwardly relied on Owen, because she still loved him and because he dominated her visions when, for instance, she woke up to challenge another long day in late-night blackness, alone, in a sweat, with her heart clobbering her from within. Owen did not call often.

At the end of November her brother, Lewis, was arrested in scandalous circumstances. Phoebe refused to believe what was publicly said about him. Dr. Straub saw in this sympathy a confirmation of her tendency to dissoluteness. He became more confidently paternal than ever.

Phoebe began her journal:

> In art we must start by eliminating all historical classifications, which only produce stifled characters. We want beauty novelty style for all ages and lands. It's Christmas, isn't it—"No Hell"? . . .

As if to acknowledge the season, her squawk box softened its tone, doubling her own voice in dreamier obsessions:

"Gounod's 'Ave Maria' . . ." *Vacation's starting—but not for Mary Stuart. Ave Maria Stuart! It's like Christmas in wartime. Oh, you remember! The dead on a picket fence at Gettysburg, and: 'Hordes across the Yalu.'* "Fronds and spines on those corteges. Wouldn't it be kindly to be reborn into happy

> Old nights of Holy Mystery
> Hearing Noel sung in Your honor
> To the ends of the earth."

You've lost your French, Maria Stuart says. "I remember beautiful Christmases. Reproductions in gifted books—Christmas was a Prussian-blue sky with Wise Men and star. Also organ and bells. Sometimes they boom death Mass—fears and pains." *We do have peace, sort of.* "Only divine hands can stanch tears. Away on country hillsides steeples are counting out solemn carols. In small-town streets they sing in a smell of snow and ozone. Here shadows are all over the snow, with shouts not hymns." *You don't dare step into a church. You'd want to kiss people, and they'd only let you sing and cry.* "Fervent wishes in the wind! Deliver our hearts and eyes from irritation. Let's raise one Christmas tree in the Morosco Theater, and another in the Beekman meat market."

She spent most of Christmastime in bed, feverish, besnotted with her entrenched bronchitis. The infection aggravated her usual symptoms. She got up for Owen, who came with an offer of help in exchange for her giving up Walter. Breaking with him left her in a morbid state, even though he sent her money afterwards. She celebrated Christmas day in bed alone.

Walter went away for a few days with Priscilla. Phoebe agreed to look after a friend's cat. She soon began thinking that it was all the society she would ever have. And nobody's fault but her own. She didn't blame anyone for neglecting her, not even Owen. Not even Louisa, who was hiding behind him.

"Look at me, twenty years old, with breasts as wrinkly as the skin on hot milk."

Phoebe gave up all thought of modeling. She painted less and less. (Her hand shook, exhaustion led to distraction and excused it.) One morning her jeans fell down, slipping off her unfleshed hips. She hugged the mess of her body. She hurt. Sometimes the ache of her thrumming heart soared into a dazzling pain that sent her back to bed curled up and enduring. Because her sensations, feelings, and thoughts never abated, she came to the conclusion that she didn't stand a chance against them. What was she proving by lasting as long as she could? Survival meant only unremitting punishment. She didn't deserve it; she didn't deserve herself.

One evening in early February, she got out of bed and on the way to the bathroom picked up an X-Acto knife from her worktable. She ran a warm bath and sat in the tub with the knife in her right hand. After a few minutes she traced a tentative incision across her left wrist, perpendicular to the veins that ran blue and swollen underneath the transparent skin. A rosary of red droplets sprang up under the point. Her friend's cat had followed her into the bathroom and was sitting on the toilet, perched on its hindquarters, staring at her. Its gaze, one of perfect attention and indifference, was suddenly interrupted by a pink-and-white yawn, during which the cat's head disappeared behind its mouth. The animal then settled on its belly, crossing its forepaws. Phoebe shifted the knife to her left hand. Leaning her neck on the rim of the tub, she began masturbating underwater. Her pleasure—faint, short, unsettling—kept her alive.

Phoebe flipped the drain open and stepped out of the tub. She put on a can of consommé to heat while she dressed. She took a long time dressing. Later she went outside and started walking, working her way east, through the clear and windless night, cold but not frozen. She felt both numb and alert crossing the city, numb to cold and filth, alert to a thrashing rhythm within her. As she passed from one streaming avenue to the next, each dark block between became a bridge that lifted her into another half-abandoned hive where beings from uncreated dreams slept and drifted, giddy from the shock of their birth. They did not sadden her, she felt no sorrow for them, and a glance from any one of them could only mean that someone wished her well; she went on. A half hour later she crossed under an elevated highway and found herself at the "river." She wiped her eyes stung wet by cold and airy dirt. Above the city glow, scattered stars glistened in a moonless sky, drooping close, teetering not unkindly over the convulsions of her thought.

She had grown cold. She hurried up to Fourteenth Street and found a coffee shop. She was wearing Russian boots, men's corduroy trousers, a Navy pea jacket with two sweaters underneath, ski mittens, and a plaid wool cap with its earflaps down. After ordering her tea, she took off the cap, the mittens, the pea jacket, and one of her sweaters. The other customers relaxed. Someone from space had become a nice girl with rather large eyes. Three young men at the counter began teasing her, betting how long it took her to get into all those clothes. And how about getting *out* of them? Phoebe hardly minded. She had attracted no attention in a week, or since wanting to die. One of the men said it was a crime to bundle herself out of sight like that—a pretty girl was what life was all about. His words gave the world back to Phoebe. She wanted to cry. When he asked if he could take her home, she said yes.

Back in her studio, he treated her gently and a little impatiently. Because of her skinniness she turned out the lights and got under the covers first. He started rubbing his hands over her. She cried out. He took this for a sign of pleasure; she meant something else. She was experiencing a visitation, or at least an unusual visit. It had begun snowing inside her room. Out of the fathomless dark ceiling, snow was falling and soundlessly pelting her. The flakes felt light and warm as they cascaded onto her and through her. "Wait," she pleaded, "it's beautiful—" The boy grunted knowingly. She let him be, surrendering to the soft tumult. She rose to meet and savor it, gliding through rings of splintery light, up, up. Where was she going? Higher, she found or mentally assembled webs of incandescence out of which the flakes came sprinkling. She guessed, she *knew* what they were: stars. The teetering stars had spilled into the gloom of her mind. She had no strength to resist that shower or the spidery filaments above it that sucked her in. She recognized where she had come: into the abstraction called love. She was being pelted with love and sucked into it—and this poor boy was still bumping against her. Sure he was. Love had been broken into bits among us, the way light was pieced out around the sky: here and there, the same thing. A showering, never fixed, except in a fixity of change, in the motion of its fragments. Each star moved in its ring, each man in his life each woman in her life, longing to touch and never able to, and still one life, one us. That's why I love cloudless nights, Phoebe thought. Truth was shining around her. She drifted into the welter of light. She laughed incredulously, "It's us!" Her body shook with glee as he lost himself inside her. For a few days she had a hard time keeping him away.

Phoebe had to talk to someone about this joy. She approached Walter as soon as he came back. When she confessed that a stranger had restored her faith in life by telling her she was pretty, Walter scolded her. She was peddling herself to bums. They didn't care a damn about love and truth: "Their guiding light is getting into your pants."

She was disgusted with herself when she left him; and the disgust permanently cured her of suicide. Her piddling life did not deserve dramatic remedies. No sooner had she thought, When I got to the river I should have jumped right in, than her squawk box barked sympathetically, *The East River? Honey, you wouldn't have drowned, you'd have choked to death.* Phoebe wrote in her journal:

> A leap into the unknown is a leap back into childishness—another dream that doesn't work, and pretentious, too.

She resigned herself to living as a sick, childish adult, as a succession of hopeful and shameful incarnations. She remembered her father, with whom she had shared years of love and to whom she had spoken viciously. She wanted to speak to him again, in some other manner.

Phoebe had not seen Dr. Straub for a month. At her next visit, in mid-February, he remarked that she had behaved irresponsibly by not keeping her appointments. Not only had she harmed herself, she had prevented him from reporting on her condition to Owen, who was greatly upset. Phoebe thus learned of the therapist's complicity with her father. She saw an opportunity to wipe the slate clean, since both she and Owen had now put themselves in the wrong: she had yelled at him, he had acted behind her back. She wrote him a letter:

> . . . I was painfully surprised that you could talk about me to someone, even a doctor, so confidentially. It's too bad you haven't observed the results. At least I now understand why he stares at me so hard without ever seeing me. (It's true I always wear the magic ring you once gave me!) Since I can appreciate your desire to talk to someone about me, perhaps you can appreciate that to me it seems fairly disgusting? I know you meant well—that's the way "your kind" behaves, you're all so *good* at that: summing up a life in a few words. Has anyone ever looked right through you and out the other side? . . .

Owen did not respond. Phoebe was afraid of saying what she didn't mean if she used the telephone; so she wrote an-

other letter, this time to Louisa. Discussing Owen, she asked for
help:

> . . . A question becomes evident: is it possible to communicate
> with a human being? To communicate what my life is—
> Life goes on and keeps becoming what it already was. There
> are differences of form, that's all. Or I may feel that I'm still a
> lot of different people, but it's still one person struggling like
> mad—madly degrading myself—. . . .
> There were moments when you smiled—you were irresistibly
> yourself, even if you checked the smile a second after it showed.
> I know all about that. . . .
> I'm getting weaker and weaker, I let things happen abjectly.
> My room is a dream. So are the things in it, including my feet.
> Sometimes I scream dream screams. What I've lost is my confi-
> dence—my "insolence." I need tenderness, too—the infinite
> tenderness that goes with beginnings. So I scream like a little
> child who's been left out. Not just left out by people, by *things*.
> However, this does not make me feel inhuman, I feel *very*
> human. . . .

Louisa, when she came to see her, found Phoebe more than
she could face. She did not know where to begin. She encouraged Phoebe to trust the medical help she was getting and
withdrew—into Owen's shadow, as Phoebe saw it. Phoebe still
refused to condemn Owen, reminding herself that he was paying for her doctors and sending her money. She reduced him
for the time being to someone who wrote necessary checks.

With no one else to rely on, she clung earnestly to herself.
That self had become more and more fugitive: she kept losing
hold of her pain, her tremors, and her explosive feelings. One
afternoon she went to a movie, *The Diary of a Country Priest*.
In one scene, an older clergyman tells the young protagonist
that anyone called to holy orders will find in the history of
Christianity a precedent for his vocation. Walking home be-

tween ridges of grizzled snow, Phoebe asked herself if hers might not be Saint Lawrence on his griddle. At home she wrote in her journal:

> If the old ways had not been hidden, we could deliver ourselves from death by death. The divine directive points toward voluntary consumption—best by fire, "to cleanse the errant soul."

Reflections such as this reconciled Phoebe to the "fire" cauterizing her from within.

Occasionally she would return to places and people she had enjoyed. Her volatile temperament prevented these outings from soothing her as she hoped they might. In the Cedar one February evening, a writer told a group at the bar a supposedly true story that amused everyone except her. The previous summer, two of his friends had traveled through New England by car. Late one afternoon, on a back road in the White Mountains, they had overtaken a line of forty-odd girls returning to camp at the end of a hike. The girls, who were ten to thirteen years old, looked tired out. The procession was led by a group of four counselors, young women in their late teens. The writer's friends pulled up near the end of the straggling group. They asked how far the girls still had to go. About three miles, they answered. Any of them like a lift? You bet! Four of them got into the back seat. The men explained that in exchange they would have to "give head." The girls didn't know what that meant; as soon as they were told, they scrambled out of the car. The men stopped to renew their invitation farther up the line. Other girls climbed into the car and climbed out. At last the men, drawing level with the counselors, asked, "A lift, anybody?" "OK." "Hop in." Two of the counselors settled in the back seat, nothing else was said, and the car drove off under the gaze of forty-six freshly enlightened little girls.

Phoebe at first missed the point of the story. When she understood the trick the men had played, she began to cry. Her friends looked at her incredulously. She smashed her beer on the floor and ran outside.

She felt angry less at her friends than at humanity at large. Men and women looked at one another and saw only the stuff of contemptuous jokes. Tag thy neighbor, and any tag would do—Pole, Jew, cocksucker. She shuddered remembering the women who had been stuck with this ingenious disgrace. In spite of herself she laughed at the ingenuity and thought of the disgrace as something less than disastrous, an impulse that made her break out in fresh tears. She was no different. Even she could forget "love divine." She told herself after a moment, "Of course I'm no different. And *that's* part of love." Nevertheless she had begun excluding herself from the world that her love embraced.

A few nights later Phoebe had a dream. She called it her "dream of dissolution." She is attending a group event in a sort of sunken theater inside a big, old-fashioned hotel in the city. A froglike man is directing the group. Again and again he tells them, "Accept things as they happen." Long sessions of explanation and mental exercise are separated by five-minute breaks. After the first break, she notices that the cat sitting near her is missing. After the second, the woman on her left disappears. No one can leave the theater unobserved.

Phoebe now realizes what she has been warned to accept: creatures are disintegrating. They are vanishing definitively, without cause, without justification. Phoebe feels a fresh confidence. Although she knows that sadness awaits her, she no longer worries about what will happen. During another break, chatting with a short, lively woman in her sixties, she senses that this woman will go next.

When only five participants are left, Phoebe is possessed with a desire for a "saving egg." She does not understand what this means. During the next break, in a hotel shop full of exotic bric-a-brac, she finds a cream-colored porcelain egg and buys it. Rolling it in one hand, she experiences an elation both austere and sensual. Nearby, the froglike leader is talking to a dark intellectual boy whom Phoebe had known at college. The three go back together and sit on the floor of the pit. Phoebe squeezes the egg, filling up with power. The frog man, who has begun a long speech, turns to her and softly tells her, "All right, lay off. I get it. You have the power."

A consoling warmth was stealing over Phoebe. She looked forward to waking up. She could not wake up because she had not fallen asleep. The dream, vivid as a movie, had come to her as she sat on the edge of her bed—the first of many such hallucinations. She clenched her left hand around the absent egg and hummed an old refrain:

> Earth is mother to all kinds,
> Crazy men and women.
> Earth is mother to all kinds,
> Crazy women and men.

Phoebe became chronically frightened. Her tenacious depression had convinced her that "she had failed." What had she failed at? Who was the "she" that had done the failing? She was frightened by the loss of anything she might call herself. Whatever she now was eluded her; "she" had dissolved into pure confusion. When she told Walter this, he replied, "Why the hell do you think I paint?" She noted:

So there you are with two fingers up your nose. Remove them. No problem.

She made herself go back to work. She decided literally to see who she was: she would paint nothing else.

. . . First, drawings of myself, in the old manner. Divide the
surface into squares. Draw fainter lines through the center of
the squares to form a secondary griddle. Insert my parts one by
one:

P. Lewison, of medium height from head to toe. The length
of her head equals the distance between her chin and her nipples, the distance between her chin and nipples equals that
between nipples and bellybutton, the distance between nipples
and bellybutton equals that between bellybutton and crotch.
Shoulders are two head-heights broad. Bones: through the skin
you can identify ribs, also knobs of femurs, humerus, radius.
Elsewhere: frontal bone, parietal bone, temples, brows. Features: eyeballs, hair, thin nose, middling mouth, rounded chin,
scarlet cheekbones. Legend: draw two horizontal lines, letters
between them in large and small caps: PH. LEWISON. Inscribed
above: ST. LAWRENCE IN DRAG. Or BLEEDING HEART OF
JESUS. Or SACRED CUNT OF JESUS.

Phoebe gave one such sketch to Dr. Straub, the person she
most talked to, someone she wanted to thank. At their next
meeting he analyzed the drawing for her. In it, he pointed out,
he noticed blank eyes, hands hidden behind the back, genitals
more detailed than the face. His comments made her cry. Because she rarely cried in his presence, he imagined that she had
come to the verge of a useful discovery. She was crying for him.
That night she wrote him a farewell letter:

. . . O my psychiatrist! The human being has turned into a
farm animal. The hands that handle her take all they find and
give nothing back to what *must* be the source of life. You
yourself pay taxes to the animal farm—you know we all end up
in the stewpot. People love to eat out of it, and orders have been
issued to the young to multiply and then suck each other's juices
right down to the marrow. First we're pigs and donkeys, then
animal suckers. . . .

This letter at last elicited a phone call from Owen: "You can't do this to yourself. You're in bad enough shape as it is, and now what's to keep you from going to pieces completely?"

Her squawk box had already been telling her this, in these words. Phoebe wondered in terror if she had not already gone to pieces. No—she still had her feelings. They rampaged through her every hour of the day. Whatever being endured them could lay claim to a real existence. Only her body, the ground of that existence, kept letting her down. Each day she tried to will it back into wholeness if not wholesomeness: "Two feet, like everybody else. Left big toe, right big toe, left ankle, right ankle. . . . Stomach with diaphragm attached, ribs enclosing me like two hands. Lungs . . ." Her lungs remained sopped; when she ate, her stomach burned; a skinned rabbit's head stared back from her mirror.

Asking the head in the mirror if she was insane comforted her, because as long as she accepted insanity as a possibility, she knew she had some sanity left. "How can the possibility of insanity be cured?" she wrote. "By food, work, and faith."

She forced soup through her teeth. No matter how exhausted, she stuck to a daily schedule of sketching, writing, and reading. Faith proved harder. A relentless awareness of loss stuffed her thin chest with dated movies of lovers, parents, and friends.

Consolation began in a book. She had become the kind of reader authors dream of, for whom each sentence revises the universe. She could have sworn Sir Thomas Browne knew her plight when he wrote that

> Thy soul is eclipsed for a time, I yield, as the sun is shadowed
> by a cloud; no doubt but there gracious beams of God's mercy
> will shine upon thee again. . . . We must live by faith, not by

feeling; 'tis like the beginning of grace to wish for grace; we must expect and tarry.

A passing cloud had come over her. This did not mean that her sun was dead.

Life is a pure flame, and we must live by our invisible sun within us.

She remembered her autumn ecstasies—"light and love divine." Others had looked at her strangely. In Sir Thomas's company she felt less strange, less alone: I don't know what it is, but I know I'm something, and it's all I've got.

The sudden spring fostered her confidence. After five months she at last stopped coughing. She imagined that soon her hands might no longer tremble. Lewis and his friend Morris took her into the Hudson River valley for a weekend, among reservoirs and rolling orchards. Sunday night she wrote:

Grapevines budding. I'm still only twenty. Yesterday apple trees opened petals of primal cream and pink. In a few months, Rubens's wreaths of fruit—vines ripening, apples on boughs. Tonight, light dripping with shadow, hill moon rising, sun withdrawing, forest shivering in the breath of summer to be. Someone told the hawthorn, Blossom!—Ph. unfolded. Someone told the whippoorwill, Sing!—Ph. sang. Brother and friend spoke hymns of farewell to this natural day. A beloved woman must speak with the breath of corollas brushed by a shuttling bird.

She went back to work in a loving frenzy. She started calling her friends again and went out to meet them. She wanted to wrap them all into her billowing cloak of love. They were busy, they were worried, they had to leave. Her work happened in visionary outbursts. Walter came to see it. He told her, "You're crapping all over the canvas. You *know* better." Even though

she had met her only ten minutes earlier, Phoebe implored
Elizabeth, who heard this judgment, to wait in her studio after
Walter left. While Elizabeth watched, Phoebe destroyed her
new work.

She then planned another self-portrait in the manner of the
old masters. But she didn't have the patience for such things.
Her hand lusted after scrawls and tangles, "dirty combina-
tions," dull orange smeared with dull green. Her brush scampered away from her.

In mid-May she gave up. She stopped seeing her friends. She
stopped painting, although she still wrote a little. Increasingly
she spent her days and mostly sleepless nights trying to guess
the cause of her disintegration. What had she or anybody done
that must be so painfully atoned for? Something—something
obvious and stupidly hidden from her: "a secret lesson any old
ocarina can repeat." She was condemned to learn this lesson the
hard way.

In late May, her brother, Lewis, again became the object of
public scandal. Louisa, who had spent months watching over
her son, collapsed and was committed to a hospital. Phoebe
went to see her. In Louisa's hospital room, mother and daughter broke each other's heart.

Phoebe stopped at a bar on her way home. She stepped from
the sweltering day into air-conditioned chill. She sneezed into
her whiskey sour. Her nose started to dribble. By evening she
was coughing violently; before morning she was burning with
fever. She phoned Walter, who took her straight to Saint Vincent's, where she was admitted with double pneumonia.

The two doctors in charge of Phoebe were appalled by her
condition. They disregarded her psychosomatic explanation
and quickly guessed at the truth. Phoebe did her best to frus-
trate them. She regarded them as mortal enemies. Whenever
they approached her, her eyes glittered with wary loathing, and
her squawk box, in a harsh mood, speaking on her behalf,
pestered them with resentful insults.

As Phoebe saw it, two strangers had decided to meddle with her secret life. Under the pretence of caring for her, they were hunting down the scurrying, tiny identity to which she was now reduced. Her mistrust of them survived their successful treatment of her pneumonia and the prodigies of tact the doctors exercised in discussing her chronic disorder. Their suggestion that this disorder might have a physiological origin infuriated her. The ecstatic pain that had grown in her over the past year had by now become the center of her reality. She could not bear having it made medically predictable. She refused to be helped. Only when Louisa arrived, four days after Phoebe's admission, was she lured out of her corner.

Louisa promised Phoebe that she would never abandon her again; she promised never to let Owen, or anyone else, interfere with her. Phoebe let herself be convinced, after exacting one more promise: she must never be left alone with her doctors. She then agreed to do what was asked of her, giving up responsibility for her nightmare illness with a relief that surprised her. For the first time since December, she menstruated.

Phoebe was given a second basal metabolism test, this time correctly administered. It recorded her metabolic rate at an abnormal +35. Methyl thiouracil was prescribed for her, one hundred milligrams to be taken daily. Louisa was told that Phoebe could leave the hospital as soon as she recovered from her pneumonia, probably in three or four days. She would need several weeks to become healthy again. During that time she should lead a restful life, she should be taken care of—in other words, she should go home.

After her first wild resentment, Phoebe endured her stay in the hospital with petulant resignation. Her fever came down, her lungs cleared; nothing else changed. Her heart still banged, she trembled and sweated, and the best pills brought her only brief sleep. When Louisa said she was taking her to their home upstate, Phoebe did not protest. She nonetheless took the decision as a defeat—the two years she had lived on her own were being written off. Her squawk box, meshed for a while with her own passionate voice, reasserted itself to denounce her surrender. It suggested that Owen had instigated what was happening. Louisa was doing the dirty work while he rubbed his hands in the wings.

Phoebe's own voice fell to a whisper. It whispered more sound than sense, as though the squawk box had requisitioned the attributes of reason. One day it started saying, over and over, without apparent cause, "I quest, request, bequest . . ." (By now she could control her own voice no better than the box's.) At another time it repeated an inexplicable succession of letters inside her docile ears: b.s.t.q.l.d.s.t., b.s.t.q.l.d.s.t. . . . Phoebe could not decipher the series. After making it yield "Beasts stalk the question lest demons sever trust" and "But soon the quest lured drab saints thither," she rejected the possibility that the letters were initials. She found it even harder to make words out of them, especially without a *u* for the *q*. No matter what she did, they refused to be dispelled. No matter what she did. Without meaning, unthreatening, merely insistent, the letters turned into a regular refrain inside her head. Phoebe had to insert her voice's other whisperings between them: "I b.s.t.q.l.d. quest s.t. I b.s.t.q.l. request d.s.t., I b.s.t.q. bequest l.d.s.t. . . ."

Phoebe quickly lost interest in the new diagnosis of her condition, which might have pleased anyone—anyone else.

Before she left, Louisa repeated to her again and again that she would take care of her until she was completely cured. She would not be sent to a "clinic." She would be protected from Owen as long as she wanted. For the eighteenth time Phoebe consented to go home. She set a condition, however: she would go alone, and by train—the way they had always come back from the city when she first traveled with her parents as a little girl. Phoebe's doctors urged Louisa to indulge her.

During her trip, Phoebe learned something about the series of letters. B.s.t.q.l.d.s.t. signified an old train careening down an old track. At slower speeds the train said,

> Cigarettes, tch tch
> Cigarettes, tch tch.

She found nothing to eat or drink during the four-hour ride. The carriage shook so hard she could not read. Before Poughkeepsie, under a three-o'clock sun, the air-conditioning broke down. People sitting near her kept moving away. When she saw Louisa, the pang of joy made Phoebe yell. Afterwards, in her unaltered room, she yanked off her clothes to slide between the sheets of her blond-pine bed. She slept.

Owen arrived the next Friday. When she saw him, pain came back—an unfamiliar pain, which Phoebe lived with for several days before she could name it.

At two in the morning, awake in her room, Phoebe sat by her window, staring out through hot moonlight at the trees, lawn, and houses that beleaguered her. She listened to the voices inside her. With obscure insistence her box kept reminding her of a photograph in her father's room. Thanks to her, that room was now unoccupied. Phoebe got up and found the photograph, a sepia portrait framed in engraved silver of her paternal grandmother, who had died of a stroke when Phoebe was two. She was dressed in black, with a wide-brimmed hat pinned to the back of her head, a jacket with enormous lapels, a tapering ankle-length skirt, and long silk gloves held loosely in her hands. Her features expressed gravity and alertness. Averted from the camera, her gaze seemed fixed on some disaster that confirmed all she had ever suspected. Phoebe put the photograph on her bedside table.

The novelty of Phoebe's pain lay less in its symptoms—the familiar ones of her disease—than in its source, which she imagined as outside herself. She could not at first identify that source, and only did so after Louisa revealed to her the settlement Owen had made on her behalf on the occasion of her twenty-first birthday.

What she then discovered would not have surprised anyone who had observed her in Owen's presence. Her every gesture and word expressed resentment and disgust. Whenever he appeared, she would draw up her knees and grit her teeth, reminding herself of demands to be made, reconnoitering opportunities for attack. Unable to see herself, Phoebe remained unaware of the obsessiveness of her feelings. She almost realized the "truth" while Owen was reading to her late one afternoon:

> Mr. Copperfield chuckled. "You're so crazy," he said to her with indulgence. He was delighted to be in the tropics at last and he was more than pleased with himself that he had managed to dissuade his wife from stopping at a ridiculously expensive hotel where they would have been surrounded by tourists. He realized that this hotel was sinister, but that was what he loved.

Phoebe would have shouted "Just like you!" if at this moment her father had not dozed off. Her rage diverted, she only growled him awake.

A few days before Phoebe's birthday, Owen deposited several hundred shares of high-priced securities in a custody account opened in her name, and ordered the monthly transfer of five hundred dollars from his checking account into hers. The news of these arrangements brought Phoebe's emotions into perfect order.

"He hates you," a woman said. In astonishment Phoebe looked at the photograph by her bed. Two ravens rose out of a summery field and winged their slow way out of sight above the house. "He'll do anything to stop you."

"Why, you fifty-pint-old drunkess," Phoebe replied.

"I know him better'n anybody," the woman cawed. "Remember the first time he stuck you with money? He'll never change."

Owen congealed for Phoebe into a repellent image of selfishness. She saw that he had pretended to encourage her freedom only to attack it better. He no longer even pretended an interest in her painting. Of course he must hate her. Perhaps he had always hated her, and he had lavished care on her as a child only to control her, to make sure she complied with his desires. To think how she'd loved him!

"Don't expect me to thank you," Phoebe told him after learning of his extraordinary gift.

"I don't," Owen answered, with a meekness that made her yearn to draw blood.

"I'm only accepting to make you pay something." Her grandmother coaxed her, "Tell him he's a fox and a pig!" Phoebe's throat choked with sobs of fury.

She sometimes spied on her parents, hiding inside the door of the terrace where they had drinks before dinner. One evening she heard Owen suggest to Louisa that Phoebe have a thyroid-ectomy. She thus made a second discovery. Her father would not content himself with dominating her life; he wanted that life itself. She thought of the ways he had intervened since last September: choosing her thyroid specialist, choosing her psychotherapist, insisting that her troubles were psychological, belittling her flagrant symptoms. He had pushed her to the limit of her disease; now he wanted to finish her off.

Mrs. Lewison Senior's black silks flapped around her fussily: "He may think he doesn't know what he's doing, but he sure is doing it." Phoebe, who had wet her pants downstairs, was sitting on the toilet in her bathroom. She had become fiercely determined. She would survive and win. Her father would die first. Or she would teach him pain. That would be even better.

Louisa never failed her. When Phoebe called, she came.

Phoebe called her more and more often. Louisa had become company, and also childhood love, belated and never too late. Phoebe wished she did not hang on to her mother so greedily. For Louisa, apparently inexhaustible, this dependence was in itself sufficient reward. That Louisa never mentioned the operation did not disturb Phoebe: it meant that her mother had turned Owen's proposition down. After all, she herself did not speak about certain matters, such as her grandmother's eerie voice.

That voice was raised urgently when, on August first, Phoebe learned that Owen had acquired the "Portrait of Elizabeth": "He's at it again. Why, he never cared about painting. And you know how he feels about Walter." (Lewis had told her that Owen referred to Walter as "the man who ruined my daughter.") "But then, maybe he's speculating. To people like him, you know, art's just a commodity. No, that's not it. He knows how you feel about that picture, doesn't he? Take it from me, *you're* why he bought it. He doesn't want to leave you one single thing. He wants you to see he's running the whole show. . . ."

Phoebe rasped, "Shut up, you old bitch!" She'd been stung. Although she was willing to see vengefulness in anything Owen did, his simply owning the portrait hurt her most. When could he have bought it? Suspicious, she telephoned Walter's gallery. The painting had been sold—to Maud Ludlam. They were sure: it had been shipped to her in late June.

"What did I tell you?" the old woman sighed. "He's a dark one—dark as the ground owl of childhood fame."

Phoebe confronted Owen with what she'd learned. Since he now approached her like a sinner at confession, she could not tell whether her words truly upset him.

"Of course," he said. "I bought it from the Ludlams."

"Maud got rid of it after a month?"

"Why not? What difference does it make?"

"What the hell are you doing with that painting?"

"If you really want to know, I got it for you."

Phoebe sensed he was lying. She would pin him to the floor.

"So why haven't you given it to me?"

"It'll be arriving any day."

"Is it mine or isn't it?"

Owen hesitated. He *had* thought of reselling the painting.

"Would that make you happy?"

"Nothing you do could make me happy. Your owning that painting makes me puke."

"It's yours."

"I want papers to prove it."

"There's no need for that, darling."

"Yes, there is, *darling.* I want to make sure it's out of your fucking hands."

"When I promise you something—"

"Uh-uh. I want a legal document of ownership. Otherwise the world is going to learn about your hanky-panky with that wharf in New London. Remember, when you got two companies to pay off one claim?"

Owen laughed. "Phoebe, stop it. That's ancient history. Nobody gives a damn. I even told complete strangers about it— you were there."

"Not Louisa."

Watching him, Phoebe could not stifle a grin. She had guessed right. He walked out of her room. She would have her way.

Louisa took advantage of Phoebe's good spirits to broach unpleasant business. She told her that her treatment had conspicuously failed and that she should consider a thyroidectomy—the sooner the better. "You haven't gained five pounds since you came up here, and you're jumpy as ever. In your shoes I'd go crazy in a week."

"I went crazy months ago. If I could know—if I could be

sure I'd get better someday, I wouldn't mind waiting. I suppose
Owen thinks I should get my throat cut."

"He's got nothing to do with it. *You* think about it, and *you*
decide. I don't want to keep secrets from you. I did find out
there's a good surgeon at Albany. He does four or five thyroids
a week, there and in Boston. I told him about you, and he's
available."

Phoebe said nothing. After a while Louisa again spoke: "I've
told you *my* secret."

"I'm scared. It's mainly the anesthetic. I don't want to face
that. It's like death."

"Not anymore, not with Pentothal. It's not like going under.
You just disappear in a second, and then you're back. No
anxiety, no memories—"

"I believe you, but that's *not* my secret."

"I don't follow."

"Momma, if I'm going to live, I have to agree to die first. Can
I be alone for a while?"

Phoebe wrote her brother, Lewis:

> . . . Louisa is all kindness—real kindness—but I feel I'm
> losing her too. The sympathetic string of motherhood vibrates
> with hypocrisy. It has to—she has to disconnect from me if she's
> going to help. Is life always going to be like this? Yes, at least
> until death. That will do for an answer.
>
> Can you understand? I need someone to understand, and you
> can—you've survived worse than I. Will you come here to be
> with me? With you at my side, I might let them cut my throat.

Phoebe's grandmother attended her constantly—a presence
not disturbing, not reassuring. She had been permanently transformed into a bird. Although large and black, the bird brought
to Phoebe's room a sense not of ominousness but of placid,
continuous movement, like the sound of planes regularly land-

ing and taking off at a distant airport. The bird spoke less and less.

The portrait of Elizabeth arrived. Lewis brought it to her room as soon as it had been uncrated. When she saw it, Phoebe was overcome by giggles. "It was mine all along! Hang it on the wall, over there. Lewis, please let me love you."

Her twenty-first birthday passed discreetly, marked only by a cake for three. The day before, Louisa had driven Phoebe to the Medical Center in Albany, where a surgeon examined her. Phoebe had taken to him at once, something that so astonished Louisa, after her lengthy precautions, that it made her almost cross. During the days that followed Phoebe thought only of her next encounter with the doctor, ruddy, plump, irresistibly confident. When she first looked into his eyes, calm as a cow's, life became manageable. Later, she experienced fright, and a familiar hatred of created things, especially herself. In her bedroom she rediscovered an owlish raven circling the ceiling, and Elizabeth in paints, whom she did not hate.

Following Phoebe's instructions, Owen brought the portrait to the hospital during the operation and hung it in her room opposite her bed. On the bedside table Lewis installed a record player that she could reach lying down.

Louisa and Lewis were waiting for her on her return from the recovery room. Whenever Phoebe opened her eyes—for a long while they merely rolled absently under half-closed lids— her mother said to her that she was doing fine, and Lewis grimly echoed her. They were not saying what they thought, only what they had been told. Phoebe's face looked bloodless and shrunken above her bandaged neck, to which two drains were taped.

Phoebe at first did not hear them and later did not believe them. She was emerging into a welter of drowsiness and terror. In spite of the tranquilizers she had been given, she had never felt sicker. The consequences of surgery did not frighten her: she simply knew that her symptoms had grown worse.

Her heart bedeviled her ribs like a spike; sweat filmed on her arms and legs; her body had disintegrated into pockets of anguish.

The operation had succeeded, and Phoebe's reaction corresponded to a new condition. Four-fifths of her thyroid gland had been removed. Left unchecked, the gland could only respond to the body's demand for the excess thyroxine, to which it had grown accustomed, by starting to grow back. To prevent this, Phoebe was given thyroxine in amounts greater than any she had secreted during her disease. In the course of her operation her pulse had not gone below 160; it now rose to 180. No one could have persuaded her that she was being cured.

For seven days she endured in virtual immobility because of the drains in her neck and the intravenous drip in each arm. She again lost all control of her thoughts and feelings.

The feeling of fear never left her, oppressive with someone at her side, unbearable whenever she found herself alone. Without either Lewis or Louisa, Phoebe would ring for a nurse every two minutes, although she soon learned that others provided only an illusory relief. Others could distract her, not calm what she most dreaded: that the next moment would prove as intolerable as the last, as it always did.

Lewis sometimes read out loud to her. Phoebe did her best to listen; in less than a minute her attention would unravel. Music worked better. She had brought her favorite records, among them some Haydn quartets. Halfway through one of them, at the end of the "Emperor" theme and variations, Phoebe grabbed Lewis's wrist: "Leave that." She played the movement over and over, at least four hundred times. She said afterwards that without it she would have tried to kill herself. Often her head filled with words that Haydn's familiar tune trailed after it, words she thought she had forgotten, a hymn from school days: "Glorious things of thee are spoken, Sion . . ."

Her bird still attended her, voiceless and mechanical, speed-

ing incessantly from one corner of her ceiling to the next as if
hung on an elliptical track. It made a whirring, whispering
noise: *essesso, essesso* . . .

These things constituted her days and nights: the whispered
essesso of the bird, the fourth variation coming to an end,
grappling with the pillow to find the bell, reaching for Lewis's
or Louisa's hand.

Before she left home, the portrait of Elizabeth had entertained if not consoled her; here it gave no comfort. Phoebe had
her room kept dark. In the meager daylight from the blinded
windows or by the light of the night lamp, the painting was
blurred and distorted. The yellow blank eyes floated above the
head; the folded hands, whose nails suggested a silver smile,
shrank to dull stumps; the fiery red of the hair streamed down
the canvas in muddy pulsations. Phoebe would look at Elizabeth, shut her eyes, and sing in time with the record,

> See the streams of living water
> Springing from eternal love

wishing for one thing: make it end.

She never cried. She never had time to collect her tears: too
busy getting the Haydn restarted, clutching the bell, watching
the door for the tortoise-footed nurse, waiting for the next
moment to be less painful, and the one after that. If she had
been able to cry, she would have cried for her poor body,
regularly devoured by an insatiable, rubber-toothed monster.

After a week, her dose of thyroxine was reduced. Although
Phoebe did not know she felt better, her sensations gradually
came off the boil, and the terror that had swamped her subsided
into a calmer sadness. The sadness filled her whole body, as the
terror had, coldly now. The whir of the bird, the inexhaustible
sweetness of the quartet, the portrait of Elizabeth assumed new
functions as emblems of this sadness to which, without realizing

it, Phoebe turned as to the purest hope. She had nothing to look forward to; she had simply rediscovered something that she could call "herself." For the first time, she accepted her disease as a reality, as her reality. If her sickness meant sadness, she would become that sadness, keeping it all for herself, in the remnants of her body. "My body lies over the ocean," she sang. She also sang,

> 'Tis His love His people raises
> Over self to reign as kings.

She smiled at the thought of loving her sadness—surely better than not loving at all, than not loving herself at all? Self-pity provided a first step towards sanity. Only a step—what next? Elizabeth's ivory cheeks and smiling hands had fallen into place. Phoebe sighed wistfully, "My Elizabeth, I'd like to set lighted candles at your feet. I'm better now." *Essesso,* went the bird.

Louisa and Lewis knew Phoebe was recovering when she made a small joke in a mode of that time: "If Stella Dallas married Roger Maris, she'd be known as Stella Maris." In their perpetual shadow, Elizabeth's unpupilled eyes became her stars.

Phoebe's convalescence remained slow. In the course of a year her disorder had disrupted the normal functioning of her lungs, her heart, and her digestive system. She had no physical reserves to draw on. Her doctors spoke about her condition with optimism and advised that she spend another week in the hospital.

Hallucinations still afflicted her. Voices neither hers nor the bird's rumbled through her darkened room: ". . . Who is she who on earth brings forth the sea? Who is he who on earth brings forth the sea? Who is she who lights up great days?" *Essesso, essesso.* "Who is he who devours? Where is the shoemaker the blue one?" *Essesso.* "Where is the red-white-and-blue shoemaker? . . ." Phoebe did not take these voices seriously. Even the bird could now have left without being missed, although she thanked it frequently for its attentiveness.

Phoebe reminded herself never to use her sadness as a pretext for not acting. Acting meant getting what she wanted, and she knew what she wanted: happiness. Happiness required a world with no monsters in it. She had said to Lewis, "Something's out there in the dark prowling around. You can't see it, but you keep getting these horrible reports," and even as she spoke she knew that she was only telling a convenient story—an excuse for giving up. She had nobody to blame. She asked Owen to visit her. She would not let him prowl outside in the dark any longer. When he had left, she thought, "So that's what heaven is: the living around us, no one left out." This recognition brought her only a distant joy, because she had become feverish again. In dog-day heat, she had managed to catch cold.

Several nights later she had another visitor. Her fever had gone and returned. She was lying in the dark, licking her dry mouth and smiling at the viola's turn:

> Who can faint when such a river
> Ever will their thirst assuage?

She became aware of a glow to one side and a sound like a voice speaking. She turned off the record player. The glow was emanating from the only blank wall of her room, to her left, beyond the window. At its center a circle of crystal had formed. Superposed rings of crystalline rock began appearing within the circle, tinged with blue light from behind. These blue rings opened inwards, brightening as they receded through a self-creating distance that narrowed into a radiance deep within the rock—an endpoint that Phoebe perceived as pure white, dazzling and warm. As she lay there smiling into that charming light, her bird flew noiselessly out of the hole. "Is my bird going to speak to me again?" The owlish raven had itself turned white. It vanished among the shadows of the room, only to reappear inside the blue-white tunnel, once more flying towards her. Phoebe again heard the voice. It was calling her by name.

"Who is it?" she asked.

"It's your old pal," the voice answered. "You know who."

"Walter?" Staring into the shining circles of stone, she glimpsed what looked like a man in profile. She could not recognize him, although he reminded her of a stranger on the train home from Belmont. "I can't see you."

"No need," came the answer. "I'm waiting for you."

"Thank you, but I'm picky about my friends."

"Come *on*, Phoebe. It's great in here." The hovering bird turned back into the tunnel, showing her the way. Phoebe's body tingled with sprightliness.

"Thanks. It's not bad out here, either."

The apparition slowly dimmed. A minute later no light showed in her room except for the glint of her water glass, the faint blue aura of the night lamp, the red dot on the panel of her record player. Phoebe lay in bed wishing for someone to laugh with.

She felt buoyant when she woke up. The tunnel's glow still warmed her, and she remembered the profiled man with intense affection. He's my mentor, she decided. He's the man I'll go looking for as soon as I leave this dump.

Her unusual cheerfulness made doctors and nurses beam. She promised herself to pay no more attention to her discomforts. Later in the day, as her temperature exhaustingly rose and fell, she realized that her body was once again in crisis. Like the medication given for it, its disorder now belonged to the world outside her. She hoped, as night approached, that her anonymous mentor would appear in his tunnel. Even though he did not, his memory continued to enchant her; and early the next morning, before dawn, she was granted some solace. Her bird, which she had not seen the day before, came back to her room, its first blackness restored, describing once again its customary ellipse. Its wings, however, made no sound. It rapidly gathered speed and soon was flying so fast that Phoebe could not follow it. She did not mind, she was elated. Out loud she said, "Look at that birdie go! Granny, you're wearing me out. I thought you were on my side."

The bird spun like the knot of a twirled lasso. Phoebe's heart raced as she watched.

"I wouldn't mind if you could just unlock the kettledrum in my chest of drawers and slow it down a notch. Granny, talk to me at least."

Phoebe sat up.

"Where is my chevalier, pray tell? Catalepsy got your tongue? OK, but someday I want to go riding again. Think of it, I can buy myself a chestnut now. Horseflesh will be mine. I'll go out riding in pursuit of my faithful bird's-eye, hear that? Meanwhile, the birthday girl is full of thirst."

She cleared her throat and coughed.

"My throat is full of thistledown. There are so many thirsts I want to do. First it will soon be time for love. I haven't had an orgy in thirteen weekends. It's a boycott, no less. And that's exactly who I want to start with—boysenberries and their big banjos."

Phoebe no longer cared if the bird was listening.

"Then a nice older piece of lettuce for salad days, full of suggestions and spinal trappings. And finally I want the man of my dreamy legs from somewhere in betweentimes. When I love that personality he'd better watch his outlooks! As former corpus delicti (almost) one will have knucklebones and depravities comparable to those of the avidest Elizabethan des-

peradoes, and you know how swank and murderous they can
be! . . . Oh . . . Elizabeth—"

She tried to make out the portrait in the gloom.

"I haven't forgotten you, not for one secret. And what if you
were the one? I can see us in our warm and lovable drawing
room, two wombs as one, wife to wife. I could fancy that.
Witnesses of each other's dreams. . . . But then who could I be
butterfly to (and housefly to, too)? Who could I waffle, who
could I babushka? I need real babes to sillytalk, and I can't help
thinking of all those malcontents with their malarkey and solo
prongs strewn around like landmarks, like pieces of forgotten
furniture."

Phoebe started laughing.

"Now there's a dimpled prognostic for a life! A dimity land-
lady turning sprung floperoo easterners into pidgin pies and
daffodils of her cosmology! Because for me myself and I, what
will they add? Noteworthy nothingness. I'm my own cosmo-
naut, thanks just the same, and my private universe spreads
from world-eaten rosaries to the swivels of skyrider Galahads—
and whatever that may mean," she added, "I swear it's true."
She looked around her. "My birds are spreading—hi there,
Granny!—or maybe it's my bod."

A shower of sparks burst along the path of the bird.

"I haven't forgotten you, either. You ever were and shall be
my ethereal booms. Zowie! You came out of my cecum, the
heaven-mapped loins, you and your flaky rinds, and it was then
I knew. What else can I ever know? East River to Long Island
Sound and out to sea, over which you so cunningly twinkle.
Winter, summer, winter again, going places we never left, and
all we have to do is sit through the movie and we're there!
Christmas! Why isn't it motherland? Granny, tell me you're a
nighthawk. I want to go outside and look, all that fun and
nonsense I'm missing—rockets zooming through bones.
Granny, where's my skylight? What's wrong?" Phoebe loudly

asked this of the circling bird, which was wearying, and she could sympathize with that, since her enthusiasm had left her breathless. She watched the bird slow down as it descended, blindingly white now, settling gradually until it came to rest on the floor next to her bed—except that, to Phoebe's surprise, that part of the room had no floor: the bird plummeted abruptly out of sight and hearing.

Allan and Owen

JUNE-JULY 1963

A S A RULE, THOSE WHO DIE YOUNG LEAVE THEIR PERSONAL
affairs in a mess. Perhaps because chronic illness had long made
his life seem precarious, the rule did not apply to Lewis Lewison's friend Morris Romsen. Long before he died at the end of
his thirtieth year, he had drawn up a satisfactory will; and he
had recently supplemented it with a generous life-insurance
policy whose beneficiary was his associate, Priscilla Ludlam.

The provision for Priscilla came as a surprise to Lewis, and
even more to Morris's sister, Irene Kramer. Particularly devoted to Morris, Irene was startled to learn that Priscilla had
known her brother so intimately, amazed that Morris had never
mentioned making her his beneficiary; and her amazement
turned to mild suspicion when she found out that the policy had
been written shortly before Morris's death by Allan Ludlam,
Priscilla's father. While realizing that coincidence, or friendship itself, might explain the fact, Irene still wondered if some

professional ethic did not forbid a father's writing such a policy on his daughter's behalf. She decided to consult Owen Lewison, since he had every aspect of the insurance business at his fingertips and she knew him well enough to trust his discretion. Owen told her, "I'll be happy to check things for you." He had time on his hands, and worries to forget: Phoebe, about to emerge from Saint Vincent's, had refused to let him see her. "I'm sure Ludlam's clean, though. I've worked with his office a lot, I even know him slightly. There's no chance he'd try any monkey business."

"I know him too, and I know how well off they are, or Maud is. It just seems strange."

From an old acquaintance in Allan's company, Owen discovered that Allan had been recommended to Morris by none other than Phoebe; that on learning that Priscilla would be named beneficiary, he had at first declined to write the policy; that he had later agreed to do so only after Morris assured him that Priscilla knew nothing about it.

Irene ran the Kramer Gallery, which had opened on the West Side several years earlier and recently moved uptown. During a subsequent meeting with the Ludlams at her gallery, Irene confessed to Allan her "curiosity" about Morris's life insurance: "I didn't know it could be so all-in-the-family."

Allan blushed. "It usually isn't. It bothered me too, you know—"

"I do know. You're scrupulousness itself."

At his office the next day, Allan asked if Morris's policy had raised any problems. He learned of Owen's inquiry. He called Irene: had Owen acted at her request?

"Yes, he did. It was dumb of me, but Morris had just died, and, for reasons I still don't understand, he'd never spoken about Priscilla to me. Mr. Lewison said your conduct was exemplary."

"Irene, it was standard procedure."

Allan was relieved by Irene's reassurances. If Morris's policy gave him no cause for worry, he dreaded the possibility of having other cases come accidentally to Owen's attention—cases that might reveal his secret career of repeated fraud. This career had always exposed him to high risks; to have an expert like Owen investigating him entailed a risk he couldn't afford to run.

Owen had suspected nothing. Allan had escaped danger unawares, as if he had casually brushed a spider from his neck and then recognized a black widow. He relished his luck. It enhanced and was enhanced by the euphoria of finding Elizabeth. For a while he abounded in a sense of the excellence of his life. He felt an immense gratitude towards Owen for having left that intact. One morning he wrote him a letter:

> . . . how really heartwarming it was to be vindicated by such a man as yourself. I want you to know that I value it highly and appreciate it deeply. . . .

It never occurred to Allan that he might more reasonably have asked Owen for an apology. Owen himself was dumbfounded. Fulsome praise was being heaped on him by a man whose probity he had implicitly questioned. Owen could hardly have guessed that Allan was lovestruck when he wrote the letter. He did check Allan's dates in Who's Who to make sure he wasn't getting senile.

Owen left the letter on his office desk. When he next picked it up, he again found himself wondering why Allan had written it. He was not about to borrow money. He needed no social favors. He was not going into politics. He must have had another reason, an unusual one, one that Owen could not suspect; one perhaps that he should not suspect. Was he hiding something—could Allan Ludlam have something to hide?

As the thought came to him, Owen was cheered: an entertaining possibility was brightening his bleak world. Sicker than ever, Phoebe had been treating him contemptuously; his son, Lewis, had sunk beneath consideration; having dedicated herself to Phoebe, Louisa had no time to spare; his work bored him. Now he had turned up a minor mystery that did not bore him at all. Owen was delighted by the prospect that someone from his milieu had guilty secrets. Would Allan's resemble his own New London ferry caper? Or would it prove a more intimate peccadillo?

Intrigued though he was, Owen would probably have forgotten Allan altogether if he hadn't mentioned him to Irene at the end of the following week. She had heard from him too: "Walter's portrait of Elizabeth was stolen. Allan called to ask if our insurance still covered it. They hadn't had time to take out their own."

"I didn't know they owned it," Owen said.

"They bought it last month." Irene explained that she had recently offered a selection of Walter Trale's best work for sale. "We sent it up to them early in July."

"When was it stolen?"

"I don't know exactly. Allan phoned me yesterday."

Owen said nothing. He knew that Allan had told Irene at least one lie. No insurance broker would leave anything so valuable unprotected for two minutes, certainly not two weeks; and from Allan, a phone call would have sufficed.

What was Allan up to now? If he *had* insured the Trale painting, why lie to Irene about it? When Allan spoke to her, why did he only ask about insurance when he might have requested information about art thefts, and even counsel? Owen tried to imagine some undeclared motive behind Allan's call. He could think of none until an unlikely hypothesis crossed his mind: could Allan possibly want to make money out of the theft? Was he trying to collect all the insurance he could, the gallery's as well as his own?

Owen liked this eventuality. It struck him as crass and faintly
lunatic; it reminded him of New London. His curiosity about
Allan's secret was rekindled. He began asking himself, why not
take a look? To Owen, as a professional, Allan's call to Irene
and his claim to have left the painting uninsured made the
existence of some kind of secret probable to the point of certainty. On the other hand, why should Owen waste time solving
an enigma that did not concern him? He found no reasonable
answer to this question, rather a satisfyingly unreasonable one:
he would enjoy solving this riddle far more than submitting to
the rituals of penitence decreed by Phoebe. Even if in the end
he found nothing, where was the harm in that? Surrounded as
he was by domestic disappointment, wasting time appealed to
him.

He decided to begin by approaching Allan himself. He had
a number of social and professional excuses for doing so, of
which Allan's letter was the most obvious. On the same afternoon he spoke to Irene, Owen started calling him. Allan had
left his office; his home phone did not answer, then or later in
the evening. Owen repeated his calls the next morning with no
more success. He rang Allan's house upstate. A delicately
mocking voice—Elizabeth's—announced that Allan was not
expected back "for the foreseeable summer."

Owen was annoyed. The man might as well be deliberately
evading him. He changed his plans. Before pursuing Allan
further, he would learn everything he could about him. He
wrote Allan to acknowledge his letter of thanks and express the
hope that they would soon meet. Owen resumed his research,
focusing it this time not on the minor question of Morris's
insurance policy but on more consequent activities in Allan's
past. If he had something to hide, it would very likely concern
sums of money greater than those of personal accounts; it
would have to do with the commercial insurance in which
Allan specialized.

Allan's respect for Owen was soon justified: Owen needed only one coincidence to uncover his trail. He had begun by looking at cases in which his office had worked with Allan's, and as he was probing these records, the *Vico Hazzard* file, which he had had no intention of consulting, fell into his hands. He then remembered that Allan had been involved in that affair.

Vico Hazzard was the name of a medium-sized oil tanker that during a storm in March 1958 had sunk fully loaded in the Bay of Biscay, a hundred miles off the French coast. Or so its owners claimed. The insurers discovered that on the day of the ship's sinking the weather had been generally clement, that only ten minutes had been needed to rescue the entire crew, and that no oil slick had ever been observed at the site of the accident. They rejected the claims, which were only settled after a long judicial fight. (The owners had arguments of their own: the ship's loading papers had been correctly drawn up; no member of the crew would testify to sabotage or negligence; storms come and go swiftly in the Bay of Biscay; oil sometimes stays trapped in sunken tankers.)

Owen reviewed the file. Allan was not listed among the brokers. His firm was nowhere mentioned. Owen asked colleagues who had worked on the case if any remembered Allan's connection with it. Fortunately, one did, although she could not precisely define it—nothing important. Pleased that his memory had not misled him, Owen called a friend at the company that had insured the ship. Could he find the time to track down Allan Ludlam's role in the *Vico Hazzard* case? The man answered, "I can tell you right now. He recommended those sons of bitches to us."

"You're sure?"

"Positive."

"Why didn't Ludlam's office write the policy?"

"He was all for it, or at least he said he was, but his partners decided they'd covered enough tankers."

"How come he was so sure about the owners?"

"They fooled a lot of people, including the judge. Well, maybe they fixed the judge. The case was tried in Panama, naturally."

Had they fixed Allan too? With Maud's small fortune, and the excellent living he made? Perhaps he had an expensive weakness, or a private one—gambling, another woman. Most people exhibited a much more obvious weakness: never having enough. Why not Allan? After all, Owen had postulated such a motive in his phone call to Irene and made it a premise of his inquiry. Owen accepted the implication of the *Vico Hazzard* fraud: Allan had been paid off to recommend dishonest clients to reputable insurers.

Notwithstanding a seemingly permanent hot spell, Owen spent more and more time in the city. His investigation absorbed him, and it soothed the sting of Phoebe's spiteful demands. He went to work early and finished his business by noon. The rest of his days, and soon his evenings as well, were devoted to the pursuit of Allan Ludlam's secret.

In his office Owen examined the files of many cases in which Allan had acted as broker. His conduct appeared consistently irreproachable—hardly a surprise, rather a confirmation that, as with the *Vico Hazzard,* Allan's improprieties took place behind the scenes. Then how could his influence be detected? Owen's enthusiasm briefly faltered as he realized that he was condemned to look for evidence only among frauds that had— at least initially—failed: those that had succeeded had vanished into the history of undisputed claims. Where should he continue his research? He knew enough to eliminate instances where the attempted fraud was too crude or too petty. Even so, assuming that Allan had stayed in the background, Owen still had to choose among the hundreds of cases of industrial fraud perpetrated by brokers other than Allan and his associates. Owen's hope revived when he saw that he could eliminate most cases by applying one criterion: with which brokers would

Allan's recommendation count decisively? Here Owen's expertise served him well—he knew who knew whom.

Eventually Owen reduced his cases to the manageable number of twenty-three. These he examined painstakingly. He exhausted the records in his office and those that had been made available to the public. In his search for information, he frequently found himself obliged to visit other insurance offices, where he claimed to be writing a historical article on reinsurance in modern times.

Three cases yielded the evidence Owen needed: the *Vico Hazzard* itself; the Watling Mining Corporation, whose coal mine near Etkins, West Virginia, collapsed from an unexplained blast in 1957; and Kayser Wineries, Inc., whose vineyards in the mountains behind Soledad were destroyed by late-spring frost in the early fifties. In each case the insurers had disallowed the claims advanced by their client because of probable fraud. Although fraud was proved only against Kayser Wineries, all three companies stood to benefit conspicuously from the disasters. Smaller tankers like the *Vico Hazzard* had become unprofitable soon after the closing of the Suez Canal in 1956. Before its destruction, the Watling mine, a marginal one, had been beset by labor troubles. When it filed its claim, Kayser Wineries had fallen critically low in cash reserves. The insurance company's investigation of the Watling claim determined that the explosion had occurred on a Sunday when the mine was empty, the electricity switched off, and no unusual accumulation of coal gas had been reported. The "frost" in the Kayser vineyards was shown to be hardly more severe than average seasonal temperatures: it might have damaged the wood of the vines, not killed them (two years later, production had returned to normal). The owners of the *Vico Hazzard,* the Watling Mining Corporation, and Kayser Wineries had all been recommended to their insurers by Allan Ludlam.

Owen had no material proof that Allan had known of the

frauds or profited from them. If questioned, Allan could rightly insist on his negligible legal responsibility in the three cases. Doubtless he could justify his recommendations. Some unexplored clues momentarily tempted Owen. A year after the explosion, the union official who had represented the Watling miners was summoned by a state committee to explain fifty thousand dollars of exceptional expenditures revealed by an audit of his personal account. Owen wondered if Allan's accounts might not disclose similar anomalies. Owen was gratified to have uncovered Allan's secret. He wasted no time speculating as to why someone so well off would risk his reputation in these illegal undertakings.

In his answer to Allan's letter, Owen had invited him for dinner and proposed as a tentative date the last Thursday in July. Two days before Owen completed his research, Allan called to accept his invitation. Owen suggested that they meet for drinks at his apartment and told him that, knowing their wives were in the country, he had also asked a woman they both knew to share their evening. He hoped Allan didn't mind: "She'll keep us on our toes. Nothing's duller than an all-male club. Sorry I only found one. Right now, ladies are in short supply."

The woman Owen had invited was universally known by her childhood nickname of High Heels. Forty-six and very pretty, she had been married twenty-four years to an uninterested husband for whom she had consoled herself with many lovers, Owen among them. He had not invited her innocently. His affair with her, begun the preceding winter shortly after his Christmas wrangle with Phoebe, had soon ended, not from disaffection but because the lovers decided that they preferred the reliabilities of friendship to the uncertainties of passion. They trusted each other intimately.

At first Owen had not known exactly how High Heels would benefit him. He assumed that the presence of an attractive woman would put Allan a little off his guard, especially since he knew her so well (he was related to her by marriage). Not until his investigation was complete did Owen find a specific job for her.

When Owen learned that Allan had successfully pursued a career of preposterous frauds, he began asking himself what light this might shed on his behavior in regard to the stolen portrait of Elizabeth. Owen was tempted to see in it the sign of yet another fraud, albeit a smaller, private one. Why else should Allan lie to Irene? Owen could not at first see what form such a fraud might take. Recollecting his own "crime," he had imagined Allan trying to collect insurance from more than one company. This interpretation presented difficulties. When a work of art is stolen, it rarely disappears; usually it resurfaces promptly, to be offered for sale if the thieves lack competence, more often to become the object of negotiations between them and the insurers. Allan of course knew this. He would not expect to be reimbursed if a work as valuable as the portrait were stolen from him; he would expect to get it back.

This suggested to Owen that the portrait had not been stolen at all. If Allan wanted insurance money, he must make sure that the painting never reappeared. What could give him such certainty? The work could be destroyed. Then why disguise the fact as theft, unless Allan himself had done the destroying? But Owen could not imagine anyone so money-smart demolishing a possession whose value would certainly grow. More plausibly, the portrait had been hidden. The possibility impressed Owen as perfectly compatible with Allan's behavior: secrecy, after all, had been a condition of his business frauds from beginning to end.

Owen knew now what he wanted High Heels to do. While Allan might, of course, have used any number of hiding places, Owen suspected that he would prefer one where he could keep his eye on the portrait. The house upstate could certainly be excluded: Maud would not be privy to her husband's illegal activities. The city apartment seemed much likelier, since it was primarily used by Allan as a place to stay during his working weeks, and during the summer he had it to himself. High Heels must persuade Allan to take her home with him so that she could learn if the portrait was hidden there.

Owen gave her a partial account of the facts, not mentioning his research or Allan's phone call to Irene, telling her only that the Ludlams claimed that the portrait of Elizabeth had been stolen and that he suspected them of having hidden the painting instead, perhaps in Allan's apartment. He had, he said, become intrigued by their strange behavior. No more than intrigued: he had nothing to gain in the matter.

Owen was not surprised that High Heels unhesitatingly accepted his request; and as Owen had correctly foreseen, Allan was immediately drawn to her. Owen's good judgment, however, was favored far more by what he did not know than by what he knew. When he gave High Heels his account of the missing portrait, he acted with unwitting shrewdness in lumping Maud with Allan. He did not know that High Heels was nursing a years-old grudge against Maud Ludlam and was delighted to catch her out in a suspicious scheme; delighted, as well, to date her husband. Nor could Owen possibly know how sentimentally vulnerable recent events had made Allan. His affair with Elizabeth had humiliated him, Maud had forced him from his own house—he was ripe for consolation. His long acquaintance with High Heels only heightened her attractiveness by removing the barrier of unfamiliarity that had, before Elizabeth, made him shy away so often from sexual adventure.

The evening with Allan and High Heels thus took Owen by surprise. He had planned to coddle his guests into mutual sympathy; he found himself with nothing to do. From the moment they met in his apartment, the two conversed in the liveliest fashion. By the time they sat down in the restaurant, their understanding had started growing into overt complicity. Owen felt almost an outsider at his own dinner. He even wondered, knowing the man's deviousness, if Allan had somehow enlisted High Heels in his cause. Were they now allied against him? What if they were? *He* had nothing to hide, nothing to lose. (The thought had no sooner come to him than he remembered Phoebe, aged eleven, running out of school to meet him.)

After dinner, Allan asked High Heels and Owen to join him for a nightcap. Owen declined and left. Allan timidly asked High Heels where she would like to go—a favorite bar? her place? his? His would do fine. In the taxi she took his hand; they kissed in the elevator; they had barely crossed his threshold when they began making love, the first of three leisurely times.

Their delight in each other had the intensity of ignorance, if not innocence. Allan knew nothing about High Heels's grudge against Maud, or she about his domestic troubles. They applied themselves to slaking a mutual thirst that had naturally and delectably inflamed them, not asking questions, not needing to know. Waking up the following morning, they spent themselves on one another before exchanging a word.

However, once they did start to speak, High Heels eventually said: "What I'd really love is a toasted bagel." She had hesitated to pronounce these words. She knew that when she did, Allan would go out to the nearest deli, and she would search his apartment. What Owen wanted her to do seemed now a little squalid: spying on her new lover might prove as great a betrayal as disappointing her old one. She stuck to her agreement. She had made Allan happy, he still exuded warmth and attentiveness, and she sensed that the attentiveness revealed something other than warmth—an awareness that, no matter how much he liked her, she would never find a place at the center of his life, not even for a season. He paid attention to her now because he might find few other chances to do so; later meetings would still remain exceptional events. Allan was assuming that she knew this as well as he did, and he was not mistaken. She did not mind his so carefully sweetening her own return to "real life"; and she knew she must expect no more of him. She too liked him, and, among other reasons, she liked him because he *would* go away, go back to Maud. She liked him for a good husband, after years with her own bad one; and she couldn't help imagining how her life might have turned out with a man like the one now lying in her arms. The thought flushed her with yearning: a yearning she loathed, brimming with regret, one she had sooner or later to cut short. When Allan proposed English muffins, she preferred the bagel that would take him away from her.

She found the portrait wrapped in a clean sheet, leaning against a wall in a doorless storage space next to the kitchen. She checked the dimensions and appearance and, after restoring her wearied face and body, returned to bed, where Allan found her.

To attest his gratitude, Owen sent High Heels two best seats for *How to Succeed in Business Without Really Trying,* a musical sold out five weeks in advance. For years, Owen had scarcely stretched his wits in business; he had now proved them as sharp as ever. Through his own flair, he had from meager evidence calculated exactly what Allan had done. He did not think of Phoebe for a whole day, he forgot his routine call to Louisa, utterly pervaded by a reassuring glee.

Late in the afternoon, four days afterwards, he kept ringing Allan's home number until he answered. Owen said he was in the neighborhood, could he drop by for a drink? By all means, Allan replied. He'd advise the doorman immediately.

Entering the apartment, Owen savored the coolness—the temperature outside had reached the mid nineties. Allan greeted him jovially, holding a gin-and-tonic in one hand and, with a help-yourself wave of the other, motioning Owen towards the bar: "I've been meaning to call you, damn it. Tonight you be my guest."

"We'll see."

Allan stared at the other man as he mixed his drink. Owen looked serious and alert. "What's up?"

Owen turned to Allan: "I came up here on a false pretense. This is really a business visit. Here's mud." He raised a glass full of chiming cubes.

"Chin chin. Well, we've been doing business for years, in an impersonal way."

"You're telling me. This is between the two of us."

"*Servidor de usted.*"

"You own a painting I'd like to . . . acquire—a portrait by Walter Trale."

"My wife and I own it." Allan walked past Owen to the bar. "I can tell you right now: Maud would never agree to sell."

"I'm not surprised. I saw it only once at Trale's studio, but I could tell it was special. By the way, for openers, do you think I could take a look at it?"

"That might be a little hard to arrange."

"No time like the present."

"You mean here? We'd never keep anything like that in town. A couple of prints, to show where the walls are, and that's about it."

"What are they? I still can't tell China from Japan. Could I see the portrait when I go back upstate?"

"Owen," Allan said with gentle reproach, "did Irene tell you the painting was stolen?" He also asked, "You don't know Elizabeth, do you?"

Allan's voice indicated that the question mattered to him; Owen could not relate it to what he knew. He said, "So what happened?"

"What happened about what?"

"How did it get stolen?"

"*I* don't know what happened. . . ." Allan did not mind playing such games.

"Then what have you done about it? Police? Private detectives? Who's your underwriter?"

"What do you think I should do? Art thefts are tricky."

"Irene was surprised when you asked her about the gallery's insurance."

"Is that why you're here—Irene again? Why should she care?"

"Irene's got nothing to do with my being here."

"Then why do *you* care?"

"I told you. I hope to own the painting."

"But that's out of—" Allan stopped. What was Owen getting at? The other man's eyes looked steadily into his, neither friendly nor unfriendly. "You wouldn't like to talk over dinner? The gin's gone straight to my stomach."

"This shouldn't take long." Owen sat down, crossed his legs, and set his drink on the floor beside him. Allan leaned against the wall, facing him. Owen had vexed him. "Would you mind telling me why we're having this conversation?"

"Sure. I think you made a mistake. You gave yourself away. You want the gallery's insurance to pay for the painting."

Allan suddenly wanted to laugh; he only said, "Wow!"

"I'm serious."

"No." Allan couldn't suppress a grin. He paused. "I don't know where to begin."

"Anyplace. It won't matter."

"I don't even know who insures the gallery—you probably do. I just asked Irene one question. That doesn't mean I'm making plans. What tickles me," Allan went on, "is that what you're accusing me of is how you make your money. You push all your claims to the limit."

"That's right. But only against one insurer for each claim." Owen mentally crossed his fingers, remembering New London. He thought: I should have never told those people about New London.

"I haven't made any claim. The painting is bound to show up. If it's cheap enough, we'll buy it back ourselves, and it probably will be." Allan was looking down at his guest with growing confidence. "If the people who stole it want to haggle, it wouldn't hurt to get the gallery involved. That's why I called Irene."

Because he held the ace of trumps, Owen had not pushed Allan hard. He had nonetheless cornered him. Allan thought he had won: the rosy assurance of his face attested it. He had once felt fear of Owen; his fear had proved groundless. If this time Owen was attacking him openly, he remained as innocent as he had been in writing Morris's policy. Allan could not help showing a slight contempt for Owen for being so mistaken.

At this point, Owen's attitude changed. He had anticipated confronting a colleague with professional irregularities. The irregularities had excited his curiosity more than his disapproval, and he had only expected to show Allan that although he was smart, Owen was smarter. He had imagined wanting the portrait only as a ploy: as a "serious" pretext at first, then as a position from which to press his adversary. Owen now found himself thinking in earnest about getting the painting for himself.

He had begun feeling a need to do more than outwit Allan. He was facing a rich, reputable colleague who for years had defrauded the system he claimed to serve, who now stood beaming with confidence because he had once again gone uncaught. Owen angrily dismissed his first intention of merely showing Allan up: values were at stake. He entertained no doubt at all that he had the moral fitness to mete out the punishment Allan deserved.

"You thought that up just now. I don't believe you. You know why?"

"No, and I'd be very interested—"

"I've been studying your career," Owen interrupted, "I don't mean your legitimate accomplishments, I'm not questioning them. What I mean—what I've learned—is that you're a chronic swindler"—Owen spoke fast enough to cut off any protest—"and you've been damned successful at it. As I see it, though, you have one problem. A swindler who's been born and raised poor knows that if he loses, he loses everything. But someone with your cushy background feels safe, and he starts thinking he really *is* safe. He forgets about the risks. He makes mistakes. Like calling Irene."

If Allan was surprised, he didn't show it: "Owen, tell me what's on your mind. Something you think I did has made for a misunderstanding. Or maybe your interpretation of something I actually did. What's the point?"

"Three names to show you I know. And don't kid yourself— I'll know *you* know I know. In chronological order: Kayser Wineries, Watling Mining, *Vico Hazzard.*"

After a few seconds, not moving from where he stood, his hands behind his back, Allan replied, "Who's arguing? Of course those were mistakes. Why me, though? A lot of other people were involved."

"They were mistakes, and you didn't make them. You let those other people do that. You advised them to."

"I advise all the time. It's part of the business—you know that. Has all your advice been perfect? My own batting average is pretty good—about nine-fifty."

"You bet it is. Remember the Circle C Ranch? They wanted you to double the coverage on their herd. Before recommending them, you made sure there'd been no brucellosis in the county for thirty years. You did your job. How could somebody like you not know the *Vico Hazzard* was sailing empty? Why should you bother with punk outfits like Kayser and Watling unless it was—"

"Look," Allan broke in, "it was investigated."

"It didn't come up roses, either. I know you're covered—you were only counsel. And we're all so busy we never bother much with the past. But I'm on to you, old buddy." Allan said nothing. Owen added: "I'm not interested in making trouble for you, truly. Why should I be? I just want that portrait of Elizabeth. And no, I don't think I know her. I may have met her before the war."

The mention of Elizabeth sickened Allan. Two weeks before, she had been his; at least, he had been hers. He had spat on her feelings by parading his dishonesty in front of her. Perhaps she had revenged herself by telling Owen rather than Maud what she had learned about him. He asked, "So you know about the horse?"

For the only time that evening Owen was baffled. "Does Elizabeth have a horse?"

"Not *that* horse," Allan answered irritably. "You'd better ask the thief about the portrait."

"That's what I'm doing."

Why did Owen care so much about this "theft"? Before tonight, Allan had almost forgotten the story he had made up for Irene. "You mean *I* stole the painting?"

"Listen, I'm getting hungry myself. I'll make you a proposition. I find the painting, I keep it. And I promise not to tell a soul."

Allan still did not understand. Owen emptied his iceless glass, got up, and walked into the kitchen. Allan heard the stretcher being dragged across the tile floor.

"Do I have to unwrap it, or will you take my word?"

Allan lost his temper. For twenty minutes Owen had been preparing to make a fool of him, holding, and withholding, his knowledge that the portrait was there. "You'd better get out."

"You're right. Leave the painting downstairs sometime tomorrow, OK? I'll send a man over. Unless you'd rather I took it now."

"Big joke. Get the hell out of here."

"Ludlam, I understand how you feel. You'd better start understanding how *I* feel. I'm not interested in shooting you down. It'd be messy, and some of your shit would stick to me.

Anyway, I'm not a policeman. I don't give a tiddlywink how you behave. But I can get you, and I will if I have to, because I do mind one thing: every time we guys went to bat for one of your crummy clients we were putting our money and reputation on the line. I risked my ass on account of you. You may never have to pay your debt to society, as they say, but you sure as hell will pay it to me. I'm letting you off cheap—one painting."

At this moment Allan remembered the toasted bagel. He spoke quickly, before dismay seeped into his voice: "Owen, the story about the portrait being stolen—it was an elaborate family joke."

"So what?"

"That's what we're—"

"That was *my* joke. I'm talking about your reputation. As I trust you realize, I am not joking about that."

Allan gave up. He hated to lose; he would hate losing; he could see nothing he might do to avoid it. For once his cleverness had failed him: the roulette wheel had been fixed by a woman he had not doubted for a moment. What he now wanted most in the world was to get Owen out of his apartment. He agreed to the price: "I'll drop it off at the front door on my way to the office."

"Perfect." Owen smiled. "Now, how about dinner? No? I'll be going. Just one thing I'd like to ask you. It's something that's had me wondering ever since I got interested in you—it's probably *why* I got interested in you." Allan stared at the bar. Owen continued: "How come you did it?"

Owen waited patiently for a response. After a while Allan looked up: "Because they're jerks."

"Who is?"

. "Everyone is. Not *you*, maybe," Allan hurriedly added. "But most of the others. They're so successful, they make so much money, they have Pucci wives, beach houses, and malt scotch, and they don't have a clue what it's all about. They don't even know there's anything to know. They're sheep."

"But not you."

"You seem to enjoy playing games. Do I have to explain?"

"I only wanted to know. It's an answer. Here's a suggestion: since we're not *all* sheep, you should be prepared to let others do unto you what you'd like them to let you do unto them—I think I got that right." Allan had again lapsed into silence. "Look, for the record, we'll need sale papers. Let's list a price two thousand under whatever it cost you. You'll get a capital deduction—not much, but every little bit helps."

At the door, Owen turned back; Allan was gazing out the window at a rug-sized plot of dirt fourteen stories below, where a forsythia and three evergreen shrubs withered in hot, eternal shade. "You know, Allan, you didn't need to prove anything. You're a better man than you think."

Outside, he entered the sweltering city night. A year ago Phoebe had reported the first signs of her disease, and at the time the news had actually brought him relief.

Allan did not see himself as a man at all, rather as a little boy dreaming his way through some stupid childhood misfortune. He loathed himself for having given up so abjectly. Why was he experiencing such humiliation on account of a painting and a glorified public adjuster? What had happened? He had barely looked inside a cookie jar, and the pantry cupboards had crashed down around him. He had phoned Irene and told her his fib because he expected her to repeat it to Maud; Maud would have been horrified, either because she believed the story or because she knew he was lying—in either case, she would have come after him, and he would have been able to resume his life with her. The stratagem recalled other, more tractable childhood misadventures, the ones he would instigate in order to recapture his mother's attention. A new shoe "lost" would do the trick. He would be scolded and punished and no longer forgotten. This time, however, a detective from the shoe store had arrived unannounced and threatened him with dungeons. It made no sense.

The intensity of his unhappiness nevertheless had its explanation. What sickened him, what squeezed his testicles up into his bowels as though he were leaning over a penthouse ledge, was the memory of High Heels. He could excuse her deceit (she could hardly have foreseen its consequences); but he could not endure having Owen to thank for his night with her. The thought unnerved every part of him, even the anger in his chest. He wished he could call her. She could take pity on him. She had no reason to despise him, not as he despised himself. He felt himself incapable even of speaking to her.

Maud, Elizabeth, High Heels—lost in one July.

Allan expected his anger with Owen to return in force, flooding and ebbing for days, even weeks. He had been too openly disgraced not to resent his attacker. Nevertheless his anger lacked the clear fury of vengefulness or moral outrage, and Allan, without noticing it, soon reconciled himself to his antagonist. Owen had fallen on him without warning, like a natural disaster, impersonally and arbitrarily (Allan never saw his error in writing the letter of thanks); and little by little Owen began to assume the mask of a one-time avenging angel, a fairy-tale comeuppance, a bugaboo, a caricature that even Allan unconsciously recognized as his own invention. At the same time Owen, the real-life businessman, took on a very different, although complementary, role as the audience Allan's spectacular frauds had always lacked.

It was Owen, in this double guise of hobgoblin and witness, who at last allowed Allan to give up his criminal career. The hobgoblin reminded him of the risks he ran; the witness, that he no longer needed recognition. The gelding destroyed on the eighteenth of the month marked the end of Allan's secret life. Later opportunities presented themselves—crop failures on un-

planted land, bank-engineered computer "errors." On each occasion he was checked by an invisible figure in his apartment
who sat facing him, a melting drink in his hand. An unpreju-
diced observer might have concluded that Allan had summoned Owen into his life for this very purpose.

That evening, however, Allan wanted only to drive Owen out
of his thoughts, preferably by retroactive murder. He stayed
home, convinced that elsewhere he would feel even worse. For
supper he made himself his next day's breakfast: eggs, toast, tea.
Neither scenes from an earthquake in Macedonia nor *The Jack
Paar Show* could temper his despondency. He went to bed
early, with some magazines, without even a nightcap.

Lewis and Morris
SEPTEMBER 1962–MAY 1963

MORRIS HAD MET LEWIS AT WALTER TRALE'S, LESS THAN a year before his death.

Lewis had lived with his parents for a year and a half after his graduation from college; more accurately, he lived with Louisa, while Owen did his best to ignore him. Although Lewis hardly felt at ease with Louisa, she tended him and forgave his moody ways. Lewis felt at ease with almost no one. He had few friends of either sex and made no attempt to keep those he did have.

He loved and trusted Phoebe. Their father had always favored her, she excelled where he endured; her absolute loyalty to him forestalled all resentment. She was three years younger than Lewis, and his rock. During his tedious months at home, Phoebe never asked him, "What are you doing now? What are you planning to do?" Lewis had answers to these questions; he knew them to be no more than shaming lies. He was doing nothing, and he did not know what he would ever do.

Lewis, anything but dull, suffered from an excess of misguided cleverness: he could disparage himself brilliantly in a matter of seconds. He knew literature, art, the theater, history; and his knowledge surpassed what a college normally provides. His knowledge led nowhere, certainly not into the world where he was supposed to earn a living. Lewis had once gone to work in the bookstore of his school because he loved handling books and looked forward to being immersed in them. He was then instructed to keep careful accounts of merchandise that might as well have been canned beans. He soon lost interest in his simple task, failed to master it, and quit after three days. Eight years later, he was still convinced of his practical incompetence. College friends familiar with his tastes would suggest modest ways for him to get started: they knew of jobs as readers in publishing houses, as gofers in theatrical productions, as caretakers at galleries. Lewis rejected them all. While he saw that they might lead to greater things, they sounded both beneath and beyond him—the bookstore again. Other chums who had gone on to graduate school urged their choice on him. Lewis harbored an uneasy scorn for the corporation of scholars, who seemed as unfit for the world as he. He remained desperate, lonely, and spoiled.

During his second autumn at home, he read, in an art magazine called *New Worlds,* an article by Morris Romsen on the painting of Walter Trale. Phoebe, who had been working with Walter since February, had recommended it to him. Lewis took it to heart for reasons that had nothing to do with Walter.

Morris began his article: "A fish begins to rot at the head; the rot in painting begins at the idea of Art." Lewis did not understand these words. They swept across his mind like an arm angrily clearing a table of its clutter. Reading on, he could not tell whether Morris's pronouncements illuminated his subject; he knew they illuminated *him.*

Lewis had had fugitive dreams of writing, soon discredited

and abandoned. Morris was showing him what writing could do. He advanced the notion that creation begins by annihilating typical forms and procedures, especially the illusory "naturalness" of sequence and coherence. Morris did more than state this, he demonstrated it. He made of his essay a minefield that blew itself up as you crossed it. You found yourself again and again on ground not of your choosing, propelled from semantics into psychoanalysis into epistemology into politics. These displacements seemed, rather than willful, grounded in some hidden and persuasive law that had as its purpose to keep bringing the reader back fresh to the subject. Lewis could not explain this effect, or why the article so moved him. When he reread it, doing his best to find fault with it, like a shy and incredulous father poking his newborn child, his first reaction held true, and his reservations were dispelled. He had found something in the world worth doing, after all.

Lewis did not tell Phoebe of his decision to become a writer; he informed her by letter instead. When he had talked to his parents about his new commitment, he had as he spoke lost hold of what he was saying, and enthusiasm could not compensate for vagueness. Louisa had been confused, Owen disgusted (did he expect them to support him forever?). Lewis wanted to make sure Phoebe understood: Morris's article had given him nothing less than a hope of salvation.

My burdens are isolation and a haunted mind. Now I can put the first to work and exorcise the second. Solitude will be my shop. Others will use what I make there, in *their* solitudes—a long-distance community of minds. I'll take the words droning inside my head and make them real—make them into things that strike, or stroke, or puzzle, or disappear. This is something I can actually do. A little something—doctors are more useful, actors communicate better—but buggers can't be choosers. Before, reading was better than not getting out of bed, but how

what I read got written was weirder than Linear A. Enter
Morris Romsen, and shazam.

Phoebe asked, would he like to meet him? She could easily
arrange it. (Already sick, for Lewis she would have rolled naked
in snow.) At Walter's next party, knowing Morris was expected, she asked Walter if she might invite her older brother.
Lewis rejoiced; refused to attend; attended.

The party, which took place on the night of November first,
included almost fifty guests. Phoebe mentioned Lewis to Morris
and quoted one or two passages from his letter. She warned
Lewis when he arrived that Morris might act aloof; he must
forgive him for that. She also told Lewis that Morris suffered
from "a heart condition, as they now call imminent death."

"But he's so *young*. Is that why he looks so sad?"

"He's had it since he was twenty-three. And no, I don't think
so."

Morris surprised Lewis, and not by his aloofness. Lewis's
poor opinion of himself made him expect worse than that, now
more than ever: if choosing to write had exalted him, writing
itself had only made life worse. After an exciting glimpse of
freedom, he found himself still trapped between a pitying
mother and an irritable father. He had written a little poetry
both mannered and crude and kept a self-sniffing diary that
could hardly qualify as a "journal." From Morris he looked
forward at best to an acceptance of the stammering praise that
constituted his only offering.

Because he liked Phoebe, Morris was favorably disposed
towards Lewis. Whatever aloofness he did show sprang entirely
from sexual prudence. He mistrusted his own peculiar inclina-
tions, especially with a younger man whose penchants he knew
nothing about. He openly welcomed Lewis's admiration; and
Lewis, with astonishment, found himself, instead of stammering, conversing almost spontaneously.

They were standing under Elizabeth's portrait. Lewis said, "From what you wrote I'd imagined it different. Maybe that's what you wanted?"

"Ah, so?"

"No? I got something like: one can't really describe *anything*. So you pretend to describe—you use words to make a false replica. Then we're absorbed by the words, not by the illusion of a description. You also defuse reactions that might get in our way. So when we look at the painting there's nothing we expected—none of your false words, none of our false reactions— we have to see it on its own terms?"

"Not *bad*. So what's the point?"

"The point, the point . . . is, what's actually there? You leave the thing intact by giving us what isn't there—?"

"Promise not to tell? They won't get it."

"I don't either—I'm only guessing. I mean, some of the things you say are *wild*. What about: 'Our original heaven is the tempestuous sky of the vagina'?"

"Just more of the same." Morris pointed to the portrait. "Imagine writing about that mouth. Even if you keep it abstract—like 'a mauve horizontal'—people will look and tell themselves, incredible mouth, so mauve, so horizontal. And horizontality means this, and mauve means something else. Goodbye, Miss Mouth. 'Tempestuous sky' gets rid of the vagina, and vice versa, even if the words are still there, doing whatever it is words do. Of course, most people can't even see the print."

"So what about them?"

"Who knows? It's a dull delirium of a world. Lewis, take care of *yourself*. That's plenty for a lifetime, no matter how short."

Morris had called him by name; Lewis did not even notice. Not since childhood, certainly not since Phoebe's birth, had he once forgotten his own feelings. He had never met anyone like Morris, whose self-assured talent was disguised by attentiveness, and his endangered heart by distractingly good looks. Lewis had not expected Morris to be beautiful. He had not expected to love him.

Later they talked again. Morris had made his rounds; Lewis had watched him. Not thinking about himself had lightened Lewis's demeanor and made him agreeable. Morris suggested they lunch the following week. Lewis silently postponed his return home and accepted.

"You probably won't approve," Morris told him in parting, "but I'm going into business with a friend. I'll be buying and selling paintings."

"A gallery?"

"Out of my apartment."

Lewis was surprised. He did not approve. At their lunch he said as much: "With your reputation? They'll say you're promoting. Think of your authority now. It's priceless."

"It could work the other way. I put money in something, my opinion's worth that much more."

"But what *about* your opinions? Isn't a work of art going to look different when you've invested in it? Even Berenson—"

"*Even?* Be my Duveen! He knew what he was doing—so do I. I'd like to do my shopping uptown for a change. And I wouldn't mind collecting a wee bit for myself."

"With your eye? It's a piece of cake."

"Lewis, you're sweet to care, but. Look: there's oceans of money sloshing around out there. All I want is a beach pail."

"I know. And you're right, I do care. There's a better way."

"You mean," said Morris, waving his glinting Muscadet through a long bar of smoky sunshine, "I can have caviar *and* a clean mind?"

"The trouble is the selling part. That's what's compromising. But if you buy—"

"And *not* sell? Like to pay for lunch?"

"My pleasure. What I'm suggesting is *advising* buyers. There are dozens of rich people around who want to own new art. It's

the latest ticket to whatever. They also want to look original
and do it on the cheap, but they only know what they read in
the magazines, and that's not news. So you find them artists on
the way up. You help the buyers, you help the artists, you help
yourself—you get a commission on each purchase. You don't
have to deal. No speculating with your own money. No tempta-
tion to promote."

"People want work that other people want, and they don't
need me to find it. Know any eager buyers for unknowns? One
or two, I daresay—"

"I've got eight." Lewis unfolded a typewritten list and read
it out loud. He had pestered the names out of Louisa. "I've
talked to three of them—the Dowells, the Liebermans, and the
Platts. The Platts were suspicious. The others sound interested."

"You bucking for Eagle Scout, little boy? *I* know you're just
being nice, but with some you might pass for a closet schmuck."

"But *you* know I can trust you."

Morris picked up the list and left the check. He liked Lewis.
He behaved condescendingly towards him because he was
twenty-eight, Lewis twenty-three and young for his years. Morris felt an irresistible craving to curtail the younger man's enthusiasm and to do this by acting hard. Acting hard gave Morris pleasure. Lewis willingly submitted. Such treatment gave
him pleasure. Morris failed to notice this. Experienced though
he was, he still hesitated to believe that anyone sincerely relished punishment, still found his own yearning to inflict it
perverse.

Lewis knew only that he would unquestioningly accept
whatever Morris said or did. He enjoyed Morris's disdain.
Watching his friend pocketing the list touched Lewis more than
any thanks. He did not guess that Morris, while showing interest in his proposal, had no intention of giving up his original
plan; had he known, he would have admired his duplicity.

Lewis had carefully garnered Morris's occasional remarks

about writing, and on his return home he tried some of them out. Morris recommended imitation as a practice as useful as it was unfashionable. Choose a model, he had said, and copy it. The model will have substance, form, and style. You can imitate all three; you can imitate one or the other; you will probably fail to reproduce any of them, and this inability will point to what you can do, to what usually you are already doing. You will begin discovering your own genius. As his models, Lewis chose a poem by Wallace Stevens, a story by Henry James, an essay by William Empson. He had a wickedly hard time and savored it: the work kept him busy, and full of thoughts of his new friend.

He saw Morris briefly three weeks later. They drank martinis in a bar off Fifth Avenue called Michael's Pub. Lewis reported his attempts to follow Morris's advice about writing. "Advice? I read that in *Mademoiselle,*" the other exclaimed. The riposte, Lewis thought, revealed the essential Morris.

Lewis had to cut the meeting short. He was expected elsewhere. He took a taxi to Second Avenue and Thirty-second Street, walked south two blocks, crossed to the southeast corner, and went into a bar. Scarcely a dozen men sat in its booths—a late place. Lewis passed through a door in the back into a smaller room. Two men by the window nodded to him. Through another door, he reached the building's service elevator and rode three stories up. He entered a loft that occupied the entire floor, now divided crosswise by a black rayon curtain. Six or seven men standing in front of the curtain smiled when they saw him. As he approached, they turned their backs to him and continued their conversation.

"I thought your friend was the one who strangled the bath attendant?"

"Only gossip, I'm afraid. But it taught me wisdom all the same—*never* be jealous of the past."

One man turned to Lewis and said, "Break a leg, Minerva— or shall we do it for you?"

Lewis had visited the loft more than once. Tonight for the first time he would star here: they were going to crucify him.

The elevator regularly swelled the group of men, until the closed space seethed.

Except for some ambiguous episodes at summer camp, Lewis had tried to keep his sexual particularity a secret. He knew that others shared his taste. He had seen proof of it, and, like Morris, hardly believed it; and insofar as his family's world was concerned, he might have gleaned his knowledge from science fiction. If he had examined that world more cunningly, he would have found as many brothers there as elsewhere. Lewis preferred the conviction that giving or receiving pain for pleasure belonged to a furtive milieu. At twenty, on a visit to the city, he had been spotted in the street by an alert big boy and properly cruised and bruised. He had then discovered clandestine gatherings where his taste was the rule. He dreaded these meetings and longed for them. They filled him with implacable sensations and the intangibility of old dreams, and they succeeded in briefly satisfying him with a melancholy peace. He attended them at long, regular intervals. They provided one place where he belonged.

He himself had chosen his part for this warm, overcast late November evening. The announcement of the event had disgusted him, and he had guessed that his disgust only gauged his desire. At a subsequent meeting, the others had shared the disgust, no doubt to encourage him—to shame him. They told Lewis that while he had no right to participate at all, the leading role struck them as too degrading for anyone else to perform. It required the lowest of the low.

He was assured that the performance would be no sham. The crown of thorns had been woven out of rusted barbed wire. He would be whipped with willow fronds peeled and wetted. High above the grungy floor, he would be nailed to the pine-log cross with real nails (needle-thin and hammered home by an expert—

with luck he might escape crippling). A Gem blade set in a bamboo pole would slit his side. The same pole would prod a urine-soaked sponge into his face. The only departure from gospel tradition (aside from a foot-square platform under his feet) was intended to keep him from seeing his tormentors. Why give him that satisfaction? "Don't expect to get gone on those upturned faces, Lulu. A rock like you could pull a real Camille. We'd rather full-focus on your cakes." They would nail him face to the cross.

Like any fledgling performer, Lewis suffered intense stage fright. It proved superfluous: he had nothing to do. Whatever was required of him was done by others. He was stripped, crowned, scourged, and lifted up by gangs of adept males; he could only submit to them, like a swimmer rolled in an endless succession of toppling breakers, or like a little boy with his head held underwater in the vise of a bully's legs. He held his breath until it was punched out of him. He was allowed no respite in his humiliations. On the floor he was pissed on, on the cross screamed at and pelted with bolts, sneakers, stinking pellets. He never had time to think or feel anything except his sensations, to which he surrendered in the certainty that they belonged to him absolutely and lay beyond his choosing. He heard himself sobbing: nothing more than the dross of his consciousness as it soared like a rocket into clouds—clouds of tar steam that choked him and made him drunk. He felt blood run down one hip and leg, not the cutting spear. He wondered if he'd shit. Pine bark chafed his swollen cock.

The voices in the room lowered. Something else was happening. A familiar ladder jolted into place beside him. The twenty-year-old who had so deftly nailed him up was setting pliers to his feet.

"Already?" Lewis moaned.

"Velma's here."

"Huh?"

"The orgy patrol. The vice," hissed the other, addressing his left hand.

Can anyone keep a crucifixion secret? The police had doubted it. (Two of their members attended these meetings.) They decided not to risk indiscriminate revelation; they staged a raid and turned the scandal to their own advantage. The raid was efficiently executed. No one was hurt. Only six of the thirty-four men present escaped to the upper floors, where they were permitted to spend an anxious night before absconding.

The police had tipped off friendly newspapermen. Early editions of the *News* carried a photograph of a nameless young man lying on the loft floor, half naked, somewhat bloody. Louisa's sister and Morris, among others, recognized Lewis.

Lewis had been taken to the emergency ward at Bellevue Hospital. After tending his wounds, the doctors on duty sent him to the psychiatric ward, where he passed a scary night. Word that he had been admitted as a pervert spread quickly. The ward's drunks and psychotics expressed no less scorn for him than his crucifixion audience, and theirs was meant in earnest. The few tired and jaded orderlies promised feeble protection. Although the violence remained verbal, Lewis waited for the morning in terror and, even after he had washed and eaten breakfast, did not da' e sleep, praying fervently and incessantly for the arrival of a doctor who might authorize his release. Shortly before noon, he saw Morris standing among a group of visitors at the end of the ward. Lewis crouched behind his bed.

When Morris found Lewis, he squatted down and tendered him a little plastic shopping bag. Lewis stood up. The bag contained toothbrush and toothpaste, shaving articles, hairbrush, cologne, and a box of Band-Aids.

"I couldn't remember if you smoked—not here, I guess. How's tricks?"

"How did you find me?"

"Your picture's in the paper. Don't worry, it's a terrible likeness. And nobody who'd mind reads the *News* anyway. Phoebe wants to know when she can come and see you. She sends lots of love."

"Phoebe!"

Lewis began to realize that his secret life lay open to the world. Everybody knew, or would know. Morris kept speaking to him matter-of-factly, and in time Lewis noticed the silver lining: Morris cared about him. His coming to Bellevue proved that. Thanking him, Lewis almost cried.

"Any plans?" Morris asked. Lewis knew what he meant: he couldn't go home. "Let me help. Not today, I'm afraid, but come and see me tomorrow evening. We'll, as one says, discuss your future."

Lewis left the hospital two hours later. In the First Avenue lobby he met Louisa, who had just arrived. Her teary consternation made him cringe. He welcomed her first words, however: "I promise you Owen doesn't know. I'll make sure he never does. Please tell me, are you all right?" Lewis's bandaged hands and feet (he was shuffling in heel-less straw slippers) gave him the look of a battle casualty.

"Yes. I'm sorry. Mother, I'm really sorry, but I can't stand being with you right now."

Louisa said she understood, put him in a taxi, promised not to interfere. She made him take the hundred dollars in her handbag. "Promise to call me if you need anything?"

Lewis booked a room at the Chelsea. Next day, making sure his parents had gone out, he fetched his few belongings from their place. At ten that night he arrived at Morris's apartment, which occupied one high-ceilinged floor of a converted brownstone on Cornelia Street. Lewis blushed when Morris embraced him. They sat down in a corner between lofty, slovenly bookcases. A decanter and two glasses had been set out on a low table beside a platter of toast and Roquefort cheese. Morris poured out the wine, one Lewis had never heard of—sweet, French, and with *Venice* in its name. With the wine a warmth of relief and contentment seeped from his throat and stomach to the tips of his toes, to the tip of his nose. He licked the rim of his glass, shutting his eyes. Opening them, he found himself sitting in the same place, naked, with his ankles and wrists bound to his chair. Morris stood in front of him, bare to the waist except for chromium-studded black leather wristbands and a set of brass knuckles on his right hand. When Lewis's eyes met his, Morris said with a grin, "Now, Louisa, I'm going to beat the pie out of you."

First visit: Morris drugs Lewis, strips him, ties him to a chair. He threatens him with brass knuckles (made of metal-painted rubber) and does not use them, finding better things to do. Lewis soon reveals certain weaknesses (others might call them preferences). Barely awake, he says, "Do anything you like, but let me loose. I go crazy if I can't move." Morris draws up an armchair. "Louisa, you're crazy anyway. But I'd love to see what you mean." Lewis begins to cry. Morris taunts him, in accidental slang: "Poor Ella, such a sad route to go! How did a swinging skinner like me pull a dorky trick like Miss Thing. . . ." Lewis interrupts, "Don't talk like that. I'm not a screaming faggot, and neither are you. It makes me puke." Morris: "Poor baby! Did you just step out of a time machine? You can suck my Jewish ass! I'll talk any way I want." Morris harangues him late into the night.

Morris had a surprise for Lewis. On the following day he took him to Thirteenth Street just west of First Avenue and there, three metaled flights up a tenement stairway, led him into a two-room apartment. Although its size forbade even one closet, it had been properly maintained, and its rent was eighty-five dollars.

"Which I'll pay till you find a job," Morris told Lewis, who moved in ten days before Christmas.

The two men saw each other for drinks, for dinner, for openings, for double features; never privately. For nearly two months Morris refused to let Lewis come to his apartment. Lewis's pleadings did nothing to shorten the interval.

Second visit: January 27, 6:00 P.M. When Lewis has undressed, Morris fastens his wrists to his ankles with short-linked metal cuffs. Unable to walk, Lewis hops after Morris at his bidding. A nudge topples him. Morris passes a rope through his arms and legs. Drawn tight through an eye-knot at one of its ends, the rope bunches Lewis's hands and feet, pressing his head against his knees, reducing him to a sack-shaped bundle that Morris drags behind him. In the kitchen, while he readies his dinner, Morris resorts to the jargon Lewis abhors and vents his disillusionment with the practice of sadomasochism, which he is planning to give up: ". . . It may mean short roses for us, but that's show biz. I mean B and D is so gaggy. And where does it all end? In a bug wing, at fat best. Just think—a nice girl like you already getting taken home! *You'll* probably end up popped. I wouldn't actually mind, except playing god must be your dream. No, this one plans to rejoin the fluff in the vanilla bars. You should, too. It's not so bad. You could always turn out spinach queen. Or why don't you just try going it alone? That's you! I'll give you a fifi-bag to remember me by. . . ." Morris continues his monologue while consuming shrimp, chops, salad, flan, Petit Chablis, and coffee. Afterwards he settles down in his study. Twenty minutes later, Lewis calls from the kitchen. Morris answers the summons with an irritated "Do you mind!" and tapes a wool sock inside Lewis's mouth. Lewis fears he will choke and starts writhing on the floor. "*Must* you be so pigeon-titted?" The cuffs keep clattering. Morris hauls Lewis across the living-room floor. Opening the window, he loops the drag-rope over the top of the railing outside and pulls Lewis upwards until his back barely touches the floor. When the rope is secured to the railing, Lewis is immobilized by his own weight. The window now cannot shut; through it pass bitter gusts and occasional fine snow. Morris returns to his desk.

Lewis had taken a temporary job as night watchman at a factory building in Queens. Afternoons, he haunted off-off-Broadway theaters, where he tried to make himself useful in any capacity that might lead to being hired. Three days after Lewis's second visit, Morris introduced him to Tom, the head lighting man at the City Center Opera. He had agreed to have Lewis apprenticed to him. This meant low pay and invaluable experience. The sudden opportunity intimidated Lewis. Tom coached him patiently, and Morris reassured him during his fits of self-doubt. After such kindness, Lewis could not understand why Morris again barred him from his apartment. He offered to run the most humdrum household errands for his benefactor. Morris remained adamant. For three weeks, Lewis had to content himself with public meetings, knowing that all the while Priscilla frequently visited the lodgings on Cornelia Street.

Third visit: February 14. Books fill every room in Morris's apartment, including the kitchen. Even the back door is hidden by a bookcase. This door is not, however, completely blocked: the lower shelves of the bookcase can swing out to allow passage of upright dogs and crouching humans. Lewis is permitted to return only if he promises henceforth to use this entrance. He is given a key. On Saint Valentine's night he makes his first appearance on his hands and knees, to Morris's satisfaction: "That's fine. *Don't* stand up. Wriggle out of your Peck and Pecks right where you are. You'll have yourself when you see what I've brought you." He hands the naked Lewis a straitjacket. Lewis bursts into tears. Morris snaps, "The party's over," and picks up his overcoat. Lewis begins obediently working his way into the straitjacket; Morris knots the drawstrings. With a short length of nylon cord he attaches

Lewis's left foot to a leg of the kitchen table. He also fits him
with a studded leather cock ring, its points facing inwards.
Morris then pulls up a chair and begins his talk for the evening. He has taken for his subject Lewis's sexual inadequacy.
Morris explains that he has tried to lessen its effect by keeping
Lewis away as long as possible. Now he must speak his mind.
He has never had so boring a lover. He describes the delights
of some earlier affairs, long and short: ". . . One piece of ivy
pie was so righteous! Never been tampered with, and he still
knew twice what you know, Zelda Gooch. . . ." However, he
will not linger over his past. After fifteen minutes, putting on
his coat, he tells Lewis, "I'm out for dinner tonight. You
won't be alone, though. Phoebe's coming to see you. She'll let
herself in." Lewis huddles under the kitchen table. He pisses
on himself.

After weeks of insistence, Morris pestered Lewis into showing him everything he had written—his poems, his journal, his
imitations. "You'll need one reader at least, and I *am* on your
side, you know." For the first and last time, Morris became a
teacher. He went through Lewis's work with him line by line.
He refused to correct; instead, he invented exercises for Lewis.
He made him rework passages in other styles. (Lewis's "breakthrough" took the form of a political polemic rewritten as a love
poem.) Morris took care to do these exercises himself, keeping
no more than a step ahead of his pupil. Little by little he weaned
Lewis from his limitations, his "individuality": favorite words,
repeated sentence rhythms, obsessive metaphors, whatever let
him shy away from the entirety of language (as a novice skier,
preoccupied with his skis, shies from the buoyant steeps that
can give him wings).

Fourth visit: March 14. Lewis finds Morris with Tom from
the City Center. Morris tells him that Tom will spend the
evening with them. Two long boards are leaning against the
mantelpiece. A small vise is screwed to both ends of each

board. After Lewis has stripped, the men spread-eagle him against the boards and clamp his wrists and ankles in the four vises. Only the loose boards hold him in place; Lewis does not dare stir. Morris and Tom sit down to dinner. They discuss Lewis while they eat. Morris speaks of his hopelessness as a writer; he reads a few hilariously incompetent passages by him out loud. Tom describes him at the theater—slow to learn, manually clumsy, so socially clumsy the entire staff dislikes him (including Tom). After dinner the two men sit together on the sofa in front of Lewis. They start kissing. Lewis falls to the floor, gashing one knee bloodily on the glass coffee table. Morris replaces Lewis's left foot in the vise from which it has slipped. Talking campily and incessantly, he and Tom caress one another. At last they put on their coats and leave. Tom's place, they agree, will be cozier under the circumstances.

The following afternoon, Lewis met Morris at an opening at the Stable Gallery. Morris greeted him exuberantly. He had sent a selection of Lewis's work to one of the editors of *Locus Solus,* a little magazine whose reputation was unrivaled. Three poems had been accepted. "You tell people you're a writer, they say 'Wonderful,' and *always* they ask next, 'And have you published anything?' Now you say yes."

The two pursued their study of writing several hours each week.

Fifth visit: April 15. The worst for Lewis so far. He picks up the evening's "toys": a full-length inflatable rubber suit that constricts its wearer whenever he struggles against it. Lewis climbs three floors of a dilapidated building on lower Varick Street. A small nervous man dumps a bundle in his arms and slams the door in his face. When Lewis crawls through the back door into Morris's apartment, he finds Morris waiting for him, naked except for a gag, a note in his outstretched hand:

Dear Louisa,
    My turn. Put the contraption on me, use the pump to blow
it up, and get out. If you do anything else, or if you come back,
I'll never forgive you.

                                                                    M.

In tears, Lewis complies with his instructions. Afterwards he
goes to a restaurant. He can't eat. He decides to see a movie,
a revival of *Twenty Thousand Leagues Under the Sea.* James
Mason doomed to submarine exile makes him cry so hard he
has to leave. He walks down rainy streets for another hour.
How can Morris's heart survive the constricting suit? He goes
back, crawls once more through the bookcase, and releases his
friend. Morris is panting fearfully. Lewis holds the sweating
body in his arms, murmuring brotherly comfort. Both men
speak words of endearment, and like all of Lewis's visits, the
evening ends in a prolific tenderness that lasts into the next
morning.

    Morris had imagined a prodigious book: for that place and
time, The Book. It was to include fiction as well as criticism,
theory as well as poetry, using the most appropriate medium to
explore each facet of its subject: the finiteness of intellect and
language confronting the infinity of the intuited universe. During the spring weekend they spent with Phoebe in the Hudson
River valley, Morris invited Lewis to collaborate on the project.
They would begin work on May 24, Morris's thirtieth birthday.
The task would take at least three years.

    Sixth visit: May 23. Entering the kitchen on all fours, Lewis
finds Morris busily stirring five plastic basins with a broom
handle. The basins contain black matter, heavy and wet. Morris
hands Lewis the stick. His efforts have left him rather pale. He
now only adds water to the basins while Lewis churns them.
The basins, he learns, are filled with quick-drying cement. At
Morris's bidding, Lewis carries them into the living room and

sets them around the edge of a small area covered with layers of newspaper. Lewis undresses and stands at the center of the area. Using a housepainter's brush, Morris daubs grease over Lewis's head and body. Kneeling down, he then starts covering him in cement, first heaping it generously around his feet and ankles to form a massive base, then applying a half-inch thickness over his limbs, torso, and head. Morris leaves an opening for nose and eyes and with his forefinger jabs a passage into each ear. When he finishes, sweating and breathing hard, Morris is visibly pleased with his crude statue, whose arms stretch out sideways like a scarecrow's, giving it an air both of solidity and of helplessness. While the cement is hardening, Morris goes off to wash and eat dinner. On his return, he tells Lewis to move his arms and legs. Tears and sweat are already dripping from the end of Lewis's nose, and his eyes now wince with effort: he cannot budge. Morris walks back and forth in front of him while delivering his customary monologue of abuse. He has hesitated, he confesses, to tell Lewis the most important thing he will ever say to him. He has spoken already of the repulsion inspired by Lewis's degeneracy, by his lack of sexual talent, by his lack of talent *tout court.* Morris has since realized that everything he has said falls short of the truth: what makes Lewis ultimately repulsive is his intrinsic self. His specific shortcomings only manifest the underlying ugliness, stupidity, and heartlessness that constitute his very being. With growing passion Morris applies his new insight in appalling descriptions of Lewis's physical, mental, and social behavior. Wherever he looks, he can discover only failure and disreputableness. Some might consider his nature something he has no control over, but this makes it no less unbearable: "Even if I don't like reading you the stations, I won't spread jam. So please, Louisa, get it and go. You're a mess, a reject, a patient—I could go on for days. And don't tell me—I have your nose wide open. I'm sorry. Spare me the wet lashes, it's all summer stock. Because the only one you've ever been really strung out on is your own smart self, and you always will be. Think I'm going to stick around and watch the buns drop? And for what—to keep catching my rakes in your zits? Forget it, Dorothy. This is goodbye. Remember one thing, though. No matter what I've said to you, no matter how I've turned you out, the truth is"—Morris's eyes become wet; he turns a surprising shade of red—"the truth is, and I'm singing it out: I lo—. . . " Morris is staring past Lewis as his voice breaks off. Has he stopped because the telephone is ringing? His color veers from red to gray. He turns to lean on the back of a chair, except that no chair is to be found where he leans: he sinks onto his knees before lying face down on the floor. He rolls himself slowly onto his back, looking up at Lewis, who watches his lips form a repeated word *(Nitro, nitro)*, then remain open and still. Morris breathes rapidly, until a moment comes when he does not breathe at all. Lewis shouts into the cement plastered across his mouth. He only makes his own head hum. Panic has started to overcome him when he realizes what has happened: Morris is playing a joke on him. He is deliberately scaring him out of his wits. Lewis's panic turns to rage. Morris has gone too far, inhumanly far. Lewis will never forgive him. Remembering their previous meeting, he knows that Morris may very well lie there half the night. He can only wait, and he is steeling himself for his ordeal when he notices Morris's eyes. They are fixed in an impossible stare. They never blink. Lewis counts sixty seconds, the eyelids do not move. The fly of Morris's shirt lies motionless over his chest and belly. Lewis keeps looking down at his friend. A grieving numbness is expanding through his body. Another minute passes before he thinks: I may be wrong. Perhaps Morris is only stricken, or perhaps if he's dying there's time to save him. Lewis screams another muffled scream, tells himself: Emotion does no good. Figure out how to get free. Earlier, Lewis has noticed a croquet mallet leaning against one of the bookcases. Morris would have used it to crack his shell. The phone is ringing again. Question: what can he use for a mallet? Answer: a fall to the floor. How can I fall when I can't move? However, Lewis can move, if only inside his skin. He can squeeze himself left and right, or front and back. Will this let him shift his weight? Seven feet away to the front and left, on the coffee table where he cut himself, sits the phone. Lewis begins pressing towards it and then away from it, right heel to left toe, left toe to right heel. He begins to sway, minimally. He senses a tapping of the cement base on the floor. His hunch is working. The statue has started to rock. He must not fall backwards, away from the table. He puts all his strength into pushing forwards. The base goes tap-thump, tap-thump. A momentum has been established. A point comes when the backwards swing does not occur. Before falling, Lewis and his carapace balance for three full seconds on the front edge of the base, precious seconds during which he twists hard clockwise, trying to swing his left arm in front of him, and the arm does strike the floor an instant before his head and chest. The cement shatters to the elbow. The phone lies too high to reach. He yanks it by its wire onto the floor and pulls the handset in front of his face. The cement around his head has cracked. With his free hand he loosens a piece over his mouth. Running his finger over the rotary dial to the last hole, he dials zero. He hears an answering voice, barely audible. He calls out Morris's address, begs for help, explains that he is immobilized. He repeats his appeal over and over, long after the operator has connected him with the police. Still speaking into the receiver, he hears someone at the front door. Who is it? Why are they ringing the bell? and knocking? "Break it down!" he starts shouting. The bell still rings. He hasn't noticed the sirens before, several of them. Ringing and knocking stop. The door is being forced, a heavy old oak door equipped with three locks. Lewis has nothing left to do. He begins sinking into a weary, gloomy dullness. With despondent irony he tells himself that Morris will never top this. He is mistaken, in the sense that worse is to come. He is not otherwise mistaken: Morris has bequeathed him a legacy that will perpetuate and compound the experience of his six visits. Their last evening has become a moment of pain that will engender further moments of pain, and these will have to be endured without any hope of Morris's returning, as he had before, from dinner or from Tom's place. In his guise of tormentor Morris will enshroud Lewis's life. Lewis will never want to forget him, and he will have no choice in the matter. A rosary of mourning, shame, and isolation has begun entwining him more finally than thongs and chains. Morris might well in these consequences be completing his last aborted sentence, which Lewis had unhesitatingly grasped in its entirety: "The truth is, I loathe you."

Lewis and Walter

JUNE 1962-JUNE 1963

PRISCILLA LUDLAM ATTENDED THE SAME PROGRESSIVE liberal-arts college as Phoebe, graduating from it, a year after Phoebe left, with a major in art history. For her degree she wrote a commendable bachelor thesis, entitled "The Female Figure in Recent American Art," having as its true subject the work of Walter Trale. (Priscilla's tutor, the same admirer of Walter's work who had taught Phoebe painting, suggested the nominally broader subject to mollify her colleagues in the Fine Arts Department.)

As soon as she had completed her paper, Priscilla wanted Walter to read it. She gave it to Phoebe and asked her to bring it to his attention. It soon occurred to Phoebe that the paper might also interest Lewis, who at the time knew nothing about Walter except what she herself had told him. She sent him a copy.

An account of Walter's early portrait of Elizabeth constituted the centerpiece of the thesis. As a teenager Priscilla had heard about the portrait, which Walter had painted in the upstate town where she still lived. Priscilla set out to gather information about its early history. In her thesis she compensated for her limited critical skills with an abundance of anecdote.

Priscilla had sharp wits. At twenty-two, however, her curiosities drew her less to analysis than to the rehearsal of life—to people, to attainment, to the city. She had not majored in art history because she thought herself scholarly or even "artistic": she was interested not so much in art itself as in those who created it. Art came as close to magic as a possession-prone world allowed. What did it take to become a magician? Priscilla's interest was encouraged by the unprecedented glamor, fostered by critics and buyers alike, of new American painting. When her tutor proposed that she spend a year studying Walter Trale, she accepted enthusiastically, because she could at once imagine him as another Pollock or de Kooning. She devoted many hours to staring dutifully at slides of Walter's work. If she came to feel at home with it, she could not be said to have ever understood it. It never touched her, at least not on its own terms. It mattered to her because she saw in it an expression of the artist's life. Her interpretations of the work surreptitiously concealed an imaginary likeness of Walter himself. He was a subject that did touch her; and her delineation of him made Lewis respond to her thesis with idiosyncratic sympathy.

Priscilla described at length the background of the "Portrait of Elizabeth": how Walter, at eighteen a precociously successful painter of racehorses, prize dogs, and cherished pets, was transformed by his meeting with the woman he was soon to portray. Elizabeth had revealed to him the "animal grace and transcendent sexuality" of a woman's beauty. Merely seeing her had initiated the revelation; but according to Priscilla, Elizabeth also intervened actively in Walter's life. She had seen *him*—seen him for what he might become—and through her friendship she had inspired him to become it. By her visionary wisdom Elizabeth made a creator of him. In Priscilla's view, it was not only through her beauty and intelligence that Elizabeth exerted her influence but by fully assuming the role of Woman as muse and genetrix. It was this experience of Elizabeth as absolute Woman that Walter had recorded in his portrait of her.

Priscilla supplied engaging anecdotes to support her claim. Defending her interpretation of the portrait proved harder. If the painting looked inspired, what else did it look like? Certainly not Elizabeth. All biographers explaining art take their wishes as facts. Priscilla made the painting conform to her need, which was to establish in it the presence of *das Ewig-Weibliche* (as, knowing no German, she insistently called it). To her, the gold and white of the face invoked a medieval Madonna. The ocher of the eyes belonged to Athena (or perhaps her owl). The mauve lips stood for mourning (notice that the bared teeth are not smiling)—a demonstrable recollection of the *Pietà*. A mouth-colored mouth with no teeth would probably have suggested to Priscilla the Cumaean Sibyl; plain brown eyes the mortality of autumn leaves; pink cheeks the sacred Rose.

Priscilla never realized that her analysis suffered from self-indulgence, and Lewis did not care. Morris would later teach him what art criticism might achieve. For the time being he was seduced by her account of Walter the man. Priscilla's absolute Woman crystalized Lewis's own feelings; women had always struck him as awesome and inexplicably different. At no age that he could remember had he been close to anyone of the opposite sex, except for Phoebe; and if other women acquired mystery by their remoteness, Phoebe had become no less mysterious through intimacy—her love for him left him perpetually incredulous. Mystery meant an aversion that differed from his hostility towards men. Lewis disliked men because, as one of them, he knew all too well how they functioned. He knew, among other things, how they experienced desire. He was attracted to men because he wanted to rediscover with them this familiar, recognizable desire. Women had unimaginable desires, and one particularly unimaginable sexual desire. He remembered at four watching Phoebe while her diapers were changed and staring at her big button. It looked anything but girlish. Lewis was not bewildered by the vagina, but by the irrelevant and impudent clitoris. He did not want it there. It was the stopper. It meant that women had been fashioned as unpredictable beings, that he could never trust them to behave in an accountable way.

With men, he knew how to provoke the aggressiveness through which he could respond to them. Even here women eluded him. Once, when he was nine, at a family gathering, he called a pretty eleven-year-old cousin a bitch. He knew the insult to be reliably bad because his mother had slapped him when he tried it on her. The cousin laughed gleefully, said he was cute, and pampered him for the rest of the day before withdrawing to Connecticut. They were not to be trusted.

In spite of dating one girl in late adolescence, Lewis's aversion never wavered. Because he kept his true desires hidden, classmates at school and college thought him merely shy, and they frequently introduced him to young ladies both nice and not-nice. He wanted no part of them.

Walter's experience of women, as Priscilla described it, confirmed Lewis's. Walter displayed generosity and ebullience, Lewis pettiness and anxiety; both could agree that in Woman mystery and power abide.

Lewis found a second reason to like Priscilla's thesis: it showed precisely the extent of his difference from Walter. Walter had recognized the power in women and faced it. Through Elizabeth, he had let it into his life. Perhaps he had even mastered it in his art and turned it into a power of his own. Walter was thus an exemplar of all that Lewis could never aspire to.

Lewis often had crushes on the men he admired. A fund of natural affection underlay his habitual mistrust. Because he was frightened by the give-and-take of friendship, Lewis expressed this warmth either by provoking those he liked or by adoring them from a distance. In Walter, Priscilla had supplied him with a new idol.

Lewis confided his admiration to Phoebe, who at once saw in it an opportunity to move him into the living world he was so determined to avoid. When, in early June, he exclaimed over the phone, "What an incredible man!" she replied, "So why don't you visit? See the work yourself."

"I don't mean the work. I mean *him.*"

"So come and see *him.*"

Lewis began commenting on the current heat wave. He heard Phoebe saying to someone at her end, "My big brother thinks you're the cat's pajamas, but he's scared to meet you."

When Walter took the phone, Lewis had fled.

Phoebe did not let him get away. She called back repeatedly to tease, berate, and beg. She even lured him with the unlikely possibility that Lewis might somehow work for Walter. The proposal flustered him at first; soon, however, he began working it into his fantasies, until his fantasies themselves changed. Instead of worship, Lewis began dreaming of servitude. He could put his own inadequacy to good use. He could free Walter from whatever distracted him from his art. He would clean his brushes, wash his skylight, scour his toilet bowl, run errands in Brownsville. He accepted Phoebe's invitation.

In the days preceding his visit, walking through the town under dying elms and heat-wilted maples, or sitting with a book on the porch of the house, or lying in bed late at night, he thought of what his meeting with Walter might bring. He did not want gratitude or recompense. He longed ultimately to become indispensable to Walter. He imagined a career starting as charman and ending as watchdog.

Walter in the flesh only strengthened Lewis's devotion. He

looked his forty-three years and looked them well. A nonchalant alertness pleasantly animated his sprawling features, his wrinkles tempered his obvious candor with an aura of lessons learned. Lewis felt a surge of tenderness when he saw him. This would normally have ensured his protracted silence, but Phoebe kept prodding him to speak.

"It's incredible," he finally told Walter over sizzling shrimp, "how you started your career with such a really profound work."

"Profound? 'Digger III' profound? Sure was a *gloomy* beagle."

"I mean—I *meant* Elizabeth. Your first woman—I mean, the first person you painted was a woman. That's probably significant."

"No shit." Walter had not yet read Priscilla's thesis; Lewis had not yet seen the portrait of Elizabeth.

Phoebe said, "Lewis thinks you're accomplices in misogyny."

"Not misogyny, not really—" ("No, not really!" Phoebe camped) "—but, you know, that power," Lewis hurried on. "It's not that it's bad, just big. You don't want to get in its way."

"That's in the portrait?" Walter asked.

"Why, sure." Lewis looked startled. "I don't have to tell *you.*"

"Tell me anyway."

Lewis discoursed on female unpredictability. He related the incident with his eleven-year-old cousin: "It wasn't as though she was genuinely fond of me. I was used."

"The trouble is," Walter said ruefully, "*they* never seem to realize." He was suffering at the time from a woman's unresponsiveness.

Although Walter liked him, and Lewis was as willing as ever to serve, he was frustrated in his aims by a rudimentary fact:

he was a man. At the studio the next morning, after Walter asked what kind of work he wanted to do for him, Lewis replied, chores—cleaning up, shopping, soaking the beans. "That's no kind of work for you," Walter said. He meant, among other things, that it was woman's work. Walter, who enjoyed chores, might have accepted another woman as helper; when Phoebe cooked dinner for him, he felt that her presence made a difference. A man could only add more of what he knew all too well.

Walter said, not unkindly, that he found Lewis's offer to play housemaid silly. Lewis was scarcely disappointed—he had been schooled, after all, in Owen's harsher ways. He readily withdrew to his first, safe role as worshiper.

Lewis did not see Walter again until the November evening when he met Morris. In the meantime, both their lives had changed. Walter was living with Priscilla; Lewis had been overwhelmed by Morris's article.

Lewis and Priscilla had once known each other well. Six years before, they had had a serious falling out, and they had not seen each other since. Before the November party Priscilla decided to bury the past. She wanted to please Phoebe, and she assumed that in six years Lewis had grown up. When she saw him arrive, she greeted him with a hug. Lewis was surprised and pleased; however, preoccupied as he was with the prospect of meeting Morris, he responded distractedly to Priscilla's welcome. She mentioned hearing from Phoebe that he had liked her thesis. He replied, "Yes, it was really nice. As a matter of fact, for a while it kind of obsessed me. But you've read Morris's piece? *That* says it all, doesn't it?"

Priscilla had worked hard on her thesis. Walter himself had praised it. In those few seconds Lewis squandered his credit with her.

Late that month Lewis was arrested in the crucifixion raid. Although a reader of the *News,* Walter failed to spot the incrim-

inating photograph. Priscilla noticed it and called up Phoebe to
check. Phoebe went out for the paper and phoned back to thank
Priscilla for letting her know. Interrupting Walter at work,
Priscilla told him, "Look what's happened to Phoebe's brother,
the poor guy!" She wondered how he'd become involved with
such freaks. "They must have given him drugs. Nobody's that
screwy."

Lewis often saw Walter that winter in Morris's company. In
his behavior towards him Walter showed an amiable lack of
concern. He knew that Morris and Lewis had become lovers,
a relationship that, according to Priscilla, was "doing wonders—just what Lewis needed to get it together." She sometimes reminded Walter that for Phoebe's sake they should be
kind to him. By this time Priscilla had become Morris's business partner.

Walter came to think of Lewis as a "case"—someone not all
that sick who you still wished would get better. Inevitably
Lewis reminded Walter of Phoebe, whom he was losing to her
own "neurosis," and of Morris, whom he respected and rather
feared. Lewis was to be tolerated and encouraged and, perhaps,
avoided.

Morris died. Public and private accounts of his death were
gluttonously sucked up by downtown gossips. Walter knew
Lewis too little to resist the vague story that many people
eagerly accepted: Morris had not died accidentally, and Lewis
had not merely witnessed his death.

Lewis had changed in the half year that followed his arrest.
Phoebe's old hopes for him had been essentially fulfilled: if
Walter had done nothing for Lewis, Morris had done everything. He had offered Lewis the chance to earn a living, to write
professionally, to recognize and express the love he felt; and,
overcoming his chronic fearfulness, Lewis had taken that
chance. He learned, for a time at least, that fearfulness could
not excuse running away. He was proud that he could now

handle a lighting console, that he was going to be published, that Morris had adopted him; prouder still of being able to get a job done, of writing for his own increasingly stern taste, of having turned his sexual addiction into a means of loving one man. When Morris died, Lewis clearly saw the fullness his new life had taken on, and how fragile, without Morris, it had now become.

Morris had incidentally altered Lewis's attitude towards Walter. While Morris always praised Walter's painting, he treated the artist himself almost patronizingly—an attitude completely at odds with Lewis's obsequiousness. At one December opening, after Morris had walked away from Walter in mid sentence, Lewis asked him how he could act so cavalierly. "I adore Walter," Morris answered, "but he says absolutely everything that comes into his head. He can be *brainless.*" Lewis said he always listened to Walter because he was so perceptive. Morris interrupted him: "In so-called life he doesn't notice anything, except the visuals." Lewis once again ventured to cite Priscilla's theory of Walter and Woman. "Louisa!" Morris exclaimed to Lewis, who shrank, "that's infantile caca! Even if Miss Priss is right, it's still only Big Momma Rides Again. Most boys feel that way sometime—like you, *n'est-ce pas,* am I not insightful? Walter probably didn't notice—Wonder Woman's name for him was Cadmium Rose. Doesn't mean anything, only words. My words for it were 'tempestuous sky of the vagina,' remember, and *they* don't mean anything either."

"I never asked you—why 'tempestuous'?"

"What's rumbling thunder remind you of? *Basta!*"

Lewis returned to Walter: "You mean good painters can be mediocrities?"

"He's not a mediocrity. I love him—warm as a farmhouse bath on a frosty night. It's only those surfeits of well-meaningness. . . . Maybe it's just been too easy for him. A good shit-dip would have tightened and brightened him. But there's nothing wrong with him. He's just not special."

Lewis began listening to Walter more dispassionately and decided Morris was right. Not knowing he painted, one might have taken him for an affable wholesaler, a well-read truck driver, a debonair postman. Lewis saw that adulating Walter did him an injustice: an extraordinary man can be expected to do extraordinary work; from an ordinary man, such work means that he has transcended his nature. If this notion still smacked of sentimentality, it at least allowed Lewis to transform his idol into someone for whom he felt affinity as well as respect. His own exertions as a writer—small compared to Walter's thirty years' diligence—gave him a sense of comradeship with the older man.

Morris's death cost Lewis his lover, mentor, and closest friend. Within days he learned how alone he had become. Newspaper reports, private rumors even less well informed, were making of him a macabre celebrity. No one seemed sure who had buried whom in cement; either way, the act sounded deranged, if not criminal. The tale of the crucifixion was revived and given wide circulation. Lewis learned that few people knew the truth about him—that he loved Morris, that he wrote, that he worked at the City Center. Many of Phoebe's friends did not know he was her brother. Tom, at least, did not let him down; and the regularity of Lewis's daily stint at the theater sustained him during the weeks that followed Morris's death. However, he valued Tom as his boss. Outside the classroom, he had never worked for anyone; he was now doing a competent job for someone who had trained him well without ever overtly favoring him. Lewis refused to jeopardize their professional relationship by making Tom his confidant.

He knew he needed a confidant. A year before he would have turned to Phoebe; she now lay in a hospital in critical condition. He dreaded facing Morris's sister, Irene. Each time he wondered, who am I going to talk to? he would think, in spite of himself, I have to ask Morris. Grief would then penetrate him, the cold, fleshly grief he had felt when he gazed down at his lover's breathless lips. Phoebe was lost for now, Morris forever. Lewis turned to their common friend.

He had seen and not spoken to Walter at Morris's funeral. On Wednesday, a few days later, he called the studio. Priscilla answered: Walter was busy, was there anything she could do? How was he?

"Same as you. Except you have company."

"Big deal. It's *awful*. There's this hole in my life I keep falling into. . . ."

"I do reruns all the time—I saw it, but I still can't believe it. Listen, when is Walter free?"

"When would you like?"

"Right away! I really need to talk to him."

"Gotcha. I'll tell him."

He gave her the number of a delicatessen that took messages for him.

When Lewis returned late that night, Walter had not called. At the theater, he had heard one of his companions ask another, "Jesus, is he still at large?" The next morning he received a letter from Owen's lawyer. It assured him that his father would assume his legal expenses. Lewis again phoned Walter, and Priscilla said to him, "Lewis! I'm so glad to hear from you. Can you come over tomorrow afternoon?"

"Tomorrow?"

"Darling, it's the best he can do."

The "darling" angered him, more because of his own helplessness than the intimate concern it implied.

Priscilla *was* concerned: she was doing her best to keep Lewis at bay. Only six months had passed since she had skillfully won a place in Walter's life, and she still considered her position handicapped by youth, inexperience, and a lack of credentials.

Most of Walter's friends had known him for years. All displayed forcefulness or originality or both—even the bums had clownish charm. Priscilla could not pretend to be "interesting." Only Walter's attraction to her justified her presence at his side. She needed to fortify this attachment. She needed to establish herself at the center of Walter's life, with the rest of the threatening world kept apart from their private sphere.

Lewis presented no threat. His disgrace served her plans, however, now that Phoebe and Morris could no longer protect him. Priscilla had already consigned Lewis in Walter's eyes to the role of psychic invalid. She now wanted to banish him conspicuously from their life so as to confirm certain benefits she would derive from Morris's death.

Walter was feeling intense remorse over Morris. He had neglected someone to whom he was uniquely indebted. He told Priscilla he wanted to atone for his neglect by befriending the dead man's lover. The impulse had so far remained only a wish, because Walter shrank from seeing Lewis, whom he wanted to like and didn't and whose strangeness in the wake of Morris's death had become forbidding. Priscilla knew, however, that Walter's generosity would win out. Mere aversion was no match for it.

Priscilla sensed she could turn Walter's remorse to her own advantage and so delayed Lewis's meeting with him. Lewis had called back on Friday morning. That afternoon she had been summoned to appear at the reading of Morris's will. She had been informed that no legacy in the will approached in value the life-insurance policy of which she had been named beneficiary. She planned to come home that evening with public proof that she, not Lewis, had been chosen by Morris as his heir.

Not knowing that the insurance policy proceeded from a business understanding, Walter reacted as Priscilla had foreseen. She had been consecrated as Morris's intimate. Unmentioned in the will, Lewis was relegated once again to the fringe of things, a pathetic, suspicious silhouette. That evening, alone with Priscilla, Walter for the first time found the ability to vent the grief he had been withholding. He cried in her arms. Morris became a precious bond between them.

Walter woke Lewis up Saturday morning to briskly excuse himself from their meeting that afternoon. He suggested that Lewis join them for drinks Sunday evening: "We're having a few friends over." Baffled with unfinished dreams, Lewis sleepily accepted. The phone rang again: Phoebe. She was leaving the hospital to catch a train upstate. He asked if he could take her to the station.

"Thanks, but no. I've made such a deal about doing this on my own. I do want to see you. How are you? Better not tell me! *I'm* awful, too. Come home, soon, and we'll hold each other's hands."

Lewis had intended to see Walter alone. He went to the studio that Sunday because he preferred seeing him with others to not seeing him at all. He regretted the visit. Those guests who knew who he was (the others were soon told) treated him with careful nonchalance, pointedly discussing their politics, their diets, their vacations, confronting him with the undisguised curiosity reserved for movie stars and youthful victims of terminal cancer, with one difference: they never touched him, not even an elbow, as though he were threatening them with terrifying contagion. A cheery Priscilla took him aside and earnestly questioned him first about Phoebe, then about his work, and last about his grief, which, she too emphatically insisted, she more than shared. Lewis sadly realized that they were engaged in the conversation he wanted to have with Walter.

Walter behaved like the others. In the features of the man he had chosen to trust, Lewis saw himself registered in terms all too familiar: as pervert and pariah. When he noticed Lewis's gaze, Walter's inane smile almost split his face. Lewis later detected something else. Walter averted his eyes from him as from the thought of Morris, of Morris-as-corpse. Lewis had become a carrier of mortality as well as disease. (That suspended look reminded him of someone else, someone he could not then recall.) Lewis wondered what Priscilla had told Walter about him. Why was she so set on keeping them apart? He was about to ask her (what could he lose?) when a great weariness settled on him. It had arisen, as well as from disappointment, from the sorrow that for ten days had followed him like a childhood dog; he had spent all his courage tending it. He looked at Walter once more. The openness of the face contracted into studied blankness. Lewis left.

He met Walter and Priscilla by chance the next morning, on the corner of Carmine and Bleecker Streets—Priscilla still cheery, Walter silent, standing behind her, contemplating Lewis with the appalled eyes that identified him as doom made flesh. As he was replying to something Priscilla had said, Lewis recognized that familiar expression: it was the way Owen always looked at him. Lewis's understanding of the couple he faced began to change. He lost track of what he was saying to Priscilla. His scalp prickled with sweat.

"What's wrong?" Priscilla asked.

Lewis lied, "I just remembered talking to Morris once on this corner." He kept staring at Walter. "You know how his being dead—you forget it for five seconds, and something brings it back—don't you, Priss? *You* know what an incredible man he was."

Thirty-seven years before, Walter had sat down conclusively on his little sister's best celluloid doll. Since that time, no one had ever looked at him as she had then, as Lewis was looking at him now. The aversion drained out of him; he reverted to his considerate, vulnerable self. Lewis did not notice this because of the tears of rage in his eyes.

He walked away. He did not see them again until early
September.

Every year during the hot midsummer drought, on the hills
overlooking the French Riviera, hundreds of acres of pine and
cork oak are laid waste by fire. At the end of one arid July, a
thirty-year-old schoolteacher, passing a spot where underbrush
had begun burning, got out of his car to observe the spreading
flames. Other drivers saw him, assumed that he had started the
fire, and reported him to the police. He was arrested. Overnight
he provided the outlet for a nation's frustrated anger. Although
he was cleared of the charge against him, to him this hardly
mattered. Six years later he declared that for the rest of his life,
no matter what he did, he would be remembered as the "Arson-
ist of Provence."

From the behavior of Walter's guests, from the remark overheard at the theater, from the exaggerated discretion of the
countermen at his delicatessen, from Owen's coldly dutiful letter, from Phoebe's pity, from the telephone calls of junk journalists, from the silence of acquaintances, Lewis knew that he
was similarly condemned. For years the mention of his name,
his appearance in a room, could only recall King Koncrete or
whatever tag stuck to him best. How many books would he
have to write to obliterate his scandalous fame? Would he have
to write them under another name? (Morris had said that Lewis
Lewison was so good it sounded made up.) To read in Walter's
face this squalid verdict hurt more than he could endure. Why
had he blamed Priscilla? She had her old reasons for mistrust-
ing him. Walter should have known better.

Lewis's situation excruciated him because he could see no
end to it. Phoebe might console him at home; elsewhere he had
no prospect of support or even sufferance, not if someone like
Walter repudiated him. Lewis's awareness that his pain would
last, that its unfairness would not modify its persistence, ur-

gently demanded comforting: he needed someone to blame. Throughout his life he had always blamed himself for the failures that, loving mortification as he did, he had in truth often provoked. Now he chose to blame someone else. He hated his pain, most of all when he recollected his happiness with Morris. He turned this hatred against Walter. Kind and candid, Morris's friend and Phoebe's, Walter should have known better. His blindness excluded forgiveness, and Lewis did not forgive him. Three months later, after the portrait of Elizabeth was brought home from the hospital, Lewis immediately noticed its disappearance and discovered that his father had destroyed it. He spoke to no one of what he had learned. Walter must be the first to know; Lewis must tell him. He waited until they met at another funeral to enact this small revenge.

Louisa and Lewis

1938-1963

$\mathcal{S}$ EEING LEWIS IN TROUBLE HELD NO NOVELTY FOR LOUISA. Since infancy he had schooled her in disaster.

When the Lewisons decided to have a child, Owen, although claiming to want a boy, was disappointed by Lewis. Soon afterwards he began saying how sad it was to be an only child, as he had been. Three years later, at Phoebe's birth, Owen saw his true desire satisfied. He devoted himself to her thereafter. Lewis was left to Louisa.

Lewis had already made her suffer. During her second pregnancy he had been afflicted with intermittent fevers that came and went without reason. He might be playing in his room late in the afternoon; Louisa would hear him whimpering and find him flushed and breathless. By nightfall his temperature would reach a hundred, sometimes rising to a hundred and four during the night. Doctors offered baffled diagnoses and prescribed aspirin and orange juice. As long as the fever lasted his head and body ached, he slept fitfully, he threw up most of what he ate. Louisa stayed in his room night and day, cooling him with wet sponges, reading stories, singing songs, talking until she ran out of words. After three days the fever would abate, leaving Lewis weak and testy. Louisa knew that, at two, he could not be expected to acknowledge her care of him; she was nevertheless pained to find herself blamed for his miseries: "I hurt when *you're* there." Sometimes he would cry when she appeared at his bedside. Louisa expected to feel surpassing love for a firstborn son. What love she felt was regularly distracted by the conviction that Lewis had come into the world with a nature she would never understand. Louisa found males strange—she even liked their strangeness, at a distance. Owen had proved a special case. Before they married, he had clearly wanted her, and Louisa did not mind that he wanted her in part for her good name and connections: she accepted his suit wholeheartedly, and her commitment to his career after their marriage maintained their mutual trust. Other men bewildered her. She found them full of abstract generosity and practical unkindness, broad-minded towards the world (and their dogs), impatiently suspicious of individuals who disturbed their opinions. Louisa may have been blinkered by the memory of her father, a big, brusque man who had died when she was five, leaving her family poor and herself haunted by a strong, elusive presence.

Even tiny, Lewis looked to her like another mysterious male. Her sense of incomprehension, and its attendant fear of motherly incompetence, made her swear to keep doing her best by him. Failures only renewed her dedication. As a result, her life with him was punctuated with "I must" and "if only." Whatever happened, she must, she must sustain him; and if only, if only she hadn't behaved in this or that way, what had happened might not have; and if only it hadn't happened, Lewis might be different. She never thought, "If only *he* hadn't," no doubt suspecting that such thinking had as its logical *terminus a quo:* if only he hadn't been born.

Fearfulness made Louisa vulnerable. Lewis learned that by demanding and blaming he could get the better of her. He learned, too, that if he could lure her into a shameful business with him, she would forgive him anything. He sensed that Louisa would always protect him from Owen.

At the age of three he discovered how to make a shameful business of his genitals. With tantrums threatened or indulged, he would force Louisa to stay with him when he was in bed or in the bathroom and squeeze his penis in a special, reassuring way. A year later, by then too "reasonable" for such games, he would harry her with questions about his member: "Will it snap off when it's stiff? Momma, promise to tell me if I'm supposed to snap it off?" Until he was almost ten, he would get up at night in tears if she had not come in to secure the bath mitt in which he lodged his penis while he slept.

These tactics reduced Louisa to impotence. She complied with them, concealed them from Owen, and at last found herself depending on them. They became her most reliable evidence that Lewis trusted her and that she could comfort him.

When Lewis was eleven, the Lewisons rented a summer house upstate, in the neighborhood where they would eventually settle. Friends with children of Lewis's age made a place for him on picnics and swimming parties, and after a few days Lewis began bicycling into the summer haze to join his new acquaintances. One day he stayed home. He sat until evening on the porch steps. After that, he never again left the house of his own accord. He spent his afternoons reading comics or hunting through the unfamiliar library for "grown-up" books. On weekends he kept to his room, out of Owen's sight. His gloominess troubled Louisa less than his utter loss of insolence. He offered to help her around the house. He behaved almost gently with her.

One morning, having dispatched him to riding school, Louisa searched Lewis's room. In the bottom drawer of his commode, twenty-two stacked issues of *Action Comics* concealed a sheet of blue-lined paper on which a doggerel poem had been penciled. Three quatrains followed its title, printed in capital letters: TO LEWIS WHO WE LOVE TO HATE. The last quatrain read:

> We think you'd be better off dead, get it?
> Cause you're really sick in the head, get it?
> You think you're sharp as a tack, get it?
> But you're really crazy as a *bat,* get it?

Louisa restored the page to its cache. When Lewis came home, she asked if he had had any problems with his new friends; he fell bitterly silent. Louisa spoke to other parents, who made necessary inquiries. She soon found out what had happened.

A few days before he began his solitary life, Lewis had asked all the boys he knew to meet him at one of their houses. Early in the afternoon, carrying a wicker hamper, he had joined a dozen ten- to twelve-year-olds in the mortifying heat of a third-floor attic.

Lewis had tried to initiate the meeting with a speech about "friendship and courage." No one listened, and he quickly proceeded to the main event. Opening the hamper, he turned it upside down, shook it hard, and kept shaking it until, twenty seconds later, a small bat emerged, soon followed by another. The two bats spent some time fluttering among the tumbling, shouting boys before settling on the darker side of a corner rafter. By then the group had evacuated the attic. Only one ten-year-old remained. He had retreated sobbing to a spot behind a queen post where he still sat clutching his knees, watching incredulously as Lewis, his hands sheathed in electrician's gloves, calmly plucked the bats from their refuge and returned them to the hamper. (Two days before, Lewis, in his own attic, had devoted three turbulent hours to techniques of bat catching.)

When he came downstairs, grinning with pride, Lewis found his group dispersing. Two or three boys whom he addressed replied with scant, nervous words before biking hurriedly away. He had plainly produced an effect; he did not worry what sort of effect until the poem was dropped anonymously into the Lewison mailbox. As far as Lewis was concerned, summer had ended. No boy would now dare to be known as his friend. Lewis felt that he had been cruelly mistreated. He had only wanted to impress the others. Having succeeded in that, he hoped (this he barely admitted to himself) that he might propose to his admiring friends that they all confirm their companionship by masturbating together. It was this half-secret, not-unsociable wish that had inspired him. It did not merit ostracism.

When she learned about the bats, Louisa told herself that the author of the poem was not far off the mark: if not insane, Lewis seemed certifiably strange. He frightened her by what he had done, and no less by his perfect secrecy. Except for borrowing the hamper, he had given her no clue about his undertaking. She could not console him—she was unsure of what he might do in return. Above all, she longed to recover his trust.

Lewis gave her the chance to do so before the summer was over. He went alone into town one morning (something he was forbidden to do) and came back with a foulard by Hermès as a present for her. Suspicious, Louisa asked where he had found the money to pay for it. Lewis told several lies, all of them transparent. He was almost relieved when he had to admit to stealing the scarf.

Louisa lost her temper. To one of her upbringing, shoplifting was the first slippery step to armed robbery and hatchet murders. She slapped Lewis hard—the last time she ever did so. He yelled, "I did it for *you!*" and ran away in tears. Louisa realized that he had in his devious way confided in her. She must not lose him.

She followed him outside, where he had hidden between two lush snowball bushes. The slap had worked. He fell into her arms, sobbing, "I'm sorry, I'm sorry." If she had been less shocked by his thieving, Louisa would have cried too. She hugged him as long as he let her. They walked twice around the house together, her hands on his shoulders. She explained that she must take the scarf back. She would look at other scarves, slip it among them, pretend to choose his, and pay for it; she could then keep his present. She made Lewis promise never to steal again and, if he did, to tell her at once. She did not mention his father.

In this manner Lewis implicated his mother in the first of many thefts, making her his ally against Owen, against a world both respectable and hostile, against his own ordinary yearnings. Her involvement enabled him to steal with zest. He knew that if the worst happened, she would suffer the consequences. Sometimes the worst did happen; and whenever he was caught, Louisa duly appeared to soft-soap the store owner, or floor manager, or policeman. Neither mother nor son ever acknowledged that they felt happiest together after these dramas.

Thieving brought Lewis another advantage: possessions. He learned that by threatening to steal an expensive object he could, once he convinced her that he craved it, make Louisa give him enough money to buy it. (He sometimes stole it anyway.) Cultural items like books and classical records best suited this blackmail, and Lewis assembled a library and a record collection remarkable for one his age. On his own, he acquired, among other things, two hundred and ten packages of chewing gum, a hundred and sixty-nine Tootsie Rolls, ninety-eight bananas, oranges, and apples, seventy-six pens and pencils, eighteen neckties, seven bottles of French perfume (although three were open samples), and five six-packs. His grandest failures included a top hat at Tripler's and a multipurpose electric tool kit at Sears; his proudest triumphs, a small dress sword filched under the malevolent eyes of a Third Avenue pawnbroker and a first edition of *Madame Bovary,* which he spent twenty harrowing minutes slowly shifting from the depths of Brentano's, rack by rack, until, reaching the sidewalk of Fifth Avenue, he made a four-block dash with it into obscurity.

He told Louisa about most of his thefts, only neglecting to mention those too trifling to outrage her. He ultimately sought outrage rather than complicity, and he discovered after two years that his achievements left him dissatisfied, because Louisa invariably proved kind. Lewis had a secret hope and fear: that Louisa, at last turning against him, would inflict the punishment he deserved—leave him to the police, send him to a military academy, tell Owen. Louisa's governing rule, however, was to keep her crazy boy within eyeshot. She did not really care what he did, as long as he stayed hers—hers to watch, to listen to, to mollify, to save from his craziness. She scolded, complained, threatened, and always bought him off. After weeks of argument, she let him keep *Madame Bovary.* (He had made a rare choice, and she hated Brentano's.) Where Lewis was concerned, the observant Owen noticed nothing.

In Lewis's eyes, each kindness of Louisa's reshaped her into a likeness of the Connecticut cousin who had loved him for his rudeness; each kindness made her less dependable. In this he judged her unfairly (Louisa was consistency itself) and resented her sincerely: she had abdicated her parental function of providing pain.

After four years, their complicity ended.

The Lewisons continued to vacation upstate in spite of Lewis's unhappy summer. In time his unhappiness waned. The bats passed into half-spooky, half-glamorous legend. One day in July, when he was fifteen, members of an unfamiliar gang noticed the solitary Lewison boy and decided to adopt him. Fearing trickery, Lewis acted petulant and unresponsive. The others laughed at him and said they needed a good sorehead. Even when Lewis had come to enjoy these funny companions, he never left himself unprepared for some cruel joke they might be playing on him.

One of the gang, a girl a year younger than Lewis, openly pursued him. She persisted in spite of his overt mistrust of her. She biked at his side, let him dunk her when they went swimming, and retrieved his nasty comments good-naturedly ("Just because I like you, Groucho, doesn't make me all bad"). One evening, while they sat together at the movies, she rested her head on his shoulder. An hour later Lewis kissed her. He pressed his jaws against hers, not feeling much, excited by the idea of kissing. He knew he should try for more.

Behind his parents' house lay a farm, whose barn he had often explored. Lewis brought the girl there two days later. Piled to the tie beams with new hay, the high building was deserted, as he knew it would be at four o'clock on a steamy August afternoon. They settled in a corner, night-black after the summer sunlight, and embraced between a cliff of hay and a tar-scented wall. Lewis kissed her harder and harder. After a while she let him squeeze her small breasts, then asked to go outside. Lewis held her. She complained. He did not know what to do. She would not let him touch her elsewhere, she wouldn't touch him. He wrestled her to the ground and lay on top of her, rubbing against her, trying to pull down her shorts, poking inside them. The girl tried to bite him. Both were gasping and sweating in that close corner. Dust from ancient harvests, roused from the barn floor, drifted into their nostrils and eyes. Lewis went on thrashing against her, unwilling to stop. The girl began sniveling. She was frightened: no light, seemingly less and less air, Lewis hurting her with his elbows and hips. She took a deep breath to scream and choked on dry hay-dust, coughing wretchedly. She shit in her pants. Lewis smelled it. The girl had begun to utter faint spasmodic cries when he ran away.

Louisa was standing in front of the barn door. She had noticed the two bicycles while walking by. Lewis did not speak to her as he mounted his bicycle to sprint off through the cornfields. Louisa found the girl inside the barn and brought her to the house to bathe and change. She made tea and talked to her. Louisa had no problems with women, whatever their age. She soothed the girl. Learning what had happened, she spoke of her chronic difficulties with Lewis. The girl had grown calm, almost content with their secrets by the time Louisa drove her home.

Louisa found Lewis waiting for her when she returned. He was wet-eyed with impatience. Once he knew that she had talked with the girl, he would not let her speak, fitfully spluttering forth his resentment: his life was none of her business, she should stay out of it, for good. . . . He ran off the porch, slamming the screen door with a bouncy clatter.

Louisa understood that the violence choking him did not represent shame for his assault. The girl had told her, "He didn't really do anything, but he got so wild trying." She had felt in danger less of rape than of Lewis's incapacity for it. He was ashamed to have his mother know this. He wanted never to face her again.

He stuck to his aversion and kept beyond Louisa's reach. He stopped speaking to her about stealing (in truth, he stole no more). In the years that followed he clung fiercely to an absurd position: he was helpless to prevent his parents from conditioning his life, and at the same time they had nothing to do with him. Louisa supposed that he would have given up eating if he had thought it put him in her debt. Lewis claimed that he owed his parents nothing, and that they owed him everything in compensation for the circumstances to which they condemned him. Louisa's concern and affection demonstrated only minimal decency, nothing to her credit and no help to him. How could she help him in his pursuit of philosophical consistency, political integrity, or whatever other distant goal he had most recently set himself?

For eight years, Louisa depended on Phoebe for information about her son. She respected her children's intimacy. Fearful of weakening it, she never pressed her daughter to tell more than she volunteered; so her knowledge remained limited while her anxiety grew large. She worried about Lewis's social life (he never brought a friend home); about his love life (she thought he was homosexual—was he at least homosexual?); about his future (bleak); about his relations with his father. His life offered her little not to worry about. He seemed locked inside himself—a place that he enjoyed no more than any other.

If, month after month, Louisa kept speculating about her son, she never guessed at his career as a practicing masochist. The crucifixion raid devastated what trust she still had in her own insight and gave her anxiety something real to gnaw on. After she rushed to Lewis's side and he fled from her, she began spending much of her time in the city. She was determined to stay near him, hovering just out of his sight, hoping that she could stave off the next catastrophe. She feared for his life.

Morris's friendship with Lewis dismayed her because the more Lewis saw Morris, the less he saw Phoebe, and the less Louisa knew about him. She wanted to believe Phoebe's assertion that Morris was working miracles on Lewis's behalf. To Louisa, however, the crucifixion had proved her son insane, and she did not see how anyone could change that. Morris might have reassured her if she had approached him; Lewis's unpredictable reactions made her afraid to risk that. She went on worrying about Lewis, rarely seeing him, pleased when she knew what he was doing, disheartened when she didn't, her imagination then inflating itself with volatile, inaccurate terrors.

One evening in late May, getting out of a taxi in front of the Washington Square apartment house where she was dining, Louisa saw Phoebe walking by. Heading for Macdougal Street, Phoebe did not look at Louisa or turn at the sound of her name. Anyone except Louisa would have been concerned for Phoebe; Louisa thought, what has happened to Lewis? When she called her an hour later and Phoebe failed to answer, she knew that something awful had happened. Louisa bravely telephoned Morris. At first his number did not answer either; it then rang busy for a full ten minutes. Louisa left her dinner and hurried across Sixth Avenue to Cornelia Street. At the door of Morris's building she pushed intercom buzzers until she found a tenant willing to let her in. She climbed the two flights to the apartment and began ringing the bell. A voice resounded far inside— perhaps shouting, she thought; she couldn't make out the words. She kept ringing and knocking. The man who had let her in came down for a look, a woman in a gym suit appeared on the stairs below. They think I'm bonkers, Louisa thought, but I'm doing the right thing.

The voice inside kept calling out. No one came to open the door. Outside she heard a siren approaching, a second and a third, each swelling to soprano frenzy before declining in a long, laggard wail. Downstairs the building door opened to thudding feet. She was surrounded by cops and unhatted firemen. Exquisitely, they lifted her to one side, then attacked Morris's door with an ax, a sledgehammer, and two crowbars. When it sprang from its hinges, Louisa was trembling with dread and eagerness.

She quickly got inside. Two objects lay on the living-room floor in a litter of newspapers: Morris's body and a long shattered stone, which four firemen promptly surrounded, chipping carefully at its black fragments. Louisa bent over Morris. He looked distracted, did not answer her, seemed not to breathe. She knew what to do. She began blowing air through the parted lips.

A policeman pulled Louisa away, led her to the large, wide-open window, and held her there. She started to lose control and swore loudly. She twisted her head around and saw Lewis lying among chunks of black stone. She screamed. Two white-suited males forced her onto a stretcher and strapped her to it; another man adroitly needled a vein in her left forearm. Louisa woke up in a hospital room on the East Side.

She was still drowsy when, late the following morning, a visitor was announced. She was surprised to see Lewis: "You're all right? It's darling of you to come here. Wherever here may be."

"You need someone to sign you out—this is the nut ward. Phoebe's on her way, but I thought I'd speed things up."

"*Thank* you. How is Morris?" Louisa asked—a lying question. She knew she'd breathed into a dead mouth.

"He had a heart attack. He died right in front of me."

"Lewis, I'm so . . ." Tears were rising fast.

"What the fuck were you doing there?"

"I didn't know . . . Phoebe wouldn't talk to me." She sniffled into a bouquet of Kleenex. "I'm sorry. It was hard enough for you without my . . . Thank you for coming, I don't deserve it. I *am* sorry."

"You don't deserve it, and you're not why I'm here."

"You said, so I could get out?"

"I'm trying to contain the damage. I hope you leave the hospital, go home, and shut up. Let's say you don't answer the phone for a week."

She recognized Lewis's manner, not its present motive: "Lewis, I just don't understand."

"Remember the policemen at Morris's last night? Policemen like to file reports. Some hotshot young prosecutor with a flea up his ass held a press conference this morning. He made, shall we say, selective use of the reports. There was Morris, there was me, somebody was buried in cement, but he didn't say who, just 'one of the parties.' And, big surprise, a certain Mrs. Lewison was there too. You know what she did? She started kissing the corpse. She was the mother of one of the parties, *not* the one who was the corpse. Get it?"

"No, I don't 'get it.' "

"You can't see how a freaked-out queer who'd let himself be crucified might horribly murder his mother's lover? What was that croquet mallet doing in the living room?"

"But no one who knows you could dream—"

"But no one does know me. Not anymore. Just go home."

"It never occurred—"

"Of course it didn't. It never does. You barge in and wonder why everything gets so distressing." Louisa stared at him. "Does it ever occur to you that you get exactly what you ask for?"

"It's *you* I get distressed about."

"You hung around all winter for *me?* You should have gone to Tierra del Fuego."

Lewis spoke quietly. He was drifting through limbo. He still did not believe Morris had died. If he had been asked what he desired, he might have answered his own death, although he was too enthralled by his sensations to contemplate suicide deliberately.

His cold words released in Louisa a flash of warmth. When he left, she thought: Perhaps he's right. Perhaps she had never helped him. Perhaps, as he implied, she had always behaved selfishly. Could she do better leaving him alone? It was that possibility, so obvious and so new, that filled her with sudden joy. "And good riddance!" She spoke the words aloud.

She did not quite mean them. She nevertheless let herself, very briefly, imagine the life she might have had if Lewis had never been born: not having to wake up every day, and most nights, convinced that the essence of life was raw fear. Louisa realized that on the previous evening she had suppressed more than Morris's deadness: entering the apartment, she had known that Lewis lay under the cement, and she had wished him dead too. As she acknowledged her wish, words again broke from her: "My poor boy!" She had been the crazy one, after all. She started laughing. She didn't want him dead, never, she didn't want him not to have been born, she didn't want anything of him. With a pang of tenderness, a silent blessing she could never speak, she let him go. Then she started singing, "This can't be love . . . ," and laughed as she sang. She would stay out of his life as long as he wished; not a second longer.

Louisa intertwined the fingers of her hands and stretched her arms over her head. Below her window the city rose pallidly in hot, dirty haze. A garbage scow spun down the East River on the ebb tide. What would she do with her life, now that she had dumped her dreary load?

She had no time to consider the question, because Phoebe arrived. She could then no longer doubt to which of the few creatures in her neglected life she might, at last, be of urgent and unquestionable use.

Irene and Walter

MAY – AUGUST 1962

Because his shows at the Kramer Gallery made Walter Trale famous, many assumed that Irene Kramer had discovered him. In fact he came to her late, less than a year before Morris died, with almost thirty years of painting behind him.

Irene had heard of him long before and had seen his paintings in group shows and in private collections. She had never found an opportunity to assess his work as a whole.

Although Irene was only thirty-four when she opened her gallery uptown, she had been selling art for twelve years, ever since she had finished four terms of art history at the New School—all the formal training she was to have. She had paid her way doing part-time secretarial work. Her father, who had started as an usher and who owned six movie theaters when he retired, might have paid for studies in law or medicine or business; to him, art dealing meant high risks and uncertain returns. He underestimated his daughter: Irene could have succeeded in almost any career she chose. She had intelligence and ambition, and she usually knew what she wanted. (She had, as well, a diminutive, perfectly restrained hourglass figure and a pretty face to which wide brown eyes could sometimes lend a melting beauty.)

While at the New School Irene met Mark Kramer, ten years her senior, a prosperous public accountant with a weakness for high culture. He persuaded her to leave the Bronx. From their brief marriage she learned that the sexual sincerity of the male may have capture and imprisonment as its covert goal. Mark soon wanted her staying at home being her wonderful self, not caring if that self demanded more. After her second year of study, Irene went to work as an assistant at Martha Jackson's. This meant not going with Mark to Europe, to the Bahamas, to Sun Valley. She could see little point in this, he in that. When they were divorced, in 1952, she told him, "Don't pay me alimony, give me a lump sum. We'll both benefit." His calculations proved her right. He borrowed the money she wanted. He felt so grateful that for five years he paid her rent.

Irene began buying paintings, which she sold from her apartment. She chiefly handled Europeans—Americans then were still condemned to being either too famous (and too expensive) or unknown. Since she had to recoup her investments in the short term, she left discovering the undiscovered till later. She struck some profitable deals; notably, in her first year, the purchase for six thousand dollars of twenty-two Klee gouaches (a year later she sold two of them for the same amount). It took her five years to establish herself as a reliable dealer, with access to works she wanted to sell and customers on whom she could depend. She then opened a small gallery on Sixth Avenue south of Fifty-sixth Street, financing it with her personal collection as collateral. The gallery barely sustained itself commercially, but it brought her into the public eye, and she made an enviable reputation for herself through her farsighted choice of painters.

(Irene claimed that a good dealer had to know how to "buy potential"—had to know how to see, in paintings actually looked at, work not yet imagined even by the artist himself.) In the fall of 1961, when she gathered twenty of her best clients and presented her plan for a new and larger gallery, they backed her without hesitation.

Morris's essay on Walter appeared in *New Worlds* the following May. He had already urged Irene to sign on this painter whose talent had been proved and who had not yet become fashionable. Irene had taken her younger brother seriously and also a little skeptically—she had seen his earlier enthusiasms wax and wane. When Morris's article was published and acclaimed (it was chosen for that year's *Trends in American Painting*), Irene decided to take a careful look at Walter's work.

What she had seen of it she admired, and if she had avoided it professionally, that had to do with commerce, not art. Walter wore his originality strangely; he was a master in disguise, even if he wore the disguise of a master. He could not be classed as an abstractionist, even when he most resembled one. His figuration had a disturbing offhand look, with none of the starkness of Hopper and Sheeler or the stylization of Lichtenstein. Now that Irene had started her new gallery, Walter's eccentricity ceased to be an obstacle. She had originally become a dealer to encourage new art. She could now do so.

Because she liked Walter's work, Irene had imagined that she already knew it, forgetting that an occasional painting provides poor insight into an artist's universe. Irene spent a week assembling in her mind a complete Trale retrospective and found herself increasingly fascinated the more she saw. She started at Walter's gallery, then visited collectors, including those with work from his animal years, and concluded her tour at his studio. Walter had kept for himself over a hundred paintings and at least a thousand drawings, many of them among his best. Irene spent a long afternoon in their midst. When she was done, she knew that she had discovered a world that revealed more than talent and intelligence and imagination. Walter's originality resembled that of original sin. He had reinvented the act of painting itself.

Walter kept away during Irene's visit, letting Phoebe play hostess. The two women spoke little. Irene was absorbed in her study; Phoebe knew better than to distract her. As she left, Irene said, "He's better than anything I can say about him. I'll be in touch soon."

Walter had never cared much for public success, which he'd already known as a boy. He had never lacked confidence in his abilities. For twenty-five years he had been satisfied with earning enough to pay for his big studio and the parties he liked to throw in it. Now his attitude was changing. Morris's article had affected him too. The art market was starting to boom. Painters half his worth were selling for twice his price. If his time was to come, he wanted it to be now. Irene had opportunely appeared. Phoebe's account of her visit exhilarated him.

He waited for news. None came. He phoned her gallery. She was busy. She did not return his call. Three days later, he called again. Irene was out. "Walter *who?*" her secretary inquired. Next morning Irene did phone and made matters worse. Her careful praise of his work sounded like a checklist of routine compliments. She mysteriously concluded that this was not the moment to talk business: "I can't explain why. You can probably guess."

Walter could not possibly guess. In her enthusiasm Irene had made the familiar mistake of assuming that the man was as clever as the artist. Her remarks aimed at efficacy and discretion; to Walter, after ten days of silence, they signified indifference. He reacted morosely. His thrill of expectation grew sour with disappointment. With resentment as well: he felt his good will had been abused.

Walter found an explanation for this injustice when he stopped at his gallery the following day. His dealer was out—

not surprising at two o'clock in the afternoon. The surprise was that he was lunching with Irene. Walter was informed by the admiring young assistant that they were meeting for the third time. "It's all about you, isn't it?" She would not tell him more. Walter jumped to a conclusion founded wholly on suspicion: the two dealers were conspiring against him. Irene knew that in her gallery his work would fetch higher prices. She had not signed him on because she was planning to buy his paintings from his present dealer and resell them. The two dealers would split her markup. Since Walter would be no better off than before, they were keeping him in the dark.

As he paced along dank, warm streets that afternoon, these thoughts kindled Walter's mind with ever-brightening hostility. At home, he called his dealer, who only said, *"You're* asking *me* what's happening?" Walter never considered that the other man's curtness might be justified. It simply confirmed his suspicions and enabled him to savor in earnest his role as intended victim.

He decided to let his enemies complacently elaborate their scheme. His pleasure in wrecking it would be all the greater. His patience proved short-lived. A few days later an elderly friend from his *animalier* days took him out to lunch uptown. As Walter sat down, he saw Irene and Morris at a table on the far side of the restaurant. Throughout the meal he observed them busily conversing, so engrossed with one another they did not notice him until they were leaving. Morris then waved connivingly; Irene blushed as she smiled at him. As well she might: Walter saw at once that the conspiracy to exploit him had broadened. The critic who had rediscovered his work would now promote it and so merit a wedge of pie. And they hadn't even bothered to shake hands with him! Their nonchalance made Walter especially bitter. He refrained from venting his outrage to his lunch companion only by silently deciding to intervene.

As he walked the fifty-two blocks to his studio, he realized that Morris's complicity aggrieved him most. He scarcely knew Irene; perhaps she had a tougher character than he'd imagined. He knew his dealer well enough. Walter liked in him above all his pleasant lack of ambition; if Irene had proposed an easy way to make money, he might understandably be tempted. Walter felt passionate respect for Morris. He thought him bright, eloquent, fervently committed to a rare idea of art held by few artists and fewer critics. Because of this commitment, Morris's essay on his work had convinced Walter that they shared an intense if impersonal affinity. Walter had been understood; he had been assigned the place he deserved, at the dark, sharp point of invention. That Morris could exploit what he had so intimately perceived jarred Walter painfully.

He called Morris and suggested that he come to the studio at ten-thirty the next morning. The suggestion had the ring of a summons. Morris deferentially ignored the tone and accepted.

Having overheard the phone call, Phoebe asked Walter what was wrong. For the first time he related his fantasy to someone else. As he spoke, he reminded her of Lewis, at age eight, on the verge of a fit. Wondering how many cocktails had preceded lunch, she did not dare speak her mind.

In the morning, she found Walter still sheathed in glum determination. Letting Morris in, Phoebe gave him a trouble-in-paradise look that pinched the smooth space between his brows. Walter mutely motioned him to a chair by the dining table, which had been cleared of everything except the telephone. Facing Morris across the table, Walter solemnly lifted the handset and dialed.

"Gavin Breitbart, please, Walter Trale calling," he declared, adding in ominous sotto voce, "My lawyer." He cleared his throat: "Gavin?" Standing painfully straight, he began delivering into the mouthpiece a long statement obviously, if inadequately, rehearsed. His voice reminded Morris of someone from the past—Senator Claghorn?

"... a very grave breach of professional ethics, which I want you to start proceedings in the matter. ...."

Walter stared belligerently at Morris while he listed his grievances: Irene's duplicity, her conspiracy with his dealer, her plan to include Morris as a highbrow publicity agent.

Listening to him, Phoebe wished she had gone to New Mexico. Morris was emerging from perplexity into half-credulous mirth. No one could have taken Walter seriously if self-righteousness were not so crassly distorting his benevolent mug. When Morris heard himself personally implicated, he bent over and cut the connection: "Stop. Stop before they come and cart you off. What have you been sniffing—Drāno?" Walter scowled. Phoebe stared at her toes. Morris went on: "Listen, maestro, Irene wants you in her shop. She didn't like cutting out your dealer, so she offered him a percentage for the next couple of years."

"Exactly."

"No, not exactly. It's out of her pocket."

"Says who?"

"She does." (The phone rang: "Oh, Gavin . . . Later, OK?") "Your dealer's a piggy. He keeps upping the ante. She even thought of making him a partner. But that's finished."

"How come?"

"No contract, I believe. Irene got fed up. *He* suggested cutting your share, you know. She says screw him."

"Yeah, and not just him."

"Walter, can't you grasp that she's mad for you? Look, I knew something was up, so I told her to drop in. You'll see."

"That's what *you* say. Why don't you admit you're in cahoots? I saw you the other day. What are you, lovers?"

"As I live and bleed! *A,* I'm queer. *B,* she's my sister."

"Kramer?" Walter leaned one thigh against the table.

"Her ex."

The doorbell rang. Phoebe admitted Irene. Morris said to

Walter, "Don't forget Gavin. He may have an emergency patrol on the way."

"OK—hel*lo,*" Walter said to Irene, "something I have to clear up." He was reddening. A moment later he was telling his lawyer, "It was a mistake. Forget it. It doesn't matter—no, the name *doesn't* matter. Listen to me. Well . . . Kramer." Lowering his voice, he turned his back to the others. They stood there politely hushed, except for Phoebe, prey to the giggles. "Look, I'm not alone . . ." Walter's voice petered out. He glanced at the others—Irene patiently watching him, Morris shaking his head, Phoebe red with restraint. He hung up. "Coffee? Beer?" He ran both hands through his hair. Irene gazed at him in nascent consternation. Walter was breaking into a sweat. "Irene, there's something I think—"

"Not a word!" Morris interrupted. "We'll never tell, will we, Phoebe? Not for lox and bagels!" Phoebe nodded as she wiped her eyes.

Irene said, "Mr. Trale, Morris thought this might be a good time to see you. Phoebe's told you how extraordinary I think your work is? I apologize for having taken so long to find that out. I'd love to show you—I'd like to give you *two* shows, back to back. A retrospective first, then new work. I can do well by you, I promise. I don't have to be told that you'll do well by me. Just having you under my roof would be a blessing."

She had spoken plainly and earnestly. Her low voice soothed Walter. He gulped her words down like lemonade in a hot spell. He made a few appreciative noises until he was again overcome by an awareness of his folly and began shaking his head in retrospective consternation. When he next looked at Irene, he realized that she was still speaking to him:

" . . . No? *You'd* rather?"

"I'm sorry—"

Morris reminded him, "Walter, it's *over.*"

Irene resumed: "What I was suggesting is, I've been having

trouble with your curmudgeon of a dealer, but if *you* agree, I can certainly come to terms. I can take care of all that, if you like."

"Great!" Walter replied. He stared at her as though he had rediscovered his beloved elephant. The bell again rang, and Phoebe went to the door: Priscilla stood there, thesis in hand. Walter never even saw her. He went on staring at Irene, who was turning the faintest shade of pink. It occurred to him that she might like to sit down. "Coffee? Beer? Please don't call me Mr. Trale. It makes me feel older."

"You *are* older, Walter," Irene replied, with a most agreeable chuckle. She was pleased to have secured this fine painter, pleased that he was so likable—a nice, big baby. "Thanks, I can't stay—I don't *want* to stay, because I'm going to your gallery right now and settle things. I'm making sure you don't get away from me."

"Who'd ever think of doing that?"

Morris and Phoebe might have been in Manitoba. Walter was immersed in his abrupt conviction that Irene should take complete charge of him. "I'll come with you. The three of us can work it out together."

Morris said, "Leave it to the pros. You'll just work up a froth."

Irene remained silent. Her smile—warm, faintly condescending—was filling Walter with concupiscent awe. "You're right," he agreed, at once asking Irene: "So I'll see you later?"

"I'll phone you as quick as I can."

"No, I mean *see* you. How about dinner?"

Phoebe shook her head. Even Lewis at four had never sounded so demanding. "Say please!" she whispered. Irene's smile widened; Morris pursed his lips.

Walter refused to be distracted: "What *about* dinner?"

"Walter," Morris chided, "this isn't Schenectady."

"What? Well—tomorrow? How about—"

"All right," said Irene. "The day *after* tomorrow. Meet me at the gallery at seven." Morris reflected that she had found a humane way of liberating them all.

Two days later, Walter arrived at the Kramer Gallery early, a bouquet of sweet william in one hand. Irene told him, "I'm pooped. Can we have a drink here and go straight to dinner? I reserved at the Polo Lounge, in the Westbury. Ever eat there? You'll love it, although not necessarily the food, but you'll need a tie. I bought you this"—a strip of raw blue silk.

Walter formed no opinion of the restaurant. When not perfunctorily swallowing food, he sat with one forearm thrust across the table and the other perched on the back of the banquette, staring at Irene. She herself sat upright and still, folding her hands between courses, glancing sideways at Walter with smiles of affectionate amusement. At first, for his sake, she had tried to smile less—she smiled as though watching a doddering colt. He didn't mind.

Walter was doing his best to be adorable. He hurriedly drank enough to break down his own reticence. He laughed often; tears sprang to his eyes readily when a thought moved him; he disparaged and praised himself without affectation; he listened to Irene's words with conspicuous attention. Walter wanted to know Irene almost as greedily as he wanted her to know him. He failed to see that she knew him already, that he could do nothing to make her like him more.

She did not mind his courting her, although his method seemed startlingly direct, like a puppy rolling over to have its belly scratched. Colts and puppies made for fondness, not desire. She decided that disappointing him no less directly would prove the greatest kindness. When he reached over to stroke her arm, she tartly exclaimed, "You're not going to make a pass at me!"

Walter's eyes shone with relief. She had been the one to broach the hot, imminent subject. "Baby, I've never wanted anyone so much!"

She saw that it would take more than hints to discourage him. "You'll get over it, Mr. Trale! I may not have many rules, but there's one that I swear by: never go to bed with an artist. *Certainly* not one of mine."

"And every rule has its exception, right?"

"Not after seven years. My God, if Norman Bluhm ever thought I was seeing you—" Walter laughed. Irene saw that she would have to speak more bluntly: "You don't interest me sexually. Not at all. And I like you. If you have enough sense to understand that, we can have a nice time."

"Maybe you'll change your mind. I can wait." He hardly seemed willing to wait. For the rest of dinner he refused to talk about anything else. Irene finally heaved a great sigh of exasperation (Walter thought: I'm getting to her) and said, "Let's move out of here."

"I'll ask for the check."

"It's been taken care of."

"I invited *you*—"

"In my league, the dealer does the inviting. Where would you like to go?"

"Wherever you say."

"Your place?"

"Yes," Walter gasped.

"It's on my way. I'll drop you." She did not forget the sweet william.

Irene refused to date Walter again. She soon learned that this decision was putting her freedom and perhaps her career in jeopardy. Walter visited the gallery once a day, sometimes twice. He phoned her morning, noon, night, and in between. He tirelessly restated his longing and shared all his thoughts and feelings, which new love was delivering daily by the gross.

Irene agreed to another dinner if Walter would leave her in peace. Their evening together turned out better than she dared hope, even though it took place in Walter's studio, even though they spent it alone. (The other hypothetical guests never appeared; Phoebe vamoosed between drinks and the cleaning woman's jambalaya.) It happened that when Walter turned on the oven, the pilot light had gone out. Lowering a match towards the burner, he ignited a soft explosion that frizzled his forward scalp and reduced his eyebrows to stubble. He thereupon withdrew into a mortified sulk, as obstinate as his lustful state and far less obnoxious.

On another evening Irene even let him take her home. She first subjected him to a demanding social round: a gallery opening, two cocktail parties, a long, late supper together. Only then, after Walter had drunk more than any stag's fill, did Irene maliciously invite him to her apartment. Walter, beaming like a prize student, didn't know what he should do with his diploma and had two more double scotches to find out. He woke up the next morning on the sofa with a friendly note pinned to his shirt instructing him in the use of Irene's coffee maker.

Walter tricked the gallery receptionist into revealing that Irene was to spend the following weekend in a resort town upstate. He followed her there but could not track her down, and in consequence he found no pleasure in a place full of old friends and memories—he stayed with Mr. Pruell, one of his first patrons; here, twenty-six years before, Elizabeth had transformed his life. Monday, in the city once again, Irene refused to relinquish her secret: "We all need a place to hide. Except you, I suppose."

Irene told him she would be busy through the coming week. Walter took the news calmly. He had a plan. Irene loved classical music; a highly touted performance of the Verdi *Requiem* was to take place at Tanglewood the following Saturday; Walter would ask Irene to drive up for it. He first had to reserve accommodations. Pleasurably furnished adjoining rooms were not easily found in that season. Fortunately, a family canceled at an inn in West Stockbridge.

Irene accepted his proposal. "What a great idea! We'll stay

at the Broffs' in Lenox." Walter mentioned the inn. "Save your bread. No, wait: let me check if there's an extra bed. They'll always find a corner for me." The Broffs were full up. They arrived in Lenox at noon. At the Broffs', Walter verified the presence of three houseguests. Lunch turned into a winy meal attended by four more guests, after which the entire party removed early to Tanglewood, where they claimed a swath of field directly in front of the shed and settled on rugs and blankets spread out in a profusion worthy of a Caucasian tribe. Walter sat down next to Irene.

A couple of his neighbors stretched out on their backs. Walter followed their example. It was a cool, sunny day. He listened languidly to the gossip around him. When the talk stopped, he sat up to join in the applause for the musicians and then once more lay down. Summer sun warmed him from his crown to his soles. Soon the sound of voices and instruments began surging over him gently, like banks of warm fog. He paid little attention to the music: he had come here for Irene. He took care nevertheless to prevent his vagrant mind from deluding him into sleep. Sleep felt as tempting as a mud-bed to a hippopotamus, and he would not disappoint her so childishly.

His thoughts pursued images of a landscape consisting entirely of her. Today she had seduced him once again. Behind saucer-large mauve lenses her eyes glinted like birds vanishing through a screen of leaves. Her small, ripe body chided his attention under billows of buff and beige. He ached to unwrap her. He began an enjoyable game: imagining her body, he let quiet passages of music suggest an unveiling of it, louder ones still closer involvements. The sun warmed his delectations.

He was swimming through warm and enchanted seas like a happy, solitary seal; and he hardly felt a quiver of surprise when he sensed something like a responsive caress, as though the point of his pleasure had been dreamily handled.

He recalled where he was and opened his eyes. A cashmere

shawl Irene had been carrying lay across his hips, in the shape of a fore-Alp. Irene herself sat gazing intently towards the performers as they stormed into the *Dies irae.* Her fingers were locked tightly together, she had decisively sucked her faintly trembling lower lip between her teeth.

Walter loudly groaned. Surely he had reached an age when he could keep his fly buttoned? He briefly longed for a dagger or an icepick to plunge into his chest. With death not readily available, he resorted to flight. Gathering as he rose the shawl around his impenitent erection, he started racing across the sunlit expanse, thick with human obstacles that he skirted with immediate expertise, like an ace slalomist or broken-field runner. He did not slow down until he had reached the city and his own studio.

For several mornings he woke up to spasms of shame, as though shame were a cat poised to leap onto his belly the moment he emerged from sleep. He did not leave his studio until Tuesday. When, early that afternoon, he appeared at the Kramer Gallery, Irene led him straight into her office. Closing the door behind her, she sat down on a leather couch and motioned Walter to sit next to her. As she observed his thunderhead countenance, she found herself smiling once again.

"I thought I'd better bring this back."

Irene accepted the shawl. "What happened to you?"

"Oh, nothing. I just wanted to die. I still do."

"Why did you run away? No one minded. *Au contraire,* we all found you very impressive."

Walter looked up at her. If it pained him to have his anguish made fun of, Irene's forgiving him offered delicious solace. He managed a small laugh. "It was all for you, you know." He looked helplessly into her brown eyes. She said nothing. He unzipped his jeans and pulled forth a now wizened penis. "It still is. It's all yours."

Irene blushed and went on smiling. "Oh, my dear!" She

shook her head. Walter took her right hand and laid his member in its palm, where it rested still as a mouse. "My dear!" she said again. "So small, so sweet!" Bending over, she brushed her lips across it, with the faint smack of a childhood kiss. Someone knocked at the door. Walter made way for business.

That evening Irene disappeared. For four weeks, almost until the end of August, she could be found neither at work nor at home. Walter pestered her friends, in vain; not even his own friends would help him, not even Phoebe.

In early August he learned that Irene was staying at a secret retreat upstate. He learned no more than that. Irene remained safe with Louisa, the old and still-dear friend who had promised to shelter her for as long as was necessary from her distracted suitor.

Priscilla and Walter

JUNE 1962-APRIL 1963

PRISCILLA WAS FIFTEEN WHEN SHE FIRST HEARD OF
Walter. Old Mr. Pruell was showing her portraits of horses he'd
owned. He spoke of the man who painted them with a warmth
that made Priscilla curious.

"He was about your age. A natural."

"Does he still paint horses?"

"He's still painting. He makes a living at it. A nice man."

"Does he still paint horses?"

"No, he doesn't. He'd have been a millionaire. But he wanted
to be a success as a, well, regular painter. It wasn't easy for him.
Funny: he could manage stallions or rabbits, but give him a
plate of apples, or a human being, and he didn't know where
to start. Elizabeth changed all that."

Of course Priscilla wanted to hear about Elizabeth.

"She was a few years older than Walter, and very sharp.
Attractive, too—big and handsome and graceful as a cat. She

loved horses. Walter met her at the track one day, and I think he thought she was part horse. By the second race they were thick as thieves. Just good friends, though, they never went—they never fell in love. She had exactly what he needed—she was a *human* animal. She posed for him every day for the next week or two. He must have done dozens of sketches, and finally he painted her portrait in oils."

Priscilla found the anecdote irresistibly romantic, even if Elizabeth and Walter had remained just friends. During the years that followed, she often asked family friends about them; and she had accumulated considerable lore by the time her professor of art history in college told her that Walter was destined for fame. Priscilla's teacher, who had already nourished Phoebe's interest in Walter, differed radically in her attitudes from the well-to-do families among which Priscilla had grown up. That Walter should be admired both by her and, for instance, by Mr. Pruell lent weight to Priscilla's sentimental fascination with him. Walter migrated from a world of fantasy and elderly reminiscence into that of flesh-and-blood heroes, among basketball stars, actors, and presidential candidates. Priscilla agreed to make him the subject of her senior thesis.

Learning and thinking about Walter almost convinced Priscilla that she already knew him. (She would later enjoy claiming that her thesis had brought them together.) As her knowledge of his work increased, she consistently translated it into terms she could call her own. Priscilla treated paintings like doors: she wanted to know what lay behind them. She sensed the power in Walter's art, and she could not accept that its source might be evident in the paint itself. It was to be found, she thought, in some extraordinary experience that the painting expressed. Thus she developed her theory of Walter and Woman.

Priscilla expected her thesis to bring her access to Walter. Her expectation was strengthened when Phoebe became Walter's assistant. Even if she and Phoebe were not close friends, they had known each other since childhood, they had gone to the same college, and as young women starting out in the world they were disposed to helping one another. With Phoebe as go-between, Priscilla looked forward to meeting Walter without delay.

Priscilla called Phoebe up soon after her graduation. Phoebe said that she would gladly give Walter "The Female Figure in Recent American Art." Priscilla should drop it off at her studio the following Tuesday. Priscilla asked, couldn't she give it to Walter herself? When was he usually home? What was he like? Was Phoebe having an affair with him? Phoebe told her, "I can't invite you in right away. One of my jobs is keeping people out. Wait till he reads it, then I'll fix something up."

Priscilla did not want to wait. One morning she showed up with her thesis at Walter's studio, where Walter was busy falling in love with Irene.

Priscilla apologized to Phoebe later that day, deploring her own ruse so frankly that she made Phoebe laugh. Priscilla knew better than to try again. Soon afterwards a new way of approaching Walter presented itself.

Going back to her parents' home upstate, Priscilla learned that Walter was visiting nearby. He had come only for the weekend, and he left Mr. Pruell's before she could catch him. She felt certain, however, that if he came back, she could instigate a meeting.

In August Walter returned for two weeks. Priscilla told Maud and Allan that she wanted to meet him, and they agreed to get her invited to any social events Walter might attend. Three such events occurred. At the first, Walter failed to appear. At the second, she spotted him across a crowded expanse of lawn; he had gone before she could reach him. At the third, she accosted him promptly, with a mutual friend to introduce them. Priscilla was wearing a dress of clinging silk jersey, its pale ground stamped with bold geometrical figures that enhanced the gentler lines of her young body. Walter looked briefly at the dress. When he raised his eyes, they stared through hers as towards some distant thing—the ghost of Irene. He spoke to Priscilla distractedly.

She was more disillusioned than disappointed. Priscilla knew she pleased men; Walter's lack of response made her doubt not herself but him. She had never imagined that the Genius might be a jerk. She dismissed her interest in him as adolescent daydreaming.

Summer ended—Priscilla's last long student vacation. She looked back on it without regret. In early September she visited the city, staying at her parents' apartment. She declared that she had come to look for work, although privately she felt uncertain what kind of work she might profitably attempt.

One evening, after a day of listless job hunting, she stopped at the Westbury for a drink. In the Polo Lounge, settled in a raised enclosure some distance from the windows, she observed through their high panes the allegretto traffic of Madison Avenue. It was almost eight o'clock. First lights winked on in the slowly fading dusk. The men passing by still wore jackets of pale gabardine or seersucker, the women chemises of crisp linen, earth-brown or olive-green. Priscilla shivered with yearning for the city around her, a yearning to belong. What part could she ever hope to play in this alluring, forbidding world? From the table next to hers a male voice unexpectedly addressed her: "It's magic out there, isn't it?"

Priscilla had been enjoying her solitary gin-and-tonic. Pursing her lips, she turned a look of definitive contempt on her neighbor, who was Walter. No line of her expression wavered as she recognized him. He did not recognize her. He winced under the look and continued to smile and even speak. "It sort of makes the locals look good."

She stared at him disdainfully before returning her gaze to

the street. "The 'locals' look great to me. You're not one of us, I presume?"

"Well, I've lived here forever. Originally, I'm from Schenectady."

"From Schenectady? How interesting! I've never met anyone from Schenectady. I imagined nobody in Schenectady ever got away—except maybe to Albany."

"It wasn't so bad. It was a long time ago."

"I can see that. Some things, though, you just never can grow out of."

Six weeks of frustration had started to blunt Walter's longing for Irene. On her return, she had called him to discuss his forthcoming shows and nothing else. She refused even to acknowledge that she had gone into hiding because of him. He could not so much as apologize. Irene had locked the door on their private past.

Tonight, coming back to the setting where he had declared his passion for her, he was commemorating something he knew had ended, indulging a melancholy that was not without self-disdain. Watching Priscilla, he became acutely aware that for almost three months he had slept alone.

"Care to freshen that?" he asked.

"Tanqueray and tonic. Schweppes, please." She sucked on gravelish ice. She had yet to smile.

He ordered their drinks—her second, his fourth. They drank. He offered her dinner. She accepted, on the condition that they stay at their separate tables: "It's cooler that way." When he started to introduce himself, she interrupted, "No names! No *last* names. What's the point, for one meal?" She refused to hear what kind of work he did: "Can't men understand? The pleasure with strangers is leaving that stuff out." She was holding names and "that stuff" as her trumps. She considered Walter as he leaned into that cool space between them, revving himself up.

By coffee she allowed herself a little gentleness. "Thanks for the treat. I'm not all barbs, you know. It's just that most men . . ." She then asked him his last name. The question thrilled Walter; it implied that she might see him again. At his answer, Priscilla released like a glittering fan the full smile she had withheld all evening. She reached towards Walter and grasped his left hand in both of hers. Even to her, the gesture seemed impulsive; she blushed appropriately.

When she in turn told him her name, his response surpassed her hopes. He had read her thesis twice. Priscilla's theory of Woman and the Artist may have made bad criticism, but it had allowed Walter to recognize himself—"discover himself," as he put it.

Some males claim to dislike women, others to like them, but all share an original, undying fear. Every man is irrationally and overwhelmingly convinced that woman, having created him, can destroy him as well. Men are all sexual bigots. The distinction between dislike and like only separates those who resist women's power by attacking them from those who try to exorcise it through adoration and submission. Walter belonged to the adoring class. Priscilla had inadvertently caught his feelings when she described Woman as a Muse who could transform him. Gratified already by Priscilla's insight, he would have been delighted to be speaking to her even if he had not been suffering from loneliness, even without her stimulating display of coldness.

Three minutes after Priscilla had spoken her name, Walter invited her to see his new work. She said she'd love to. A taxi took them to the studio, where she stayed the night.

Once again Priscilla judged Walter accurately. Knowing that with her almost-beginner's experience she could hardly surprise him sexually, she divined that the gratification Walter most wanted was the gratification he might give *her*. She let herself be gratified, let herself pass again and again, with outspoken delight, from readiness to passion to affectionate gratitude. Priscilla did not have to feign. She did not like boys her age, who always seemed intent on proving something. Even if Walter was older than any previous lover, she had no reluctance to overcome. She had only to confound her animal and her personal desires. She wanted Walter, and wanted him to want her. This need expressed itself in profusions of pleasure. The next morning, Walter shyly invited her to stay on.

Priscilla accepted, with some anxiety. She had idealized Walter, schemed to meet him, given him up as a loss. Now she had possessed him after a single encounter. She scarcely knew what sort of prize she had won, and she moved in with little idea of what to do next. When she told her parents, Maud acted astounded and concerned, Allan astounded and hurt. Priscilla listened to them patiently (she had already transferred her clothes, books, and records to Walter's studio). Certain words of her mother's concentrated her own preoccupation: plainly an attachment so hurriedly formed could be no less hurriedly ended. How, if she wanted to, could she make sure her new life would last?

Priscilla had no doubt that for the present her strongest asset was Walter's heaven-sent desire, his desire for *her* desire. During that first night with him she had discovered, almost accidentally, a powerful way to express her excitement. She had begun talking out loud while he was caressing her and felt his fingers and tongue quicken as she did so. Afterwards, remembering the effect, she spoke at greater length, as roughly as she could: "My cunt never felt so hot, darling, I'm turning to jam inside, put another finger in, yes, baby, and in my ass, too, how did you know. . . ." Her talking turned into a fond harangue, a running commentary suitable for some blind voyeur with an insatiable craving for detail. To Walter, her words magnified their acts with impersonal erotic grandeur, and he was never less than shocked to hear them issue from this expensively educated young mouth. They made the mouth and the body breathing through it all the more desirable, and the voice itself was an almost threatening sound, one that demanded stilling. This became Walter's delectable task, at which he never failed.

Walter's first weeks with Priscilla followed one another in a stagger of satisfaction. He made her his one and only drug. Priscilla grew more confident. Years before, however, she had noticed how different from their ecstatic beginnings marriages became, after two years, or one year, or three months. She knew that while the contractual solemnity of marriage (real even when taken lightly) might dampen enthusiasm, it also provided a barrier to ending a relationship casually. No such barrier protected her. She would need more than passion to keep him. Priscilla decided to go on playing the self-possessed woman Walter had met in the Polo Lounge. She demanded, she refused, she disagreed. She knew she was acting. Even if she made her part convincing by insisting on it, she never forgot how vulnerable she remained. Out of bed, she had nothing to offer that Walter could use. She had brains and energy, in a city stocked with efficient women. Her family's connections were rapidly losing their allure now that Walter had reached the verge of fame. She almost regretted having money of her own, since Walter might have enjoyed supporting her. Undeniably, she possessed youth and good looks; they were not enough. (Sadly, perhaps inevitably, Priscilla in her accounting ignored what to both Walter and herself mattered supremely: she liked him better than anyone she had ever known.)

Her anxiety was sharpened by the success of Walter's first show at the Kramer Gallery, a large, well-chosen retrospective. She gauged the extent of that success by the almost smug contentment of the guests at the opening. They knew they were witnessing a rare conjunction of history and current taste. Women in shantung pantsuits, men in cashmere jackets and silver-buckled moccasins, after a minute or two spent in rememberable conversation with Walter, descended avidly on Irene, whom some of them actually knew. She could have auctioned the show for three times its stated price. As she had foreseen, she and Walter were doing well by one another; and that day she perhaps deserved to outshine him. She had hung on her walls paintings that had long been accessible, making their private value public. Priscilla felt towards her an admiration almost free of envy. Irene had achieved all that she herself might aspire to. She was the masterly intermediary. At that moment Irene's power impressed Priscilla as even more compelling than Walter's genius.

That power frightened Priscilla. Walter had loved Irene (mightn't he still?), and she was making him famous. She treated Priscilla with a plain politeness suggesting that the young woman might someday soon be gone. After their first meeting Priscilla was convinced that Irene had penetrated all her ambitions and doubts. Priscilla asked her if she had read her thesis. Irene answered, "I read it, and I liked it—I love good gossip. I wouldn't push your line downtown, though. They're all into Schapiro and Greenberg." She added, not unkindly, "You might try reading them."

Priscilla's fear revealed what she needed. It led her to imagine a day when she might offend Irene, who would promptly destroy her in Walter's eyes. (In truth, the two women misjudged each other. Priscilla thought too much of Irene's influence, Irene too little of Priscilla's pluck.) Priscilla saw that she must find someone Walter trusted who would side with her in a crisis.

She had hoped to make Phoebe such an ally. Priscilla had taken pains to anticipate any resentment her intrusion might have provoked, consulting Phoebe systematically about household matters, staying out of sight when she was working with Walter, reiterating her admiration of Phoebe's painting. Phoebe may have been surprised to find Priscilla at the studio on that mid-September morning, but she accepted her at once; and her ready acceptance finally discouraged Priscilla from enlisting her. Phoebe manifested no disapproval of Priscilla, and no approval either. She responded to Priscilla's advances amiably and with indifference. Phoebe was preoccupied with her own life and her burgeoning disease. She did not care whether Priscilla stayed or left.

Morris visited Walter shortly before the retrospective opened. Priscilla had read his article in the summer issue of *New Worlds;* it had left her more bewildered than enlightened. Walter reassured her: no one would ever understand him as she had, "but this is about something different—where the work's going, not where it's coming from." She kept a wary distance from Morris when they met.

Morris was Irene's brother—a fact, ominous at first, that eventually brought her Morris's friendship. At the opening, she saw him standing alone in front of a Manet-inspired "Canoeing Couple," staring disdainfully at the crowd around Irene. She went up to him: "Looks like a smasheroo."

"Mmm."

"You must be pleased."

"I am. But what a roadhog!"

"You think so? I feel Walter's happy staying in the background."

"I didn't mean *Walter.* Oh, why do I have such a wildly jealous nature? But you, little princess, have every right to kvell."

Priscilla clasped the revelation to her. Clever Morris had a foible. He was not "wildly jealous," except of Irene.

A week later she had a chance to exploit this discovery. Morris phoned: could he stop by and see them? Come right over, Priscilla told him. Morris found her alone and untypically morose. He asked what was wrong. Her first evasions stimulated his curiosity. Apologetically, she admitted to being worried about his sister. She was a brilliant dealer, Walter was happy with her, and there was something wrong. She wasn't sure what. Perhaps Irene had only guessed that Walter was great, without really understanding him. In a way, and not intentionally, she was exploiting him. "You know she's selling 'Spruce Fox' to Chase Manhattan? It ought to be in the Whitney."

In fact the building's architects had only made an offer for the painting; it had not been sold. Her half-lie, however, only sharpened her point, which had touched Morris. Even as he disagreed, gently assuring her that Walter was in good hands, he told himself that she was right. He advised Priscilla to keep her doubts to herself. Walter entered, and the three of them talked of other things.

If Priscilla did not again mention Irene to Morris, she took care to cultivate the sympathy she knew he felt for her. He had been pleased to be confided in, pleased to give advice. She asked for more. She phoned him for critiques of Walter's friends. When they met at social gatherings, she begged a few minutes of him to be taught what Stella or Judd was trying to do. She consulted him about where to buy the best smoked salmon below Fourteenth Street. She paid extraordinary attention to everything he said. Irene aside, not since childhood had any woman so fussed over him; and Priscilla had wit and looks and youth. How could he resist?

Over a lunch Morris said to her, "You may be right about Irene." Priscilla bit her tongue to keep from grinning. She had been waiting in strenuous silence for these words.

"Do you think I'm good for Walter?"

"You're better than good." Morris was joking, Priscilla saw her goal within reach. She had her ally.

She still needed a treaty of alliance. Like Walter's loving her, Morris's liking her could be ended by a whim. She needed a partnership of acts and facts.

Soon after, she asked him why he had never made money

from his expertise. "Do you really like doing the spadework and seeing people cash in on it?" He replied that he liked his freedom. He could work when he wanted and sleep till noon. The prospect of dealing with framers, shippers, and accountants hardly appealed to him. "*I* could do all that," Priscilla said. Why should she bother? "To know what you know. I've got to learn about *something.*"

She lured him with young painters excited by the prospect of his sponsorship and with works that looked like sure bargains. After a week he confessed to being interested. He consented to a trial run.

Priscilla then took a critical step. She suggested to Morris that, given his competence and his high commitment, he should consider handling some of Walter's work. "Irene would never agree," he objected; "*Walter* would never agree." Priscilla said, "Let me try."

Walter had become a minor celebrity. Three glossy monthlies were scheduling articles on him. Museums were showing interest. Phoebe half-seriously proposed that he hire a social secretary. Elated by the public attention, Walter knew how to protect himself in private. His success never impinged on his attachment to Priscilla, and he even associated it with her advent: the unexpected happiness she had given him seemed to have expanded into the excitements of fame. Whatever he was doing, he remained peripherally aware throughout each day of the unharvested vocalizing with which she would rapturously conclude it.

Artists and their dealers are sure to have occasional misunderstandings. For Walter, any disagreement with Irene tapped a reserve of passion that his affair with Priscilla had not quite emptied. In November Irene sold "The Prepared Piano," one of his favorite paintings, to a collector in Des Moines. Walter was appalled: "He'll stick it in his silo, and it'll never be seen again."

That evening Priscilla suggested to Walter that such trouble should be avoided. Did he have to entrust all his paintings to one person? Walter replied that as he kept so many for himself, he felt obliged to give Irene the rest. Still, he agreed with Priscilla "in theory."

This gave Priscilla an opening. She had not yet told Walter that Morris had become a dealer. She broke the news the next day. Morris was exactly what Walter needed: a friend who understood his work, and who would never be irresponsible about selling it.

Maybe, Walter said; but what about Irene? When Priscilla again brought up the subject, he said Morris was a great idea, except that Irene would be dead set against it. Priscilla asked, What if she agreed? Why, said Walter, it's a great idea.

Priscilla made an appointment to see Irene. She knew what she had to do. Irene had no reason to share Walter's success with anyone, not even her brother. Priscilla would have to disguise the nature of the understanding between Walter and Morris—she would have to lie. If the truth came out later, Irene would know who had misled her. Priscilla accepted the risk because she had so far been winning. She had successfully courted Morris, she had held on to Walter, both men had accepted her plan. If carrying it out meant lying, she would lie and cope with the consequences when they occurred. If caught, she would claim that she had been misunderstood by Irene, or by Walter, or both. She might have to fight. She would have a position to fight for.

Priscilla reassured herself by declaring her problem to be essentially semantic. If I can find the right terms, Walter will think my proposal one thing, Irene something else. How will they talk when they discuss it? What words will they use? What questions will they ask? Certain words, like *sell,* could wreck her plans. "Irene, Morris has just sold my 'Last Duchess.' " The probability of such a statement made her shudder. She experienced moments of extreme doubt. She drew up lists of all

the words that might serve in discussions of commercial trans-
actions. So many other words could replace the coarseness of
buy and *sell: manage, handle, look after, take care of* . . .
Weren't such words the very ones Walter and Irene would use?
The proposal had sprung from a tense situation; it was bound
to remain slightly embarrassing to them and so encourage eu-
phemism. Priscilla chose to trust her luck and her lists. She
could monitor Walter's communications with Irene well
enough to anticipate danger.

She prepared a version of her proposal to accommodate, for
Irene's hearing, whatever Morris and Walter might say. Arriving at the Kramer Gallery for her appointment, she felt a new
confidence: she was representing Walter professionally.

Priscilla told Irene that Walter deeply regretted their disagreement over "The Prepared Piano." He felt that neither he
nor Irene should be blamed for what had happened. Couldn't
such misunderstandings be averted by asking a third party to
act as arbiter in the case of special paintings? He was proposing
her brother for this role. What did Irene think? Morris's discre-
tionary power would affect them only rarely. . . .

"Morris would be perfect," Irene interrupted. "I'd been hoping he'd do the same for me."

Priscilla did not understand this remark. "Walter will be—"

"He didn't need my approval. I wish the darling would grasp
that I'm working for *him.*" Irene paused. "Why didn't he talk
to me himself?"

"Because," Priscilla promptly answered, "he was embarrassed about your fight. So I agreed to stand in." Feeling like
a pro, she decided to gamble her stake forthwith: "If you called
him now, he'd love it." She watched Irene dial their number.

" . . . so I'm not good enough for you, Mr. Trale?" Irene said.
"You need a *man* to look after you. . . ."

She was smiling when she hung up. So was Priscilla as she
went out the gallery door.

"I made it sort of ambiguous," she ambiguously told Morris. "You'll be 'making decisions' about certain paintings. She got the message."

"Miss Priss, you're a star. May I wonder why?"

"I told you—to pick your elegant brains."

"Be my guest. Just one tiny *nasty* reason to console me?"

"I want Walter, you know that. It's tough out there for a brat like me."

"Sho 'nuff. And something to show Mummy and Daddy, too?"

"Oh, maybe. It should keep Maud out of my hair."

Priscilla was to receive more tangible rewards. Morris insisted she be paid money for work done; her willingness to help him for nothing merely reflected the condescension typical of her class. He offered her a percentage of the sales she prepared. She agreed to this. In time she pointed out how dependent this had made her. She had begun earning appreciable amounts of money, and he had recently been having some cardiac "discomfort": "Don't you go and die on me, I've still got lots more to learn! And you know I'm not employable, except by you. Without you, I'm nobody."

He said nothing at the time. A few days later he mentioned taking out a life-insurance policy that named her as his beneficiary. Priscilla burst into tears. Morris gave her one of his rare hugs. "Dear Priss, think how ecstatic I'd feel bankrolling you from the void!"

In her conquest of Morris, Priscilla perhaps achieved her most impressive exploit. Intelligent, cynical, mistrustful of women, he let a little shiksa win his confidence by sheer will. He had justified adopting her by her charm, her loyalty, her usefulness, hardly noticing her strangeness to him, and how strangely he himself had yielded to her bizarre determination.

Priscilla's dealings with Irene impressed Walter, reinforcing his attraction to her with an element of respect. When she asked for work to bring to Morris, he found it hard to say no to her. Although she did not ask often (in the end, Morris never sold any of his paintings), the works sometimes mattered greatly to him, if only because they were new. Priscilla fought him tenaciously on these occasions, making his consent both an instrument and measure of her strength. Hadn't he promised her? Couldn't he trust her? Didn't he love her? Each victory left her a little surer of her place in Walter's life; and as if to prove that place supreme, she challenged herself to convince him that he should give Morris the portrait of Elizabeth. It took all her prowess, and a little over a week, to wear down his refusal, resistance, reluctance. One morning she got up to find the portrait gone from the studio wall and standing by the front door, wrapped in a plastic sheet. For the first time since her arrival in September, Priscilla felt that she could call the city in which she lived her own.

Walter undoubtedly loved Priscilla, and he may have even enjoyed giving in to her. If he was annoyed at having to relinquish certain paintings, he lived too actively, and such losses came too rarely, for him to worry for long; and he was, after all, helping Morris. He saw the portrait of Elizabeth, however, as his primordial, self-made totem; as Priscilla herself had once written, not only his but him. Early that morning, he had remembered Phoebe's brilliantly faithful copy. She had painted it as a labor of love, love for him and for his work. She would not mind if he used it for a while to defend himself. While Priscilla slept, Walter, having put the original out of sight, left the copy where she would surely find it. She jubilantly transported it to Morris's before the day was out.

Irene and Morris

1945-1963

Even before his lover's death, Priscilla had caused Lewis pain. He had become morbidly jealous of her for having persuaded Morris to sell paintings. When playing the tormentor, Morris never failed to describe Priscilla's long and frequent visits to his apartment, which Lewis was allowed to enter barely once a month. Lewis thus pieced together the story of their unlikely friendship. He incidentally learned about Morris's lifelong relationship with Irene.

A week before Morris and Lewis met, Irene asked her brother to become artistic adviser to the Kramer Gallery. She had considered her offer carefully. The possibility had first occurred to her when her study of Walter's work had allowed her to admire the range and depth of her brother's insights. If Irene hesitated to hire him, it was only because she mistrusted her prejudices in his favor, and not only as her brother: as the person she had always loved most.

Irene approached Morris tactfully. She made it clear that she was not acting out of sisterly kindness. She emphasized that he would receive a good salary as well as a commission on sales, and that he could set his own schedule. She explained how deliberately she had made her choice. For months she had felt the need of bringing in an adviser. She had eliminated several eminent prospects—Rosenberg and Hess would have seen a threat to their independence in being associated with a gallery; Greenberg had tied himself up with the Rubin gang. She had concluded that Morris suited her perfectly, even if he was her brother. If the fact might harm him in the opinions of some, she had decided that such opinions belonged to fools. She would not settle for less than the best.

Irene's tact expressed both her esteem and her affection. For perhaps the first time, she was acting towards Morris without a trace of solicitude. She was recognizing him as her equal, not in intelligence (she had known that for years), but as an adult in charge of his own life. Irene had sometimes doubted that she would ever know this happiness. She had been watching over Morris since he was twelve.

Their parents were almost forty when Morris was born, six years after Irene; they were in their fifties when he reached adolescence. They had difficulty understanding their moody son, and he them. Irene became close to her brother when she began mediating the family stalemates that more and more frequently punctuated his teenage years. She had always liked Morris, and her liking developed into love as she came to recognize him as a gifted, erratic boy.

If Irene helped reconcile him to his life at home, she could do little for him in school, where in spite of her coaching his work remained mediocre. During Morris's freshman year of high school, she began to be seconded by a powerful confeder-ate: a history teacher called Arnold Loewenberg. This scholarly Austrian, whose studies had been long interrupted by the Anschluss and the war and who was only now finishing his doctoral dissertation, perceived beneath Morris's indifference to study a passionate and talented mind, which he set out to raise to its proper level. He befriended the boy, introducing him to the pleasures of painting and music, lending him records and books of reproductions, telling him stories of life in Europe, where history lay all around you and works of art were recognized as emblems of that history. Almost in passing he showed Morris how to work—how to analyze what he read, how to organize what he wrote. Mr. Loewenberg also demanded exceptional results of his pupil: first that he become the best in his class, afterwards that he meet the standards of a *Gymnasium* or *lycée*. After a while Mr. Loewenberg began giving Morris failing grades whenever his work fell short of these standards, and Morris's other teachers followed his lead, with varying and sufficient severity—a benevolent conspiracy that turned Morris into a prizewinning student by the end of the year.

Arnold Loewenberg and Irene became friends. He provided her with valuable advice during her days as a student of art history and invaluable encouragement at the start of her career; even so, she felt most indebted to him for adopting Morris. "You must never forget," he once told her, "that he is an intellectual"—he pronounced the word with lip-smacking emphasis—"perhaps will he someday become an extraordinary one, but in a land of greed and ball games he will of course experience hardships." From him she drew confidence that she was not tending a talented misfit.

Morris was strange, and enjoyed being strange. Unlike Lewis, he never suffered from friendlessness and related despairs. He judged his fellows shrewdly, knowing how to make them admire or fear or befriend him. At heart he kept distant, relishing distance as a privilege; and this, more than anything, worried Irene. She foresaw him doomed to the bitterness of the unloving.

The summer following Morris's first year with Mr. Loewenberg, his parents rented a cottage on Kiamesha Lake. Irene sometimes came for a weekend. One Friday she was given an unexpected ride and arrived in the country several hours early. It was mid afternoon. Her parents had gone out. Standing in the empty house, she heard Morris's voice. She looked for him outside, then in the garage, where she did not at first see him, because she found herself face to face with someone else: Morris's younger friend Irwin Hall, dressed in his undershorts. His hands had been tied behind his back with wire; he was standing on tiptoe, so as not to be choked by the noose of thin white rope strung from a joist above his head. As Irene, sustaining Irwin with one arm, began loosening the rope, she heard Morris laugh and saw him standing in the shadows by the wall.

"Don't worry, pardner," he said, "just my big sister."

The rope came free. Irene exclaimed, "You guys are wacko. Morris, get his hands untied."

Panting slightly, Irwin said, "We were playing." The noose had chafed a stripe under his chin. His cropped blond hair set off the liquid, greenish-brown eyes cheerfully turned towards his friend.

Irene blurted angrily at Morris, "You're a goddamned creep."

Normally fearful of her, he only grinned: "You don't know it, Irene, but this man's dangerous." He was rocking from side to side with excitement. Irene unfastened the wire.

Afterwards Morris explained to her that all his friends played "outlaw and sheriff." Several months later, in the attic of their house in the Bronx, she found a mail-order kit hidden under a jumble of old cartons. It included leather-and-chrome thongs, two whips, and a zipper gag. The implements looked new. They had never been used. Morris had ordered the kit, like the magazine in which it had been advertised, to nourish fantasies, not acts. Acts frightened him. Irene's reaction in the garage confirmed what he had already surmised: kit and magazine might belong to the public domain, his desires were still abnormal. They shocked him as they might have his father. After Irwin, he kept them to himself for two years. He then occasionally picked up a boy downtown and let his fancies free.

Once he mistook his prey and was himself beaten up. The damage proved hard to conceal, especially from an affectionate sister. Irene was again dismayed, less because of his sexual bent (she knew that sadomasochism was hardly "abnormal") than by a fear that it would reinforce his essential remoteness. She decided to encourage him forcefully in the activity to which, having proved his merits, he might be best tempted to commit himself; and with Arnold Loewenberg still her willing abettor, she persuaded Morris during his last year in high school to start seriously preparing for a scholarly future. Luckily, such a future had a special attraction for him: it inspired consternation in his parents. They feared it would permanently estrange their son. They could not, however, deny him the higher education so often proclaimed as one of their goals; and they were comforted when, of the colleges that accepted him, Morris chose NYU in preference to Harvard and Chicago. The choice would keep him closer to home, they felt, foolishly estimating in miles the distance between the Bronx and Washington Square.

Two years later Morris began majoring in art history. Irene played no part in this decision, which was initiated by a reading of Hegel's *Aesthetics:* art appealed to Morris as a historical register of society's metaphysical struggles. Irene continued nonetheless to influence his development. She had by now completed her studies, completed her marriage, begun her professional career. She introduced Morris, full of old theory and practice, to art that was local and fresh and to a society of artists still poor and unpublicized, bustling with experiment, with debate, with a sense of urgency worthy of a futures market. Morris was forced to confront his studies with present realities. He thrived.

That Morris should go to graduate school seemed obvious to everyone except his father, who said he should come home and manage the movie theaters, and his mother, who said he should just come home. Irene helped Morris win a scholarship and find a part-time job. She counseled him in his dealings with their parents. He won their approval at last and began his graduate studies at Columbia in the fall of 1954. He would have earned his doctorate in three or four years if his progress had not been arrested by an unexpected and serious heart attack.

Morris spent much of the next two years in hospitals. Times between confinements came to seem like vacations: for him, the reality that mattered was engendered by medical routines, by administered survival procedures. Morris's parents paid whatever the best care cost. Irene made sure he did get the best, in moments of crisis calling on specialists from other hospitals, from other cities. Irene saw Morris through tests and through days of waiting for their results, and through weeks when he was instructed to "do nothing but rest." She made him keep studying. She arranged for him to take examinations and write papers months late. When he was tempted to use his illness as an excuse for giving up, she did not let him forget the joy he found in the exercise of his gifts. Thanks to her, over the course of four and a half difficult years, he did much more than survive.

During this time Morris learned to think for himself. Now that he repeatedly had to face the possibility of dying, his studies took on new relevance. Because he might never see this drawing again, he looked at it with uncompromising attention. Words he heard or read or wrote reverberated like final declarations. He did not give up his philosophical bias, but he began looking at works of art less as symptoms of cultural history and more as individual actions. This change in his attitude did not concern subject matter, or symbolic values, or even form in any general sense. As far as he was concerned, the "individual actions" that interested him were always rendered in terms of appearance—touch, grain, and tone. Morris became uncannily sympathetic to contemporary art; as though the threat of death had cleansed his eyes of all that kept him from seeing it as its declared self: an enterprise dedicated to shifting the center of art to the surface of its medium, where it properly belonged. When he discovered Walter's painting, he knew how to do it justice.

The change in Morris was hidden from Irene by the unevenness of his life. She noticed the events of particular days: how he slept, what he ate and didn't eat, the strength of his voice, the hints for the future in his doctors' pronouncements. Like a mother with her child, she relegated questions other than those of health to some hypothetical future time. She wanted Morris to endure the least pain, his nights to pass restfully, his recovery to be assured. After relapses had brought her many moments of hopelessness, his seemingly unending convalescence ended at last, and he finally recovered. Her devotion had been rewarded. In the meantime she had lost touch with him. Her brilliant younger brother had turned into someone to be nursed. Having encouraged the development of his powers, she came to doubt their importance, thankful to have him alive.

His article on Walter astounded her. Morris had cultivated her surprise, telling her nothing about it, not even mentioning his study of Walter, whose work he had first seen while finishing his dissertation on Lewis Eilshemius. As soon as it appeared, Morris brought Irene his first copy of *New Worlds*—a gesture that made it clear whom his essay was intended to please. Not even he had foreseen the delight it gave her. It so absorbed her that she had to keep reminding herself who had written it. The later approval of Morris's fellow critics strengthened her conviction that even if one article did not make an oeuvre, Morris had fulfilled his promise. Irene continued to wake up thinking about him, but with jubilation now, not dread.

In opening her uptown gallery, Irene knew that her career

was at stake. Although she did not doubt her own capacities, she had often imagined during the first months of her venture having a counselor who could share the pressure of crises and in calmer times encourage her initiatives. She now asked herself, who could be fitter than Morris for such a role? He had endured crises of terrifying proportions. He had led her to Walter and to her success with him. She asked him to become her collaborator.

A month earlier Morris would probably have accepted her offer. He had loved Irene since childhood; he possibly owed her his life. Her response to his essay had satisfied him gloriously, and he recognized her subsequent adoption of Walter as an acknowledgment of his acumen. Against these bonds, however, were arrayed darker feelings no less tenacious. Irene was someone he had always been obliged to admire. She had been bigger, then older, always a model at home and at school. Even his debts to her confined him. As his protector, his mentor, and finally his guardian, she had proved herself strong and good; Morris had been condemned to strangeness, perversion, and sickness. The strong have the privilege of giving. The weak remain dependent and grateful. But was Irene really the stronger? Who had done the surviving?

When Priscilla insinuated that Irene was exploiting Walter, her words spread through Morris like a stain. Irene was exploiting him, too. He had discovered Walter, and she was turning the profit. When Irene made her proposal to him a few weeks later, it occurred to him that working for her would restore his old dependency in a new guise. Priscilla had shown him that he could make money on his own doing precisely what Irene wanted from him. Forgetting his success and his promise, playing the resentful orphan instead, he declined her offer.

Initially this refusal did not surprise Irene: she understood the reticence a big sister might inspire. She did her best to mitigate it. She invited Morris to set his own terms. She enlisted outsiders to plead her cause. Her efforts only hardened his position. (Robert Rosenblum declared that trying to change Morris's mind was like pushing gin at an AA convention.) He avoided Irene and her emissaries. A week and a half later, when Priscilla announced that Walter wanted Morris as *his* adviser, Irene gave up.

Even then Morris kept his distance from her, although she never again referred to her offer. He sometimes did; once to remark, in the worst faith, that even Lewis condemned her idea. Irene came to think of Lewis as an enemy.

At Morris's death, Irene cried all the more bitterly for the estrangement that had preceded it. She blamed herself harshly for it.

One morning in early June, Lewis met Priscilla and Walter on Carmine Street, and his disappointment in the painter turned to disgust. He went to see Irene that afternoon. Hoping to get rid of him, she met him in the gallery lobby. Lewis told her he knew the truth about Walter's business understanding with Morris. So did she, she replied. You don't, Lewis insisted. Irene said that she was too busy to argue; if he didn't agree, that was his problem. (She could hardly bear looking at him. He might have killed her brother.) Lewis lost his temper: "It's *your* fucking problem."

Irene left him standing there. Later she began wondering what might lie behind his outburst. When he called to apologize, she agreed to meet him again the next day.

This time Lewis showed patience. He told her about his affair with Morris, saying in conclusion, "I loved him more than I'll ever love anybody, and I know you did too." She asked him how Morris had died. Lewis supplied every painful detail. He then returned to the subject he had broached the day before: "Priscilla set up this deal—"

"Not really. It was Walter's idea."

"It wasn't. I thought you knew *that*. Morris would anyway decide which paintings of Walter's to sell—"

"Which *not* to sell."

Lewis explained the arrangement. Still bewildered, Irene was reluctant to understand. Lewis suggested they visit Morris's apartment. She could see for herself.

"It's impounded. We have to get a permit."

"*I* don't. How about Sunday night?"

Lewis had the key to Morris's back door, concealed by its bookcases from the police. Irene and Lewis crept through it, each with a flashlight.

Morris had hung Walter's five paintings in his bedroom. The portrait of Elizabeth faced the bed. Lewis went off to look for a sales list. Returning, he found Irene exploring the portrait with her mobile beam. Darkness hid her face; her voice revealed a changed mood. Lewis thought of his mother when he'd given her the stolen scarf. He shivered.

"Morris would never have sold—" he began.

"Of course he wouldn't."

"Even Priscilla—"

"Oh, Priscilla!" She paused. "As they say, the course of true love is paved with good intentions. . . . Let's get these things out of here."

"The paintings? *Now?*"

"What else? When else?"

Later that night, Irene justified her preposterous, no doubt illegal, ploy: if Walter was selling these paintings, she was contractually bound to help him. She spoke with the resolution of solid outrage.

On Tuesday Irene began discreetly offering Walter's paintings to reliable customers from out of town. On Friday Maud bought the portrait of Elizabeth. Three other paintings were sold before the end of July, the last on August first. Irene then phoned Walter to tell him what she had done.

She did not blame him for his role, or excuse herself. She thought that probably he would angrily announce that he was leaving her gallery. He only sounded perplexed. Hadn't Priscilla told her about the deal with Morris? Hadn't Irene called him to say she approved? "Look," he said, "basically it was so Morris could make some money. Is that so terrible? He certainly deserved it."

"I agree. Now, tell me, *cher coeur,* how did Priscilla deserve it? Oh, no, spare me the sordid details. . . ." Irene was finally grasping the truth.

"Priscilla?"

"There's something I'd like to know: what did she say I'd agreed to?"

"Every so often Morris would sell a painting of mine."

"To me she *never* said anything about selling—just giving you advice. Of course I know he was selling other work and splitting the proceeds with her." Walter's silence filled up her pause. "You know he and Priscilla went halves?" Another pause. "Ask her."

"She's away for the day."

"I'm sure she can explain it all. Still, I'd listen to her very carefully. You don't happen to own a tape recorder?"

Walter asked who had bought the portrait of Elizabeth. Irene began feeling remorse. She had behaved unfairly to Walter, who had only acted foolishly, not betrayed her. However, she had not behaved unfairly to Priscilla.

Walter was not thinking of Priscilla, not yet. After Irene hung up, he at once called Maud and told her that the real "Portrait of Elizabeth" had remained in his hands.

Pauline and Maud

SUMMER 1938

Maud Ludlam once told Elizabeth that she'd had two children: her daughter, Priscilla, and her sister, Pauline.

Their mother had died when Maud was eleven and Pauline five. Afterwards, their father retained the best governesses for their care. When governesses began losing authority, Maud gradually turned into a foster mother. By then she had emerged from the worst of adolescence. She liked her role.

She also liked Pauline, who was sweet-tempered and zany, with whims that she clung to indomitably. From the age of three until her first brush with a policeman she went swimming bottomless, clad only in a strikingly superfluous bra. At six she started taking riding lessons; for her first horse show, she was given English riding togs, which she wore happily enough, except for the boots: if she dressed up, she said, it was going to be heels or nothing. For years she startled judges by riding in black cap, black coat, white shirt and stock tie, jodhpurs, and high-heeled dress shoes (usually Maud's, padded with cotton). When Pauline was eleven, an elegant Chinese guest of her father's showed her how to handle chopsticks: thenceforth she refused to eat with anything else, carrying her own stainless-steel pair wherever she went, using it, to the stupefaction of one and all, to neatly dissect thick pies and steaks.

Pauline's quirks sometimes embarrassed others, never Maud. She admired Pauline's spunk. Far less daring herself, she aspired merely to pass unnoticed. Her mother's death had bequeathed her a chronic doubt as to her own reality.

Like a coach training a natural athlete, Maud encouraged Pauline through puberty into young womanhood. The sisters enjoyed themselves, Pauline dashing around, Maud feeling useful as her loyal supervisor. Close though they were, they showed tolerance rather than understanding towards one another. They often said they should do more together—go to Europe, for instance.

Their father, Paul Dunlap, had had a long career as a sensible investment counselor. He had increased tenfold the small capital inherited from their grandfather, a real-estate developer in Buffalo. He had speculated on America's entry into the Great War, foreseen the postwar boom, guessed at the crash. He retired a millionaire.

After his wife's death, Paul Dunlap for several years gave up family life. Later, impressed by Maud's grades and her seriousness, he began confiding in her. Pauline stood outside adult concerns, with all the charm, and all the impertinence, of the household cocker.

Paul Dunlap established his preference for Maud in practice and in writ. He taught her what he had learned as an investor, or tried to—Maud had earned her good marks in literature and languages, not economics. When he gave her money so she could learn about handling large sums, Maud only learned that large sums made her long for professional advice. She did not see that her father, muttering vague praises of primogeniture, intended to leave her nine-tenths of his estate. He was making her the head of the family.

Pauline was not instructed in money matters. From Maud she gradually found out that she would have little control of the family fortunes, while Maud would have a great deal. After their father's death, Maud and one professional trustee became responsible for Pauline's capital. Pauline told herself, better Maud than some fathead at the bank. The disproportion of their inheritance did not distress her. It did not affect her life: Maud gave her the money she so happily continued to spend, and she readily acquiesced to Maud's suggestion that, to enhance Pauline's "eligibility," they pretend that their father had left them equally rich.

Maud had qualms. She asked Allan if he couldn't devise a way of evening their fortunes; Allan told her that it was clearly impossible. For the time being, Maud knew, problems existed only in her conscience. She nevertheless could not forget that a wall of almost a million prewar dollars had been raised between them and that it might someday prove more rugged than sisterly scrupulousness and trust.

In the shadow of that wall, Pauline had already changed. She had stopped growing up. Now twenty-two, she once again began deferring to Maud as she had at fifteen. By the time summer came, Maud felt as though she had been depressingly consigned to an older generation. Pauline came to her for every kind of advice. She refused to buy clothes without her, refused to wear them without her blessing: whenever she left the house, she would exhibit herself to Maud with a cheery "How do I look?" that for all its apparent impulsiveness soon became an ineluctable rite. Like any dutiful young girl, Pauline provided Maud with unasked-for, meticulous accounts of all she did; and she flattered her (Maud could find no nicer word) with equally needless attentions, with notes and even little gifts of flowers or a book, on every faintly memorable occasion in Maud's life—the day their mother died, the day she first met Allan, the day her next period was due. Maud groaned inwardly at each of these tributes, never daring to tell Pauline how much they saddened her. She had once courted their father in similar fashion, until one day he firmly stopped her: "It's love insurance. Save yourself the trouble. You've got mine."

Pauline had Maud's love and must have known it. What she wanted, what she feared losing, was permission to go on playing as she always had. She did not want to talk or think about money that Maud had and she hadn't, just as she averted her eyes whenever she drove past the treeless, set-back, economy-size supermarket that had wrecked the alignment of their town's main street. She was determined to pretend that nothing had changed.

Her attitude reinforced Maud's own reluctance to set matters straight, as Allan kept urging her to do: Pauline would not live with them much longer, she must start taking care of herself. Maud protested, "I'm part of the problem. How can I help her solve it?"—a good excuse for doing nothing.

Early in July, in this summer of her twenty-third year, a few weeks after graduating from Wellesley, Pauline met Oliver Pruell. He began taking her out. Ten days later Pauline rose early to catch her sister at breakfast:

"He's giving me a big rush. I guess he's serious. He's infuriatingly proper."

"That's not necessarily bad."

"Two years out of college, and risqué means holding hands?"

"He's not a fairy?"

"No. Maybe. I have a feeling he 'knows' I'm rich."

"What's his name?"

"May I keep that one secret from you? He's from a good family. He works on Wall Street, too. If he's not after my charms, though, he must want . . . Maud, how can I tell?"

Maud considered herself a poor counselor concerning men; during her adult life she had known only one intimately. She had met Allan three years earlier. They had quickly fomented a friendly complicity: her self-doubt found a perfect complement in his assurance. They had "had fun," going to the theater, dancing late. He had proposed to her as though he were doing her a favor he enjoyed. Her friends warned her that he was thinking of her wealth to come. Her father disagreed, and she, knowing Allan, knew better. She was a little surprised when, three weeks after they had moved into their well-appointed East Side apartment, she found the bill for the rent on her desk. Allan took for granted that she would pay for that, for their trips, for their box at the Met if she wanted it, while he assumed the cost of their cars and his clubs. Maud hardly minded, because Allan was otherwise proving the best of husbands. From their courtship Maud had expected that he would last as a companion; and he had. She had not expected passion. Months passed, and Allan came home to her every evening like a sailor on liberty. Maud found herself in love with him.

(Later, when the war abducted Allan to the Pacific and she turned a horrifying thirty, Maud took a lover. Or rather he took her; or rather he did *not* take her. A slightly impoverished Baltimorean, of exquisite extraction and no less exquisite sensibilities, began pursuing her ardently. At last she yielded. Maud wanted to be confirmed in her bodily beauty; she got homage of a more speculative kind. Michael, capable of satisfying her, explained that he treasured that consummation so highly that only marriage could properly enshrine it. He knew her true worth—he had a friend at her bank, as she learned before showing him the door.)

Maud gave her sister evasive counsel.

A month later, Pauline was ensnared by the losing streak into which Oliver and the martingale had lured her. She owed her beau six hundred and thirty-five dollars, as well as her virginity. She decided to earn the money and asked Maud to help her find a job. She said she wanted to work: "Anything. Selling Fuller Brushes. I'm a disgrace as it is."

Maud was pleased. She foresaw wonderful benefits in Pauline's decision. She might discover the value of money (by which Maud somehow meant its irrelevance). She might earn, if not her living, at least her rent. She might leave Maud and *her* money behind her.

Maud sent Pauline to one of her oldest friends, a man of wealth and local influence, the president of "The Association" (the Association for the Improvement of the Breed of Thoroughbred Horses). Maud had failed to observe that Pauline had taken his son as her constant companion. She could not guess that it was because of this young man that she wanted to earn money.

Mr. Pruell, however, had often noticed Oliver and Pauline together, most recently sharing a bag of chips as they sauntered under the high elms of Broadway. He agreed to see Pauline (who told herself that, after all, a job was a job), but he had no interest in finding her work. He wanted her to look after his son. He confided his concern for him; he showed her Oliver's erotic hymns to Elizabeth. She fell definitively in love.

She wanted to marry. Oliver said they couldn't afford it. Pauline decided to involve her sister. She intercepted her on her way out to dinner.

"Did you get your job?" Maud asked her cheerfully.

"I love Mr. Pruell—I never really knew him."

"He's a dream, isn't he?"

"I'm dating Oliver Pruell—the one I told you about a month ago? It's serious?" The questions in Pauline's voice invited Maud's approval.

"How wonderful!" Maud answered, in dismay. How could she not have known?

The next morning she learned that she had no companions

in ignorance: her "discreet inquiries" about Oliver became comic as each of her friends volunteered straight-to-the-point evaluations at the mention of his name. According to most, he was handsome, polished, very much a Pruell, less admired than liked, no rogue—not one to marry a girl for her money, not with his expectations. Not absolutely reliable: two years ago, after a summer-long affair with Elizabeth, he had ditched her.

Pauline again spoke to Maud. She wanted Oliver to marry her. ("Of course I'm not pregnant!" "But you're sleeping with him?" "It was like pulling hen's teeth, but yes.") Although "mad about her," Oliver thought it greater madness to live on his present salary.

"He says wait till I'm twenty-five—till I 'come into my own,' as he puts it."

"How patient of him!"

As Maud feared, the problem rapidly got worse. Allan went back to the city the next day. With no invitation to rescue her, Maud dined with Pauline, who promptly asked her: "Can I talk about Oliver?"

"Will it help?"

"Something wrong with him?"

"Don't be silly."

"He says it's no dice." Maud wondered why this could not reasonably end the matter; however, they would not then be having this conversation. Pauline went on, "It wouldn't take much to change his mind, I think. Or do I mean 'I don't think'?"

"Are you sure he wants to marry you?"

"Oh, yes. He swears he'd marry me if only—" Pauline stopped.

"So there's a bill of particulars?"

"Oh, Maud, *he* promised me and *I* looked for the answers. I thought that maybe—"

"Could you explain the appeal of someone who insists on more money?"

"I should never have put it that way. Anyway, we *have* the money, don't we?"

"That's hardly the point."

"What *is* the point of having money if you can't use it to get what you want? You always said I should be happy."

"*That's* the point. And after all," Maud continued, knowing she could not ward off Pauline indefinitely, "what could we do?"

"If I got my share now, that would help—even if it's not as much as he thinks."

"It's impossible. Legally, I mean. You must know that."

"Sure. So what if I took my share out of what you have, and I pay it back to you at nine-oh-five A.M. on my twenty-fifth birthday?"

"I can't."

"You say you never know what to do with it all. And think: from now on I wouldn't cost you another penny."

"It isn't up to me. It's Daddy's money—"

"Oh, come on!"

"He *cared* about what happened to it. I don't like what he decided, but I *promised* I'd respect it. Even if I didn't, you know most of my money is in trust, and I'm only one trustee. It wouldn't work. I can't go against his wishes. Not to mention his will."

"Darling, who knows what he'd think now? Why don't you stop using a dead man to hide behind? If you disapprove of Oliver, just say so."

"It's not hiding. I'm responsible—that's the way the money was left to us. I wish *you* had it. My disapproving of Oliver has nothing to do with it."

"You see? That's why you're talking this junk. You wish I had the money! Do you think you'd have gotten Allan without it, with your big feet?"

Pauline left the table. The front door presently slammed. In the living room Maud refilled her glass with the dregs of shaken martinis. Sitting down, she told herself: I mustn't let her think such things about me. The glass sloshed in her hand. She had been blindsided by Pauline's attack.

She came down early in the morning to wait for her sister. Maud said to her that she had forgotten something they could do. The house in the city had been left to Maud outright. It was now rented. If Pauline wanted it, the tenants could be moved out by the spring.

Since the night before, she added, she had realized that she could ask to have the allowance from Pauline's trust fund increased, even doubled.

Pauline accepted. While she was pleased to have more income of her own, she reckoned it was the handsome corner house on Sutton Square that would appease Oliver.

During the night her feelings towards Maud had undergone considerable change. After rushing outside, she had promptly divested herself of her years of submissiveness; and like a snake in springtime, resentment had at once raised its sullen head. Again and again she angrily reminded herself of the unfairness of her position. She was as clever as Maud, she was prettier, and she was so much poorer! She would never have let *her* sister suffer from an old man's whim.

By morning, practice had hardened her indignation. When Maud made her offer, Pauline found it less than her due. Maud's concessions chiefly gratified her by putting Maud permanently in the wrong.

Soon afterwards, before the engagement was announced, Maud chose to travel. The season was ending, and she had time before the wedding to make a long-postponed excursion to Europe. Offended by her departure, Pauline let her resentment flourish. If Maud had stayed, even an angry sister might have noticed that she only wanted peace for herself. Instead, Maud allowed Pauline to turn her into a kind of witch. The happiness of Pauline's engagement, the publicity of her marriage, glittered against a dark background of indifference and betrayal.

Or, if Maud had stayed, Pauline might at least have been able to vent her resentment. Maud would have suffered and survived, and Pauline's anger would have expired into acceptance, if not understanding. Maud left. For many years Pauline saw as little of her as she could, altogether avoiding the familiarity that had so long sustained her. Her indignation had nowhere to go except into a sodden pit of recollection and foreboding, where it lay, impotent and alive, year after year, waiting to emerge on some marvelous day of wrath—a brooding existence, exuding ropy feelers of revenge.

Or, if Pauline's happiness with Oliver had lasted, her rancor might have simply been forgotten. Pauline never interested Oliver except as a prize. He soon neglected her. He discouraged her from working, from having children—when he learned the truth about her inheritance, he declared that in such difficult times children cost more than they could comfortably afford.

So Pauline's resentment lived on, a ponderous beast dormant in its gloomy trough. Twenty-five years after her marriage, her friend Owen Lewison told her one evening that Allan and Maud, for reasons unknown to him, had sequestered a valuable painting by Walter Trale, improbably claiming that it had been stolen. He asked Pauline to find out if the picture had been hidden in Allan's apartment. "High Heels" accepted, with a vengeance, with no illusions about her task: she would seduce Maud's husband and implicate her sister in a dubious scheme. Her night with Allan, however, left her dissatisfied. She liked him more than she wanted to; and this inexplicably reawakened her age-old attachment to Maud. She was confused. She told herself that sleeping with Allan could not be counted as revenge if her sister did not know about it.

She must pay her a visit and make sure she knew what had happened.

The beast had come forth from its pit. In the light of day, it looked less like a dragon than like a lost lamb.

Maud and Priscilla
1940-1963

Maud, no fool, did not regret that she had money to be liked for. She hoped, less shrewdly, that it might inspire in others tolerance for her ordinary self. She did not like talking about money, because the subject made her feel foolish, and her foolishness made her cringe for her father's sake. She had learned so little from him, and forgotten so much. Maud had tried managing the far from negligible sums her father had left her outright. She had even had conspicuous successes: in 1938, she added oil stocks to her portfolio after they had shrunk to half their value and before their precipitous rise. Her prescience, however, was invariably based on irrelevant facts. She had, for instance, no inkling of the oil industry's forthcoming boom, only observed that its stocks provided a higher yield than her other securities. She made costly mistakes, such as missing a chance to buy early into natural gas. After the third such mistake, she abandoned investment policy to her advisers.

Her withdrawal from finance sadly recalled to Maud her

father's long efforts to train her. A difficult master, he had taught her by examples from which few rules could be drawn; and the prime rule read: in money matters, do not look for rules. While she had believed everything he said, her belief was grounded in faith, not understanding. In resisting Pauline's demands, she had, exceptionally, acted with a reasonable conviction: she could accept as plain good sense her father's dictum that fortunes should be kept intact. Declaring this to sentimental Pauline would have sounded like rank hypocrisy; so Maud had taken refuge, with lesser hypocrisy, in the letter of her father's intentions.

In promising to carry out these intentions, Maud implicitly subjected her future offspring to the rule that had favored her over Pauline: one of them would inherit the bulk of her fortune. As it turned out, Maud had only one child.

When Priscilla came of age, Maud told herself, I know too much and too little about money, but at least I know something. I might have done worse. Priscilla should find out what money can do. Of course, Maud could not teach her. On the other hand, if efficient Priscilla had inherited her grandfather's flair, simply using money might be training enough.

Maud had mostly let Priscilla solve her own problems since, from infancy, she had proved so much better at it. All the same, Maud had looked after her conscientiously. Tempted though she may have been to leave her clever daughter to her own devices, she realized that even the cleverest child cannot foresee the measles or the injustice of lower mathematics. She provided Priscilla with the elements of a healthy life, she found good doctors to supervise her growth, at school she persuaded sympathetic teachers to monitor her progress. Otherwise, Maud simply kept herself available, although she hardly knew why. At eleven Priscilla had her appendix removed. Maud sat with her through her recovery, noticing ruefully that it was Priscilla who kept *her* cheered up.

Diffident Maud enjoyed having a bright, athletic, sociable

daughter. She had what many parents strive for: a child who surpasses them. Maud's own successes always struck her as due to luck, like her timely purchase of oil stock, or too secret to qualify as achievements. Her house, even her garden belonged to this domain of secrecy. Allan pleaded with her to show them to the world; Maud insisted on keeping them in the family.

Behind the house there had once stretched an acre and a half of lawn, conventionally hedged and planted with a few unsurprising trees. Within this space Maud plotted an arrangement of outdoor rooms, cunningly varied and juxtaposed. One room was shaded for sunny days, its neighbor wide open to the skies; some were planted by color (white, blue, rose); others flowered according to the seasons, from the primrose-speckled spring oval walled with high rhododendrons to the autumn rectangle, which was bordered with a multitude of chrysanthemums set against severely clipped hedges of golden-leaving beech. She favored old-fashioned plants—lilies, dahlias, Portland roses; syringa, deutzia, sweet shrub—perhaps because at the heart of all her design lay a simple experience of her girlhood. One day in May, playing hide-and-seek at her Massachusetts cousins', she had concealed herself between two ancient lilac bushes in full bloom. For a long minute she saw the world through their sun-fretted clusters, half suffocating in their heady stench. At the farthest corner of her garden she raised a small room that to her justified the rest: a perfect square of lilac hedges, trimmed along their sides and growing freely at their tops, each May modulating around their perimeter through every imaginable gradation of blossom, from wine-red to palest mauve and back again, the transitions tempered by flowers of the white lilac with which the other bushes were interspersed. Only Allan and Priscilla ever accompanied Maud there; and, of course, John. John had come to work as handyman for her father and stayed on. Not because of loyalty to the family or a predilection for gardening: the intensity Maud brought to her tasks inspired him with a lasting enthusiasm of his own. Except for Allan, no one knew her as he did.

Outside her private world, Maud had rarely experienced the special satisfaction of seeing what she wanted and getting it. Weather permitting, Priscilla did nothing else. One day her fourth-grade teacher called her a dunce; two weeks later she moved to the top of her class. At eleven she saw a movie with Sonja Henie; by the end of the winter she was competing as a figure skater. She successfully pursued popularity, even at boarding school, where she showed a tendency to collect boy-friends. Her classmates forgave her because hers were too old for them.

Any parents would have taken pride in her. For Allan, with his busy career, pride sufficed. Maud, with much less to do, wished she'd had a live mother whose example she could follow. While Priscilla's successes reassured her, Maud suspected that whatever her upbringing Priscilla would have become a prodi-gious achiever. A pang of regret sometimes transfixed her when she thought of her daughter: had she ever been truly useful to her?

Priscilla showed self-reliance from the time she could crawl. She saw the world as a nest of probable satisfactions. Obstacles like her fourth-grade teacher pointed towards bigger opportuni-ties. Only once had she known complete helplessness. When she was fourteen, during her summer vacation, she had made friends with Lewis Lewison. Drawn to him by his unlikeness to other boys and by a shyness close to surliness, she had given up her hefty eighteen-year-olds to pursue him. At last he kissed her, and on one hot afternoon took her into the empty barn behind his parents' house, where he came to grips with her strong, skinny body, and with his own. Her resistance to his assault enraged him less than his inability to carry it through, which made him wild as he lay on her, rubbing against her flesh like a child trapped in a closet and banging the door. She had been terrified and, finding herself trapped, had lost control of herself.

Lewis ran off. Louisa found, washed, and consoled her. She promised to attend to Lewis and urged Priscilla to speak to her mother. Priscilla agreed. Maud would certainly show compassion, and Priscilla's "accident," if childish, had been provoked by grown-up business. She could talk to Maud as an equal.

Priscilla was less sure of this when she saw her mother. Maud appeared in the door of the house and looked at Priscilla with a not unfamiliar, not unaffectionate, not unwary look: Tell me everything is fine, it said, and I'll go away.

Priscilla was sitting alone in the front room. She had never done this. Perplexed, Maud stood still in the doorway: "I think I'll have some tea."

"Want me to make it?"

"That would be lovely. Darjeeling, please."

"I saw Lewis this afternoon."

"What a lucky boy! How does Gene feel about your leaving him for a fifteen-year-old? *I* saw Phoebe. As far as I could tell, she was teaching her counselors knots."

"I'd have done better going on that trip with her."

Maud put down two teacups and closed the cabinet doors. She groped for words that would invite Priscilla to go on, and succeeded in not finding them. Irritation with what she could not say made her voice tremble: "You should have a brand-new sleeping bag, at least." She laughed foolishly to cover the tremor.

Priscilla laughed too and squeezed Maud's arm. "It's no problem. The other guys will take me whenever I want. Show me what you're wearing tonight?"

They drank their tea. Maud never heard about Lewis in the barn.

As a rule, Priscilla confided in Maud. She told her all a mother might want to know. In delicate matters she often spoke after the fact, leaving Maud with foregone conclusions. When, a few months after her college graduation, Priscilla announced her liaison with Walter, Maud was not surprised that she had already moved in with him. As usual, she had to like it or lump it.

Maud missed Priscilla during the following winter. She missed what they had never had together. It seemed to Maud that her daughter had grown up in one brief flurry of yesterdays, while she was gazing out the window at an Adirondack sunset. Maud had borne her; Priscilla had grown up without her. She could do little about that now.

She could do something. She remembered her father (oh, with him things *had* happened, she had been mixed up with him, she had hung on his words and arms), she remembered her father's determination to train her. If nothing else, she could at least teach Priscilla that money was an opportunity to be mastered. Priscilla might then emerge from the blindness that afflicted Maud and Pauline. Maud knew that, like the moon in the sky or the trees in the woods, money surrounded them too naturally to ever be thought about. Maud could not blame Priscilla if she "didn't really care" about money—she never asked her to go out at night to make sure the moon was shining and the trees growing. Such things looked after themselves. Even Allan, who himself knew and cared about money, showed no anxiety concerning Priscilla: "She's fortunate *not* to have to worry. That's what 'fortune' means. She'll learn when the time comes."

Allan's opinion was wasted on Maud. She brooded over the problem on melancholy winter days. She finally came up with a scheme. She could hardly influence Priscilla directly. She must create a foregone conclusion of her own: a situation where Priscilla would be obliged to use money and make decisions about it.

Maud conceived her project in early May, when spring was

warming belatedly the upper reaches of the Hudson. Several
weeks later, she went to her bank in the city and put it into
effect. She gave instructions to have twenty thousand dollars
transferred yearly to Priscilla for the next ten years. Priscilla
could spend the income; she could only invest the capital. She
would *have* to invest it.

As she made these arrangements, Maud thought less and less
about Priscilla and more and more intently of her dead father.
When she had done her part, she asked the bank officials to
inform Priscilla. The scheme should be presented to her as the
working out of an old covenant. Maud told herself she should
spare Priscilla the nuisance of feeling grateful. She had performed her duty in the manner of an invisible guardian, as an
agent of impersonal benevolence.

These mildly insane precautions at once aroused Priscilla's
suspicions. She recognized Maud's hand. Priscilla recalled that
one afternoon when she was nine she had returned from school
two hours late and found her mother conferring on the terrace
with a policeman. The next day Maud had a television set (then
new and rare) installed in Priscilla's bedroom: a bribe never to
come home late again. Priscilla thought, I have now committed
a bohemian cohabitation, and Mama is bribing me to give it up.
That much Priscilla could understand. But the scale of the
gesture! Giving away two hundred thousand dollars suggested
motives less generous—a tax break, for instance. Priscilla did
not mind. She simply wanted to know.

The early summer had been vexing to her. Dedicated to her
partnership with Morris, she had not sold anything since his
death—their paintings had all been impounded in the dead
man's apartment. She hoped eventually to recover them, at
least those by Walter; after all, no one else knew about them.
With such a stock, and with Morris's life insurance as working
capital, she could look forward to the future. Meanwhile, she
had to abide the slow course of the law. She had little else to

do. Walter spent his days hard at work. Most of her friends had
gone away. When the bank told her of Maud's scheme, she
decided to get out of the city and unearth her mother's secret.
She phoned Maud to announce her arrival on August first in
time for lunch.

Priscilla's call surprised Maud only passingly. She had suspected that her precautions would prove wishful. Initially resigned to her visit, by the time Priscilla arrived Maud had come
to resent it. Elizabeth had distressed her by leaving for the day.
Later, Allan had called to make a disagreeable confession.
Watching her daughter emerge from a taxi and stride buoyantly
towards the house, she shuddered. My God, she's like Pauline.

On the shady west porch the women settled into upholstered
white wicker armchairs. Declining a drink, noticing that her
mother's glass was filled with green chartreuse, Priscilla tilted
her chair forward, sat pertly upright, and declared her thanks:
whatever Maud's reasons, Priscilla was stunned by her kindness. She spoke at length, underscoring her gratitude.

Maud did not respond. She appeared hardly to be listening.
Something, Priscilla thought, is unusually wrong. She nevertheless kept up a cheerful monologue. She talked enthusiastically
about her life with Walter. "I see, I see," Maud at last interrupted, only then referring to the pretext of her daughter's visit:
"They made everything clear in the letter, didn't they? They put
everything in the letter?"

"Yes, the letter was absolutely clear. They put everything in
it, Mama, except you."

"Oh, me—" Maud sighed, waving to a ghost beyond the
lawn.

"I came here for you."

"You're sweet, but you know, I only had to go through the
motions—hardly worth taking credit for."

"But you deserve credit. As for going through the motions—
Mama, isn't your elbow getting a little sore?"

"What do you mean?" Maud wrily answered. "It's only my seventeenth drink."

"Can you tell me one thing? Is it Allan?"

"He spoke to *you* about it?"

Allan had called Maud earlier. Fearful she would learn about the doomed gelding he had helped insure, he had described his part in the business. Although Maud did not fully understand him, Allan's discomfiture became painfully apparent to her.

"He didn't speak to me. Someone saw them," Priscilla explained. "I'm sorry, Mama. Who would have dreamed it of Aunt Paw?"

Even unwily Maud had the sense not to budge. She sipped her chartreuse and stared through the beetle-butted screen: "Tell me what you know."

"Oh, 'know'! When was it, the night before last, a friend driving across Sixty-third Street had to stop behind a taxi, and she saw Papa and Aunt Pauline get out together, outside the apartment. They were acting—" Maud had risen and started crossing the porch. She tripped over a board as smooth as any other. "Oh, Mama!"

Maud was stumbling with humiliation. Not because of what she was hearing: because she was hearing it from her daughter. She felt outraged by Priscilla's presence, and losing her balance didn't help. She kept silent.

"Mama! It's no fun, but it won't matter. Papa adores you and always will." She barely paused. "You don't have to drink brandy before lunch."

"It's not brandy. I was up at five, and I had my lunch at eleven," Maud declared. Her own anger bewildered her.

"OK, Mama."

Maud squeezed her crystal snifter so hard that it splintered. "Damn you!" she blurted, meaning to say, Damn it.

Priscilla stared at her eagerly. "It's awful seeing you—"

"So why bother coming? I've been so much better since— hah!" Maud chose to steam rather than explain.

"Mama," Priscilla went on, her voice dropping a minor third, "I can't enjoy your becoming a lush."

"Is that what you came here to tell me?"

"I came here, and it *is* a long ride, to tell you—I've already said it. Or maybe you weren't listening."

"Of course I was. I'm glad you're pleased."

"Aren't *you* pleased? I thought my coming up might mean something to you. I didn't know you'd just been 'going through the motions'—as usual."

"Anyway, enjoy the money." Maud had cut her left little finger.

"Mama, you're such a dope!"

"Is there something wrong with enjoying money?"

"Shit! Why do I sit here talking to this flop? Listen, I just inherited a hundred thousand dollars. Not to mention what I've made on my own, you'll be glad to know."

"I *am* pleased. You never said a word—"

"I've been selling paintings. I've been working with Morris Romsen—you know, the critic. Walter Trale gave us an option on his best paintings."

"Not all of them, surely. He didn't give you the portrait of Elizabeth."

"Oh, yes, he did."

"How funny. I bought it last month, and not from you, Miss Kahnweiler."

"What are you talking about?"

"I mean that I bought—that five or six weeks ago Allan and I bought Walter Trale's 'Portrait of Elizabeth' from Irene Kramer. I can't show it to you because your father's taken it elsewhere. Give him a call."

Wasting no time in conjectures as to how Irene had recovered the portrait (she was Morris's sister and heir, after all), Priscilla made silent calculations. She could get back to the city by six; that afternoon an opening was scheduled at the Kramer Gallery. Her father could wait. She had to see Irene.

"Mama, can you drive me to the station?"

"Ask John. He's out in back. I'm going to have a little lie-down."

At two-thirty Maud called her bank in the city to cancel her scheme. She had completed her new instructions and was about to hang up when unforeseen grief overcame her. She asked the bank official to wait and muffled the phone while her sobs subsided. She then said, "Disregard what I told you. Don't change anything, except for one thing. Change the name of the beneficiary. Please delete 'Priscilla Ludlam' and write in 'Pauline Pruell.' Née Dunlap. Send the papers for me to sign as soon as you can."

Maud and Elizabeth
JULY - SEPTEMBER 1963

" . . . ONE WEEK," MAUD WAS SHOUTING PRECISELY, "what's a week in a lifetime?"

No less loudly, no less deliberately, Elizabeth answered, "A lifetime? And you still want that milktoast?"

"That's for me to decide!" Maud cried (quickly whispering, "He's coming downstairs").

"(Nice going.) It's him or the portrait, you can't have both!"

"You're disgusting!"

"It's my portrait, isn't it?"

"*Of* you—hardly yours!"

"Cut the crap, Mrs. Miniver. I need something to show for my week. (Where *is* he?)"

"(I'll go look.)"

Tiptoeing out, Maud at once noticed that the portrait of Elizabeth was missing from the library, where for a week it had stood unpacked and unhung. After looking into the music

room, the den, and the dining room—all empty—she rejoined
Elizabeth. Together they watched Allan, encumbered with the
painting, walking to the station wagon that he had parked on
the public road.

"I was sure he'd come charging in."

"What was that phone call?" Maud asked.

Until today, Maud had not seen Elizabeth since the year
before she married, and she had forgotten ever meeting her. She
would not have recognized her name if, a year ago, she had not
read her daughter's thesis on Walter Trale. Its account of his
friendship with Elizabeth touched her because they had met in
this very town, where Maud had been summering with her
family. She vividly recalled the evening parties where men wore
white double-breasted dinner jackets and women organdy and
organza. She had gone swimming that summer in a new elastic,
white-belted bathing suit, and she had become engaged to Allan
(when he proposed, she had on high-waisted, pleated slacks,
with a lawn kerchief over her hair). Her father was still alive,
Pauline still her happy protégée. She remembered Walter, then
only a boy, younger even than Pauline, his talent all the more
glamorous for his youth, so that he was lionized by the horse-
and-dog set. Maud felt less sure about Elizabeth. An image
came back to her of someone beautiful and a little "wild,"
someone she could not place with certainty; someone in an
older crowd who had disappeared after a few years; someone
with the bright precarious youth of those not altogether young.
What had that woman now become? (Like Maud, Elizabeth
must be past fifty. What had she herself become? What had she
done to attain this once-faraway age?)

During the months that followed her reading of Priscilla's
account, Maud sometimes remembered to ask acquaintances
about Elizabeth. Their answers whetted her curiosity. Elizabeth
had married a Brazilian—or was it a Lebanese?—millionaire.
She had married a carpet salesman from Topeka. She had

remained single. No man could win her. No decent man would have her. She had turned into an alcoholic, or a drug addict, or a nymphomaniac. Hadn't she proclaimed herself a lesbian? Purest rumor—a rumor probably started by Elizabeth herself, after she had gone into business. Career women often find it best not to marry. Elizabeth had had a brilliant career. Not as a businesswoman: as an actress. Or perhaps as an artist. Remember those banged bronze monsters in Brasilia, or were those the Brazilian's first wife's? Elizabeth had done none of those things. She had disappeared. She had come to nothing.

In June, on a visit to the city, Maud stopped at the Kramer Gallery. Irene, whom she had known for years, confided that she was offering rare paintings by Walter Trale to her best customers. Among them was the portrait of Elizabeth H.; Maud asked to see it and scrutinized it for the symptoms of Walter's fabled passion. She looked for Elizabeth as well, who only veiled herself in fresh mystery. Recognizing a windfall, Maud bought the painting on the spot. Her burgeoning fascination with Elizabeth left her, she felt, little choice. The fascination continued to grow.

It occurred to Maud, a few days later, to question Irene about Elizabeth herself. Irene said: ask Barrington Pruell. Louisa Lewison had once told her that he and Elizabeth kept in touch.

Maud thought that likely. Old Mr. Pruell had befriended Elizabeth in those early years. On the morning of July tenth she paid him a visit.

Maud and Mr. Pruell had a longstanding friendship. After her mother's death, Maud had turned to him for support. He knew her father well and understood, if he did not condone, his withdrawal from domestic life. He did his best to explain Mr. Dunlap's behavior to his young friend, and he encouraged her to keep up her grades and take good care of Pauline. Maud had trusted him. After her marriage they saw each other less. Maud frequented Allan's friends, city people, business people; publicly, at least, Mr. Pruell belonged to the horse-and-dog world. They now took each other for granted. When they met at parties, they hugged, exchanged "news," promised to meet privately, and never did.

When Maud announced the reason for her visit, Mr. Pruell said, "It's your lucky day. No point my telling you about Elizabeth. She's coming to lunch."

"She's here?"

"She arrived last week. Stay and see for yourself."

Maud phoned Allan to tell him that she would be out for the day. She begged Mr. Pruell to talk to her about his friend: "I'd like to be the tiniest bit prepared."

Mr. Pruell laughed. "Ask *her*. You'll have more fun."

Elizabeth called to say she couldn't come after all.

Although Mr. Pruell promised to arrange another meeting, Maud felt a disappointment verging on anger. She felt betrayed. It was then that she realized she had been nourishing a small passion, one for which she could find no name. She knew that it included a trace of envy. What had made Elizabeth so different? How had she won friends like Walter Trale and Barrington Pruell and left in her wake the enticing confusion of her reputations? Elizabeth's failure to appear for lunch clinched Maud's obsession with her. She made up her mind that they would meet.

The next days brought Maud only frustration. She learned where Elizabeth was staying, what friends she saw, which parties she would attend. If Maud had called Elizabeth at her hotel, she could have met her in a day; but without a plausible excuse she was embarrassed to approach her. She did not hesitate, however, to get herself invited to every social event in town. And wherever Maud went, Elizabeth did not appear. After a while, Maud began wondering if the woman wasn't avoiding her. (She could imagine no reason for this. Elizabeth could hardly guess that she was being perversely pursued.) Without getting even a glimpse of her prey, Maud consumed a surfeit of olives and jellied ham and enough drinks to afflict even her seasoned metabolism.

After four days, she grew so discouraged that she actually gave up all hope of knowing Elizabeth. They were, she still felt, linked by destiny: but their destiny was to never meet—"a conjunction of their minds, an opposition of their stars." One morning—the fifteenth of July—she picked up her phone and broke her engagements for the day. At eleven o'clock, after trotting into the driveway, dismounting, and tethering her bay mare to a convenient birch, an unfamiliar red-haired woman in riding cap and jodhpurs walked up to Maud's front door and rang the bell.

To Elizabeth, an hour later, watching Allan drive off, Maud declared, "If anything happens to that picture, I'll roast him."

"In the meantime, why not settle for the original?" Elizabeth slipped her arm into Maud's.

Maud took five seconds to understand. "You don't mean you want to *stay* here?"

"I'd love to. If you don't trust my friendly sentiments, I can honestly confess that I'm broke. Bone poor till September sixth. So it would also help."

"I do love to be useful—how did you guess?"

"Allan told me, of course."

"But you do see—"

"We can always finesse the drama. Although I'm pretty much stuck with it in any case."

"How come?"

"Allan was a discreet visitor but a frequent one. The help at the Adelphi are turning sort of frosty. It's hardly your problem, I know—"

"I suppose not. Then why *do* I feel responsible? I guess I'd rather be on your side than theirs."

"If it's not fun, I'll disappear. I promise. Instantly."

Maud surprised Elizabeth, who had called on her out of impulse, although not without a reason: she had heard that Maud was trying to meet her. Allan had described Maud to her misleadingly. Instead of a devoted homebody, Elizabeth discovered a woman whose clean-edged prettiness had been sweetly softened by the faint wrinkling of years. Her disconsolate politeness inspired Elizabeth with an intense longing to make her giggle.

Until Allan's back-door entry, the two women had talked like schoolmates making up for half a lifetime's separation. Maud soon discovered what they had in common. When she brought up Allan, Elizabeth could not help committing a pause; which Maud of course noticed.

She had thought that Allan might be having an affair. For a week he had acted towards her with distracted impatience; he had also twice brought her home voluptuous masses of her favorite Jeanne Charmet dahlias. What this behavior might signify she had inferred from the solicitous phone calls of not-very-dear friends. When Elizabeth brightly followed her pause with talk of certain attractive men she'd just met, naming names and detailing qualities, Maud interrupted: "Aha! *That's* what my girlfriends haven't been telling me. There's another woman, and it's you!"

Maud recognized something like relief in her voice: as if she were thinking, If he had to cheat, better her than someone else.

Blushing wildly, Elizabeth said, "I won't say, 'If only I'd known—' I *am* glad we're talking to one another."

"But I've been chasing you for days!"

Elizabeth smiled. "You see why you never caught up?"

"You mean you were running away?"

"No. I was meeting Allan. I'd plan to go to the McCollums' from five to seven, then Allan would call to say he could get away from five to seven—"

"Because of course *I* was going to the McCollums' from five to seven, because *you* were."

"So I would call Mrs. McCollum, or anyway not go."

"The first time was Barrington Pruell's lunch?"

"*You* were the dear old friend so anxious to meet me? Oh, no! You do get it?"

"Yes, I do." Maud felt stupid. Elizabeth was overwhelming her.

Elizabeth leaned across the coffee table and took Maud's hands. "I *didn't* know. I only learned you were looking for me two days ago." Maud glanced up warily. "I never schedule things. Actually, coming here was my horse's idea."

Maud sighed. "I can see how funny it is, my making it possible . . ."

"What's funnier is us, right now." Elizabeth paused. "I'm sorry you wasted all that time. But so what? New game today."

Maud smiled as if to say: You're very kind. "Look at it this way: thanks to Allan, we're friends."

Maud gazed into Elizabeth's eyes, thinking, What can I lose? They heard Allan treading carefully through the kitchen. Familiar with house sounds, Maud reported his movements. Elizabeth said she had to phone the stable—her mare was overdue. When she lifted the handset, she clapped her hand over the speaker and for several minutes kept the receiver at her ear. After hanging up, she said to Maud, "Let's blow his mind."

"You mean *shoot* him?"

"No, sweetie pie. Just wow him." Elizabeth proposed a portentous dialogue for Allan to overhear; they thereupon performed it with operatic gravity and gusto.

Maud told Elizabeth she was welcome to stay. Elizabeth thanked her with an embrace. Now she must ride her mare home. "She's probably girdled the birch."

"The 'ladies of the forest' grow like weeds here. It's expendable."

"I hope you like to ride."

Raising her eyes in woeful ecstasy, Maud answered, "Oh, Elizabeth, it's out of the question. Horses don't like me. Or I don't understand them."

"You never met the right horses. Come on out. This one's a dream."

Maud moaned and followed. On the lawn Elizabeth introduced her to the mare, Fatima. The two greeted each other genteelly, if noncommittally. Elizabeth ambled away into summer haze.

She moved in the following day. She told Maud she had everything she needed. "Enough for a week is enough for a summer. Not that I'll stay *that* long." Maud didn't think she'd mind. She had missed her already.

That morning Allan called Maud to ask her if Elizabeth had said anything "about a horse." Maud cut the conversation short. Allan had run away; he could stay away.

In the evening Elizabeth suggested that they go into town for cocktails. Maud demurred: "How about drinks on the porch? I recommend it highly. I do it all the time."

"You haven't been out in two days."

"But I love it here." Maud was reluctant to be seen with her husband's lover.

"So do I. But soon? I've missed some promising bars."

Safe for the night, Maud acquiesced.

The previous morning, from the moment she began eavesdropping on the telephone, Elizabeth had been sure that Allan knew she was listening. He had played the tough guy for her, bringing their brief story to a pitiful end. She said to Maud, "I couldn't quite make it out. He has a devious side, you know."

"You mean," Maud said belligerently, "last week was only the tip of the Venusberg?"

"I don't think so. I've known womanizers (and they have their attractions), but not Allan. Definitely not. He's had a successful career, hasn't he?"

"Very." Perplexed, Maud dropped the subject.

Elizabeth asked, "Whose bedroom is the one next to mine?"

"My daughter Priscilla's. Or it used to be."

"Did I tell you I met her at Walter Trale's? She's sharp. She knew so much about me I almost felt my age. Whatever that may be."

Maud told Elizabeth about her recent largesse towards Priscilla, explaining, "So she'll know *something* about money." She reddened, remembering her friend's "bone-poorness."

"I bet she makes a fortune with it."

Maud drove Elizabeth to the stables the next morning. She had agreed to accompany her if she could just sit and watch. She enjoyed seeing Elizabeth take her mount through its paces: animal and rider looked equally content. After unsaddling, Elizabeth introduced Maud to a few more horses. Maud conceded that with Elizabeth next to her she might, someday, give one of them a try. As they were leaving, a man arrived from the racetrack with a depressing tale about a destroyed gelding.

That night, after dinner, they chose to read. Even though the light was weakening, they sat on the west piazza, their reading glasses perched on their nose tips, reluctant to forsake the evening sky behind the panoply of blackening hills. After ten minutes Maud heaved a sigh of delight. Elizabeth closed her book expectantly. "Well—" Maud said and read aloud:

> An extreme languor had settled on him, he felt weakened with the cessation of her grasp. . . . He heard himself quote:
>
> " 'Since when we stand side by side!' " His voice trembled.
>
> "Ah yes!" came in her deep tones: "The beautiful lines . . . They're true. We must part. In this world . . ." They seemed to her lovely and mournful words to say; heavenly to have them to say, vibratingly, arousing all sorts of images. Macmaster, mournfully too, said:
>
> "We must wait." He added fiercely: "But tonight, at dusk!"

He imagined the dusk under the yew hedge. A shining motor drew up in the sunlight under the window.

"Yes! Yes!" she said. "There's a little white gate from the lane." She imagined their interview of passion and mournfulness amongst dim objects half seen. So much of glamour she could allow herself.

Afterwards he must come to the house to ask after her health and they would walk side by side on the lawn, publicly, in the warm light, talking of indifferent but beautiful poetries, a little wearily, but with what currents electrifying and passing between their flesh. . . . And then: long, circumspect years. . . .

"Were the Edwardians ever more neatly skewered? Perhaps they were Georgians by then."

"It's dazzling. How about this?"

I finished my cigarette and lit another. The minutes dragged by. Horns tooted and grunted on the boulevard. A big red interurban car rumbled past. A traffic light gonged. The blonde leaned on her elbow and cupped a hand over her eyes and stared at me behind it. The partition door opened and the tall bird with the cane slid out. He had another wrapped parcel, the shape of a large book. He went over to the desk and paid money. He left as he had come, walking on the balls of his feet, breathing with his mouth open, giving me a sharp side glance as he passed.

I got to my feet, tipped my hat to the blonde and went out after him. He walked west, swinging his cane in a small tight arc just above his right shoe. He was easy to follow. His coat was cut from a rather loud piece of horse robe with shoulders so wide that his neck stuck up out of it like a celery stalk and his head wobbled on it as he walked. We went a block and a half. At the Highland Avenue traffic signal I pulled up beside him and let him see me. . . .

The western light had shrunk to a band of dark green. Maud asked, "What was in the parcel?"

A few days later, Maud consented to ride. At the stables, tucking her slacks into a pair of borrowed boots, she adjured Elizabeth, "You're responsible!"

"Tell that to the horse."

Faced with a beast like an overstuffed pony, Maud was driven to confess that she had once had "endless" riding lessons. Elizabeth chided her for a sneak. "I have the know-how," Maud explained, "it's the performance that gives me the willies. Jumping especially," she incautiously added.

Maud was then assigned a proper horse. For an hour and a half she walked, trotted, and cantered around the ring behind Elizabeth, who at last led her onto the infield grass, on which stood three jumps of whitewashed wood. Elizabeth dismounted and set the bar of the lowest jump at barely a foot above the ground. She led Maud over it at an easy lope. She repeated the procedure with the bar at two feet. Setting it at three, she saw Maud's knees clench on her saddle and thought, she's afraid of taking a spill.

Elizabeth decided to show Maud that she had no cause for fright. When she took the jump herself, she nonchalantly slipped out of her stirrups and slid off her mount onto the turf. Intent on making her fall look natural, she distractedly caught her right foot on the pommel and landed on her capless head. Maud, right behind her, was so unsettled by the mishap that she forgot her own anxiety and took the jump smoothly. Propped on one elbow, Elizabeth cheered.

On their way home, Elizabeth invited Maud to a bar on Broadway. Maud never went to bars. She would again have refused if surviving an hour on horseback hadn't drained her power to resist. Entering the P's-and-Q's, she nervously inquired, "You know this crowd?" She dreaded meeting people she knew, and not meeting people she knew, and meeting people she didn't know. She was reminded of childhood visits to her father's office, full of strange men in shirt-sleeves. She drank too fast and had to pee twice in half an hour. When they left she felt sweaty and sick.

Elizabeth ignored Maud's discomforts. At six-thirty the next evening, appearing in a pale-yellow voile blouse that wreathed over a white sheath skirt, she proposed going back into town. Maud gazed at her admiringly and shook her head: "You go on without me."

"It wouldn't be the same."

"You saw what happened yesterday. I'd rather get sozzled at home."

"How come?"

"I don't like being stared at by strangers."

"It's half the fun. Especially if you give them something to stare at. What about that green Norell shift?"

"Why not a bathing suit?"

"You'd be surprised. Most of them never notice you—you 'one,' not you Maud."

"And the other half? You said 'half the fun'?"

"Staring, just like you said. Or anyway looking. It's pleasant to watch other people. That's what they invented bars for—pleasure."

As they drove to the Boots 'n' Saddles, Maud vowed to remember those words. It was true that, once seated, they attracted scant attention.

Maud talked about Allan: "He sounded eager to come home. I think he should stew in his juice. I have no desire to pass the sponge. Not right away."

"You mean me?"

"I'm glad it *was* you. I still don't like it."

"If you think he needs to squirm, he can manage that by himself."

"Tell me about his devious side."

"How should I know?"

"Why did you ask about his career?"

"I've come to a conclusion about men: they're usually nuts. I'm not sure about this horse business, but it sounds like he's playing dirty games. Don't ask me why. Maybe to prove he doesn't need your connections. Shall we try the neighboring hole before going home? He'll come back when he really wants to."

It was almost nine when they left the second bar. In her kitchen, forgivably bumping into unclosed drawers and dropping an occasional fork, Maud assembled a meal. "May I leave the garlic out of the salad dressing? You know the Italians do, at least the ones in Italy." A Bibb lettuce in each hand, she came to a stop in the middle of the kitchen and there uttered a dreadful sigh.

"Baby!" clucked Elizabeth, "I thought you'd enjoyed yourself tonight." Glass in hand, she was leaning against a varnished-oak counter, swaying dancelike from side to side.

"Yes. But after you've gone—Allan, my friends, they're not like you at all. The future looks, well, uninspiring."

"You have everything you need to be happy. You do know that?"

"Ohhh, happiness . . ."

Maud walked over to the sink. Elizabeth followed her and hugged her from behind. When Maud looked around, Elizabeth kissed her mouth. The lettuces dropped into the sink.

"It's nice of you not to resist."

Maud turned on the cold water. "Don't you think we'd better eat something?"

"I love you, Maud."

"I was having such a good time!"

"You're a *glorious* woman."

"No. I'm not."

"I know. You've lived through forty-nine-and-a-half years of minor disasters. How about joining the party?" Elizabeth held her tight.

Maud kept shaking her head while she plucked a lettuce to tatters. "You're kind, you're a marvelous friend, but you have to accept me the way I am." She looked over her shoulder into Elizabeth's face. "I'd love to love you. It's frightening, though. I've never been with a woman before."

"Look, kissing you was . . . 'I love you' means you inspire me." Maud's subsequent laugh recalled Saint Sebastian at the loosing of the arrows. "Can't you tell I'm happy being with you, 'the way you are'?"

"I have this recurrent impression that I'm a bust."

"No kidding? I admit that sometimes you make me feel sane and efficient, which doesn't happen often. Maybe you could turn into a genuine bust and I'd really be on top of things."

"I'm going on the wagon this second."

"Don't you dare! Anyway, it's too late to start today."

They watched television after dinner. Mandy Rice-Davies followed a newly crowned pope. Elizabeth switched to the Mets, only thirty-two games out of first place and showing progress.

"There goes the Duke."

"He's very graceful. If only I knew what he was doing."

"It doesn't matter. Do you think he could fancy an older woman?"

Maud glanced shyly at Elizabeth and did not answer.

Maud came to like pub-crawling. She enjoyed speculating with Elizabeth about the lives of other patrons. Sometimes, to settle disagreements, the women consulted the patrons themselves, making friends of them for an evening. Maud discovered the easy society flourishing in public places.

One such evening, sitting on a bar-stool next to Maud, Elizabeth said to her, "You know I originally came to see you because you were my lover's wife?"

"Of course."

"I bet you don't know why I liked you right away." Maud

pertly tilted her head. Elizabeth pointed to their reflections in the mirror behind the embottled rear counter. "We have the same nose."

Later that night, the tenth since their meeting, Maud took Elizabeth into the music room, sat her down by the upright piano, and rendered Schumann's *Warum*.

"I haven't played since Priscilla graduated, heaven knows why. I never dared ask you—I've always longed to find somebody to accompany or play four hands with. You don't perchance play anything?"

"Just the one-holed flute, darling."

"Is that the baroque instrument?"

"It is if you treat it right. I'm a musical dunce."

"It really doesn't matter. I like playing alone. Just promise not to listen less than two rooms away."

The Mets tied the record for consecutive losses on the road. An earthquake wrecked Skopje, capital of Macedonia. Arlene Francis was arrested after a car accident. Priscilla called to announce her forthcoming visit.

Still later, Maud asked Elizabeth, "You know my bed's the size of a putting green—would you consider sharing it? It's when I'm drifting off that I recall what it was I wanted to talk about."

"I toss and turn like a seal, I'm told."

"And the morning after, they're vanished. I myself suffer from wakefulness in the dark hours. Can't we try?"

Maud was immediately cured of her insomnia, which Elizabeth immediately acquired. At four o'clock during their first night Maud opened her eyes to see her friend sitting crosslegged at her side. Since her fall in the riding ring, Elizabeth's neck sometimes stiffened painfully when she lay still.

Elizabeth woke up in the morning cradled in Maud's arms. She declared, "I need to get laid."

"I wish there was more I could do."

After breakfast Elizabeth made two phone calls. She told Maud she would be spending the next day and night in the city.

In the afternoon, while Maud was hoeing her herb garden (a task she delegated to no one), Elizabeth's voice streamed through opened windows into the steamy air:

> But this is wine that's all too strange and strong.
>   I'm full of foolish song,
>   And out my song must pour.
> So please forgive this helpless haze I'm in,
>   I've really never been
>   In love before.
>   Ba ba doobie,
>   Ba ba doobie,
>   Ba ba doobie
>   Ah bah.

Her clear tones had a seductive faint breathiness.

Maud told Elizabeth over dinner, "You could sing opera. Or at least operetta."

"Theater! Music! How I'd love it! Honey, I'm strictly bathwater pops."

For Maud, the following day bristled with event. Up with the sun, in the garden by seven, she drove Elizabeth to the bus station to catch the ten-o'clock southbound and came home in time for Allan's call. He confessed his role in insuring the lately destroyed gelding. Maud could not grasp the facts of his story, even after he repeated it, and she concluded by saying, "What a depressing business! Why tell *me* about it?"

(Allan drew two small consolations from talking to her. She did not mention the portrait, which two nights before he had shamefully surrendered to Owen Lewison. By confirming Elizabeth's presence, she lessened his pain at not being asked back.)

Soon afterwards Priscilla arrived. Maud then learned of

Allan's night with Pauline. She fought with her daughter. Torn between anger and remorse, she decided to give Pauline the money she had intended for Priscilla. At three in the afternoon Walter Trale called to tell her that the "Portrait of Elizabeth" she had bought was a copy. There had been a string of crazy misunderstandings. . . .

Maud believed him. Human communication was going to the bow-wows. Why today of all days had Elizabeth abandoned her? She thought of telling Allan about the painting, then remembered his fling with Pauline. She drove to the Boots 'n' Saddles. Finding the place empty in mid-afternoon, she drank two more solitary chartreuses. At home she was given a message from Elizabeth, with a number to call in the city, of which she did not avail herself.

The next day, Elizabeth arrived earlier than expected. In time for another free lunch, Maud told herself. She had difficulty responding to her boarder's embrace. Elizabeth seemed not to notice.

"Nice enough," she replied to Maud's polite inquiry. "I feel sort of dumb missing a day here."

"It's sweet of you to say so," Maud said, staring into her coffee cup.

" 'Sweet'? Hey—this is *me.* "

Maud pursed her lips. "I've been thinking there's something we really ought to discuss. It's been marvelous having you here, and I want it to go on being marvelous. So don't you think— don't you think it might be better if we decided exactly how long it is you expect to stay? Open-ended arrangements are so awfully . . ."

Unable to go on, Maud shut her eyes. Sneaking up on her, Elizabeth slid fingers under her dirty-blonde curls and took an emphatic grip on her ears. Maud was immobilized. Elizabeth said to her, "Little girl, you're jealous."

"Oh, really? Jealous of what? Of you?"

"It won't hurt to say so."

Maud began to cry. "You move in and take over as though you'd been here all your life. All I know about you is that you spent a week putting out for my husband—"

Elizabeth squeezed Maud's ears to shut her up. "I implore you to forgive me. I'm an unfeeling jerk—"

"Everything's easy for you. You don't have a family to worry about. You don't have any money problems—you don't even have any money."

"My beloved, listen, please, I promise you that starting right now I will never again do *anything* without you—" She let go of Maud's ears.

"If you knew what I've gone through since you left!"

"I'll arrange something right now," Elizabeth said, walking across the veranda towards the front parlor. At the door she turned: "Think of it—our first double date!"

Maud, still snuffling, at these words looked up in astonishment. "What do you mean?"

"I'll find you somebody delectable."

"Elizabeth, stop it! That's not what I meant. I'm past fifty."

From the gloom beyond the door Elizabeth replied, "I'd never have guessed it. But you'll see: at our age, it's a picnic."

Over lunch Maud begged Elizabeth to revoke her good deed. Elizabeth could then play the offended party: "I got three dates broken to make sure you'd have the best." She ended the discussion by saying, "If you don't like him, you say no." Maud consented and began a recapitulation of the previous day.

In the afternoon they went for a ride, starting from a horse farm to the west of the house. Instead of climbing into the foothills as they had planned, they kept to the unpaved roads that ran between level fields of blossoming potatoes and newly harvested corn. Elizabeth questioned Maud about Pauline, and Maud told her about their childhood years, her foster-motherhood, the bitter falling-out over Pauline's engagement to

Oliver. Her voice trembled, she spoke of "principles of money and responsibility."

Elizabeth remarked, "The two of you turning a million dollars into a problem—it's hilarious!"

"It didn't *feel* hilarious! Why are you stopping?"

Elizabeth was staring across broken cornstalks. "Did you see the lark? If that's what it was. Just like one, the way it fluttered into the stubble."

"I was stuck back in nineteen thirty-eight."

"I lived in Bavaria once. A romance. Skylarks came singing down out of the sky and settled into the wheat, same as these. That was summertime."

"I know that bird, but I don't know what it's called."

"Not lark, anyway."

"Well, they don't get eaten here, either. You must understand it *wasn't* both of us, only me. It took me a fortnight to ruin everything, and she never understood. Never." They rode through a stand of hefty cutleaf maples. "Hearing about her night with Allan . . . I told myself I deserved it."

"You sit a horse very gracefully, you know."

"And now I'll make it up to her."

Suppressing an impulsive Bronx cheer, Elizabeth replied in cold tones, "You make a mess, and you pay for it."

"And I'm happy to pay for it!" Maud explained that she was settling the money on Pauline, not Priscilla.

"That's great," Elizabeth said, "but why not forget about the Dark Ages? You can shoot a brand-new movie."

"You're a hopeless optimist. Twenty-five years aren't going to simply disappear."

Elizabeth vented her Bronx cheer and replied, "In the twinkling of an eye!"

Maud shrugged.

At dinner, Maud gave a confused account of Allan's phone call. Elizabeth made her understand (she herself had only now understood) that Allan had arranged insurance for an aging racehorse knowing that it would soon be killed. "But that's not like him at all," Maud said. "That's ghastly."

"I've seen worse. But it's what I meant—"

"I'm glad he's not here. Especially after Pauline. I can understand *her,* but how could *he?* Twice in a month! What *did* you mean?"

"Funny-business like the gelding wouldn't happen out of the blue. As for Pauline: Allan's pushing sixty, he's suffering from multiple upset, and Pauline was familiar, attractive, and available."

"My God—I forgot to tell you about the painting."

Later still, the two sang songs from musicals. Elizabeth's snapping fingers perked up Maud's somewhat Schubertian accompaniment. Maud sang along as well as sight-reading allowed. They repeated numbers they liked, and one they rehearsed until they could sing it in duet:

> . . . I hope that things will go well with him,
>   I bear no hate.
> All I can say is, the hell with him,
>   He gets the gate.
>   So take my benediction,
>   Take my old Benedick, too.
>   Take him away,
>   It's too good to be true.

"Poor Allan!"

Elizabeth had made their date for the following evening. Maud remained dubious about it, but they set off in midafternoon, detouring to the city down the rural meanders of the Taconic Parkway. Near the first Poughkeepsie exit Maud again brought up Allan: "Should I divorce him?"

"No."

"He's been small comfort lately."

"So divorce him."

"Oh?"

"You have a problem."

"Once a day and twice on Sunday."

"You like him."

Maud sighed. "I know. We've always gotten along so well."

"What's he like in bed?"

"*You're* asking?"

"With me he had unusual difficulties. He isn't the first. Never mind why. I liked him."

"That's why you said he was no hardened cheater?"

"Exactly. I'd like to say he was a novice, except nobody can be expected to go twenty-five years—"

"*I* have. Elizabeth, why am I doing this? That's one reason it's hard to answer you."

"Look, once a month obviously scores low. So does always resorting to the same—"

"He treats me marvelously. He always has."

"By this time tomorrow you may have a broader basis—"

"I'm not listening."

They drove in silence along a half-empty reservoir. Elizabeth said, "I know you're no spendthrift—all the same, you do have your gardens and your 'conventional benevolences.' Are you sure what you're giving Pauline won't hurt?"

"Not really. In certain brackets the graduated income tax is a great leveler. Priscilla's the one who's losing out. If she hadn't talked the way she did the other day . . ."

"It was that bad?"

"She treated me like an old drunk."

"Children make stern disciplinarians."

"She told me about Allan and Pauline. I hated her for that."

They had stopped at a toll station. Elizabeth started briefing Maud on her date.

By ten the next morning they were on the Thruway north. Maud spoke little, apparently content. Elizabeth asked no questions. As they crossed the Tappanzee Bridge, Maud said, "I've got to get into better shape. Riding's invigorating, but there are specific areas . . ."

"I believe you were a great hit."

"What do you mean?"

"George called to thank me. He also said you'd made it—"

"Hush! He might have let *me* tell you. In any case, that's to *his* credit, isn't it?"

"I know it's hard to accept—he found you *very* attractive."

"But imagine having to turn out so many lights. I didn't dare leave them on. I had a hard time being sure what was happening. If I can't tell what's making me feel so good, how can I ask for more?"

"You have a point."

"How do you keep so svelte?"

"Ballet basics."

"When do you dance?"

"I don't, just exercises. And riding. If no horses are available, I walk for hours."

"Well: the attic gets too hot in summer, and it's too damp in the cellar in any season—where do I put the barre and mirror? Now that I think of it, I'll skip the mirror."

"Don't. It's a necessary torment."

Glimpses of the Hudson revealed water bluer than the sky it reflected.

"I called Allan. I felt peculiarly fond of him this morning."

"You changed your mind about him?"

"He's not dying to come home. He's afraid the two of us will tear him to smithereens."

"But you're not getting rid of him?"

"That was yesterday."

"He'll make a loyal stud and gofer, provided you give him

a hard time." Maud frowned. Elizabeth nudged her: "Think what you've got on him!"

"Don't even joke about it."

"He's not a bad man—even if he tries to be. Interesting, though. Not many wives of the gentility can claim bona fide criminals as husbands."

"If only I could be sure you weren't serious. When he comes home, I'm counting on him to help with Priscilla."

"She needs help?"

"You don't understand, I have no regrets about taking back the money—I only thought if Allan could set something up to take its place. Something small. . . ."

"You dodo, money's the last thing she needs. She just got a hundred thousand dollars in life insurance—"

"She did mention that."

"That's a fortune for somebody her age. You people . . . Sometimes I think they should make inheritance taxes total."

"She's going to hate me."

"So? You already tried buying her off. Please, darling, look at the road, not me. Your getting angry means she matters to you. Tell her that."

"She won't believe it."

"She doesn't believe you now."

"I simply can't phone her."

"Write a letter."

"All right."

"Promise?"

"All right."

"Today?"

"Today." Maud's promise recalled to her a childhood pledge to write a thank-you note—the first time she imagined someone actually reading what she wrote. That afternoon, when she sat down to her letter to Priscilla, she fell asleep. She needed another day to complete two handwritten pages fit to mail.

Benefit expositions of "The Horse in Contemporary Art" had opened at the Spa Music Theater and the Hall of Springs. Oliver La Farge died. Police brutality during a CORE march was being "probed." At Kamp Kelly, Mr. Grimmis and Miss Crystal did their best to protect Ira and Arthur from the insidious Marcia Mason. Maud and Elizabeth lay in the sun, Maud deepening her tan, Elizabeth shielding her freckle-prone whiteness with a floppy hat and a gauzy, long-sleeved chemise.

Maud reported, "Mr. Pruell plans to journey on a sailing yacht from Cape Cod to Mount Desert. Tempted?"

Nothing appealed to her less, said Elizabeth, than cramped quarters amid infinite space. Perhaps the two of them might travel. . . .

They drove to town for misleading guidebooks and uninformative maps. They speculated about Mexico, Sweden, Afghanistan. They fancied an ocean liner followed by a panoramic train, rucksacking forays over exotic mountains—the Carpathians, the Kazakh Hills. They called Maud's travel agent, who proposed charter flights to Venice or Majorca. By evening their house had become the traveler's joy.

Maud posted her letter to Priscilla. Elizabeth asked, "What about Pauline?"

"Am I to have no peace?"

"If you're going to play Santa Claus . . ."

"But I'm Scrooge making amends! Did I tell you she's coming here in two days? She wants to talk."

"About the money?"

"She implied something darker."

"So—you can still make peace."

"I'm in a letting-the-chips-fall mood. But I'll think about it. It could hardly get worse, I suppose."

Maud avenged herself on Elizabeth by making her sing Blondchen's first aria in *The Abduction from the Seraglio*. Elizabeth labored to hold the long high notes. She afterwards described to Maud another Mozart aria she remembered—one that had falling in love with love as its theme and sailed along under a wind of pure desire. Maud found Cherubino's *Non so più,* and Elizabeth, at her third try, learned to hold long notes out of pure desire. Maud wished sometimes that she had been born a man.

Priscilla had not responded to Maud's letter. Elizabeth pointed out that it had been mailed only yesterday. "But I sent it special delivery, and I went to the post office myself." Maud phoned Walter. The letter had arrived that morning.

"I'm so relieved. Is Priscilla all right?"

"As far as I know."

"What do you mean?"

"I haven't seen her lately."

"I still don't understand."

After a moment Walter said, "She's not living here anymore."

"Oh, dear—where's she gone?"

"She's at Phoebe Lewison's studio. I put your letter under the door."

Maud wrote down the telephone number. "I'm sorry, Walter."

"It's OK. And don't worry about her. If anybody can take care of herself, it's Priscilla."

Maud knew what he meant. She rang Phoebe's studio. At the sound of her voice, Priscilla hung up. "Oh, my God, what have I done?"

"Come on, you expected it. Anyway, you told me she thrives on obstacles."

"She's twenty-three."

"If she needs help, she'll ask. Concerned parents drive difficult children crazy. I'll go see her on our next date if you like."

"You're an angel. You wouldn't like to take care of Pauline, too? I know, I know. . . ."

"I want to meet her, though."

"Tomorrow, provided I survive. No, I'm glad she's coming. I'll tell her everything. And listen, too."

After Pauline's arrival the next day, Maud and Elizabeth had no chance to talk until evening. The sisters had settled after lunch in the lilac garden, each oppressed with her dissimilar, unspoken confession. Pauline had not yet heard from the bank. Learning from Maud of the provision made on her behalf filled Pauline with jubilation, soon followed by shame. ("She'd come to tell me about Allan," Maud later said to Elizabeth, "and she began worrying that I'd take back the money, then almost wishing I *would* take it back, since she'd behaved like such a skunk.") Sitting up very straight, Pauline at last informed Maud that she had slept with her husband. Maud said to her ("It made me feel proud, as though you were watching"), "How could you possibly do such a thing to me?" The coldhearted falseness of these words released in Pauline a twenty-five-year-old accumulation of rage. Maud endured her sister's vehemence, only nodding her head attentively, and at the end said to her, "I've never dared apologize. You'd be inhuman not to feel the way you do."

"When she saw I meant it," Maud told Elizabeth, "she started crying. She said to me, 'Maud, that's nonsense! You don't have a mean bone in your body.' So it became my turn to be pitiful and cry—I haven't cried like that since Mummy was buried." Tears were again running down Maud's cheeks: "Why did it take so long?" She glanced at Elizabeth, sitting on the floor next to the bed where she lay, with something like reproach. "Why did they raise us like that?"

Elizabeth got to her feet and embraced her friend. "I was lucky. I had a real-live, no-bullshit mother."

They heard a discreet knock. The door opened, and Pauline's head appeared. "Sorry!" she exclaimed at the prospect of these two women entwined. She saw Maud's tear-streaked face. "You OK?"

"Fine. I'm just debriefing. You don't mind?"

"Not a bit."

The three had planned to go riding the following morning. High Heels appeared in real boots. To Maud's consternation, Elizabeth backed out. Her neck was still sore, she had a persistent headache. . . . Maud scolded her for acting so irresponsibly. Her fall might have done her worse damage than she thought: "We have an ultramodern Medical Center in Albany. Use it."

Elizabeth agreed, Maud made an appointment, and the next day they stopped off on their way to the city. An orthopedist prescribed strong antispasmodics, forbade any kind of exercise, and gave Elizabeth an appointment for tests the following week. Pauline spoke of a wizard acupuncturist behind Carnegie Hall; they arrived too late to find him, too late as well for Elizabeth's promised visit to Priscilla.

Maud enjoyed her second night out, although she wished Elizabeth had let her date George again. Her friend had told her, "Knowing you, you'd only start getting attached. Anyway, you have a lifetime of monogamy to atone for." Driving home the day after, Maud asked Elizabeth, "How'd you get the way you are? Your no-bullshit mother? Was there a revelation that struck the scales from your eyes? I assume you once had scales, like us common mortals."

"My mother! She never let me imagine I wasn't a 'common mortal,' especially days when I wanted to be a dancer or a movie star." Elizabeth, at the wheel, accelerated through sparse midmorning traffic. "I thought she meant I should be like other people."

"Fat chance."

"I *sort* of had a revelation. You ever watch ladybugs?"

"Elizabeth, please—no nature stories."

"You asked, remember? OK. Let's say I came across a nameless creature of indeterminate size in my back yard—"

"I'm skeptical, all the same."

"—and after watching it doing namelessly insane things for

a while, I started laughing so hard that my—another, larger creature came out to see what was wrong with me. I can't really say what the first creature had to do with what came next—I'm only describing—"

"No *post hoc ergo propter hoc* for us!"

"—I saw the second creature standing there, not worrying, either, I mean about who she was or the way she looked. She stood there staring at me skeptically (just like you), and at the same time so obviously in love with me. I thought: That's the way I'm in love with her. I saw that what I most wanted out of life was to be her. And I was. *That* was what she meant about our all being 'common mortals.' "

"She was hardly common. She was special."

"So it doesn't make sense. Still, right then I stopped worrying about being *like* anybody else. 'Love came to Elizabeth'— it felt like going barefoot on the first day of summer. Maybe that's where the ladybug comes in. This happened forty years ago, about, and I gave up being anxious for the future, and I haven't lived a boring minute. You know I love you, Maud?"

"I hope you never stop!"

"You know that if I love other people, I don't love you any less? I love you totally, I don't know how to love somebody more—*and* I may meet some man and go love him for a while, or forever, and you'll know even if I don't talk to you for months that I love you the way I do now? Maud, Maud, if you could see how beautiful you are!"

"That's what doesn't make sense. I know why I love you, but who am I?"

After supper Elizabeth picked up a fat old biography she had unearthed from Maud's eclectic shelves and read from a letter by a certain Miss Savage:

. . . I like the cherry-eating scene, too, because it reminded me of your eating cherries when I first knew you. One day when I was going to the gallery, a very hot day I remember, I met you on the shady side of Berners Street, eating cherries out of a basket. Like your Italian friends, you were perfectly silent with content, and you handed the basket to me as I was passing, without a word. I pulled out a handful and went on my way rejoicing, not saying a word either. I had not before perceived you to be different from anyone else. I was like Peter Bell and the primrose with the yellow brim. As I went away to France a day or two after that, and did not see you again for months, the recollection of you as you were eating cherries in Berners Street abode with me and pleased me greatly, and it now pleases me greatly to have that incident brought to my recollection again. I shall hear from you someday soon, n'est-ce pas?

"What a start for a romance!"

"No romance. He refused, she died, he regretted."

"How could he resist? I was thinking of reading you a lovely bit from Hawthorne, but not after that. Not even on a night like this. Shouldn't we be outside?"

"Just one peek at the ball game. The Cards are playing. You know Stan the Man is retiring."

Halfway through the fourth inning, Maud went outdoors; as though the night were expecting her, and she it. Her unread words sang on her tongue—*So sweetly cool was the atmosphere, after all the feverish day, that the summer eve might be fancied as sprinkling dews and liquid moonlight, with a dash of icy temper in them, out of a silver vase.* . . . From the grass at her feet to the Pleiades, she read the night entire. A three-quarter moon was shining through a low thin stratum of haze onto deserted swards, onto geysers of leaf billowing about the stems they concealed. The warm air had coolness enough to be felt as a benign exhalation. The air carried no sound, none at least to be listened to; no night bird, no droning car. As Maud deciphered patterns she had learned by daylight, the imperturbable scene expanded. Each recognition dissolved its object and invited her awareness to claim what lay beyond, past this line of hedge or that swerve of road. Maud went back to fetch Elizabeth; glimpsing her crouched in front of the raw-colored screen, she let her be. She walked around the house and stopped at its far side. Looking up, she saw the looming gabled roof silhouetted against the barely hidden moon: her house, her very own. Towards the woods, where her low shrubs and ground cover had run into entanglements of softer wildness, she sat down on an old swing—she had sat there with Priscilla in her lap, perhaps here her mother had swung her as a child. In Russia they must have nights like this. Maud thought of Tatiana, late on such a night, writing her letter to Onegin. Maud had no letter to write, no longing for love. Her father's house had been bequeathed to her: not a possession so much as a space in which memory and dream escaped division. Inside it sat Elizabeth, who loved her, knowing her as she might never know herself, and there all her people would return: Pauline, and Allan, and Priscilla. She would welcome them back into her life. She would not let them settle for less.

She set apart her future for them, and this night for herself. She looked up at the stars, prickles of longing, few tonight. The light belonged to the moon as it displayed the summer earth, irregularly suspended around hummocks and columns of thickset silver leaves. Maud pushed her heels into the ground, swinging back, then forward. Straightening and bending her legs, she wondered if she could lift herself high enough to catch sight of the moon. Above the roof's peak the bright haze glowed stronger the higher she swung, as though the house hid an immense city. The clogs had slipped from her feet. For ten minutes air breezed mildly between her toes.

"I wish," she said back inside, "I wish summer would never end. At least, not for another two months."

They discussed future dates. Elizabeth asked about local resources.

"It's too small a town," Maud said. "I haven't got the nerve."

"How about the neighboring boondocks? I hear the bars in Hoosick Falls are bursting with trade."

They gave up the idea. "Men" seemed hardly worth the trouble.

Elizabeth woke up the next morning exhilarated by a dream. She had become a bird flying low over old countryside: villages of graying stone, irregular patchwork fields, clumps of deciduous woods. She had flown mile after mile; she was still filled with the elation of her flight. Sunlight penetrated her bedroom at the edges of its curtained windows, accumulating at its far upper corners in orange pools that generated a brightness of their own. Incoming beams formed luminous bridges between these glowing pools and the light outside, and across these beam-bridges crowds of larks now began to stream. In her dream she had been a skylark, and now her companions were following her home. Her room had become a gathering point for the larks of the earth. She imagined them rising in Bavaria out of yellow fields, from copses of English beech and ash, from shrubs on the edges of Eastern deserts, from reedy shores: skylarks, woodlarks, crested larks, and the nameless creatures she had seen with Maud in the stubble nearby. The birds did not sing, but their wings filled the room with an agreeable thrum.

In time she took a closer look at them. The swarming larks began separating from her awareness of them. She had recognized larger creatures between the birds and herself. Against the placid shadows of her room she noticed shadows that moved: people. She addressed herself to identifying them. The faint light made that hard. Curtains were opened, sunshine flooded the air, revealing close to her a body stretched out under a petrified sheet, on whose white ground was stamped, with what struck her as almost drunken obsessiveness, as

though one might somehow miss its point, a pattern of blue
whorls representing twined wildflowers: pinks, she guessed,
counting the figures down her legs, past her curled, upright
toes. The pattern did not distract from her own grotesque
sprawl in its midst.

A few skylarks fluttered around her fussily. The people or
person came nearer.

After a while, which she estimated as only minutes, Elizabeth sensed that she was causing fearfulness in the people or
person near her. She then saw clearly that not near but next to
her sat her beloved Maud, holding one of her hands and clasping her shoulder. Her face showed undeniable fright. Elizabeth
longed to comfort her. She could understand the fright of
watching somebody inhabited by so large a number of birds.

Now calm, the latter had withdrawn to the upper reaches of
the room, perching on moldings, skimming peacefully about
the brass chandeliers. Elizabeth appreciated their discretion, as
well as their presence, which recalled her to realities beyond her
own feelings. The lessened wingbeats allowed her to distinguish
other sounds. She had seen that Maud was speaking to her. She
could now understand her words, so loving, so frantic: "Elizabeth? Elizabeth, please tell me what's happening. Are you all
right? Tell me you're all right?"

Speaking struck Elizabeth as inappropriate for her, smiling
no less so, much as she would have liked to gratify Maud with
a smile. She found another solution. If her eyes could see Maud,
Maud could see them (not only stare through them, as she was
now doing). Elizabeth's eyes could communicate. She opened
them wide to signify that, of course, she was all right.

Maud pressed a cheek against Elizabeth's before leaving the
room.

She walked down the corridor in a state of furious apathy.
She sat down at her desk and cracked her knuckles while she
cried. She knew what to do and wanted to do nothing. She felt

a fierce need to discuss this matter with Elizabeth. She had difficulty admitting that she yearned to take Elizabeth's head in her arms and stifle it.

Elizabeth had not looked at her like a doomed animal. Maud found her list of emergency numbers, called an ambulance, phoned the Medical Center.

She sat in the ambulance at Elizabeth's side. Elizabeth, who had fallen asleep in her bed, slept while being shifted to a stretcher and through the hot half-hour drive to Albany. At the Medical Center she was committed to waiting orderlies. Around noon, in a bright air-conditioned room, with a drip in a vein of her left forearm, she reopened her eyes.

To ward off teariness, Maud began speaking at once. She soon noticed that Elizabeth's eye movements were following a pattern. She was teaching Maud a small, sufficient vocabulary: a blink meant *yes,* looking left and right *no,* looking down *I don't know* (this took Maud longest to grasp). Looking up kept its primordial sense of *What will they think of next?* Maud forgot her urge to smother that inert, pretty head. Holding it in one hand, she brushed its thick red-gold hair until it glistened.

A neurologist told Maud that the stroke indicated subdural hematoma, caused perhaps by falling off the horse, more likely by an earlier shock. Options available included an exploratory operation to determine the extent of the damage. Treatment might also require surgery. In either case the results could not be guaranteed. He had little else to propose.

"How about doing nothing?"

"Speaking frankly, it's not a bad idea." The specialist had unintentionally lowered his voice. "Cases like hers usually result only in hemiparesis. Fairly soon she should be able to move on her left side. An operation *might* facilitate . . ."

When Maud mentioned the possibility of an operation, Elizabeth's eyes snapped upwards. Maud said, "I couldn't agree with you more. You'll come home with me?" Elizabeth hesitated before answering with a decisive blink.

Maud by now saw that regret and despondency would only exasperate their difficulties. She could not deny that a terrible event had taken place. She could not deny that Elizabeth had survived it. For Maud, pretending that she hadn't—committing her to the hopeless and comforting isolation of the terminal case—would only signify that Elizabeth's existence no longer counted. It would invalidate the presence that for so few and so many days had suffused Maud's own life. Maud promised herself not to let the disaster, having ended her time with a healthy Elizabeth, put that time in question. She would confirm her promise by not renouncing the fullness of time to come. She declared to herself that her life with Elizabeth had only begun.

After two days of interviews, Maud engaged a permanent day nurse. She persuaded her housekeeper to reschedule her hours so as to come early and stay late. She bought an electric wheelchair that Elizabeth could later run with her good arm.

Two days after coming home, Elizabeth was taken out of bed, installed in her chair, and wheeled onto the veranda where, for the next two weeks, she was to spend her daylight hours. She often slept. When she woke up, she always found Maud at her side. Elizabeth soon made clear her dislike of Maud's unfailing presence. *She* was the invalid. The greatest solace Maud could provide was to live a busy life, for both their sakes.

So Maud went riding; called on Mr. Pruell; went to "their" bars. She set out on these excursions dreading the reminders of Elizabeth she was bound to meet on her way, and of the opportunities lost because Elizabeth had not accompanied her. The awareness of her friend only intensified her experiences and sharpened her powers of observation. The most trivial events now mattered, and Maud noticed them unremittingly: chance accumulations of clouds, traffic jams, silly remarks, the least of her feelings. She came back with too much to tell, and told it, so that the eyes in the stricken head would shine, flutter, and sometimes cry. Maud learned that tears stood for laughter as well as grief.

Maud began taking Elizabeth out. With the nurse in attendance, John, now chauffeur as well as gardener, lifted the patient into the front seat, then drove through the countryside: west through the Adirondacks, east to North Bennington, north to Lake George. Maud bought a second, collapsible wheelchair, small enough for the trunk. Elizabeth sat in woodland shade, surveyed the world from hilltops, went window-shopping. Maud proposed taking her along on her own outings; Elizabeth refused. She wanted to be seen only where no one knew her. She made an exception of the riding stables, where the well-bred horses ignored her infirmity. Maud would leave her by their stalls, or at the edge of the field where they were pastured, while she cantered around the ring, hoping Elizabeth was watching her jumps.

Maud came to understand that, if she lived her life completely, Elizabeth's would not be wanting; but she could not yet bring herself to make another date in the city.

In the last week of August, Walter Trale arrived, bringing Elizabeth's portrait. The confusion he had created with Phoebe's copy had cured him of his obsessive attachment to the original. He had decided that Maud deserved it—she had paid for it in good faith, and she would make a worthy custodian—and he was now putting the painting in her hands.

Walter planned to leave as soon as he had hung the portrait. He was frightened of seeing Elizabeth, whom his imagination had transformed into a freak. He needed only a few minutes to change his mind. After Maud taught him the eye code, he had his first conversation with Elizabeth; and soon afterwards, at Maud's invitation, he agreed to stay on.

On the evening of his arrival, when Maud quizzed him about Priscilla, he refused to discuss their breakup. "That's finished. Guess what she's doing now."

"Do I really have to guess?"

"She's working for Irene."

"I thought Irene was involved—"

"You're so right. It was Irene who zeroed in on her. Priscilla deserves an Emmy for chutzpah. She went to Irene and said, I behaved like a little punk, I apologize, please teach me the art business."

"And she hired her?"

"Priscilla knows how to lay it on. She told Irene about her basic training with Morris, nothing to what she could learn from her, she was the best in the business, etcetera. Priscilla promised to work for nothing, lick stamps, mop floors, just give her a chance. Irene called me up about it, I told her I couldn't care less, only don't ever leave her alone in the gallery. Sorry, Maud. Irene bought it. She told Priscilla she'd pay her what she was worth and promised to work her ass off."

"Walter, I'm terribly worried. You don't think she has the makings of a professional criminal?" Maud had been thinking that she had Allan's blood in her veins.

Walter set up a worktable on Elizabeth's veranda. He began a life of drawing, writing, and reading, sometimes interrupted for sketching out doors or visiting old friends. Once he drove as far as Peterborough to work on a set of prints. He liked Elizabeth's company, as she herself soon realized. She let him talk to her, read to her out loud (*Memoirs of a Midget;* books by Cornell Woolrich), or simply sit quietly nearby. In the evening they watched baseball together. One day, looking at her while she slept, he reflected that in spite of the pallor, the blankness of feature, the saliva trickling from her mouth, she had kept an unforeseeable beauty.

Walter had rehung the portrait on the veranda wall, close to where Elizabeth usually sat. The bright daylight lent its colors a forgotten vividness.

Maud took Elizabeth back to Albany for examination. Three specialists spoke of her condition with optimism.

Pauline returned. Maud went out to meet her on the front lawn and brought her straight to see Elizabeth. But when Pauline spoke to her, Elizabeth shut her eyes tight, thus introducing a new idiom: *No small talk!* Elizabeth saw that Pauline was bursting with news and should be allowed to tell it. She batted her eyes in mimic excitement. Pauline understood, laughed, and announced her tidings: for several months Oliver had been having "a *very* serious affair. With a not-so-young thing. Yesterday he decided to confess. You would have thought he was doing me a favor. It's true he hardly knows anymore who he's taking for granted. He made one big mistake, though. In his best how-can-you-manage-without-me manner, he said he hoped I wasn't thinking about a divorce. I said right away I wouldn't settle for less and threw the creep out. Can I hide here while my lawyer gets a stranglehold on him?"

When she wasn't out, Pauline often joined Walter and Elizabeth on the veranda, reading magazines or doing crossword puzzles. Elizabeth was pleased to be at the center of the household.

Pauline paid little attention to Walter, whom she scarcely knew. Elizabeth saw Walter frequently staring askance at Pauline. Since her stroke, Elizabeth had been determined to ignore her incapacities, but they now filled her with impatience. An attractive couple freshly sprung from domesticity, the man drawn to the woman, the woman unawares. . . . Before, Elizabeth would have needed minutes to unite them. She wanted to unite them now, in one family—her own. Her family had become her passion. Mere callers, even old friends, were sent away.

She resigned herself to taking whatever time was necessary. At last her mischievous eyes caught Pauline's and pointed towards Walter, bent innocently over his work. If only she could have winked! But Pauline had understood. She blushed with understanding. Elizabeth watched her realizing that for the first time in twenty-five years she was accountable to no one but herself. She could take any man she wanted, for as long as she wanted. And Walter, the affable, undangerous genius, had put himself at her disposal, under her sister's sheltering roof.

What happened next left Walter bewildered. He was not only seduced by Pauline, but doubly seduced: she unwittingly spiced her availability with the contempt for males that her marriage had taught her. For Walter, the mix was irresistible.

Early in September, Louisa Lewison called Maud to tell her that Phoebe had spent the last three weeks at the Medical Center, and that her condition was still critical. Maud drove to Albany the following day. Walter was hard put to accept the news. He knew how sick Phoebe had been—he had taken her to the hospital in June. He had assumed that since then she had been properly cared for.

He talked to Elizabeth about Phoebe, forgetting they had met. He described the genius with which she had reconstituted the portrait. "At the end, she knew more about it than I did. She would have loved you."

He made the trip to Albany two days later, early in the afternoon. Alone on the veranda, Elizabeth thought about Phoebe. She had heard all the others deplore sickness in one so young. For mortal illness, is one age better than another? The living die at all ages; a death sentence is handed down at our birth.

In May, when they'd met, Phoebe was so weak that Elizabeth expected her to crumple like a Raggedy Ann doll. Nevertheless, she had had all the time she needed to be "Phoebe." In her fearful thinness she was still beautiful, like a solitary water bird—a plover, perhaps (why not?) a prim shore lark, even if Elizabeth had never seen one.

She wished she could be with Phoebe now. Elizabeth considered that she herself might well be doomed. Anyway, she wouldn't sit on Maud's lap forever; and as for a home, she'd go on a breathing strike first. Why not bring Phoebe here, or go back to Albany herself? Two dying women staring madly at each other . . . "There's holy communion for you!"

She'd rather get well. So many things to do again. Like going riding—not in the cards, she knows. Then what about one more man? Elizabeth remembers distant, silhouetted figures with inexplicable affection. Thinking of Maud and George, she laughs. She can't laugh. A growl is stifled in her chest, tears spring into her eyes and flow down her throat, making her gag or cough or suffer an unpleasantness of some sort. She thinks, my trachea is full of soap wrappers!

A wave glides across her eyes and up through the tip of her cranium. Larks once came streaming into her bedroom. She hears them returning. This time perhaps they might sing for her. The birds start uttering their long, liquid flourishes as they land on the upper story of the veranda, where she cannot see them, although she hears them clearly enough. She congratulates herself for having summoned once again the lark diaspora.

Now, what about that last man? She wishes the larks away. They go on singing as they alight above her head. She laughs again. From her belly she hears an unmistakable growl. Something new is happening inside her. She feels a nibble of lust.

Christ, how she'd carried on! And now? She'd settle, Maud willing, for another tumble with Allan. Not likely, though. Couldn't she at least touch herself, one more time? Her growl bubbles up into her throat as she relinquishes her vow not to struggle with her affliction. She concentrates her energies into a lurch that will flop her right hand onto her lap. She shudders. Shut *up!* she admonishes the incessant birds. She lets go. The larks are hushed.

She hears her bowels blurt. She sees through the ceiling of the veranda as though it had changed to glass. The speckling of birds dissolves in a cloudless sky, early morning or late afternoon, she can't tell; the sky at first filmed with lavender, the color calmly drawing away (what a goofy place to lock up her life!) so that only brightness remains, white so faintly blued

the blue makes it whiter, Maud in the middle of it, speaking
from a recognizable and measurable distance, her voice a
muffled enunciation of Elizabeth's rejoicing.

Maud's face almost touched Elizabeth's as she called to her.
The nurse was saying, "She's soiled herself."

"I know," Maud replied. "Help me clean her up. Help me
clean my darling up."

Pauline had followed Maud onto the veranda. "I'll phone the
doctor."

The nurse shook her head. Maud said, "We'd better take her
to her room. Please get John." Maud was holding Elizabeth in
her arms, cheek against cheek. Elizabeth's eyes stared past her.

Pauline said, "Maud, my poor Maud! Perhaps it's better—"

"It isn't," Maud declared. Someone tapped discreetly at the
screen door. "John? Could you give me a hand?"

Allan kept peering through the screen at the blurred figures
beyond.

In a New York movie theater, Oliver watched *Dr. No* with his friend Jollie; since Pauline's departure she had dwindled in his consideration. Leaving Priscilla in charge of the gallery, Irene was visiting a young painter in his studio. Phoebe lay alone in her hospital bed, while her parents waited in the visitors' room, Louisa in an armchair, Owen standing at a window.

In the morning Barrington Pruell and his party had weighed anchor in Harwichport for Mount Desert, rounding Monomoy Point in auspicious conditions. As they turned north, a strong following wind swelled their sails, a hot wind that drove them towards their destination with disagreeable speed. In glum inactivity the crew slouched at their stations, the helmsman hardly touching the tiller, neither they nor the passengers sweating or shivering in the warm, brisk air.

I myself was proceeding, on foot, to the railroad station. Although it lay a few miles from the center of Saratoga Springs,

I carried no luggage, having come up from Albany for the day, and I had time to spare. I walked past houses and lawns of diminishing size until, with the town behind me, I found myself flanked on either side by an unkempt wood, a tangle of oak, maple, and birch, hedged with a stiff rank of staghorn. Spread out below and in front of me, fields of hay in rich second growth extended to a line of darker hills, the earth's wetness rising from them in steady vibrations. As I walked, I reflected on a question, virtually the only one of interest still unanswered: how had Allan's letter to Elizabeth come into the hands of strangers? At the station I bought my ticket and walked through to the benches overlooking the tracks. About to sit down, I noticed a tall gentleman standing on the far platform. No one else was to be seen on this second Monday in September.

The man had dressed, as for an afternoon lawn party, in a costume of conventional perfection. A blazer of not-quite-navy blue followed the slope of his shoulder and the fall of his slack right arm with uncluttered smoothness. Above the flattened collar of the jacket appeared a neat ring of off-white crepe de chine shirting, its points drawn together with a glint of gold beneath a rep tie of plum and pewter stripes, whose mild bulge was nipped by a more visible clasp of gold above the open middle button of the blazer. From a gently cinched waist fell pleated trousers of dove-gray flannel—my mental fingertips fondled their imagined softness, confirmed by the delicacy with which they broke, an inch above their cuffs, against the insteps of brown-and-amber saddle shoes. To complete the array, the man in his left hand held a high-crowned, pale-yellow Panama hat, using it to fan—so solemnly I wondered any air was displaced—his sweatless head.

Tipped forward, turned a little to one side, the head looked strong and sleek, although, in its details, less than handsome: the aquiline nose was too thick at its tip, the space between the eyes too narrow, the lips too thin. These flaws hardly mattered.

It has been said that being perfectly dressed provides a satisfaction no religion can give; and from this man, even in our nondescript surroundings, such satisfaction emanated like light from a filament. The way he assumed his elegance implied an imperiously debonair attitude to the world around him. He seemed to be inventing his very presence here, imagining himself in some sublime farce staged for the amusement of knowing friends, and for his own.

This impression, as it turned out, contained an element of truth. A few days later, returning for the funerals, I learned that the man I had seen in the station was a professional actor, not particularly well known or successful except in his secondary career: he appeared as a paid extra man at fashionable parties. He could supply a stylish presence, he spoke well (and not too well), he charged a reasonable fee. I had seen him at work, perhaps waiting for a lady due on the northbound train whom he had been hired to escort for the evening.

I was relieved to have this apparition explained. He had disturbed me more than I cared to admit. I was twenty years younger then, and no doubt my own uncertainty exaggerated the actor's effect. At the time, I still hoped that life naturally engendered life, that death, no matter how devastating its losses, could be overcome or circumvented by the living as long as they themselves remained alive. If I knew that Morris could never be replaced, I expected that his memory sooner or later would grow flat, surviving only as a reminder of a time that could be safely called the past.

I thought, in other words, that I could always recover. I was only beginning to learn that the dead stay everlastingly present among us, taking the form of palpable vacancies that only disappear when, as we must, we take them into ourselves. We take the dead inside us; we fill their voids with our own substance; we become them. The living dead do not belong to a race of fantasy, they constitute the inhabitants of our earth. The longer we live, the more numerous the inviting holes death opens in our lives and the more we add to the death inside us, until at last we embody nothing else. And when we in turn die, those who survive embody us, the whole of us, our individual selves and the crowd of dead men and women we have carried within us.

Your father dies: you hear his laugh resounding in your lungs. Your mother dies: in a store window you catch yourself walking with her huddled gait. A friend dies: you strike his pose in front of an expectant camera. Beyond these outward signs, we take up the foibles, the gifts, the unrealized failures and successes of those we have watched and watched die.

Of course we do everything in our power to deny this. I shall deny it to you and to myself as long as I speak, still pretending that you are only you, and I I. In this way I can become altogether blind and go on groping my way through sunlight and darkness, with only my uncomprehending complaints to furnish names for the things I trip over and for the other sightless bodies I stumble against. In such circumstances, I sometimes think that only the residual strength of the dead beings inside me gives me power to survive at all. By that I mean both the accumulated weight of the generations succeeding one another and, as well, from the first of times, when names held their objects fast and light shone among us in miracles of discovery, the immortal presence of that original and heroic actor who saw that the world had been given him to play in without remorse or fear.

New York, January 27, 1987

ABOUT THE AUTHOR

HARRY MATHEWS was raised in New York City and graduated from Harvard, with a B.A. in music, in 1952. *Cigarettes* is his fourth novel, following *The Conversions* (1962), *Tlooth* (1966), and *The Sinking of the Odradek Stadium* (1975). Harry Mathews is also the author of two collections of short fiction, *Selected Declarations of Dependence* (with Alex Katz) and *Country Cooking and Other Stories,* as well as several volumes of poetry and numerous translations. He divides his time between Paris and New York.